I0818038

FALLEN SHARDS

MICHAEL S. JACKSON

@mikestepjack | mjackson.co.uk

OTHER BOOKS IN THE RINGLANDER SERIES

BOOK I
The Path And The Way
Audiobook | eBook | Paperback | Hardback

NOVELLA
The Battle That Was Lost
Audiobook | eBook | Hardback

First edition in Paperback 2025
First edition in Hardback 2025

Edited by Dom McDermott
Cover illustration by John Anthony Di Giovanni
Cover design and interior maps by Michael S. Jackson
Character images by Jonathan McEnroe
Kyira's diary sketches by Jenny Hunter

978-1-7399149-4-3

www.mjackson.co.uk | @mikestepjack

CONTENTS

ACKNOWLEDGMENTS

I couldn't do anything without the constant stream of support and love from my family and friends. You know who you are.

The artists who produced visual art for this book are of such a high calibre that it made design very easy. John, Jonny, and Jenny (The three Js) Thank you so much for being so good at what you do. This book wouldn't be half of what it is without your absolute skill.

The fantasy community is a thriving and creative place and I count myself extremely lucky to be a part of it, even in the changing face of social media it powers on, a force of passionate souls who live and breathe fantasy.

The editor and beta readers who read this book before any other and stuck out all of the tpyos and missing words, gave me their very valuable time and effort. Thank you all for being a part of my little world.

Dom McDermott (editor)
Jennifer Freestone (beta reader)
Thomas Turner (beta reader)
Kayla Yetman (beta reader)
Peter Hutchinson (beta reader)
Michael Sugarman (beta reader)

The Outer Reaches
Nord
Nortun
The Laich
Telast
Makril
Daertuca
Dali
(The Valleys)
Drakemyre
Tyr
Fairsky
Krask
Port Ataska
Ston'rer
Raeven's Torr
Hatar
Anake Bain
Koroeil
Zunqai
Groudil
Calfs Malon
Horn dol Zunqai
Ferrho
Iron Road
Kemenem
Kaem'aor Sea
Kroth
Kereat
Kort Areta

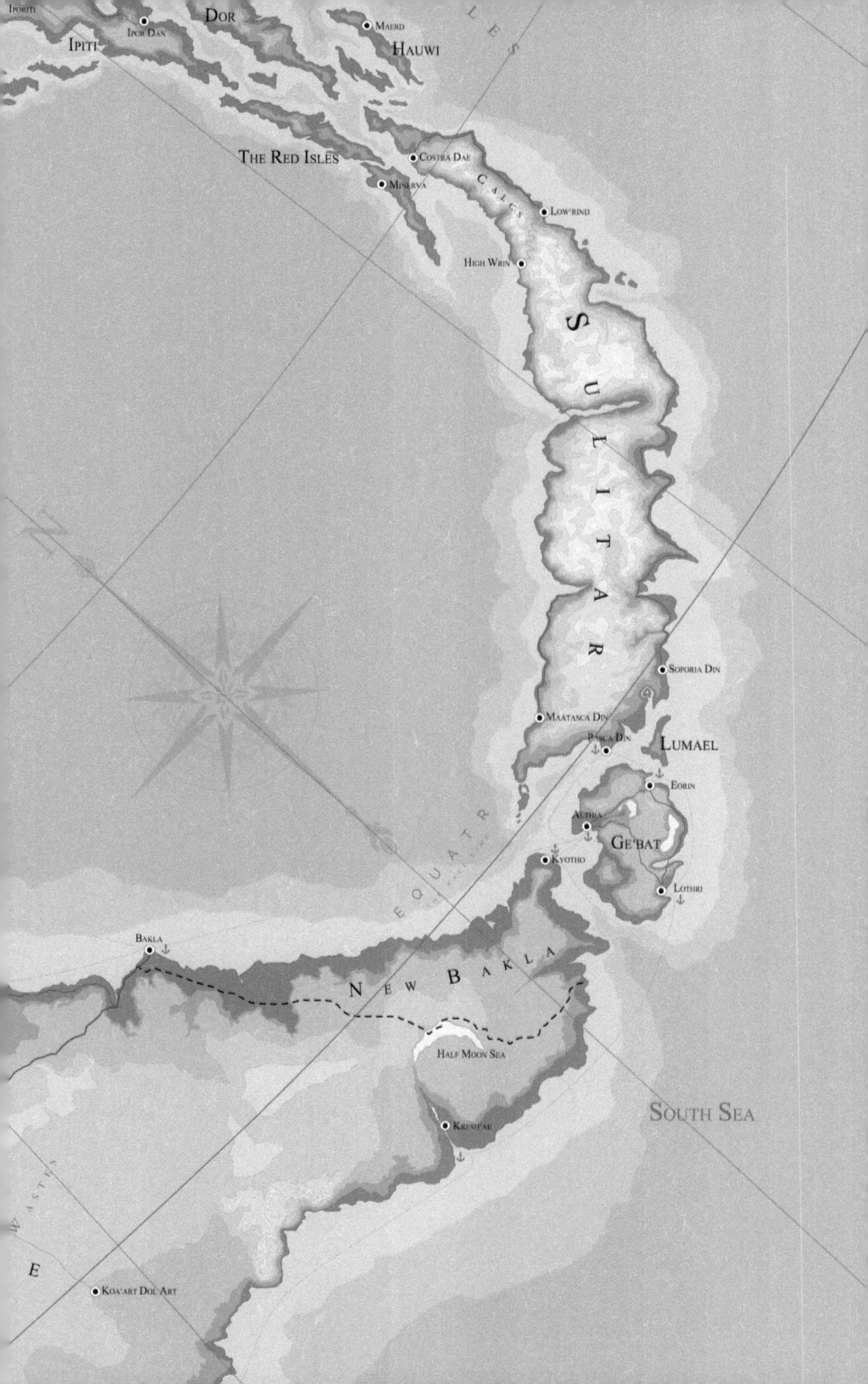

Iporiti
Dor
Ipor Dan
Maerd
Ipiti
Hauwi
The Red Isles
Costra Dae
Minerva
Calus
Low'rind
High Wrin
Sulitar
Soporia Din
Maatasca Din
Basca Din
Lumael
Eorin
Authra
Ge'bat
Kyotho
Lothri
Equator
Bakla
New Bakla
Half Moon Sea
South Sea
Kresip'ae
Wastes
Koa'art Dol Art

SERIES SUMMARY

RECAP OF BOOK 1 - THE PATH AND THE WAY

After her father and brother's disappearance, Kyira, a Sami Pathwatcher, tracks her father and kills the kidnappers. In a case of mistaken identity, she realises that one of the men she has killed was an innocent rebel captain of the Tsiorc, the rebel resistance brought together under the triangle/cross sigil to fight the monstrous Bohr, the inhuman oppressors of Rengas. The innocent's partner, Lyla, who is pregnant with his child, Captain Bryn and Captain Tri reveal that Kyira's brother Hasaan has likely willingly joined the Bohr's army under a conscripted branch called the Kin. Kyira sets off with her father to find her brother, but quickly finds that their world is struggling against a battle of its own.

The Forbringrs (the gods of Rengas) are fighting in the heavens, tearing holes in reality. Each portal brings catastrophic consequences where it opens and Kyira sees firsthand what the power of the Forbringrs can do as fire comes to life, mountains crumble and the never-changing tides of the Way channel turn dragging ships to the depths.

Meanwhile, in the great city of Tyr, the rebel spy Fia experiences painful loss as her partner (and Kavik's daughter) Janike's life is taken by the great Banèman, Jagar. The Banèmen are bred until the exceptional qualities of the Bohr become focused into tools that can be wielded like blades. Strength, telepathy and pure energy come together to make the Banèmen efficient warriors and ruthless killers, and Jagar was the strongest Banèman of all.

Jagar is hunting rebel captains, and kills Captain Bryn and Tri, before changing form and disguising himself as Jaem, a refugee fleeing from the stricken Nordun town of Makril. Still stricken with grief and loss, Kyira follows remaining Captain Lyla, travelling with the Makrilaen refugee convoy until reaching the rebel Tsiorc camp. Jagar uses his disguise to get close to Tactician Laeb a Sulitarian captain who has famously bested the Bohr in battle numerous times. Within the heart of the camp Jagar reveals his true self, almost killing them all. Kyira gets to Jagar first, slaying the slayer with a shard from a broken blade. Jagar's spectacular death lets loose a stream of pure energy which kills Kyira's father and sets fire to the Tsiorc camp.

The rebels and the Sulitarian fleet, led by the clever Commander Laeb and former comrade, Kai, sneak into the Bohr stronghold of Tyr. The prosperous trade city of Tyr straddles two continents connected by the Waybridge, where the human rebels and the Bohr lord's army face off. The Tsiorc rebels meet the lord's army, while Eris, a Teräväen resident living on the poorer side of Tyr, has formed a rebel faction of her own, surround and overcome the lord's army upon the Waybridge.

As the battle reaches its zenith, a portal opens in Tyr and rips the city apart, and the Bohr King and Commander Laeb both fall into the raging waters of the Way along with the whole of Vasen, the opulent wealthy half of Tyr, crashing into the watery catacombs beneath.

Kyira survives the battle upon the Waybridge but the rebel Captain Lyla does not, after she is killed by Kyira's brother, Hasaan. Her family now disowned, Kyira takes the only coure she has left, protecting Lyla's baby daughter Abika from the battle and her treacherous brother, but as the portal above Tyr rips open, it drags Kyira and Abika in. The internal forces of the portal should have crushed them both, but Kyira fights on, denying the Gods, and both Kyira and Abika emerge unscathed in a new place, surrounded by orange trees as the portal dies and winks out of existence.

PART I

ABIKA

1

BREAKING BREAD

It seemed the world just hated certain people. Mutta stumbled around the kitchen like a chicken with no head, clanking pots, burning skin and food alike while a trail of damage stalked behind her. Cooking smells were lost to fume and fire, and everything that could go wrong was going wrong.

It amazed Abika that someone as old as Mutta hadn't mastered simple tasks like cooking. She had just opened her mouth to say as much when Mutta spun towards her, that long nose following shortly after.

"The bread!" squawked Mutta. "It's burning!"

Abika stood defiantly. "Of course it is." Mutta never stopped moving. It made her hard to predict, so Abika just assumed she was in a bad mood all the time. Which was mostly true anyway.

"There are those—" Mutta lifted a huge pot of boiling vegetables. "who eat the bread, girl. And those who make it." Abika watched her struggle with the pot, pouring the steaming water into a deep basin. After a long moment of saving tubers and carrots from a mushy fate, she turned to Abika red-faced and sweating. "I think we both know which you are to be."

"Why make bread, when you can just eat it?" The logic felt flawed somehow, but it was more important to Abika to have something to send back. She couldn't just stand there and be bullied. Mutta shook her head and turned away, muttering.

Aki's hand touched Abika's shoulder, his heavy clay ring warm against her neck. "Daughter," he whispered, "must we fall out every mealtime? It gets tiresome."

"Yes. I know." Abika pursed her lips together to hide the smile.

Aki was not the biggest man Abika knew, but he was the strongest. He could also be as soft as a woman. "Do as Mutta tells you. Now."

"She's not my mother."

"And I am not your father, and yet you are our daughter and you *will* heed us." Aki glowered at her. "These are the rules of the Avere."

Abika plucked her response from a full basket ready and waiting. "Avere children are given a namesake to pass on knowledge aren't they? Well, my name was given by another. My mother." She stared at Mutta, still skipping around like her apron was on fire. "My real mother."

It was Aki's turn to stand defiantly now. Those usual wrinkles that appeared when he laughed, very much hidden. "Don't quote the rules to me, child."

Abika cast her eyes down. "She is *not* my mother."

Aki's expression didn't change, those greying eyebrows no longer betraying him, but the grip on her shoulder tightened ever so slightly. "Still, girl, she loves you just the same. As we all do." He nodded at the basement trapdoor tucked into the kitchen corner. "Now move." The softness disappeared in those final words, then his eyes darted to the sides and his voice rose. "And be quick about it!" He left her with a quick wink.

Abika scowled as hard as she could, then turned and descended down the short ladder into the low basement. Almost bent over double she scurried about in the musty air until she found the oven's bottom. Aki once said that the ancient oven was built first and the commune grew around it as more and more children came to live here. Children like her, with no parents, no home, and no possessions. Abika opened the bottom drawer and found the latest breads. Five loaves, well-fired to kill the weevils within.

Abika was twelve now, but she could still remember the smell of good bread, which was something she rarely ate in this house.

"BREAD!" roared Mutta from the kitchen above.

"It's coming!" growled Abika. She grabbed two dark loaves, one in each hand, then stood and cracked her head on the underside of the stone roof, cursing and damning the bloody birdwoman back to her bloody cage. "It's bloody coming!"

"Thank you," said the kitchen worker Meorith from the top of the ladder. "You made it then?"

Abika rubbed her head. "Yes, I made it, you bloody—"

"Ah, ah, come on now, Bee," said Meorith, pulling the other loaves from the oven drawer. "None of that. What's the matter? Did you bump your head?"

Abika bit her tongue and forced a smile.

Meorith smiled warmly back at her. "See, back to your normal self already. No one likes to get bread, but until you find yourself wearing an apron like this one you may as well grow a callus on your scalp." She began walking away. "It's the only way you'll survive." Meorith tapped her own head to drive the point home.

"And I suppose that will be my lot in life? To be a—" The trapdoor fell shut. "To be a bloody kitchen maid?" The last words were muttered in the dark. There was no one around her. In fact, there was never anything around her, except routine and hopelessness. She threw one of her loaves onto the ground and it shattered like it was made of charcoal and chalk. She hated this. She hated all of it.

"You made it then?" said Mutta, once Abika had ascended. "I'll take that. Burned. Of course. Do you destroy *everything* you get your hands on Abika?"

Abika rubbed her head. "You're welcome."

"Where are the others?"

"Meorith took—"

Mutta dropped a heavy board on the kitchen's wooden side, cutting Abika off, then handed her a large bread knife. "Here, make yourself useful and get slicing." Then she was stirring and buzzing about the kitchen again.

Abika stared at the knife for a long moment. Was it a weapon, a tool? It just depended on what direction she was holding it. She started sawing.

"I know I'm not your mother," said Mutta.

Abika focused intently on the bread.

"The whole of this commune knows it, child. As Aki earns his name for the role he brings, I earn the name *Mutta* because I look after you, all of you. We are mother and we are father." She pulled her necklace out from her shirt and kissed the shining stone, murmured a prayer then put it back.

That crystal must surely have been worn out by now, the amount of times Mutta had kissed the thing. "Wait! He told you?"

"Yes he told me!" she said, pointing the spoon and splashing Abika with soup. "You said I am not your mother. Twelve cycles it's been, child, and you still haven't realised that I hear *everything*. Twelve cycles of food, warmth and shelter. I may not have birthed you, but I damned well earned the title. And while I'm at it, don't talk down to your father." Her eyes were fierce, but there was a hint of begging in there. She wanted Abika to talk back, she wanted a fight.

Abika folded her arms and waited for the air between them to thin. "I want to work in the kitchen."

Mutta shrugged. "This is a kitchen."

"No, this is a pantry with a gas stove. Meorith is—"

"Older than you." Mutta blinked slowly, then turned back to the pot. "And more respectful."

"Meorith is a suck-up."

"Well, it works for her. And for me."

Bitterness filled Abika's mouth. She wanted to take that bloody spoon and whack Mutta around the head with it. She pointed the tip of the breadknife towards Mutta's back. It would only take a few steps. How hard would she have to lunge? Cutting meat was one thing...

"Until you respect me, child, you'll never work in the kitchens. You will stay in this *pantry* of yours while the rest of the children earn their keep." She paused the clinking of her big spoon in the hope she would hear some sort of challenge, but Abika would not give it to her. She would never give this woman what she wanted. "Besides, child, the kitchens are for the more mature children. There are many hazards in there that—"

"I am not a stupid little girl, I can look after—"

Mutta spun, holding the ladle out like a sword. "And THAT is why you will never grace those walls, child. Because you don't respect us!" Mutta glanced at the knife held out in her direction. "We know what the trials of life have to offer, for we have been through them. We know how to navigate those waters, because we have done it already." Aki appeared at the door, and something unreadable passed between them.

"You should listen to her, Abika. There is logic to what she says."

"Logic?"

"Don't back-chat, child!" snapped Mutta, splattering soup everywhere.

Abika felt the sting of tears behind her eyes, but she would not cry. Not here. Not in front of these people. She swallowed it back and straightened her shoulders.

Aki broke the silence. "Freja. We will need to do a town-run soon. I'm running short of burn stones. And the gas pipes...They are corroded."

"It's spread?"

Aki nodded.

"You said it was safe!"

Aki sighed. Clearly he had been dreading having this discussion. His gaze flickered towards Abika before he answered. "Well, it isn't safe. Not anymore. We cannot ride out this winter with faulty pipes, and I cannot fix them without supplies. We've still two months of the cold." Mutta turned to him, and he stepped towards her. "It'll be the last for a few months."

Mutta held the spoon above the pot. She always held herself strong. That strong jaw, high cheeks, and dark hair that seemed to stay up regardless of the activity. The spoon shook.

"Freja?"

Mutta threw the spoon back into the soup. "We will have to do without new pipes, my heart. We cannot afford them, and we cannot leave a family of twelve to fend for themselves against anything that may decide to creep along the shoreline."

"The shoreline? Freja, when was the last time anyone came out this far? The bay is safe. *We* are safe."

"How do you know that for sure, Jekob? I asked you to put up fences, I asked you to dig pits. None of which you have done. And the amount of trips you've made to town this past cycle...surely you must have the supplies somewhere to fix the pipes? What else is there to do in Ipor Dan really?" She waited for him to answer.

"I wouldn't ask if I didn't think it necessary." Aki looked sullen, but he spoke softly. "And don't make this about me, Freja."

"As you say," said Mutta.

Abika wished she had that ability to calm herself like Aki did—maybe she and Mutta would have gotten on better.

Aki cleared his throat. "So, this is your word?"

"It is my word." Another pause. Then the hands went on the hips. Aki had no chance. "We will wait until the warmer months."

"As you say," said Aki. He glanced at Abika, then turned and left the pantry kitchen.

2

THE SHARD NECKLACE

Abika kicked open the door to the playroom to find Aki lying on the floor amongst toys and children recounting tales.

"Ah!" said Aki, "Just in time." The child in his arms stuck his tongue out at her.

Abika shook her head. "I'm not changing him."

"Guess again!" laughed Aki. "We're telling stories!"

"I've heard all of your stories, Aki."

"Not all of them, I can promise you that." He shot her an unreadable expression then sat up with the child nestled in his crossed legs. This was the childish side of her commune father. Jekob had many sides, of which Abika was certain there were yet to see.

"Come, Thio," said Aki, pulling his eyes from Abika's. "Let us talk of the great storm of the cursed city of Tyr. Once upon a time, the Great Mother—"

"Baeivi! Baeivi!"

"Yes!" said Aki. "That's right! Baeivi is the Great Mother. She made us all, and without her we would have nothing at all. Clever boy. Well, about a decade ago, little Thio, the Great Mother Baeivi became angry, and when the gods become angry, we can only stand in their shadow and hope that their wrath does not reach us. As it was, she tore Rengas asunder with her might and main, sending storms so powerful they tore holes in the air. Firespirals, hurricanes and tsunamis that whooshed and whirled and—"

"And killed."

Aki shot Abika a look. "Yes, Bee. Thank you."

Thio missed the point, naturally. "Then what happened?" asked the toddler.

"Then?" said Aki. "It's said that someone was pulled into the hole. Shortly after though, the hole disappeared. In fact, they all just closed up. All of them. Gone."

Thio looked aghast. "Gone?"

"Gone," Aki's expression grew thoughtful. "The only evidence that anything happened at all was the loss of the biggest city in Rengas, and the great tower of glass that grew from its ashes."

"Wow!" said Thio, reaching upwards. "I'm a tower too!"

Abika sighed. "It's not there anymore though, silly boy."

Thio stuck out his tongue again. "Shut up, Bee!"

"Now, now," said Aki, standing. "Bee's right. The tower fell into the deep waters of the Way a few cycles past. I think the Bohr did it. They're very powerful the Bohr. They deserve our respect. Others say the Great Mother just left, which is why most of the shard towers fell."

Abika shook her head once more in disapproval. "The Great Mother couldn't just *leave*. She's a Forbringr. They're supposed to be everywhere."

Aki ignored Abika. "The only truth is that the holes disappeared, never to be seen again."

"Why?" asked Thio.

Aki winked at Abika. "Why? Why? I'll tell you why, Thio, because the Great Mother was scared of your father!" Aki roared and ran in circles, then both child and man disappeared out of the playroom doors and into the hallway before the kitchens.

"And peace," said Abika to herself.

Abika often thought about Tyr. Her real mother had apparently lived near there, but that was as much as she knew. Or at least, that was what had been written in the note that accompanied Abika's baby basket, the day she had been left here to rot. The news of Tyr's downfall travelling so far across the Middle Sea spoke of the scale of the city's fate, which spread fear around the island of Ipiti like fire through cottongrass. The stories from across the sea quickly subsided, but the rumours of great earthquakes and storms were not so easily forgotten.

"Bika! Bika, up!"

Another little boy appeared at Abika's feet. "No, Elrith. I'm not playing I've got—"

"Bika!" Soon the whole room, even the eldest of the five children, were shouting her name over and over.

"No! Look, I'm just—" A wooden nara cracked her painfully on the side of the head. "Ow! Alright, that's it!" She grabbed Elrith. "Come here, you little ratface!" She picked up the snotty little boy and threw him over her shoulder. "Let's see how fast we can go!"

The little boy screamed half in delight, half in terror as Abika spun on the spot with him. Say anything you like, but no one could spin like Abika. She was the greatest, and the fastest. It was all in the technique. Eventually the screams began to subside, and she put Elrith down, laughing as he stumbled around all dizzy.

"Now," she said. "Let's not be throwing chunks of wood at people's heads, boy. Alright?"

Mutta appeared at the door. "What is going on?!"

Elrith burst into tears, wiping snot all over his face to highlight his anguish. "Bika spin!"

Mutta's glare hardened. "Abika, you know he doesn't like it."

"He threw a toy at my head!"

"No, I didn't!" Elrith blubbed.

"You little—"

"No, that's enough. Abika leave them be."

"Mutta—"

"Don't you Mutta me, child. You're the eldest here. Act your age!" She slammed the door behind her, leaving Abika fuming.

"Act my age?" she roared. "I don't even know my own birthday! How can I act my age!" It was a perfect comeback, and she stared at the door, hoping that Mutta would appear, belt in hand. She would fight her and hit her and spit and scream.

But nothing came. There was no fight.

Aki and Mutta's room was the largest in the commune, and the most secure, but with a little rattling around, the tang of the bread knife made short work of the old lock. She slipped inside and pushed the door, waiting for the familiar click, then hopped left onto the only floorboard that didn't creak, before leaping up onto the frame of the wooden bed. This room was full of noisy traps that signalled to anyone and everyone in the old house that someone was in here, but Abika knew them all. She held her breath and listened. Birds, wind, water, then talking. Both parents were still chattering outside about something or other, but she should still be quick. Her eyes fell upon the sacrificial redula blade above their bed, it looked sharp, but she knew it wasn't.

The tom'ra leaves were what she was here for, and they were in a jar at the back of Mutta's dress cupboard. As plain and obvious as last time she saw them. The lid popped off easily enough and she took two of the leaves out, inhaling the musty aroma that followed. Aki loved kaldi, he would wake a good half hour before the rest of the house and spend the time brewing it, fussing over each process like the witch-doctors of stories, concocting potions of all sorts. She didn't understand his fascination with the stuff, it smelled like old wood and tasted twice as awful. These leaves though, were something special. She knew their smell was easily forgotten or overlooked by most, and in all honesty, she might have even overlooked it herself had she not caught Meorith smoking them one wet day on the shores of the bay.

There was a bump downstairs and the memory was torn from her mind, replaced by panic. The lid went back on the jar, the jar went back into the clean ring on the dusty shelf, but then she stopped. A twinkle of light had caught her eye. She moved her head just so to see it again, then again. There behind the cupboard wall.

With a little prying, the short slat came free, revealing a shelf about a hand wide and long. On it sat an array of Mutta's jewellery: a steel ring with soft runes carved into the metal that said *My heart, forever*; a timepiece made of some yellow metal; and the necklace with its iridescent crystal. It shone, catching the light just so and willing Abika to take it and keep it forever. Up close it was just the most beautiful thing she had ever—

"Abika!"

"Shit." That came from the stairs. Abika grabbed the necklace, replaced the slat, then threw herself across the room to the door and slunk back out into the dim hallway. She padded to the wall to her and Meorith's room, as footsteps boomed up the stairs.

Abika opened the landing cupboard and pulled out a fresh towel and hung it over the top of the stairs. "What!"

"What are you about?" asked Aki, stopping halfway up.

"I need to bathe, Aki."

Her father shook his head, a deep frown settling upon his forehead. After a moment's pause his greying eyebrows raised. "Fine," he said, more quietly. "But be quick. Mutta wants us out. We have pits to dig."

3

STORMS

Two baths in a week was all of Abika's penance for stealing the shard necklace, but at least the secret was still hers. Being so clean made absolutely no sense after a day spent digging holes near the beach, and if there was anything more boring than digging holes it was fencing. The day was blessedly cool at least, but it wasn't long before Abika was sweating anyway.

"Aki?"

"Abika, this is the last post, and we'll get along a lot faster if we just get on with it. No talking."

Abika frowned, moving her hands quickly out of the way as Aki hammered."Aki, do you think it's possible to be connected to things?"

Aki sighed. "Connected, like how?"

"Like the path to the house, like mother to son."

Aki let the hammer sit at his side, resting against his leg. "You're not still on about this Abika? You really riled up Mutta with your arguing with everything she says and does. It's getting tiresome, I can tell you. And worse, you're putting me in the middle of you both."

Abika shook her head, but couldn't stop a scowl forming. "No, this is different. I mean connected to things. Objects."

Aki lifted his hammer. "You know, my father helped me make this hammer. It's always served me well, and I know it as well as I know my own arm."

Jekob was a romantic at heart, and once you got past the father in him, he enjoyed the back and forth of mental exercises. It might just have been one of Abika's favourite things about him.

"But can it change you?"

Aki's eyes narrowed again as the thought took shape. "You mean does it change who I am? As a person? I guess so. I do feel connected to this hammer more than any other. I'd be inclined to choose it over another. Is that what you mean?"

It wasn't what she meant. Not at all. As a child people expected her to ask questions, but she was of an age now that most of the time her questions had adult meaning behind them. It was something she had become more and more aware of the past couple of cycles. As her questions became bolder and more complicated, so did the answers. Sometimes her foster parents would outright lie to her, purely because they didn't have the time to answer truthfully. Abika didn't blame them for that though, in fact she had even used it herself as an excuse to start fights with Mutta.

"Why did you tell Freja?" As soon as the words had left her lips, she regretted them. She hadn't warmed him up enough.

Her father stared at her. "It's *Mutta* and told her what? That you said she wasn't your mother?"

"Well, you did. That wasn't fair. I told you in confidence."

"Confidence? This is what I mean, Abika. Why are you being like this? Do we not love you and look after you? Do we not provide and care for you?"

"Of course, but—"

"Then why do you disrespect us? Why do you disrespect me? Turning Freja and I against each other will only widen the chasm that is your relationship."

Guilt. A wave of it broke over her. So deep she could barely breathe. "I don't want a relationship with—"

"Don't you dare say it, girl," hissed Aki. He pointed the hammer at her. The muscles in his forearms were twitching with the effort but the hammer hovered above her breast bone like Aki's arms were cast of iron. That hammer was a part of him. It was his iron will, his resolve, his strength and passion, and now his anger. "To disrespect Freja is to disrespect me."

Abika had no words, but she stared back defiantly. Swallowing, she dredged up the only thing she could. "I just want *more*."

Aki's stare remained as hard as the hammer. "It's getting dark. I'm going in. Make sure all of this is put away before nightfall."

———

The sun had dropped quickly and Abika had barely finished cleaning her hands when the succulent flavour of tom'ra smoke drifted over from their favourite smoking spot. There was a large green space to cross before the beach, but even through the thorny bushes and trees, it was easy to spot the telltale cloud of blue smoke being blown up into the chilly evening air.

"I see you Meorith," said Abika, approaching.

Meorith jumped. "Gods! Bee? Is that you?"

"It's just me," said Abika. "You'll not be switched."

"Good," said Meorith, passing Abika the pipe, and almost falling off of the stone beneath her. "I'm so bored of digging pits! Here, there's still a puff or two left."

"It's alright," said Abika, beaming. "I have some leaf myself tonight."

"They'll catch you one day, Bee," slurred Meorith.

"No, they won't." Abika took the pipe and dipping into her pocket, pulled a handful of crushed tom'ra leaf and pressed it tight into the dying embers. She puffed it a few times to get it bright again then sucked in a long draw of hot smoke. It was delicious. Breathing through her nose helped enhanced the high, even when the air was damp.

The bay was misty, and cold, and beyond the great ocean storms of the Middle Sea roiled and tumbled like the great Forbringrs were fighting. A flash lit up the horizon, and she held her breath, waiting for the low rumble of thunder to reach them. Sometimes her chest would grow so tight, when the storms were far away, but it was always wonderful in between the flash and the thunder, where it felt like anything could happen. A time of action and then thought, too often it was the other way around.

Abika's eyes rolled in her head, the world swimming as she swung to look at Meorith. "What's it like?"

"What is what like?" said Meorith, groggily. "The world? Boys? Sex?"

"Uch," said Abika. "Gods no. The kitchens. What are they like?"

"They're like kitchens." Meorith shook her head. "I don't know why you're so eager to work in a dirty, smelly, hot kitchen. There's so much more out there. The world is much bigger than our little commune."

"That's not what I meant."

Meorith flicked her dark hair. "Yes, it was, Bee. It's written all over you."

"What is?"

Meorith pulled her legs up so she could sit more rigidly. "You think you deserve better than everyone else, Bee. It oozes out of your pores. The stink of it follows you around."

"That's just the bread." Abika sniggered.

"Don't make fun. I'm being serious. *This* is life and you need to get used to it. The only thing I look forward to is an occasional visit to the city. But you expect the world to be handed to you, that is why you and Mutta will never get on. She fought for everything..."

Abika sat back against their large rock and took a long breath ignoring Meorith's lecture. The calm was with her now, like a friend. It felt like a smoothness, like the glassy surface of the bay when there were no storms, but more solid like a windowpane. They were thirty or so feet above the water on a stony embankment, but if she were down by the water she could run her fingers over those smooth peaks and dips, little waves in her mind, and each time she did, the calmness would hold her close and look after her. She rolled the pipe between her finger and thumb and concentrated. Little dots of light appeared on the grains of wood like tiny firebugs, leaving black spots where they settled. Their presence should have shocked her, but she had seen them many times before. The first time it ever happened she had been sitting in this very spot, she had assumed the tom'ra leaf's embers had dropped on her fingertips. But they hadn't. The lights were her own. Abika had conjured them out of the calm to live in this world.

She rubbed the pipe stem to hide the new pock marks and held it out for Meorith. "Here. You finish it. I don't care about going to Ipor Dan, Meorith. Aki might go to the city all the time, but I don't care about it. At all."

"You're such a liar!" Meorith took a long draw and then smiled drunkenly. "Why are you so bad, Bee?"

Abika's head felt like it could just lift off her shoulders and float up into the sky. "Bad?"

Meorith nodded. "Bad. You are bad, Bee. You killed that pig. Your remember don't you? How old were you?"

"Nine? No it was my eighth."

Meorith laughed bitterly. "Bee, you can't just be killing things when you want. It's disgusting. Lorith raised him from a piglet. Aki was happy for us to keep him alive through the winter, even if it meant eating oats for three months straight."

"Lorith didn't raise him, he might have said he did, but he lied about everything Meorith."

Meorith's mouth fell open. "Bee, you just killed it. It doesn't matter if our bloody brother raised him or not! I don't think either I or Lorith ever understood why you did that."

Abika shook her head. "Lorith is and never was my brother just like you are not my bloody sister. Besides how is killing a pig any different to an offering?"

"An offering is to appease the Great Mother. You were just being selfish. And cruel."

"It was four cycles ago, Meorith."

"That doesn't matter! Why did you do it, Bee?"

Abika wanted to melt away into the calm. "I wake up every morning wondering who I am, Meorith. Where I come from. Your parents died, which is sad, but at least you know. I don't know, and I never will. All I was ever told was that a woman who worked the fields near Ipor Dan left me for dead here at the commune." Abika tried to picture the woman's face like she had a hundred times before, but all she saw was a broken memory of a hooded figure.

"Left you for dead?" Meorith looked disgusted. She took another draw of tom'ra and coughed it out. "Hardly. It doesn't matter where you come from, Bee. All Avere children are lost! What would you prefer? Living on the streets of Ipor Dan selling fruit? Anyway, give any excuse you want. You murdered that poor animal."

"It kept me up with its bloody screaming!" snapped Abika. "And one day I'd just had enough. I woke up early, went down to the sheds, found a fishknife and cut its throat." Meorith stared at her. "I used the sharpest blade I could find, Meorith. It didn't suffer. Using a dull blade, now that would have been cruel. And messy."

Meorith scoffed. "Sometimes I wonder who you even are, Bee. I'm serious. Who does that?"

"Tollo! He kills pigs all the time. And chickens."

"Tollo is a cook, Bee." Meorith pulled her knees up again, but this time she was hiding behind them. The damp stone was probably making her behind cold, as it was for Abika. "It just bothers me is all. We take turns stealing tom'ra from Mutta, we sit here, we smoke, we laugh. And I still don't know who you are. We are sis—"

"We are not sisters!" snarled Abika. "How do you know who you are? You don't know me."

Meorith sucked from the pipe and inhaled deeply. "Actually, I do know you. Or at least I know you enough."

"No, you don't."

"Try this on then," said Meorith. "You think you're desperate to work in the kitchens? You're not. You want *out*. You want to change, and see things, but you're so confined to our little commune. Five adults, seven children, and they have you under their spell. Because that's what Freja wants. That's how she works. It's how she controls you. She's like a witch. A witch from the Red Isles. And don't tell me they don't have witches there because Tollo told me they do."

Abika frowned. It was one thing to want something, but to hear the actual reasons come from someone else's lips was terrifying. "That doesn't mean anything." She snatched the pipe away from Meorith's fingers.

"I'm in my fifteenth, Abika. Four cycles older than you."

"Three."

"I've been through this," said Meorith. "Freja is testing you."

"She hates me." Abika's resolve tightened. "And I hate her." She pulled the crystal necklace from her pocket and held it up, watching it glint in the lightning that flashed around them.

Meorith's eyes widened. "You stole Mutta's necklace? She's going to kill you."

"See!" Abika poked Meorith in the chest with the pipe end, pushing her off her little rock. "You think you know me, but you don't. I don't care about what Mutta thinks. I don't care what you think." Abika was up, and the world spun, but she made it to the rock on which Meorith had been sitting and draped the necklace over it. Abika grabbed her own rock, and held it high. "I don't care at all!"

Meorith's eyes widened as Abika drove the stone into the necklace. The crystal reverberated with the force of the impact, sending a shockwave up Abika's arm. A scream burst out of her, filling her waking soul with chaos and imbalance, shattering the calm that the tom'ra had given her. She reeled as the world tipped on its side.

It was fuzzy, but the colours and shapes were clearly that of a woman. They swirled and coalesced into a shape she knew. A face. Her lips were moving. Her eyes gazing down at Abika with such warmth that she felt completely secure. This person would look after her, forever.

"Abika! Wake up!"

The air was still fresh and salty, and Abika's back was freezing cold. Meorith shook Abika by the shoulders and a wave of nausea followed after. She turned on her side, and the shore spun with her. "I'm alright, Meorith. Leave me be."

"You smoked too much!" moaned Meorith, barely able to keep her balance. "You're too young to be smoking tom'ra."

Abika lifted herself onto her hands and knees. "Whatever you say, Meorith."

"Whatever I say? Stupid girl. You'd better find a way to get this necklace back into Mutta's room without her seeing. And be thankful that you have barely the strength of a lake weasel, because if you'd marked it, Mutta would have actually killed you. Sharp knife or no!" Meorith dropped the still-intact necklace on the ground and disappeared behind the old tree muttering something about pigs.

Abika sat back down, feeling like she might empty her stomach. The world was brighter, like she'd just woken up from a long sleep, but her head still felt thick. Images of a face she didn't recognise flashed in and out of her mind, and she couldn't blame the calm of the tom'ra leaf either. That had been shattered the moment the stone had touched the crystal on Mutta's necklace. She held it up against the light. It was still whole, with not a mark on it.

"What sort of glass stone doesn't crack when you smash it?" she muttered. She kicked the big rock she'd used and it rolled down the short embankment to the water.

Perhaps Meorith was right, maybe she should try to get the necklace back behind the dressing cupboard before Mutta found out. Or maybe she should just bloody keep it.

The island of Ipiti was a trove of gas, and the towns were built upon the largest reserves. Meorith had told Abika that Freja and Jekob had found a gas well here which was why they had built the commune, quietly taking advantage of the Great Mother Baeivi's gift.

It was getting late as Abika staggered up from the smoking spot. The darkness beyond the house was almost absolute, but Abika had snuck out often enough that she knew the path well, and it wasn't long before she was standing, feeling her way along the pipes just to stay upright. The pipes were silent—the house did not draw gas unless the heating was on, and Mutta did not approve of heating at night-time.

"Just wear a jumper," said Abika, in her best impression of Mutta's silly voice. "You wear a bloody jumper, you haggard, old Red Isles witch."

Abika followed the lengths of metal until she felt a join near the tap that controlled the flow and heating. There was the faintest taint of the gas's stink in the air, but it was wound tight. Even in the darkness Abika could see the long line of piping as a straight line all the way to the well at the bottom of the path. There was not a spot of rust anywhere. Aki must have been mistaken about the corrosion he mentioned to Mutta. Unless he just made it up—maybe he was just as keen to get out of here as Abika was.

Shrugging, she thought no more about it and stumbled off to bed.

4

EXPLOSION

Breakfast was always a chore in the commune. More so when your head thumped with every footstep. The dining room was cacophony of shouts and bleating; the air thick with steam and cooking smells. There was fried oats in butter, peppery nightflower stems steeped in tea, and even meat. Bacon was such a rarity, but Abika could do nothing more than push it around her plate.

Tom'ra shouldn't have affected her like this, but there was no denying the horses galloping around inside her head. Hooves crushing. Brain compressing—Abika winced and placed the tray down on the table. Thio was just tipping the last of his nara milk upon the tiled floor, when angry voices rose above the din.

"It's gone, Jekob. Gone!"

Abika left the breakfast table and sidestepped along the hallway towards the kitchens, listening.

Jekob's voice reverberated through the pantry kitchen door. "Could it have fallen down the back of the cupboard?"

"No," said Mutta. "I searched everywhere."

"I always said we should have double backed that shelf. If it has fallen then—"

"It hasn't fallen, Jekob! It's just gone."

"Well, I can buy you another. It might be a good reason for a visit to town."

Mutta slammed the spoon down, making Abika jump. "You can't buy another! I'd rather not go back there."

Aki's silence was famous for drawing the truth from people. He'd used it on Abika as long as she could remember, and he was using it now on Freja.

"I took it..." uttered Mutta. "From Vasta."

"Vasta?" snapped Jekob. "How...Why would you buy anything from him?"

The door was pulled shut and Abika pressed her ear to the wood.

"It was in the window," said Mutta. "I thought it was the most beautiful crystal I had ever seen, and I wanted it. That's why."

Abika wanted to burst into the pantry kitchen and point at the woman who ever dared ask to be called *Mutta*. To shame her and show that Abika had been clever enough to hide and hear her confessions.

An explosion of sound and vibration tore through the house, shaking pictures from the wall, and knocking dust from the low ceiling. A pot fell to the floor, followed by a scream from Mutta that was almost as loud as the boom itself.

Aki barrelled out of the door, locking eyes with Abika before yanking open the front door, almost pulling it from the hinges. A few dumb seconds passed before Meorith, Mutta and Abika fell out of the commune in pursuit.

A fountain of blue and orange flame burned hard through the trees that stood between house and well, easily visible in the early morning light. The pipes were no longer connected and straight but broken and bent at each join. Aki was already running along the path towards it, shirtless but with sheets thrown over his shoulders. "Come on!"

Abika rubbed her eyes. "Is that fire?"

Meorith planted a heavy punch on Abika's arm. "Wake up, Abika! The gas is alight!"

"Are we safe?"

Meorith pointed at the gas pipes disappearing under the foundations of the house near the kitchen window. "What do you think? It's bloody gas, you fool."

Mutta shouldered Abika out of the way, and Meorith sprung after.

Aki was already chest deep in the well, which was completely open to the air. He stood upon what looked like an upturned steel bowl that sealed the hole about half way down, but who knew how deep it went. The pipes that stuck out of the centre of that upturned bowl were all jagged and broken, and that was where the flames were, roaring out of the thin tubes higher than the commune roof. On the ground around them was a huge black scorch mark in the shape of a star.

"What happens if it goes out?!" roared Mutta.

Aki dropped to his knees yanking a spanner against the pipe on the metal seal. "I don't know—There's too much force!"

The fire stuttered, and the air was filled with a horrible smell. "Jekob?"

Womf. The flame caught again.

Colours and wind rushed by as Abika's limbs were set free, then ground, turf and gravel. Ears ringing, she lifted her head from the ground to see Aki pulling himself up and scooping up the metal seal which had landed nearby. He grabbed a tattered-looking connecting pipe with a right angle on it. The well was fully open. The wet hole in the ground roaring as gas rushed out, distorting the commune behind it.

Mutta limped back towards the well as Aki reached it on the other side, their words lost in the wind.

"...switch the pipes...?"

"No!" shouted Aki. "No, no, no!"

Meorith looked like she had escaped unscathed. "What do we do?" she shouted, as Abika joined them. Aki held out his arm to stop them getting too close, but Abika could see into the hole now. It was immediately clear why the seal was so important. The ledge the seal had been jammed into was now too big and all the gas was escaping around the edges.

Aki frowned at her. "We need to plug it back up and repressurise before it runs out!" Carefully, Aki dropped himself onto the large stone, his hair flapping as the rushing gas blew up and out into the air. He nodded at the metal seal. Abika went to grab it.

"Meorith help her!" shouted Mutta.

"I don't need—" But the seal was much heavier than it looked. Abika tried to drag it towards the lip of the hole before Meorith reached her from the other side.

Aki grabbed the huge metal bowl with one hand and hefted it into the hole. The seal was now too small to do its job.

"Freja, get a spade! And a pickaxe." Mutta ran off, back towards the commune up the path, while Aki began tearing at the inside of the hole with his bare hands. "Stand back, girls! I need to collapse this hole."

"Can't we just let it burn?" shouted Abika.

"Not if you want to survive the winter," growled Aki.

Meorith slid into the hole and started scrabbling at the side like Aki was doing, pulling lumps of earth and rocks into the hole. "We need to bury the sides," said Aki, dragging the seal back into position. "Go and check the connecting pipes, Bee."

Abika jogged over to where the pipes ran along the ground, she grabbed one and then immediately jumped back. "Ow!"

"It's fire," shouted Mutta. "Silly child! Use some of the sheet! Is the air pipe damaged?"

Abika picked up some chewed rags and lifted the blackened end of the connecting gas pipe as high as she could. "No, it's alright."

"Thank the Forbringrs!" said Mutta. "Abika, there should be a spare pipe somewhere near there. Can you see it?"

"Yes, it's here." Abika a length of pipe from the grass.

"Connect it to that one."

The pipe moved easily when Abika pulled it, sliding along the dewy morning ground. Once she had the far end, she lifted it as high as she could and carefully slotted to the two ends together.

"Don't forget to close over the clasp, Bee!"

Mutta rushed by her with a spade and pickaxe. Aki and Meorith immediately began tearing down the walls of the gas well to bury the seal and stop the leaking gas from escaping. The pipes that went below ground were still intact, but the other connecting pipes had been blown right back, and were all bent. Anything with a join or right angle had come completely loose.

The pitch of the escaping gas began to change as the hole slowly disappeared beneath and was channelled up through the hole in the top of the seal. Aki handed Meorith the spade and grabbed a connecting pipe sitting nearby.

"Freja!" shouted Aki. "Get ready to switch the pipes back to the house. You need to reverse the flows. The pressure needs to be equal!"

Mutta grabbed Abika's arm. "Abika, come with me!"

They both ran up the path a hundred or so paces to a small tap. Mutta immediately started wrenching the rusted tap, then stopped, and put her ear to the pipe. "Right, Abika. Go to the next valve, it's about twenty paces up. And when I say, I want you to turn it all the way. It will close the air pipe and stop the pumping."

Abika frowned. "Air?"

"Yes air! The well is drawing air down from the house, which is displacing the gas in the well. The two pressures need to be equal or the house will fill with gas."

A new light drew Abika's eyes back towards the well. There was a thin blue flame roaring from the centre of the hole through the ruined right-angle connection. Muscles straining and hands wrapped in sheets, Aki attempted to bend the glowing seal pipe to meet the others while the fire still burned like a blowing torch.

Mutta pushed her, "Just do as I say, child! GO! Sprint!"

Abika ran, and stopped at a red-painted lever, and pointed at it. "This one?"

"Turn!"

Abika took hold of the red tap and turned. Air hissed through the pipe, and the flame near Aki grew in intensity, lighting up the walls of the commune.

"The other way, Bee!" roared Aki. "The other way!"

Abika turned the lever slowly the other way, the air changing pitch as the tap slowly cut off the cycle of air. One last turn and the sound disappeared completely. Except the flame from the well was still going strong. "I did it!"

Frowning Abika reached down, noticing that the cloth joint she had seen the night before was lying on the ground at her feet. She picked it up, but any new thoughts were struck out of her head.

A boom tore through the air from behind, shaking Abika's bones, turning her bowels to water. She jerked around to see a fireball rise up from the well, higher than the trees, flames ripping and reaching through the air. Mutta screamed, and tore away back down the path, but Abika was frozen to the spot.

Aki and Meorith were nowhere to be seen.

5

THE LOST

Jagar wrestled against the forces that held him. How long had it been since he had died? And what did it matter, in a place where time was a landscape that could be traversed as easily as one could walk? Jagar couldn't walk. He couldn't walk, for he was without form, though not without purpose.

Whatever he was now was pushed and pulled and stretched to breaking as he moved through the ether. How much time had passed since his death? A moment? A lifetime? A hundred thousand lifetimes?

His memories were there, like papers and maps and notes strewn over a desk. He reached out for the brightest one. The scene played out as a diorama inside a transparent box. It was a room with canvas walls—a tent. Two brothers fighting valiantly against an assailant, the captain's man moving faster than any other, drawing blood before being burned to cinder. The Sami pair. The scene shook, moving around the Sami girl as she stepped forward and stabbed the assailant through the head. Lightning burst forth from the assailant's face smashing into the Sami father.

The mist of the father's soul drifted up away from his body and out of the scene, to float alongside Jagar, dispersing and coalescing again as was the wont of the lost. Jagar turned back to watch as the girl who had killed him fell upon the smoking corpse of her father. He should have laughed, but there was no mirth to be had. The Sami girl had struck Jagar down at his most power-

ful, finding an opening that should not have been. Jagar's anger glowed hot and bright and the father's soul struggled away.

The scene returned, replaying once more. The excited opening of the Maelta box. Pictures on paper. Jaem revealing himself as Jagar. The fight. The death. Repeat. A hundred times Jagar watched as those men's souls drifted up and away. A thousand times. A million. Whenever he drew close enough to capture one of those souls, it would vanish as clouds in sunlight. He had to trap one. The only way he would see past his own death, was with power. And the only source of power within the ether was from the Lost.

Each of those souls held a unique flavour as they scurried away from Jagar's grasp. The soul of the Sami father, a man named Iqaluk, was too broad and spread apart to consume. The captain's man, Duga's was too thin to even see against the dark red of the ether. But the brother Eoin's soul was shining and almost solid. If Jagar could position himself just right...

Eoin died for the last time, and Jagar grabbed at the mist that left the scene below, sucking it in, drawing power from the remnants of the man's life-force. Purpose erupted within Jagar like a fire renewed. He concentrated, and the diorama shook beneath, denying him. Jagar concentrated, channelling all that he had left into the fringes of the scene, sharpening the blurriness like whittling a stick to a skewer. It denied him again, but it was breaking. The diorama, the tent, the frozen beings inside vibrated, and he urged them on, until finally it broke, and the Sami girl was pulled from the tent away from the diorama scene. He had done it! He was watching the events after his own death.

Colours erupted all around as the tent vanished, replaced by green grass and blurry figures running towards the bright orange tongues of flame, jumping between the other tents of the rebel camp. Jagar moved, and jerked around watching as the scene unfolded, watching as the Sami girl cried for her father. It was she who had killed Jagar, and it was she who he wanted more than anything else.

With fresh vigour, Jagar pushed further beyond his own death. More scenes sprang into being like pocket worlds with fleets and forces fighting. Jagar floated around them watching the Tsiorc, their forces on the Way, as the first ship of the rebel fleet was dragged down into the depths by a wave of water too high to escape. The scene of the Bohr King's demise appeared next, playing out in front of him: the fight in Tyr upon the Waybridge as the humans fought; the Bohr King, caught in a trap! Her outline blurred by the light of a thousand suns. The Bohr, the Kin, the lord's army, all slain by the people of Terävä.

Jagar wanted to kill and maim and dismember. It had all been for naught! The scene blinked and vibrated, the effigy of a point in time struggling against the forces of the realm of the ether. The realms were thinning, melting into one another.

He closed his eyes, letting go, searching for something regular and familiar that he could tie his consciousness to.

There! Little Bird. He could sense the kumpani so strongly she may as well have been floating right next to him. Jagar urged himself on following the waves of Fia's heartbeat pulsing through the air until he reached an old building with a single broken chimney and an old weathervane. She was in there. He knew it.

Jagar reached out with his mind, channelling the remnants of the power the brother Eoin's soul had given him, sending it towards Fia's location. Then he was there. He could see everything in the room as though he was looking through a fish's eye. Guardian Rathe stared at Jagar with an intense expression of greed upon his face, while Fia sat at his feet equally incredulous.

Abruptly, the Sami girl burst into the room. Jagar exalted at the thought of finishing off every single one of these beings. He would destroy them, and then consume them. Rathe lifted a blade high above his head to kill Fia. His Little Bird.

Through the tangled web of energies Jagar took hold of the tendrils of his Rathe's mind, but he could only hold the Bohr, he couldn't control him, because the laws of causality wouldn't allow it. In the end though, that was enough—the Sami girl burst forward against the stillness of the room, that God-Killer blade of hers ready to purge once more. She stabbed Rathe in the crotch and the Bohr stumbled forward dumbly, straight into Jagar. The Guardian's half-blood heart and organs pumped in fear. The thinning realms were so close together here that all it took was a pinch, and the realms tore inside the fool Bohr's own body! Jagar laughed with delight as the Guardian was sucked through the tiny hole to float with the ether of the Lost.

The hole between realms widened and the room fell to dust. Jagar felt more energy leak through, as the realms shuddered like wounded animals. Further and harder did Jagar push forward until that opening was as large as the building, and all of those beings swirled and orbited around it. Around him, the centre of Rengas, the centre of the realms!

Jagar urged himself through the hole, perhaps he could change it all! His energy took form and he pushed through into Rengas as black lightning that snatched and dragged at the heels of the Sami girl. Over and over she fell, tipped and ducked below his grasp as she orbited around his influence, then finally Jagar's forks of black light found her, reeling her in. She was holding back! But how?! She was fighting him with her mind. Jagar sought out her mind and forced the words into her.

LET GO.

But she would not. She spat blood, growling through gritted teeth.

LET GO.

Her strength was something Jagar could not fathom. No human could be so strong!

LET GO.

The Sami girl's grasp faltered and she flew towards Jagar. She was his. And he would consume her soul and her body as one.

The ether flickered, as the Lost attacked, darkening Jagar's vision, flying in front and denying him access, then the rip was closing. The girl, the bundle of rags clutched in her hands, fading. Jagar screamed as the darkness swallowed them both.

6

THE FOUND

"Jæk'ob!" screamed Mutta. "Theäerdän dur Jæk'ob!" Mutta never spoke in Redula, the trade tongue of the Red Isles, because she was adamant she was no longer of the Red Isles. She was Sulitarian and that was all there was to say about it.

Abika stood at the bottom of the path where the gas well used to be, not remembering how she arrived there. The well was now a crater so wide that the path to the commune had been swallowed up by it. A fine mist floated over a chamber that descended into darkness further than Abika could see. There was no more flame, but then that might be because there was no more gas. The smell of it was all around, hanging heavy in the dank air.

Mutta was scrambling around the edge of the crater screaming Aki's name at the top of her voice. "Jæk'ob! Dur Thæ Jæk'ob!" Her eyes fell upon Abika's. "Come here, girl! Hold me!"

Abika rushed over, tears falling. "Where are they, Mutta?"

Mutta grabbed Abika's arm and lowered herself into the crater, immediately digging and shovelling soil and stone away. "Jæk'ob, Urlä Thærmuallakan!" Her hands were spades, her arms drawing strength from her grief. She lifted huge boulders away from where the hole had been as though they were made with nothing but papermash.

Abika and Mutta had once made masks with papermash. It had

involved cutting the bark from the trees along the shoreline and mixing it with water. Her mask had been a devil daemon. They didn't exist of course, but for many nights after, Abika had struggled with sleep, imagining what their fangs could be like, and those red eyes in the dark. She wished she could be back there now, she and Meorith and Lorith chasing Aki with masks on. Aki would turn and laugh and fall and they would jump upon him and pretend to eat him alive.

The buried slab atop which the seal had originally been sitting had shifted from the force of the explosion, closing the well.

"Aki is gone."

"Jæk'ob." Mutta turned towards her, her eyes red like Abika's mask, a devil daemon with teeth bared. "Urlä Thærmuallakan! Forrthath Maearll!" Then those eyes looked beyond Abika.

"Jæk'ob?"

"Freja." Abika turned to see Aki, standing tall. Strong. Blackened around the edges, and with a smear of blood across his chest, but very much alive.

"Jæk'ob!" Mutta scrambled up the side of the crater and threw herself into Aki's arms. "You're alive! My heart, I thought...I thought you had gone. Thank all the seas and the Forbringrs and...Oh, Jæk'ob."

"I am still here, my dearest," said Aki. "I am not quite ready to leave you. Not yet."

"I'm fine too, thanks Mutta." Tears streamed down Abika's face at the sight of Meorith. She quickly wiped them away but found she could not speak.

Mutta buried her face into Aki's muddy chest and pulled away. "What happened, my heart? How did you live? That explosion was big enough to kill a whale."

"You are not wrong," said Aki. "It was Meorith. She heard a large hiss as the air pumping down the pipes turned off. There was a surge, and she threw herself onto me and the seal tossed us out of the hole like a bottle cork popping." He stuck a finger in his ear and waggled it around.

Meorith was yawning widely too, apparently trying to stretch out the ringing in her ears. "We were lucky," she added, with a wince.

Aki shook his head and laid a hand on Meorith's shoulder. "Luck?

No. The Great Mother smiled down upon us. There must be an offering to thank her for our lives."

"What about the heating?" It felt like such an obvious question to Abika, but none spoke. Instead, they just stared at her, black and dirty and smeared with blood. "Are we to be cold now?"

"Abika!" roared Mutta. "Your father almost dies and you are talking of heating?"

"No, she's right," said Aki, looking under his brow at her. "Every problem must be addressed, otherwise they will stack upon each other and bury us."

Mutta shook her head. "Let us not talk of burial." She brushed the dirt from her hands. "I thought you were both taken below the ground. I thought I would never see you again."

"I saw those rocks you were moving, Mutta!" said Meorith. "You truly have the strength of the Great Mother!"

"Yes, well. You wait until your heart is taken from you and see if you could not lift a mountain to save them."

They wandered back up the path to the commune, Mutta and Meorith recounting the day's luck in excited chattering, but Aki never took his eyes from Abika not until they reached the battered old front door.

"Pour the tea," he said to Mutta and Meorith. "It might be a while before we're drinking anything hot." He held out an arm to stop Abika from entering the commune and quietly closed the door. "Wait a moment, Abika. I need a word." He studied her a moment, the gears of that quiet, introspective mind turning behind deep-set blue eyes.

Abika's heart pounded. She replayed everything she had done. She was in trouble, but what could it be? Perhaps he had worked out that she'd taken Freja's shard necklace. "Yes, Aki?"

"It seems that we are now due a trip into town. I want you to stay here, and—"

Abika shook her head. "No, Aki. Please, I want to come." The whole world lay behind her, and yet all she could see was the door, and Aki. There had to be more out there, and she wanted to see it, and something deep within her told her that she had to. "You always said you would take me to town one day, when I was old enough."

"You've been before."

"When I was too young to remember it! I am old now."

"You are twelve, child."

"Don't talk down to me, Jekob."

Aki stood up straight. "Jekob? You use my name now?" His eyes narrowed. "You're right. You are old enough. Old enough to smoke. Old enough to snoop around our room."

Abika swallowed. If you were going to be caught between two lies, it was better to be caught in the smaller. She made her lie obvious. "I...I don't know what you mean."

"Yes, you do. I know how much tom'ra was in that jar. Adults do not steal."

Abika bowed her head and put her hands in her pockets, fingering the shiny surface of Mutta's shard necklace. "Yes, Aki."

Aki placed a warm hand on her shoulder then lowered his voice. "You can buy some of your own leaf tomorrow. In town."

7

OFFERING

It was late afternoon by the time preparations had been made for the offering. The sun was barely thirty minutes from setting over the bay, but all was ready. Abika tugged on the leash around the pig's neck to keep the animal from pulling.

"And we give thanks," said Mutta, her arms swaying above her head, "for the lives of Meorith, and Jekob, and for your wisdom in keeping them true." Her face was a mask of powdered white, with a tribal design of red and black daubed across her cheekbones and down beyond the neckline of her wispy dress. It was less a dress and more a dirty white full-body wrap, with faint stains of brown around the shoulders.

"Bee, go!" Meorith shouldered Abika forward towards the plinth Mutta stood behind.

"Upon which," groaned Mutta, her voice taking on a more of-the-heavens quality now. "We offer this sow graciously..."

Abika stopped at Aki's side, keeping clear of his naked torso. He was painted from head to toe in white too, with red and green splatters that were still wet.

"The rule is just before sunset, child," whispered Aki.

She frowned up at him. "I wasn't thinking that."

"I was," breathed Aki.

Abika smiled despite herself.

"May her flesh sate your hunger, and her blood, your thirst," repeated Mutta, with more arms than were probably needed. She took up the long knife that usually hung over their bed and threw a fold of her dress over it. The material floated down and fell apart as it touched the blade.

She must have made an audible noise because Aki nudged her. "It has to be that sharp, Abika. It is only fair to the pig." He raised his eyebrows at her, and Abika nodded at the subtext.

"Why a sow? There's a male in there." she asked.

"An offering has to be something you will miss," whispered Aki.

Abika blinked. "And we'll leave her to rot? I was looking forward to crackling."

Aki exhaled slowly. "So was I, Bee. So was I." Mutta shot them both a look. "Go, you're up."

Abika approached the plinth, rolling her eyes at Mutta's wild gesticulating. It was so funny that Abika was having trouble keeping the smirk away, until all at once those movements took on a new purpose. The long blade moved this way and that, dangerously close to Mutta's painted skin, slicing through Mutta's clothes as it went, reducing it to shreds that fell about her feet, and leaving only her nakedness. Her entire body was painted to look like the body of a Ruffin, a terrifying and gargantuan lizard-like creature that could change colour at will. Just the thought of it was enough to give Abika nightmares, but thankfully there were none in Ipiti.

The design had been carefully applied daubed Mutta's white skin, from her thighs to the horns at her neck. Her breasts were part of the design too, making the slightly protruding eyes of the beast, with yellow slits painted around the nipples.

Mutta's expression became one of the daemon mask once more, more terrifying as it was someone Abika knew, morphing slowly into the undead, brought back to life to feast on the flesh of those who foolishly offered themselves up to the gods. Mother Baeivi and the Stallo were creators but what business did they have creating life from death? Sacrificing made no sense. The thoughts taking shape made no difference to Mutta's resolve, and Abika had to abide as the blade grew bigger, whipping around her and cutting the evening shift Aki had asked her to wear. Soon both she and Mutta stood as naked as the day they entered this world.

"We offer to the gods," said Mutta. "We appease their want this day for the gift of Jekob and Meorith's life."

Abika glanced over her shoulder and both her father and Meorith had abandoned their clothes also.

"Today is no ordinary offering," bellowed Mutta. "Today, Abika, we also give upon your name to the Great Mother. We never knew your day of birth. The woman who gave you to us never revealed it when she left you here for me. But I name you on this day as a sign that you are no longer a child in the eyes of this family, and even though you are not mine, you will be ours after today. We will drink, and we will tell stories to each other, and we will sleep long into the morn." Mutta held the blade out to her. "Take this, Abika."

Abika took the blade without question. The ritual demanded it. "I am to be named," she said.

"She is to be named," muttered Aki and Meorith from behind.

Mutta nodded and took the pig's leash. "You are to be named, Abika. A name which means literally, *Gift of the Great Mother*. And gift to us and to—"

The blade was heavy and awkward, but perhaps it only felt like that because of how sharp she knew it was. Holding it with both hands, Abika let the blade drop and pulled it across the pig's throat, spilling the animal's blood to the mud. The pig's squealed, then coughed. The legs went soon after, and stupid animal thudded to the mud.

Mutta's face was one of fury itself. "Abika! We were not ready! There was still a reading—"

The pig interrupted her with a squealing protest bubbling from the animal's open neck. The warm blood pooling at Abika's toes was a strange feeling against the cold muddy shore of the bay.

Mutta snatched the blade from her. "Jekob, take Meorith."

Abika heard the two behind her shuffle together their things and make their way back through the trees to the commune. Mutta might have redressed herself, had her clothes not been cut to ribbons, instead she just stood there unashamed.

"You are not mine," uttered Mutta, her eyes on the distant storms of the Middle Sea. "You know, those words are not scripture. In fact, they're not even a part of the offering. They came from me, Abika." She held her hands over stomach. "I am unable to bring life into this world, but still, I wanted to be a mother. Even as your foster parents, I could never understand how a mother could just hand over her child to strangers."

Abika balked. This was beginning to feel uncomfortable. She knelt down to pick up her ruined shift.

Mutta pointed the blade at her. "Stand up. You are an adult now, Abika, and you will be punished so."

Abika shivered despite herself. "Will you cut my throat?" The knife didn't waver.

"We give you so much, Abika, and yet you still dishonour us at every turn. I thought today might go some ways as to repair our relationship, Abika. I thought we might finally become like mother and daughter."

"Like Meorith?"

Mutta shook her head. "Meorith had five cycles on you when she came to us. Jekob found her wandering the streets in Maerd."

"Meorith is from Hauwi?"

Mutta nodded. "A Hauwi girl, imagine that. Though, you wouldn't think it to look at her." Mutta smiled, but her eyes were filling with tears. "I just don't know who you are anymore, Abika. You're not mine, and it seems you never will be."

"You're right there, Freja." Abika knew she shouldn't say what was in her mind. It would cut deeper than any blade, but as sure as the sun she couldn't help it. "I will never be yours. And one day I will find my real parents, and I'll not think of you ever again."

Mutta nodded slowly, then the tears fell. She closed her eyes and took a deep breath, as though she wanted to say something. When she opened them again, that flat smile was back again. "Good night, Abika." She spared Abika one more glance, then turned and left, leaving her standing on the beach alone.

There were birds still chirping in the air, but it was mostly quiet. Even the road behind the distant trees, which often had cart traffic, was silent. Abika watched Mutta until the trees stole her from view, then sat herself down on the dead pig's fuzzy body until the sun had long since vanished behind the distant storms.

VASTA

8

PITY BE UPON THEM

The sinew strings of Vasta's guitar rolled off the end of his fingertips, releasing sound out into the warm evening air. The music notes flattened out, becoming one with the thin smoke of his crackling fire, joining a chorus of lapping waves from the nearby seashore, the soft cawing from the duskgulls, and the rustling of new spring leaves hanging from the birch tree behind him. It was a song that tied Vasta to the world with a tether of natural music.

Tuning his mind to the strings, he relaxed into it, with no particular tune in mind, just an idea of which notes should join with which. He kept the chords major, but that was the extent of his purpose; he was merely a conduit for this section of the piece, and this newly crafted guitar was his medium.

The sound had yet to bed in, the strings and wood still strangers, but come the moonrise, they would be lovers, intimate in ways that only the two could be.

His fingers were no longer a part of him as he played. The memory of cycles of scientific experimentation running through his carpals had clearly not dulled despite his tendency to think otherwise. His hands were his most prized tools, capable of dropping even the smallest measures of mercura, or separating hair filaments of hearthsalt from iron. As far as he knew, he had been the only Bohr capable of doing so, yet now a smattering of musical notes were the extent of their success. Annoyance crept into his heart at his mind's proclivity to wander. He acknowledged the emotion and let it evaporate, embracing a diminished fifth, before letting the major return as a soft harmonic.

The tune calmed his soul, but not his mind. The trees were moving in the wind as they had done since they had been old enough to flower, and still Vasta's heart lurched. He scanned the fauna, searching for eyes, faces, weapons, but there were none. The road to Ipor Dan was far enough away that he shouldn't be bothered, but it didn't stop his mind playing and replaying a thousand possible occurrences and conflicts. It had been almost a century of exile, living away from his own kind, but it wasn't the isolation that so ate at his resolve. It was the hostility of humans. The White Dragon were at his door. Threats lurking, fights starting. They wanted him.

His fingers stumbled—was that all he was now, even after so long? A Bohr standing afraid. Hiding away from the humans who wished him nothing but harm? Where might he have ended up had he been truly left alone? What might he have achieved if had he stopped running and stayed to fight those would only use him? Perhaps the worlds truly did have a plan for him.

A deep red cloud of anger swallowed him whole. What business was it of the worlds to dictate his life? The worlds were not sentient! They could not choose. Fate was a lie, a reflex of social evolution regurgitated from human minds far less capable than his. So why was he afraid?

"Why?!"

Vasta had stopped playing, his fist tight before him. The echo of shout was deadened by the trees behind but not the water in front, and the sound rippled away from him and bounced around the valleys.

He splayed his fingers, extending his thick black claws, hoping it might diffuse the tension but the lightness of the moment had gone. He had wasted it, as he had wasted all else. The evening air seemed no longer a symphony of sound but rather a damp, oppressive cage with the ocean on one side and the hills behind. Anger caught in his throat, too deep to ignore. It could be quelled, because it was only anger at his own foolish choices, but one must not quell the natural forces of these worlds.

He stood up and lifted the guitar above his head, and it bumped into the low branches of the birch tree and fell behind him, dropping awkwardly over the uneven ground with the unmistakable sound of cracking wood.

“Fool,” he whispered, with a shake of his head. He lifted the guitar carefully, but the tension of the strings pulled the damaged neck splintering away from the body.

Anger rose up like magma filling the chambers of a volcano. He should have smashed that guitar into the ground, and torn the very fibres of wood until they were but particles of matter floating away over the Middle Sea. Instead, he took a long breath and placed the guitar back into its case, ignoring the broken sounds, then turned towards the road. All that awaited him between here and home were the White Dragon night guards.

Vasta lifted the case up onto his back and licked his lips. “And pity be upon them.”

9

WORD OF THE WHITE DRAGON

The road into Ipor Dan could barely be called a road. The commune was so far out of town that any excursion meant crossing at least four livestock fields first. Hadaya, their strongest nara, pulled their cart slowly forwards, but she was still smaller in comparison to the other nara that passed by, swinging their antlers and stomping as they did.

Hadaya's clip-clopping drifted in and out of Abika's head as her thoughts jumped between the necklace tied around her wrist and the prospect of being in town. What would she do? Who would she meet? She knew where she was going first, at any rate.

"You go to town a lot, Aki," asked Abika. "Why?"

"Many reasons."

Abika held her hand out, letting the wind whip over it. "Any you'd care to share?"

Aki snorted. "You were right, Abika. You are older. But no. Those are stories I shall keep to myself."

"Until I'm what... thirteen? Twenty? One hundred."

"We can only hope to live so long," said Aki. "You are nervous." He nodded to her leg bouncing beneath her hak.

Abika shrugged. "It always does that."

"Don't be. I am here. Though we have much to do."

Aki didn't speak much of these *dangers*, whatever they were, but it was impossible to hide fear. It was such a powerful emotion, that even Aki couldn't manage it. Mutta was much better at it, hiding it within layers of seething scorn and nagging.

A torqa flew past them on the down hills at the cliff road, the man dragging it used the weight of the cart so that each second step was a long leap. It looked like fun, until the wheels clipped the cliff's edge and both man and cart were almost sent plummeting down into the river below. Heated words were exchanged with Aki, but then that was Sulitaria for you. Foreigners were few in Ipiti, but they still referred to Sulitaria as the Outer Isles. Aki often spoke angrily of the term. *"The outer of what! There are too many islands within Sulitaria to just name them the Outer Isles. Bloody Ringlanders."*

The road eventually flattened out into the stream moors and finally the last forest before Ipor Dan. It was near mid-morning when the tight road opened out into a vibrant market square split by a long canal. The colour and life was astounding. Bright birds dipped and dived between vendors and archways, around corners and streets that buzzed with activity and the smells of cooking meat, spice and perfume. Compared to the commune, Ipor Dan was paradise!

"Stay here with Hadaya. Abika, are you listening?"

"Yes, of course. No, wait! Why do I have to stay?"

Aki strapped Hadaya to a fence outside a long building where a long line of other beasts sat chewing cud and yoke. "First stop is nara feed. Hadaya loves us, but will stray without food." He slapped her rump, drawing a snort. "I'll be back soon. We have a lot to do today."

"Yes," muttered Abika, as Aki walked off. "So, you keep saying."

Abika held the shard necklace around her wrist up. The morning sun shone brightly through the crystal changing it from a green to red. She waited until Aki was far enough away then took one hesitant step forward, then another, until soon the cart and Hadaya were lost behind her in the crossing traffic.

Ipor Dan was a sprawling city. Even here, before the market, Abika had never seen so many people, and so much skin! And not all old and wrinkly like Mutta or Aki, but young people walking around with their tops off, their chests on display to the world. A pair of boys walked by her talking in the city tongue about a lost round of the dice game Briš. She watched them until they disappeared around a corner.

The dusty road was strewn with dung, so she spent most of the time watching her feet, but when she did look there was always a building, twice as high as the commune, looming above her. Háongs were thin homes that lined every street, but it was the energy that struck Abika most. Everywhere was so fresh and filled with bright promise.

Skipping around traffic and nara shit, the háongs eventually led her to a main street that was split down the middle by the canal. She moved to the side to let the bustling people by and to get a better view.

Canoes lined the canal, vividly painted and laden with baskets of seeds, fruits and sizzling meats. Anything Abika could possibly need in life, she could buy right here, if she could navigate the narrow paths either side of the canal without misstepping, of course. Chances are she would land in a canoe filled with dragonfruit before the water.

The buzz of barter became louder, the sound bouncing between the háongs on either side where children played. Abika's nose caught a familiar smell as groups of young men sat smoking leaf near the entrances, laughing and jibing with each other and taking up big areas of space that forced the crowds closer.

As Abika stepped down off the bridge over the canal, she noticed that most still wore their ceremonials from morning prayer. Wide-brimmed hats called dangs kept the bright sun out of eyes and were so numerous that Abika could have raced across the top of the crowd.

"Itraeka!"

Abika snapped around and a man shoved by her. Abika followed in his wake down the busy street. Aki had joked once never to make eye contact with the infamous canal vendors, or you would be hounded, but every stall glittered with promise and gold drawing Abika's eye like a hungry magpie.

Abika tucked in at a stall that wasn't so busy which sold cheeses of all kinds and smelled like a wet goat. "Excuse me?"

"Yes!" cried the woman, as rotund as she was loud. "We have an eastern blue here with your name on it. What is your name, my dear?"

"It's Abika."

"Abika," repeated the vendor. "God's gift. And indeed you are, but

I'd wager you have some Kemen blood in you with those big brown eyes of yours. What do you need today? We have blues, and some very ripe goat's cheese. Fresh this week. What about this?" Before she could protest the woman had thrust a yellowish curd into Abika's mouth. "Isn't it wonderful? It's from the Isle of Dor. Imported." The last word she said with a slow nod, as if importing anything explained the cost.

Abika swallowed the foul lump. "No, I'm looking for—"

"The Dor is very strong, I'll admit. Maybe you'd prefer something softer and less intense. Try this, it's from the north—the city of Iporiti."

Abika's mouth was suddenly full of white cheese.

"It's good isn't it? Now this one—"

Abika stepped back, and was almost swept away by the current of people. "No!" she said, swallowing the curds. "No, please! I'm looking for Vasta's shop." Abika held up her wrist and the shining shard necklace. "He sells things like this—"

The vendor's mouth twisted. "Go on! Be gone with you!"

"What, I—" A piece of Dor's finest flew by her head and into the face of a gaunt man walking by."

Abika backed away and joined the rushing lines unsure what she had said. She tried again with other vendors: an unclean looking man who sold fish heads; another who sold raisins and dried fruit, although she actually managed to catch some of those discards; and even a leather tanner who threw a handful of rivets at her head.

By the time Abika reached the end of the market street she had at least eaten well. Tired and browbeaten, she looked back down the canal. "Whoever you are, Vasta, it seems you are not popular amongst the locals."

The afternoon sun dipped beyond the tall streets plunging the city into shadow. The canal wound its way around Ipor Dan, but there were so many twists and turns that leaving the water meant getting lost in a maze of dusty streets. Aki would know by now that she had left Hadaya. Maybe he was looking for her out here in the dark alleyways.

Paper lanterns shone above the main roads, but an hour had passed since the last one. Two young boys looked out at Abika from a dark doorway, their faces and intentions hidden in shadow. She hurried on, trying to look as though she knew what she was about. The roads continued, each street identical to the last until Abika stumbled over something.

"Fruit baskets?" There was no one around, so Abika grabbed the yoke between the two wicker baskets and resumed walking. "I'm just a local on her way home." Inside one of the baskets was an orange which would keep the hunger away.

Eyes followed her wherever she turned. Maybe one of them knew who Vasta was. Maybe they could show her the way to his shop. Either way, she wasn't going home tonight. Mutta would moan, Aki would despair—

"Girl." The word was simple, but it froze Abika's blood.

She turned to see two boys standing behind her. "What are you doing?" said the oldest boy.

"Eating." Abika popped the last segments of orange in her mouth then licked her fingers. "Why? What's it to you?" The first boy had dark hair and blue eyes, with full lips, while the other had mousy-brown hair with blue-green eyes. "I've come from the market."

"No, you ain't," said the older boy.

"Yes, I have."

The older boy took a step forward. "Them's our baskets."

"Nope."

The older boy nodded, smiling a line of wonky teeth. "It is. We collected a whole cart full of them from the port in the south of Ipiti just yesterday. We spent the whole morning filling up a hundred of those crates with oranges to sell at the market. We delivered the rest ourselves and finished an hour ago. I could pick that exact crate out of a sea of crates just like it!"

"You deliver oranges?"

"And you ate the last one!" snapped the younger boy.

"Oh," said Abika with a shrug. "Well, it was good, if that's any consolation."

"It should be," said the older boy, reasserting himself. "They're from the Red Isles." He waited as though Abika was supposed to understand.

"Red Isles oranges are the best oranges in all of Sulitaria! Who doesn't know that?"

"I know that," said Abika. "Because I'm from right here." She gestured to the street around her.

"Where?" said the oldest boy. "Point to your house."

The younger boy grabbed at the older. "Alar, look!"

A woman and two men had marched round the far corner moving in a triangle like wolves prowling, straight towards Abika and the two boys.

"Come with us," pleaded Alar.

Abika shook her head at the older boy. "No."

The younger boy stepped closer and pulled at Abika's arm. "Please, girl. Please," he whispered. "The Dragons hurt people."

"Hello there," hissed the woman. Her ceremonials whipped around her as she rounded upon them. "It seems we have some children out after dark."

"It's barely sun-down," said Abika.

"Cheek too," said the man at the back. He sounded like the woman looked, dangerous.

Alar pulled on Abika's hak. "Come on," he breathed.

"What's your name, market girl?" asked the woman.

"It's Itraeka."

"Well, Itraeka. Anyone who works at the market knows that all business needs finished by sun-down. By order of the White Dragon."

"Those who ain't," said the man at the back, "get punished."

"Punished?" said Abika.

"You heard me." His knife made no sound as it was released from his sheath. He produced a rag from his sleeve and began wiping the blade, making it dirtier.

The woman tilted her dang showing black painted lips. "Where are you from, Itraeka?"

"Dor."

"See, Losa," said the man at the back, pointing out each word with his knife. "She don't know! How many times ought I bloody say it! Ohalo's been keeping the word of the White Dragon to hisself. Maybe's we should educate her—"

The second man struck out, knocking the other's knife clanking to the stone. "Don't be abusing the Speaker around me, Dolum."

"Stae...come on now," said Losa as Dolum picked up his knife. He held it up, inspecting it and muttering under his breath. "We don't assault our own. Even a bastard like you knows the rules."

"I thought we had squads in Dor," said the one called Stae. "If she was really from there, she should know the rules by now. She's lyin."

"We've no squads in Dor, not yet." Losa's tongue licked lips like a snake. "What about them two?"

"Naw," gruffed Dolum. "I recognise these two shits. They're regulars in the market."

Stae stepped forward. "Where abouts in Dor are you from, girl?"

Abika pretended. She was good at pretending. "Out of town. I'm a bit lost." She looked to her hands, fiddling with the lashing around the baskets like she was nothing but a nervous and lost little child.

Stae placed a hand on her shoulder and squatted down to meet Abika's tear-filled eyes. "Look girl, you can't be walking around after dark. It's dangerous. And you absolutely shouldn't be near these two." They were about to let them go, Abika could feel it. But that was no good to her.

"Do you know Vasta?" she asked.

Stae stood back up. "I know Vasta. Do you know Vasta?"

The trick with lying was keeping it as close as possible to the truth. If you could convince yourself, you could convince anyone. "Not as well as I should," said Abika, "but well enough."

The other two guards glanced between each other, but Stae's eyes never left Abika's.

"It would seem that luck is with us on this beautiful spring night! Stae took out a coin and started flipping it. "I like it when luck visits, it's like rain and sun at the same time." The group laughed with him, and the air felt suddenly dangerous. "Tell me, Itraeka, what do you want with the Bohr called Vasta?"

Abika's heart thumped. Vasta was a Bohr? "I need to see him is all." Abika fingered the necklace in her pocket. "If you could take me to him..."

Dolum stepped closer, looming over her. "We'll not be taking you anywhere, market girl. Especially not to the facking Bohr. Not until you tell us what it is you need from him, and why."

"I have something of his." Of all the things to say, Abika knew immediately she'd chosen poorly. Three pairs of eyes started scanning her, deciding and probing and—

Abika ducked her head and swung the shoulder pole into Losa's guts. The guard stumbled back into the other two and they all fell together in a heap. Abika turned on her heel and bolted, following the two brothers through the streets, through dark alleys and past dark doors until she heard the sound of water. They emerged from an alleyway with the canal in front of them, near the cheese woman's stall, but on the opposite side. Abika peered down the canal to the street that led back to where Jekob had dropped her off.

"What are you doing?" snapped Alar. "Angering the Guard of the White Dragon? Do you have a death wish?"

"A death wish? Who are they?"

The two boys glanced at each other. "You're no market girl, otherwise you'd know who they were."

"No, I'm not. I'm from a commune near the bay but what difference does that make? Who are they?"

Alar blinked. "Just go home, bay girl. Your parents will be worried."

Abika snarled. "Don't tell me what to do, *Alar*. You don't know me. And it doesn't matter who you are anyway, and I don't care." She turned then stopped. "Unless you can you tell me how to find this Bohr. This Vasta?"

The younger brother shook his head. "Alar, she outsmarted the Guard of the White Dragon!"

Alar frowned, then shook his head. "So what if she outsmarted the Guard! It's not hard, Kalim! Look, bay girl, I don't know where this Bohr of yours lives, but Lorith might."

Abika's breath caught. "Lorith, you say? Who's that?"

10

HARD GRAFT

The shanty town was a bruise on the body of Ipor Dan. Rot and decay claimed all, so that none willing would have stayed there. Were it not for the thin strands of smoke rising from each crumbling shack, Abika might have even believed it. The shoes on her feet and clothes on her back drew many lingering stares.

"Lorith has kept this place going," said Kalim, pulling up a wire fence.

Abika crawled through. "What was it like before?"

Kalim held out a splayed hand showing three fingers missing at the top knuckles.

Abika swallowed. "What happened? Was that the Order of the White Dragon?"

"Just a fight," said Kalim. "The guards leave us be, mostly."

Alar rounded on them. "Unless we give 'em cheek." Alar was a typical big brother, defiant and proud. He reminded Abika of Lorith.

"That wasn't cheek," scoffed Abika. "People are easy to manipulate. You think I was crying for real back there? You just give them what they want, or at least a colour of it and watch as they bounce from one foot to the other. Keep people talking and they're not likely to be thinking much. Don't you know anything?"

Alar pouted. "Of...Of course," his gaze flicked over Kalim. "I knew that..." Frowning, he turned and led them on, kicking a loose stone with his big toe.

Abika grimaced. "What's up with him?"

"He's used to being in charge," whispered Kalim. "And you know more than he does! Itraeka, can you really just cry? Without being sad?"

Abika pressed her lips together at the use of her fake name. It probably wouldn't hurt to keep up the act. "Sometimes, if the moment calls for it—Uch!" She had stepped in a wet patch and her moccasin had disappeared into an inches deep puddle of stinking, oily mud. She yanked it free and sighed long and loud. "Where is Lorith? How long do we have to trek across this awful place?"

"We'll get you to him," said Alar. "It just means walking for a bit."

Kalim clapped his hands together excitedly. "Itraeka, you're amazing! What a power to cry on demand like that. I wish I could do that."

Abika shook her head. "It's not a power you idiot. I'm not a Bàneman!"

"You don't look like a Banèman," said Alar, "but I've heard they can take the form of others."

"Don't look at me like that, Kalim! I'm not a bloody Banèman! Look, Alar. I already know Lorith. So, please, let's get to him."

Alar turned, and Kalim nudged her. "You're a good person, Itraeka," he whispered. "I can see it."

"No," said Abika. "I'm not."

The makeshift shanties and sheds eventually became boxes of brick and stone, still shabby but more familiar. Some even had doors and windows.

Alar brought them to a stop outside the tallest building on the block, even before the blanket entrance had been pulled aside, a foul smell of piss burned Abika's nostrils.

"It's us."

"Alar! Is that you?" The voice came from above. The ceiling was gone, leaving only beams showing. Suspended across the beams was a large bed. A young man's smiling face appeared, looking down at them over the mattress.

"Lorith," said Abika. "Imagine bumping into you out here." He looked exactly like he had the day he'd left Freja and Jekob's care.

"Lorith," announced Alar. "This is Itraeka."

"No, it's not," said Lorith, climbing out of the bed, hopping over the beams and dropping down in front of them like a chimp.

Abika gave Alar and Kalim a sheepish smile. "Sorry I lied. I used you to get here to see my brother."

"Brother now is it?" Lorith stood in front of her looking as ratty and unkempt as the last time she had seen him, if not a bit taller. "You were never so nice to me. Tell me, has Tollo learned to cook yet?

Abika shrugged. "He cooks better than Freja."

Lorith scoffed. "I never thought I'd see you again, Bee. I mean, you always hope to run into your old life so that you may smash it into pieces."

Abika wrinkled her nose. "Don't you dare try and hug me."

Lorith made to put his arms around her then, ran a hand through his black hair. "We're all just meat bags, *Itraeka*. Plus, I don't know what diseases you bring with you."

"Diseases?" said Abika. "Meat bags? You've been by yourselves too long, Lorith."

"Perhaps you're right about that." Lorith threw himself onto a dirty old chair. It creaked loudly and blew out a foul-smelling cloud into the air. "Where'd you find her, Alar?"

"She found us. Stole my baskets and whacked some Guards with them."

Lorith looked impressed. "Guards, Bee? Go you. The Guard of the White Dragon are not so easily distracted. My guess is that you will see more of them before long. Ipor Dan is—"

"A dangerous place?" nodded Abika. "So everyone keeps telling me."

"They're not wrong, Bee," said Lorith, laughing. The fool boy took nothing seriously. "You should listen to them. Since the Tsiorc disbanded after Tyr they've been growing in power. They control much of our fair city of Ipor Dan all the way to the city of Iporiti in the north."

He shrugged. "What's next, Arcez, Dor, the whole of Sulitar? Look, Bee. The Bohr are still out there. Granted, their presence on the many isles of Sulitaria is not as strong as it is across the Middle Sea, but their supporters are here and they are organised. The Guards of the White Dragon *are* dangerous."

"So," started Abika. "The Guard of the White Dragon actually want the Bohr—"

Lorith nodded along with each word. "To take over. Yes. The Guard of the White Dragon are humans who actually *want* to be enslaved. You couldn't make it up."

"Lorith, I didn't come here to share stories. I came because I need your help." She held up the necklace.

Lorith scratched at the scraggle beneath his chin. "That is Freja's."

"Mmhmm," nodded Abika. "Vasta sold it to her, and I'm trying to find him."

"I'd leave Vasta to his own, if I were you, Bee. The Bohr bring nothing but trouble. Especially that one."

"Vasta is the only Bohr in Ipor Dan," added Alar.

"On the whole island, Alar," said Lorith, dismissively. "Possibly the only Bohr in Sulitaria. Imagine being the only one of your kind and being surrounded by smelly humans to boot."

Abika fingered the necklace, wishing the calmness was upon her. She'd give anything to just disappear. To leave and fly away like a bird.

Lorith ambled to the back of the shack and opened a cupboard. It was filled with oranges, bananas, dragonfruit, and even plums. He plucked out a couple of fruits and closed the door. "You hungry?"

Abika wanted to say no, but her stomach rumbled in protest. Before she could say a word, a plumfruit was hurtling through the air towards her. Alar caught it first and handed it to her.

"The Bohr owns a pawn shop on the far end of market street, beyond the canal." Lorith took a bite out of a dragonfruit. "He makes all sorts of tools and things there. I hear he's a real expert."

"Great." Abika turned to leave. The smell was making her feel sick.

"Bee. Have you even met a Bohr before?"

Abika shook her head. "No. I only know that the people of Ipor Dan hate him."

"Because he is a *Bohr*!" Lorith placed his dragonfruit half-eaten upon the dirtiest table Abika had ever seen. "Granted, as Bohr go, Vasta is easier to look at than most but all Bohr are dangerous, Bee, and the Guard *want* this one for some reason. They're always sniffing around his shop, and that makes him unpredictable and dangerous." He stepped closer. "You know how to look after yourself, Bee, even when you were five and you killed that pig for no bloody reason, which was damn impressive by the way! Still, just be careful." Alar and Kalim looked suddenly afraid, and Lorith ambled over and placed an arm around each of their shoulders. "It's true brothers. I swear it. We had to eat that poor sow. First meat of the cycle. All fatty and tasty." His expressions became serious again. "Bee, Ipor Dan has many shades to it, and some are less visible than others. You do not want to get caught up between the Guards of the White Dragon and the Bohr."

Abika smiled and pocketed the plum. "Thanks Lorith. I'd say you should clean up a bit, but you were never really good at that were you? Alar, you look after Kalim. You hear?" She stepped out into the fresh air, breathing deep, and started walking.

Abika had barely finished the plum before Lorith appeared behind her, a pipe clasped between his teeth. "You'll be needing some company, I presume."

"To keep me safe, Lorith?"

Lorith slapped his lumpy leather jacket. "Protection. The only downside is you might get a bit sweaty, but it's well after curfew. And even I don't go out after curfew, Bee."

Abika sucked the plum pit dry and threw it into a drainage gutter, watching as the dirty water carried it away like a ship out to sea. "Stop calling me Bee."

"That's your name."

"My name is Abika." She was angry, annoyed and impatient all at once. "Is that tabac?"

"It is. And no you can't have any, before you ask. Wait." Lorith stopped her. "It's a bit late to be browsing the stalls. Vasta's shop will be closed."

"I've spent all day looking for him, Lorith. I want to get my answers and go home. Jekob will be ending himself."

"Jekob." Lorith shrugged. "Well, I imagine you still call him *Aki* but he barely ever spoke to me. He doted upon you and Meorith though, right from the start. That's when he wasn't working out along the bays and in town, of course. You know, I remember when you came to us, Bee. He gushed over you. Loved you he did. Mutta was...well, Mutta, but then I always got the impression Freja never really had a heart in that tomb of a chest. Maybe a stone, or a lump of nara shit."

Abika pulled up the wire fence. "After you."

Lorith didn't duck under. He was frowning. "You're punishing Freja, aren't you? That's why you have her necklace. You're going to sell it to Vasta."

"She bought it from Vasta,' said Abika. "I'm just bringing it back to him."

"Forbringr's ashes, Abika! You can't be serious? You're still trying to punish your mother?"

"She's not my mother!" Abika's anger threatened to blow out of her like a steaming kettle. She pushed Lorith, but the boy she had once known so long ago was much bigger now, though perhaps not quite a man. Abika caught herself from stumbling over herself, and realised that Lorith was rigid. "What is it?"

"Quiet." Lorith held out an arm, blocking the way. He stumbled back from the street corner. "It's the Guard."

Abika peeked out to see three Guards of the White Dragon walking towards them. It wasn't the three she had encountered, but these three looked equally dangerous, investigating windows and doorways with hands on hilts, as if the shadows themselves might attack.

"They're all like that, Bee. Ready to kill first and ask questions later. Lorith pulled her back again. "Abika, we need to find somewhere else to go."

"You know somewhere?"

"I know a place."

Abika grimaced. "Does it smell better than the last place?"

Lorith shook his head. "Worse."

Lorith led Abika up the narrow, stone stairwell of the háong that stood off the canal. Abika peeked in through an open door and at least ten faces turned towards her. It was like the commune but with a fraction of the space.

Lorith opened the door to a tiny room on the third floor, barely wide enough for four people standing shoulder to shoulder. Other than a wall-mounted water tap, there was no water works, no privy anywhere to be seen. She moved the curtain at the back and peered down into a courtyard, where some adults were milling back and forth. A man was sitting at a firepit near the back of the adjacent building, roasting meat.

"If you need to piss," said Lorith, "then go downstairs." He pushed past her and pointed beyond to an outhouse beyond the firepit. The man looked up and waved and Lorith waved back. "But if you can hold it I would. I wouldn't trust him down there as far as I could throw him." Lorith let the thin material fall and began rummaging around the room looking for something.

"He doesn't like you?"

"Not really. Not after..." He paused, bent over a tower of papers sitting carefully balanced on top of a chair. "It's probably not worth getting into to be honest. Boring really."

"Is that why you were in Iporiti?"

"Iporiti?" Lorith glanced sidelong at her, then a slow grin formed. "I thought I snuck that one past you." He reached behind the chair and picked up a single square piece of paper just lying on the floorboards.

Abika shook her head; suddenly it was all so clear. "Leaf?"

"Leaf," said Lorith sitting back on the bed. "Tom'ra. The good green. People have to smoke, Bee. What would you prefer? Spend your life stealing it from your parents?"

"They're not my parents."

"Alright, alright." He sat up, excitedly. "You know, we're growing something much stronger than any leaf Freja smokes these days." He opened the paper wrap and held it out. "Gardeners, they call us."

"No thanks, Lorith. I'm here to do—"

"Ah yes. The necklace. Well, you can always do it tomorrow."

"Give it here then." Abika opened the folded paper to reveal a square of blue powder. "What is it?"

"It's tom'ra, though maybe not as you know it. I met someone who taught me how to graft. It's where you connect two—"

"I get it, Lorith," said Abika. "So what, you took two plants and just..."

Lorith nodded, clearly pleased with himself. "Grafted them together. Yes. The grafted plants turn blue when picked, which is why the dried, crushed leaves are blue."

"And this is what you get from it?"

"Oh no," smiled Lorith. "Those plants got bigger, sure. The stalks changed colour too, but the leaf stayed much the same strength. So, I grafted upon grafts. And eventually the high got so strong! We had to peel it back in the end, after one of the gardeners overdosed. His heart got drunk, and just stopped."

Abika closed the paper and handed it back. "This stuff killed him?"

"Oh, Gods no. This batch is only about four grafts deep, rather than the twenty that got him. Four grafts is the sweet spot, enough bite to be interesting, but not too harsh, and still sweet enough to enjoy. Here, look." He pulled his well-blackened pipe from his pocket and used his long pinkie nail to drop some in. "You can mix it with tabac if you want, helps it taste better, but I usually don't bother. Tabac prices have shot up around the canal, and any you buy outside of the canal is probably more oak than it is tabac!"

Almost unconsciously Abika had removed Aki's pipe from her pocket. She held it out and Lorith took it and loaded it, before handing it back. "Now what?"

Lorith took a flint from his shirt pocket. "Just light it. You'll get one soft puff, called the head, one strong called the body, and one soft but hot, called the tail. I wouldn't take too much of the tail or the head. Ease into it." Lorith struck a single spark expertly into the little cone of powder sitting in her pipe, then stepped back and waited.

He was right, the first puff tasted powdery, but by the gods it was strong. Her head was already swimming when she lifted the pipe to her lips for the body. It was like being immersed in sweet confusion. A familiar lightness infused her soul as she took in the room. There was a rip in the curtain and through it she could see high above in the night sky where the stars shone like candles, twinkling in the vastness. The moon was nowhere to be seen, but she didn't miss it. She could make her own light anyway now the calm was on the way.

Nothing mattered anymore. The necklace, Lorith, the room. They all vanished behind a veil of blue smoke that swirled around, caressing her. Her throat felt dry, so she got up to get a drink. She stepped towards the tap and reached out for it. She blinked, and she was back on the bed again. She hadn't moved. She tried again. Each time it got harder, then she forgot what she was trying to do. The water was shimmering, but just out of reach. Life could shimmer, like air, her blood, her mind. With a huge effort she turned her head and the room spun in the other direction. Someone was there. Was it Lorith?

Her fingers were getting warm.

Lorith's smile slipped and slid and floated up, he was standing above her, he moved to the tap then he was back again, holding out a sea of...A glass. Of water. She wanted to drink. But her hand.

Her hand would not obey her.

Lorith brought the cup to her, and she sipped at the wonderful liquid.

Her fingers.

Perhaps she should try and bring the lights from her palm, now she finally had some calm about her, but she was suddenly so tired. Each blink dragged like her eyelids were lifting. Nausea followed—she'd had bad trips before so she knew enough not to move.

She always wished that the lights would stay longer, but they never did. Conjuring them was easy enough, it happened without thinking nowadays and only when she smoked, but only once, and only for a moment. There was no one else she'd met who could do it, or at least who talked about it, but why would you ever tell someone you conjure sparks out of thin air? What possible benefit would it ever bring to her life? She tried it again, focusing the calm into her fingertips and concentrating. Nothing. She fancied see could stars, like at night time.

The room melted away in front of her, replaced with a beach long and sandy. There was some nearby, sitting with her. "Meorith, what makes the stars move?"

Meorith looked at her. "The stars? Bee, that is a thunderstorm."

Flashes filled the clouds like water in a cup, burgeoning with blue light. "There is no thunder."

Meorith laughed. "Of course not. It is far away."

Abika tried to say she didn't understand.

"The sound comes later. There is a delay between the darkness and the light. You can delay them, Bee. You just have to know how."

"And the thunder always comes?"

"Always. There must always be balance, little bird."

"Little Bird? My name is Abika." Meorith snarled and Abika found herself laughing uncontrollably. "You look ridiculous!" Despite the laughter and Meorith's scorn, Abika felt the fire of a burning question. She reached for it, and the little spot of light opened into her like a flower blooming. "How do I stop the thunder from coming?"

Meorith's eyes grew wide, her face was changing. "You ask the right questions, but only the most powerful can stop it. The force of the flash is as pure and true as the earth, the sun and the sky. If you trip, you fall. None can stop the light. The flash to the thunder. They are two parts of the same thing. The head to the body."

Abika shook her head. Even as Meorith's features began to melt away. "There is always a way. I must find out."

"Power," said Meorith. "That is the way. Fill yourself with power."

The grafted tom'ra was playing tricks with Abika, but something else was happening. She knew what was real. And this was very real, but still she had to ask. "Who are you?"

Meorith's features had changed completely. The warm expression and kindly round face that Abika knew so well was now sharp, pointed and chiselled. Meorith's long hair was now short and mousey brown and she looked more masculine. Her face was not hers any longer, nor was it Lorith's. It was a daemon's face. And when it opened its mouth, fire and heat and darkness poured forth from it.

"You will know me soon enough. Now. Wake up, little bird. Wake up."

11

BARTER AND SALE

I'm going to Vasta's. Get more of the blue stuff for when I get back
Abika

Abika put down the charcoal and set the slate upon the shelf in front of the bed Lorith was currently unconscious in. It was heartening to see that the grafted tom'ra had a similar effect on Lorith as it did Abika, but there was something worrying about the depth of that sleep, not to mention the night images that still plagued her waking thoughts. She doubted it would have taken too much more to have made her own heart drunk, then all she would know was sleep and those daemon eyes, forever.

The red-gold square of light shining through the dirty shawl at the window beckoned her over. It lit up the wall above Lorith's bed, shining like a window into a dreamworld. A doorway to another place. Promise and riches. Maybe her real parents might be there, waiting to greet her. Eager to see her. Gods. What would become of her, staring at the grubbiest wall in Ipor Dan as though it shone with the aura of some fantastic world.

She turned to the window and shifted the shawl. The rising sun filled the market street below with golden light. The balcony of Lorith's room stood high above the street, giving her the perfect view of the canoes as the vendors made their way to the canal edge, ready for a day of barter and sale. The colour and variety of the market thrilled her imagination, so many lives living, working, and striving for something better!

Was Aki down there? Looking for her? Abika wanted to care, but whenever she tried to, the concern just slid away.

In bottom of her pocket, past the shard, lay the last of her own leaf, the very same she had pilfered from Mutta's cupboard. Tom'ra was a funny plant. She had never found one, but they were out there, ready for smoking by anyone lucky enough to come across them. Aki and Mutta probably grew the stuff, or Aki simply picked it up whenever he came to town, which was regularly, considering how often Abika stole leaf from them.

Her eyes adjusted as she stepped back inside from the balcony. She had already searched high and low for more of the grafted leaf powder that Lorith had given her. He was clearly a skilled gardener. Her memories were foggy, but she remembered the respect she had for Lorith clear and bright. He had carved out a living for himself in a world that was cruel. He could eat, he could sleep, he could afford to live, or at least squat, in this room. The bunched blanket beneath his head was growing wetter with each laboured, slumbering breath, his neckbeard was flecked with dried skin, and from the ribs jutting out of his chest he looked barely a week away from starvation, but the boy she knew was now grown. And if he could make it, so could she.

"You're gunna teach me how to grow that stuff, Lorith, and together we'll make enough to buy this whole town."

Lorith grunted.

"What a life you have here. I wish it was mine." She retrieved the flakes of her own leaf but there was barely enough tom'ra to blow away the cobwebs, let alone bring a high. She doubted it would even light, so she dug through Lorith's discarded breeches and pulled out some of his tabac and mixed it with the leaf before stuffing it into her pipe.

"Damn," she muttered, pipe in mouth, tapping the pockets of her breeches. There was no way she would find a flint in this mess, not nestled amongst the rags in the corner, not the dirty bowls filled with dried noodles.

"No!" Lorith was talking in his sleep.

Abika crossed the room and replaced the sheet over her commune brother's shoulders. "You're a fool, Lorith. A bloody fool."

Fresh, cool air greeted her when Abika stepped outside, and then the delicious scent of pipe smoke, which drew her to a game table where she borrowed a flint from one of the players.

"Thank you," she said, handing it back.

The boy nodded and returned to the table to take a go. Abika watched as the game took hold, and the men grew excited at the prospect of winning the neatly stacked chits in the table's centre. There was enough there to buy a whole new outfit. Gods knew she needed one herself. The dice tumbled off the table and all the players leapt to the floor at once to grab them. With barely a blink, Abika snatched up a column of chits and walked away. Not a soul had seen her. No one ever would either—she was too fast for that.

"Only four," she said, counting as she walked. "Not bad, but not good." She took a deep toke instead—it might be better to skip breakfast. Four chits might at least see her some of the way back to the commune. The opposite side of the market had no crazy cheese lady, in fact there was barely any food on this side at all. It was all cloths, beads, buttons, wood carvings, and metalwork—different produce on different days.

She stopped by a stand near the end, admiring the spinning patterns catching the light and the bright spots that coloured the shadows all around. "How much?"

The kindly faced vendor smiled and sat up from his canoe. "This one?" He held a hand beneath the many spinning blades and tugged a string beneath. Soft music played from it. "More than you have," he said. "But worry not, life is a circle, and one day you will find yourself with more money than you will ever need. Then the meaning of this spinning roof-sing will be lost, because you could buy a hundred if you so wished."

"Life is ridiculous," said Abika, taking another toke. A low calmness was on its way.

"And as irony would have it," blabbed the vendor, "when you do have enough money to come back, you won't. Life will take over your thoughts and actions, and the passing fancies of childhood will be but a distant memory of a forgotten life." The vendor unpicked the roof-sing from the stall's housing and held it out. "Take it. Business is slow today and this one has been hanging here a few weeks with no interest. My daughter won't mind."

Abika's heart skipped a beat. "I...thank you. Your daughter made this?"

The vendor's face lit up. "Her hands move faster than mine ever could, and I was the best metal worker in all of Iporiti."

Abika clenched her pipe with her teeth and held up the hanging metal sculpture. She pulled the string, but nothing, no music. "What is this? It's stopped! Your daughter must not be very good."

The vendor's smile slipped away. "It needs looked at. Like yourself, there's a stiffness inside that I cannot fix."

"Fix it," said Abika, handing the hanging blades back. "Then I will take it."

The old vendor shook his head. "I think not. It is yours now. If you want me to fix it, it will cost you twelve chits."

"Twelve? I only have four."

The vendor retired back to the low seat on his canoe and picked up a book. "Goodbye!"

"Yes, but—"

"Goodbye!"

Abika carried on until she reached the bridge at the end of the canal, which flattened out into a road that was the end of the market. Below, the water slid away through the water gate. It was tempting to throw away roof-sing in. It was beautiful though, and would look perfect above her own bed. For the first time, she wished Aki was here. She could put the sculpture in the cart and they would carry on back along the road home, laughing at those who drove too close to the cliff edge. The pipe had burned dry, and the calmness had not come. Together it all made for an annoying morning, and she hadn't gotten to Vasta's shop yet! Her stomach rumbled, adding insult to injury. She looked at the roof-sing, then back at the stalls. "But then," she said, "that might just work. Let's see."

The tiny window on the front of Vasta's shop held no sign, and if it wasn't for the word of those passing by, Abika wouldn't have believed anyone lived here, let alone sold anything. She pushed open the door and stepped inside.

The Bohr's shop was less a store and more a home that had been hollowed out, with high ceilings and no internal walls. There was a makeshift room within a room at the back with its own lighting, and walls made from glass. It might have looked out of place except for the fact that there was just so much *stuff*. The building was longer than it was wide, with every shelf and cabinet filled with boxes, stacked high but all neatly arranged. Loose items were stacked in pyramids all over the place. Abika wanted to explore, but she was scared of bumping into something. One fall here and the shop would collapse like dominos and she would be buried beneath it all.

She shuffled sideways towards a counter which had less items stacked upon it and peered over. On the other side was a strange looking instrument, a curvy box with a long neck held together with seven strings, but it looked broken. Beside it stood a bundle of swords wrapped in wet leather. One of the blades had blood on it.

"What are you doing?"

Abika started. It wasn't that the voice was terrifying, but the deepness of that tone shook her to the bone. "What do you think I'm doing?"

A great hulking shape stepped out of the room at the back. How had she not seen him? His horns almost touched the ceiling, but it was his face that held Abika's breath. He looked like a cross between a wolf and a goril. Gorils were native to the jungles of the Red Isles, and she had heard that occasionally a trapper might catch one and skin it for meat or keep it in a cage to show off. This Bohr was different, and those eyes were almost human.

It cleared its throat and the very air seemed to vibrate. "First time meeting a Bohr then." The Bohr blinked at the roof-sing in Abika's hand. "What have you there? Is that to be fixed?"

Abika found her voice somewhere in the pit of her stomach. "Of... Of course it is, why else would I be in here? I bought this with money and...and it's broken."

"Let me see it, then." The Bohr took the sculpture from her with a wide, clawed hand. "You bought this from Al'Duong."

"The metal worker on the canal? Yes. Yes. I bought it from him for twelve chits."

"Twelve?" Simply repeating Abika's lie back to her turned her legs to jelly.

"That's what I said," she glanced around the shop, trying not to stare. "How do you move around in here without breaking anything?"

"Not all of us rush through life unheeding," said the Bohr. "Al'-Duong does good work. For a human."

"His daughter made it," said Abika. The skin of the Bohr's face looked hard, almost scaled, but it creased around the brow. Was that a look of surprise?

"The daughter?" He let out a low chuckle. "I always wondered if it was him who worked the lathes—he has the hands of a child. A human child, anyway." He stepped behind the counter and moved the broken instrument out of the way. "A fix for this will cost two copper coins."

Abika shook her head. "You mean chits? I only have one chit left."

"That's fine." The Bohr seemed even less interested in money than Al'Duong had. Although maybe, in hindsight, the old vendor was just trying to get rid of some old crap.

"There we are," said the Bohr, putting down a long and thin tool. "It's a nice piece. Dreamcatchers are more of a human tradition, but as far as the metalwork goes it's been built with love. It has a nice balance, and all things must have balance."

Abika rolled her eyes. "Sure."

"I don't currently have a tool that will make it sing again though. I'll have to make said tool before I can fix it properly. Unless you just want to look at it, in which case, consider it fixed." He motioned at the door. "Now, if there's nothing else."

Abika frowned. "If it sings, it needs to sing."

"Alright, but the materials alone to lathe a tool will cost five copper coins. Do you have that?"

"No."

"It's good work. You should keep it. Once it is fixed, I imagine it will still be playing when you're an old woman. Come back when you can afford it."

"I don't want it, Vasta." Abika placed the sculpture, tinkling, onto the counter.

He approached her. "Do I know you? You speak like you've said my name more than once."

Abika drew a ragged breath but stood her ground, craning her neck to stare up at Vasta's horned head. "I am Abika." Vasta's expression twisted again, it looked like amusement. "You are the first Bohr I have ever met."

"And."

"And, you are taller, and smellier than I could have imagined."

"Smellier?" Vasta blinked. "Perhaps the dust dunes of Kemen's Cracked Wastes have evolved the Bohr into creatures who smell. Who are you to argue with evolution?"

Abika wasn't sure how to respond. "You sound like a scholar."

"I am. Amongst other things."

Abika looked around once more, seeing the shop with fresh eyes. "Aki once told me of scholars, studying the world, looking for the patterns of Baeivi's creation. You do not look like a scholar."

"Baeivi's creation? This world is just a side effect of a larger piece. Far larger than I, or even you, child, with your great mind, will ever understand. But yes, you are right. I do study the laws of the land. Of your gods."

"And?"

The Bohr's small eyes narrowed. "Your *Great Mother Baeivi* is a social reflex, like the rest of your gods. A conjured spirit to help ease the pain of death. Ironically, life is much more interesting than can be simply explained away by the Great Baeivi."

"So, you're a heretic to boot."

Vasta laughed, and Abika's bones vibrated. He took a long breath. "If you say it, then it must be so, Kami."

"My name is—"

"Kami means 'God's Gift' in Kemenese, Kemen. Which is where your name hails from." The Bohr's face twitched and moved as he talked, giving his animalistic features a strangely human appearance. "There is of course, the school of thought that as trade makes our world smaller, that names take on less meaning. Interbreeding and the like watering down tradition, but I think in your case that you actually have Kemen blood running through you. I can see it in your eyes. Have you ever seen the dunes of Kemen? Or the long flat beaches of Bakla? I'm sure you'd find them as beautiful as I do. Evolution's gift."

Abika scowled. Being spoken about so openly was grating on her. "You don't know me."

"No, but I can surmise, as is a scholar's wont. Kami is more a direct translation of God's Gift, but whoever named you was probably from Kemen."

"Stop it."

"Your parents understood that Kami would better suit a boy, and Abika a girl. I don't know much about the colour of humans, but your skin and your eyes are darker than most here in Ipiti, so I am led to believe that either your mother or father were Kemenese. Your mother probably."

"Don't talk of my parents!" growled Abika. "You don't know them. And you don't know me."

"You are a curious creature," said Vasta. "And so full of anger."

"Just...do not talk of what you do not know.

"People often mistake me as angry, or violent. Especially in Ipor Dan."

"And you say you are none of those things?"

Vasta blinked. "I try very hard not to be."

Abika glanced over to the swords behind the counter. "Do you?"

Vasta followed her gaze. "The road can be a dangerous place."

"Dangerous for whom?"

"For those who bite off more than they can chew."

Abika searched for a way to draw Vasta in, but this creature was cleverer than she was, so she found another way and pulled Mutta's glittering necklace from her pocket. "I was hoping to talk to you about this."

Vasta stood silently, looking from the shard to Abika and back again. "That is mine."

Abika held it away as Vasta reached for it. "No. I took this from my Mutta. She bought it from you."

"She stole it from me," said Vasta. "Many cycles ago."

Abika laughed. "She stole it?"

Vasta nodded. He looked serious. "It is mine, child."

This was Freja's necklace, even if Abika did steal it. She couldn't just give it away. "How much?"

Vasta was watching her intently. "You wish to sell it to me?"

"More or less," said Abika.

"To get back at her?" Vasta held out his huge, clawed hands. "Do you even know what it is?"

"It's a cryst—"

"It is a soulshard. It is inert energy."

Abika stared at the shard. It was beautiful the way the light bounced off of it. "I tried to break it and it made me sick."

Vasta blinked at her. "It made you sick? Were you drawn to it? How did you find it?"

"Look Bohr, I'll sell it to you for a good price. I *am* getting back at someone...but I still won't let it go for less than two hundred chits."

"What is it exactly that you—" Vasta's gaze flicked to the shop entrance, then he rushed by, somehow missing Abika. He placed his heavy claw flat against the door. "Abika, I suggest you find a place to hide."

There were people outside talking. Someone pounded on the door. "We hear you! Let us in, Bohr. In the name of the White Dragon."

Abika turned and looked around, the counter, the room at the back. No, she wanted to listen. She squeezed herself between two sets of cabinets just as the door began to creak open.

"Bohr," came a solid voice. "It is good to see you on this warm, spring morning. The Great Mother has again gifted us."

"Another of God's gifts?" said Vasta. "Luck does indeed grace me today. Hello, Vard. Come in, why don't you."

Two sets of footsteps entered the shop. Abika moved a little to try and see, then stopped as a pyramid of stacked boxes above shook.

"Good morning, Bohr" said the other voice. Abika recognised her as the female guard with the dark lips, Losa.

"No Zular today?" Abika could hear Vasta scratching. "In fact, I haven't seen Zular in some time."

Vard seemed to hesitate. "Uhm. Zular...Zular is busy. He is away. Somewhere else."

"Recruiting the next White Dragons?" said Vasta.

"Never you mind about Zular, Bohr," said Losa.

There was a slight pause, then Vard continued. "You are still closed? Why? This is the best and most fruitful part of the day!"

"Not all of us are trying to sell as much as possible, Soldier Vard."

Vard scoffed. "Soldier? It is Senior Soldier now, Bohr."

"Really?" replied Vasta, amusement spiking his tone. "Good for you then."

"Indeed, it is," said Vard. "Indeed it is." Somebody stopped by the worktop, barely a foot from Abika. She could see the white uniform, and the dragon sigil sewn into it. The leather armour he wore over the top showed he was prepared for a fight. "Tell me, these little boxes, what do they contain? I have always wondered."

Vasta padded over, his back casting a deep shadow over Abika. "Gems, stones, rocks."

There was the faint sound of a tiny box being slid open, and its contents being plucked out. "Gems, you say?"

"Not that one," said Vasta. "That one is called mear'pid."

"Sounds exotic,"

"It's not."

"How much is it worth?"

"Nothing really."

"Then why have it?"

"I like to study the rocks and gems of this world. They give a clue as to how it was made."

"The Great Mother made the lands, Bohr. The sooner your kind understands that, the sooner we can all get along."

"Is that why you're here?" said Vasta, sharply. "So, we can...get along."

"In a way," replied Vard. He sauntered around the shop and picked something up. "Where does this little rock come from then? Underground and forged by the Maker. The embodied soul of a Stallo giant perhaps? Tell me, Bohr. What is this tiny gem I hold."

"It didn't begin its life underground," said Vasta.

"No? Then where?"

"Probably as grass. Or hay. The fibres in it suggest that."

"Right," said Vard, clearly out of his depth.

"That is," said Vasta, "until a cow or some other large animal from long ago came along, ate said grass or hay and defecated."

"Argh!" Vard dropped the small, mostly circular piece of brown, petrified shit, and it rolled to a stop against Abika's foot.

"That explains the smell," said Losa, laughing.

Vasta interrupted them. "Not that I don't appreciate your visits Senior Soldier Vard, and Captain Losa, but what is it exactly I can help you with today?"

"We've come to give you one more chance," said Losa.

Vasta took a long breath, which, from behind, sounded like a sky-balloon being filled with air. "And what makes you think that this week I will change my mind?"

The door opened again, and someone else entered the shop. "Because, Vasta, now is the time." Abika froze at that voice. That familiar Ipiti accent, the warmth, friendliness and confidence of the way he spoke. It couldn't be.

She shuffled to get out, but Vasta leant back pushing his bulk against the worktops and pinning her in. Abika shuffled her way to the edge and pushed against him, but she may as well have been pushing against a wall. Then everything happened at once. Vasta moved, the worktops split further apart and Abika crashed to the shop floor. There was barely a moment to look up before two high pyramids of tiny stacked boxes rained down upon her. Stones, gems, and petrified cow shit rained down.

"Who's this?" barked Vard.

Vasta lifted Abika free of the piles of boxes and stones, and over the floorboards, before placing her down.

"Abika?" Aki stared down at her in confusion. He was dressed as Losa and the other Guards were, all white cloth and belts and steel.

Vard jerked around. "You know this girl?"

Aki faltered, but barely a hair. Abika saw it, because she knew him. He was Aki, and had been since she was left sitting on his doorstep.

"I do," said Aki. His hand strayed to his chest, where a dragon lay printed upon his coat. "She sold me a steamed sweetbread. Yesterday, in the market."

Losa frowned. "Leader, she told us she was from the north. We met her a last night in the slums. She attacked us."

"I did not—"

"Northerners are not allowed to sell within Ipor Dan's market area." Losa cut her off, and touched the spot on her stomach where Abika's pole had caught her.

Aki turned towards her. "How should I know where she's from, Losa?" It was so real Abika almost believed it herself.

"Alright," said Losa, raising her hands. "Peace. It is our duty to see that the rules are abided by, Leader."

"Why is she here?" asked Vard to Vasta. He looked like a child in front of the Bohr.

"This is a shop," said Vasta. "I sell things, mend things. This girl inquired about a guitar that her mother broke."

Vard squinted. "I see no guit—"

The Bohr lifted the broken instrument Abika had seen earlier from behind the counter.

"But why were you hiding, girl?"

"I'm afraid of you," said Abika, as meekly as she could. She dropped her head and sobbed.

Vard smirked. "That is something I understand, at least."

Aki moved to close the door but Losa turned and stopped him. "Bohr," she said, sidestepping back into the centre of the room. "Let me see that guitar."

Vasta handed over the instrument. "It does not work."

"Yes, Bohr. I can see that." Losa held it up. "This is intricate work. A classical instrument if ever I saw one." Her eyes fell upon Abika's. "You play classical guitar?"

Abika shook her head. "It's my father's."

"He must be good," said Losa. "This is a fine instrument. Maybe I have heard him play. I do so like to watch the musicians of Ipor Dan. If you ask me, they are the best in all of Sulitaria. Tell me child, what is his name?"

Aki's face was drawn and his lips tight. "Losa, it is time for us to leave. We will return tomorrow to discuss our business with Vasta."

"Not until the girl tells me whose guitar this really is."

Vard kicked a cabinet, sending more trinkets to the floor. "Answer her, girl!"

"I...I..."

"Her father's name was Isak," said Aki.

"Isak?" said Losa. "I have never heard this name before."

"He was Nordun," said Aki.

Abika swallowed. "Was?"

"He died at the hands of a slaver in the mountains of Nord."

"And she told you all of this while buying a sandwich?" asked Losa. "It must have been a long chat, although apparently nothing came up about where the girl actually lives."

Aki's hand dropped to his waist, and for the first time Abika noticed that he was wearing a sword. "We're not here to discuss a silly little market girl."

"No, we're not." Losa stroked Abika's cheek. "Was that his name, girl? Isak?" Stares lingered on her, none so intense as Aki's.

"My father was Isak." Abika glared at Aki as she spoke the name, as though each word was a blade she might stab with. "His head was caved in by a slaver near Tyr." Tyr was the only place in Nord Abika knew.

Vard shook his head. "This is ridiculous." He shouldered by and stood in front of Vasta looking up. "Bohr, we have asked you repeatedly to join the Guard of the White Dragon and yet you still deny us?"

Vasta shook his head. "I'm afraid I would not be much use to you. You want a fighter. A figurehead. A Bohr to help your cause would be worth a million humans."

"A million?" laughed Vard. "You certainly think a lot of yourself."

Aki's eyebrows raised. "No, Vard. He's right. The Guard of the White Dragon believe that Bohr rule will release Sulitaria." He turned his gaze on Abika. The words only for her. "That is why we exist. To further that goal. The Bohr are free of corruption. Pure. A Bohr King will unite the islands, Ipiti, Dor, Hauwi, Taraunteen, and The Red Isles under one banner." He turned away, and started pacing between the door and the counter, the only bare bit of floor left. "Imagine a world without poverty, hunger, or grief. We could push forward as a force to be reckoned with." He turned to Vasta. "What say you, Bohr?"

"No."

"Why not?!" scoffed Aki. "This city hates you. Ipor Dan is housing the only Bohr that lives in Sulitaria."

Abika studied the shop again. There was a door to the back, but it was hidden behind more piles of boxes probably full of rocks and metal. The only exit was the one that Losa and Vard stood in front of. Her only way out.

She tried to not think about Aki's words, but they echoed inside her head.

Isak.

ISAK.

Her breathing slowed, her chest rising in rhythm within the throbbing of her pulse and the pounding in her head. Her fingertips felt hot, but that couldn't be. The pipe she had smoked was long gone, and the distinct lack of tom'ra leaf would not have left her with a high, so what was this? Questions took form in her mind, solid things bumpy and brassy.

"He's a liar!" roared Losa. "And so is she!" Losa poked Abika hard for good measure, and the feeling of power evaporated.

"Now, now," gruffed Vasta, his low, boomy tone filling the room. "Don't involve the girl."

"This shit?" Losa might have been quite beautiful if it weren't for the constant snarl. "This rebel?"

"A rebel?" Vard pulled his sword. "Dolum! Get in here." A fourth Guard rushed into Vasta's shop. He had his shortsword out already.

Abika kicked Vard hard between the legs, and the man bent over double. Aki reached out for her, catching nothing but air.

Losa didn't bother with her sword. She just threw her arms around Abika in a bear hug. "Got you, rebel!"

Aki rushed forwards, but Vasta grabbed him. The Bohr pulled the sword from Aki's sheath and flicked it clattering into the dark depths of his shop.

Abika leant forward and snapped her head back, trying to hit Losa in the face. "Not me, rebel. You're coming with us!" Abika's feet lifted off the ground again as Losa dragged her to the door. "Don't just stand there Dolum, help me!"

"Right you are!" Dolum grabbed at Losa's arms. "Here, let me take her—"

"No! Dolum!"

The grip loosened and Abika's feet found solid ground. She wriggled out of Losa's hold and escaped out of the shop door.

12

CUTTING MEAT

The street outside Vasta's shop was so bright Abika didn't see the six Guards of the White Dragon standing outside until she was falling into the arms of one.

"Argh!" roared the guard, dropping his sword clattering to the cobbles.

"Let go!" screamed Abika. She found the skin of the guard's hand below the gauntlet and bit down, tasting blood and feeling hair on her tongue. The guard let go and Abika ducked below five pairs of grasping arms, she made for the gaps and then into the crowd that was rapidly filling the narrow street.

Losa tumbled out the door with Vard in tow but Aki was nowhere to be seen. "Get her!" Tears fell freely as Abika sprinted back along the canal; the market looked like it was in full swing, both sides dense with ambling people. From the bridge she scanned the pointed hats looking for a way through, looking for something—

"There! She's there." The soldier she had bitten had recovered quickly and was barrelling towards her. There was nothing for it. Abika threw herself over the edge, landing heavily in a basket boat filled with lettuce and choi.

"Away! Away!" shouted the vendor, jerking around from the stall. He grabbed an oar and started poking her with it. "Away!"

Abika pulled her foot free, and water began pouring in from the hole she had made. The canoe rocked from side to side as she and the vendor danced around each other. He pushed past, grabbing armfuls of vegetables, throwing them to safety on the canal side. The canal streets on both sides erupted in shouting as White Dragon Guards pushed their way through the crowds, knocking stalls and people into the water.

Abika threw a handful of choi leaves into the vendor's face and dived over to the next boat—a canoe full of fish. As the shouting caught up with her, Abika leapt again, heedless. The basket boat rolled sickeningly as she fell into it, and her hand plunged into something wet and smelly.

"You!" came a familiar shout. The cheese woman managed a few swears and threw two of her best Dor cheeses at her.

"Abika!"

Abika snapped around at Lorith's voice directly across the canal. "Lorith! Help!"

Lorith pushed his way onto a canoe and, between smacking away the protesting owner with his own oar, managed to push the boat away from the edge. "Abika, jump."

"Come closer!" roared Abika.

"Jump, Bee! Jump"

There was noise behind her. A guard. She had no choice. Using a solid wheel of cheddar as her footing, Abika leapt outwards as high and far as she could. Lorith and the canoe vanished from sight, and she plunged into the water, scrabbling at the canoe's side. She tried to surface, expecting air, but her head banged painfully on the underside of a boat. Panic. Kicking out again, she looked for a gap, but her hands met only the thick weave of the boat's underside. Her own air bubbles blocked the view. The water was full of fruit, apples, cloth. Abika kicked her legs the other way and saw sunlight. Air.

"Abika! A guard!" Lorith was slapping the water to block the way from the Guard of the White Dragon standing amongst the cheeses. The crowd at the side held the cheese woman hanging over the canal wall, blood streaming from her head, hauling her away as the guard pushed the cheese boat from the wall with an oar. It floated towards Abika and Lorith in their canoe, and the guard's snarl became a smile. "Rebels!" he growled, clasping and pulling his way up the basket boat. "I'll fucking drown you!"

"Get her, Dolum!" came a shout from the bridge.

Abika prepared to dive once more as the boat slid towards her, ready to crack her head like a nut between the two canoes, but Lorith struck out, and shoved his oar into the guard's face. Blood and teeth went flying, followed by the guard himself who disappeared into the canal.

"Lorith!" screamed Abika. "Help me out!"

"Come on, girl!" Arms were reaching out for her from the side. It was Al'Duong, the vendor who had given her the roof-sing. "Come on! The rest are coming!"

Abika grabbed the metalworker's outstretched arm and he and Lorith dragged Abika out of his canoe. It was Al'Duong's boat, and the water around was littered with his possessions. Leather, cloth and the twinkling of metal deep below.

"Your sculptures!" said Abika.

"Go!" said Al'Duong, pushing them into the bustling throng. "Leave now, both of you! Lose yourself in the crowd."

Lorith grabbed his bag and started throwing seemingly random items inside. Papers, old plates, a small trowel still caked in red clay.

Abika was still breathing heavily. "What happened to the soldier?"

"He was a Guard," said Lorith, without looking. He opened a drawer full of pipes of all different shapes, sizes and colours.

"Was?" Abika's stomach churned. "Did he die?"

Lorith stared at three identical pipes in his hand. "You stole my tabac."

"So?"

He rounded on her. "So? You know how much I had to work to buy that tabac?"

Abika swallowed. "I needed to smoke."

"Nobody *needs* to smoke, Bee. It's a luxury. Something that reminds us all that there is more to life than this thankless struggle."

"Did that soldier die?" Abika's mind was stuck in a loop. "Lorith? LORITH!"

Lorith paused at the black dresser in the corner. He looked up into a broken mirror, then looked away. "He was a Guard, Bee, and guards shouldn't go jumping into canals with full armour on." He let out a strangled laugh. "It's his own fault. You know what, that's immaterial. You stole my tabac."

Abika couldn't stop the tears. "Aki is a Guard. He's a Guard."

"I know, Abika. He's been one of them long since before you arrived." Lorith pocketed more papers and small trinkets, emptying drawers and looking under the bed.

"I just...I don't understand."

Lorith pressed his lips together, he was on the verge of tears. "Jekob is not who you think, Abika. He's a liar."

Abika opened her mouth to speak, but the crashing of wood stole her words away. Footsteps sounded in the hall downstairs, storming up the stairs.

"Lorith!"

The door burst open, and five soldiers filled the tiny space, faces grim and hard. They spread out, forcing Lorith and Abika back against the wall with the window. Shining steel and matt leather strapped to sweating bodies made for a concoction of smells Abika had never experienced. But worse was the staring. Five pairs of eyes beheld Lorith and Abika as though just awaiting a command before attacking. Only one had a weapon out, a brass-coloured dagger, and he held it up at Lorith's chest. Abika was apparently not a threat.

Abika felt an urge to break the silence. "We didn't mean—"

More footsteps echoed down the hallway and up the stairs growing louder with each footfall until Losa walked casually into the room. "Cosy."

Vard came up behind her, dragging Al'Duong by the collar. He threw the old man to the floor. "Very cosy. Just a couple of little love birds up in here."

Lorith spat. "Love birds—"

Abika held his arm. "Don't."

Losa smiled. "Oh no, please do. Don't mind us. You certainly didn't mind us when you let Dolum sink to the bottom of the canal."

"I'm not sure they were wholly to blame—" began Vard.

Losa rounded on him. "I'm telling you, Soldier," she hissed. "It was their fault. They pushed him and let him drown. Plain and simple. Did anyone else see different?" The other guards did nothing but blink.

Vard's expression looked drawn. "As you say."

"We did no such thing!" shouted Abika. "If the fool thought it wise to go swimming in full armour, then—"

Stars burst in Abika's eyes from Losa's slap. "Tie her and gag her. Now!"

A dagger hilt dropped in front of Abika's nose. It was almost too easy. Lorith caught her eye, his neck held tight by a muscled, leather-bound arm. "Meat bags, Bee." He croaked, nodding to the dangling blade. "Meat bags!"

Abika slid the knife from the sheath, turned it and pushed it beneath the two plates of steel. There was a hint of resistance as the point cut through the layers of cloth and leather beneath, but it soon found skin, and then it was going in. It was cutting meat, plain and simple. Like the pig she had killed, it was all so easy to do. Abika pushed the blade right to the hilt into the guard's side. The female guard screamed and fell.

"Grab her!" screamed someone.

It was too late now. Lorith joined in from the back, using the distraction to pummel faces and steel helmets alike with his bare hands. Losa had pulled her sword, but Abika was hidden, moving like water between the legs of this one and that, ducking towards the exit with the wet blade still in her hand. Al'Duong was suddenly there in front of her. She jerked to a stop in front of him and Al'Duong stared at her, terrified.

Maybe she could save the man. Lorith would look after himself as he always did, but Abika would save this one! The door back to the street was only a few paces behind him. Soon, he would be back on his boat, telling his punters how he was saved by some young hero who single-handedly—

Al'Duong's terrified eyes grew wider as Losa's blade skewered the old man through the back. All of Abika's strength left her in a moment.

"NO!"

Shock filled her head as Al'Duong fell forward.The world dimmed around the edges, then someone was lifting her, wrestling the knife from her grip. All Abika saw was him. All she saw was Al'Duong's innocent eyes closing, forever.

Diary entry

The Gilded Docks of Lothri, Ge'Bat

A nameless dread haunts my heart, leaving me tired and confused. After only a month in Ge'Bat, I'm moving on once more. The guilded docks of Lothri are beautiful, but everyone has so much currency to their name that the trials of life no longer matter to them. To me they seemed cold, grey and empty, so here I find myself in the hull of a smuggler's vessel.

The news is that the Bohr may have finally pushed as far east New Bakla, but we should be safe in Kyotho. Apparently, the shores of Kemen are all white beaches and green waters, belying the violence of the Bohr inland within the towns. What lies ahead of me?

Iqaluk, my dear father, if only you were here to guide me...

the Gilded Ducks.

KYIRA and MILLI

13

THE SOUND OF BATTLE

Kyira closed the journal and slid the pen inside the spine, swallowing back the bitterness that had collected in her mouth. How long had she spent in her youth defying her father's word? She would give much to his voice once more outside of her dreams.

The boat lurched and she bumped into the woman next to her. No words were exchanged. There was no point—there was nothing anyone could do except bear it.

Kyira pulled the candle close, but it made no difference to the thick smell of body odour, pine and salt pinching her nose. The needlepine hull of the smuggler's boat should've given off a fresh smell, but it was old wood, shiny from a great many behinds that had sat upon it. Oh, how she wished to just run! Milli, her hound, blinked and Kyira scratched her guiltily. This was only their fifth day locked in the dark, whereas some of the others had not seen sunlight for two weeks. Through sparse details in hushed Sulitarian, Kyira had learned this boat had left Soporia Din with twenty-three, added another forty at the smuggler's beach in Lumael, and now after Lothri in Ge'Bat they were back up to fifty. Fifty people forced from the poor lands of Sulitar, drawn by the promise of gold and riches along the gilded coasts of Ge'Bat.

"Put that out!" rumbled a male voice from the stern.

Kyira pulled the candle closer. Without it, there would be nothing but darkness and she couldn't do that. She couldn't deal with the darkness as well. It would be too much. "No," she murmured. "The candle stays lit."

A young bald woman, dark-skinned and dangerous, eyed Kyira from the opposite side of the leaking hull like a tigre might have stared at a duck.

Kyira scratched the thick white fur of Milli's head soothing her growl. "Easy, girl. Let us not draw blood. Not here."

The refugee crawled towards them. "I'm a friend," she said, white teeth flashing. "Friend. Undastand? Don't listen to them. I don't like the dark either. Trust is hard won. Undastand?"

Kyira nodded once, replying in Sulitarian. "I have no friends, other than Milli here. But don't be fooled, she'll still take anything of yours that ventures too close."

The refugee stretched out her hand, and Mill snarled all the way until the fingertips were beneath her nose. After a sniff, the teeth vanished, and Kyira relaxed. "Friend." The refugee felt at the furred hood hanging over Kyira's shoulders. "This a good idea. Warm at night, cool in day? I see many freedom fighters who wear the same." The refugee shuffled back, forcing her muscular arms and twisting to reclaim her old spot. The two men either side grumbled, pulling their blankets closer. "You going to fight?"

"I've done enough fighting," said Kyira.

"Haven't we all." It wasn't a question. "You a Ringlander, me a Sulitarian. We should fight. You see? For freedom and for glory!" she added the last in a mock tone. "They say we don't like each other, and so we must fight. Is this the way? I lost my family to war." She showed her leg. "And a piece of my thigh. For what? To sit ere, with strangers looking for my place again."

Kyira found herself nodding along despite herself. The scar on the women's inner thigh was long and wide and barely a half cycle old. "I am beginning to wonder if the paths laid out before us truly are written into the fates of the lands. The gods. Whatever. I am yet to see anything that proves to me any of us can change them."

The refugee nodded to the journal on Kyira's lap. "Are you a writer then? I undastand. Writers think, no fight."

"I observe. Record."

"My sister used to write before they killed ha," said the refugee. "Ha pen would move like swallow chasing moths at dusk. I asked ha once, why she did it. Why she would write down ha thoughts. You know what she said? She told me it helped ha see." The refugee tapped her temple. "Not with ha eyes, but ha mind. Undastand? My thoughts are all tangled like reedweed, she would say, writing things down helps unpick it all. Undastand?"

Kyira did understand. All too well, but she didn't show it. She didn't give any more away. What was to happen? They become friends and travel the roads of Rengas mapping the world together? In truth, Kyira couldn't say why she was bothering at all anymore. In her youth she spoke of Culdè, but perhaps some people just stopped caring. When life meant nothing anymore, never mind the paths ahead of us.

The refugee woman began murmuring to the man next to her, and the unhappy silence of waiting minds settled back upon the hold of the vessel, broken only by the slapping of water and Milli's sleepy yelps. Kyira soothed her, rubbing her head, and used the dog's pulse as a marker for her own. Space grew inside her like a flower blossoming and with it came peace. Her mind became a canvas and she ran her fingers across it, feeling the colours and ridges of the paints of her memory. The ridges rose up, becoming green, growing larger than she could see, and then she was running up the side, as the hill formed, between ridges, feeling free, following the wind of her raeven's wings, blessed be Vlada's shadow. The sky bruised and toiled above, wrestling with sunshine that burst through, only to vanish, taking the patterns across the land with it. A figure drew her forward, and she followed, beckoned by it like bees to honeycomb. She stopped near the edge of the Hammer, the cliff that had been Hasaan's favourite climb, and stared at the back of the old man. From behind, his hair was darker than she remembered, and as she stepped closer she realised he wasn't old at all. He was muscular, but then he always had been.

"Iqaluk?"

The view was snatched from her, disappearing into a spinning wheel of colour and confusion.

"Haha, there is only one reason you walk to Soporia Din," said the refugee. "To leave! You undastand?"

Milli was looking up at her. "Yes," said Kyira. "Yes, I understand." But the words hadn't formed as usually they might've. There were noises outside the boat. The sound of war was one that never left you. The battle upon the Way Bridge had been over a decade ago, and still she could remember it all.

The sounds now outside upon the beach chilled Kyira's blood. Humans roaring, metal clashing. Moans of pain—

The boat lurched to a stop, with the sound of wet seabed scraping the underside of the hull. A bell rang, then light burst in through the trapdoor above.

"Out!" roared the boatman. "Git!"

Kyira stood, but there was no point reaching for either of the two knotted ropes thrown down. She stumbled away from the ropes into the seat the refugee had been sitting, dragging Milli away from the stampeding feet, as near fifty people tried to climb at once.

"Git!" The boatsman shoved an oar down the trapdoor. "One at a time! One at a time."

Then it was Kyira's turn. Reluctantly, and with Milli strapped to her back she hauled herself out onto the deck. Smoke. Fire. The usual green waters of Kemen were red with blood. The bodies were all young men, burned black and lolling in the slow surf, while the cause of it, a huge ball of burning clay, smouldered upon the sand. It might have been terrifyingly peaceful were it not for the battle taking place over the top of the hill. A long dark line marked the flora where a squad of soldiers had been smashed through and sent tumbling down onto the beach from high up on the tall dunes.

The boatman's oar banged the deck at Kyira's feet and she hopped down smoothly off the deck into the bloody seawater.

"Let me back up!" shouted the refugee woman from the water. "You undastand? You—"

The oar smacked against her hands as she tried to clamber. "Git!" roared the boatmen. "Git! Go fight with the freedom fighters!" The oar caught her in the nose, sending her flying onto her back in the water. Kyira twitched, she should help her, but instead she squatted low, and unlatched Milli from her back as another refugee helped the woman up, dragging her to the dry sand, leaving a line of fresh blood to join the red sea.

14

BROKEN TEETH

There were only two paths before Kyira and Milli now: swim after the departing smuggler's vessel, along with the other stubborn pairs of arms already nearing the bay mouth; or take her chances with the rest of the refugees escaping up the single twisting track. Towards the sound of battle.

A new sun appeared above, flaming and real as Kyira ran along the hard sand, Milli sprinting and howling alongside. Iqaluk would have bid her to stay where she was until she knew where the fiery projectile would land, but fear took hold first. She had almost reached the bottom of the twisting path when the fiery torv smashed into the beach where the boat had been, ruining already black and broken bodies.

They topped the rise, looking out over a black cornfield which stretched for leagues in all directions. The war machines, Bohr and fighting men grappling in-between made it impossible to see just how far. Kyira gasped. "The rebellion has come this far?"

"No rebels," said the Sulitarian woman in front.

"Then who?"

"Onwards the Republic!" came a shout from up front. "May you always fight!"

The line of refugees all hissed at the man in front, dragging him down to hide with them as they picked their way through the long grass of the cornfield's fringes.

"He'll get us all killed," hissed the Sulitarian refugee over her shoulder. "Freedom fighters, from Bakla. Undastand?"

Kyira crouched low, hiding between broken walls and skulking between the mounds of earth and pits that peppered the ground. The outskirts of a ruined town stood atop the hill beyond the war zone, and there was only a handful of buildings left standing like broken teeth against the jaws of the gaping bay.

The group snaked forwards into the killing fields, and Kyira and Milli followed between craters full of spikes and bodies. A Pan guard had fallen in one, face first, but was seemingly so thick the javelins beneath hadn't penetrated all the way through. It looked as though it had simply fallen asleep in the hole. Kyira carried on, ducking low beneath an upturned war machine. It was impossible to tell how the contraption worked with its ropes, pulleys and weights tangled and out of place. More fire crackled above, then blue light as though the Gods themselves had joined the fight. Kyira dropped low, looking at how she could reconnect with the group ahead of her. The refugee woman held Milli by the scruff, shaking her head and holding a finger to her lips, then footfalls. Wide and heavy. Pan guards were the hardest and most loyal of Bohr, and a squad of three were walking by between Kyira and the group. Kyira held out her hands, hoping Milli would understand. One bark would see them set upon.

Water seeped in through her breeches but Kyira dared not move. Shouts blew in with each breath of wind. You could tell much about the battle from the noise, but never who was winning, just the hurt that was all around.

The wooden beams of the war machine lifted off the ground in front of her as a massive Pan Guard, larger than Kyira had ever seen, raised the full weight above his head.

"Here's one!" rumbled the great Bohr's voice.

Kyira scuttled away like a mouse, barely stopping for breath, dodging and ducking and sprinting as fast as her legs would carry her. Heavy footfalls pounded behind her, stumbling and throwing muddy iron and bricks over her head. A boulder the size of her chest splatted in front and Kyira dove to the side, her feet catching on something. The mud came up to greet her, holding her close in a sticky embrace. The tangled limbs of dead men were all around like a forest of stubborn and rotten roots. Their dirty, muddied expressions held in perpetual pain and fear.

Only one Pan had given chase and he came closer, slowing, his footfalls squelching beneath his bulk, breaking wood and bone alike.

"Not now," uttered Kyira. "Not here. Please." She hid her face in the stinking mud, leaving a tiny hole to breathe.

"Careful, daughter, this path leads to death."

Kyira opened her mouth and muddy water tipped in. She imagined the words instead. *"What other paths lie before me, Iqaluk? What else can I do?"*

The sounds of the world abruptly changed. Echoes, dry air and the laboured breathing of the Pan Guard standing over her.

"There's life here. I can smells it." It sniffed, snarled and growled, murmuring of awful acts. "...Mounting your head. Eating your body, roasting your..."

Kyira tried to tune out words, delivered like scraping steel upon stone, staying as still as she could, imagining as the Pan's eyes raked over the bodies at his feet, looking for her.

"What other choice do I have?"

"There are always other ways, daughter. As the raeven flies, so the greenbeetle crawls. Each avoiding danger by being smaller than they are."

And Kyira waited there, face down, as the ground trembled, shuffling herself beneath those bodies to hide her shape. Shuffling and hiding from the predator that stood above her, sniffing for her. The snarling stopped and Kyira's breath caught.

It had found her.

It would pick her up, taunt her, and then pull her to pieces. The feet moved, side-stepping away from her. The muffled sounds of steel on steel in the distance became clearer. The Pan Guard was leaving!

An immense weight pressed upon her arm. Kyira wanted to scream out loud, as the full weight of that Bohr Pan Guard pressed down, squashing her against the body of an unfortunate soldier. Tears flowed freely but she couldn't wail or scream or he would hear her then it would be over. All of this, for nothing. He would assume she was yet another of Bakla's freedom fighters and then end her life faster than she could protest.

She tried to pull back, but the angles were wrong, the soldier's armour was flared and thick and she had buried her arm well below it. Then, all at once it didn't matter. The soldier's body caved at the chest, crumpling in like he was made of nothing but paper, and the Pan toppled to the ground.

She could feel the thing's massive limbs flailing around! Kyira needed to run, to lift herself up and make for that old village where there was shelter, but fear kept her glued to the ground. The Pan would get up any second and discover her!

A voice like tearing paper sounded nearby. "Hold, Pan. Hold."

The flailing stopped as though the Bohr were suddenly unable to move. Someone was controlling it.

Kyira swallowed. If there was any time, it was now. Now. NOW.

The bodies gave her purchase.

Beat.

She pulls herself forwards, crawling through mud and grass until the holes obscured her.

Beat

She stopped. Listening.

Her feet took her on.

Beat.

She was an arrow, purposeful and correct. There were others around, but they were blurry smears.

Beat.

A white blob stood out amongst the black hills like a beacon of light, and Kyira ran as hard as she could towards it. The wind whipped the tears away from her as gifts for the fallen back to the mud.

The group ducked into an old farmhouse, jars of food sitting on blackened shelves. "Is this Kyotho?" whispered Kyira, still panting.

"Kyotho is four leagues west, undastand?"

Kyira peered through a hole in the wall. Fire tore through the air above the roofless building, the heat of it blooming for a moment. She took out her journal and flattened the pages before scratching her pen against the canvas, lines of hatching and shadow picking out the details of burning men and women, of Bohr fighters standing like wheat amongst the grass, of war machines catapulting loads of burning torv into the human fighters and scattering them like burning sticks. Kyira studied the fight, watched as the pointless game played out, as more of her kind lost their lives for nothing. Who had started this fight? It didn't matter, the outcome was the same. Like Laeb's designs, all plans eventually led to a bloody end. Her pen scratched out the gruesome details of those lying dead and dying at the feet of the Bohr, the smoke, char, fire and blood, and something caught her eye though in all that madness. Something too fast to be human.

A blur of soft light rushed between battles, leaving lines of dead humans in its wake. The dark figure of a man struck against blue light, winding its way towards the unfortunate souls. Another plume of living fire burst forth from the south end of the field, catching the freedom fighters on the far side, cutting off their flanks.

"Milli, you have to move fast. Go!" Milli blinked at her. The hound moved like water around the farmhouse, sniffing then moving on. She returned after a few moments and sat. The refugee appeared from behind Milli, and gave her a scratch.

"Where you running to, Sami?"

"Away," said Kyira. "

"We stronger if stick together, undastand?"

Kyira didn't want to stay. "Milli is all the company I need." She took the woman's hand. "Good luck. Look after yourself."

The refugee nodded at her. "If you sure. You too, Sami girl. May you always fight."

The words echoed in Kyira's ears as she dipped out of the farmhouse and along the rough roads. There were other houses, some in better condition than others, but they were all empty. The town had abandoned the place, and rightly so, considering the Bohr had brought war to their doorsteps.

The last building beckoned her in, a spark of hope held high in her breast, but as Kyira forced open the thick door she regretted her haste. Bodies littered the floor. There was no ignoring these, piled atop each other in huge mounds, charred looks of pain and anguish forever cast upon their blackened faces. This was the reason why the town was empty. They had been imprisoned here, in a town domst, and then the building had been set alight. Kyira stepped back, unable to look away.

"Awful, isn't it?" It was the same tearing paper voice.

The man shifted his long dark coat, and flicked a strand of black hair from his eyes. "You're not from Kyotho." He held no weapon, but he didn't need to, it was as clear as death what he was.

"You're a Banèman."

The man nodded. "A slayer, yes. If you had to put a label on it. On me."

"So, that was you?" Kyira nodded beyond Akosh to the hills below. "You were controlling the Bohr. Is that another *gift*?"

Akosh seemed to bristle, as though uncomfortable. He strafed, stepping towards Kyira. "You know, it's not often we Banèmen meet someone who has not heard of us. Least of all, someone who is seemingly unafraid."

"You can sense my heartbeat?" asked Kyira, stepping to the side like they were two sparring swordsmen. She urged Milli on with a knee, only to find the silly animal as stiff as stone.

Akosh shook his head slowly. "No. I don't need to see inside you, to see that you are unafraid."

"You alright, Sami girl?" The refugee woman appeared from between two ruined homes, followed by the other refugees. The group, easily twenty-five strong, stood behind, plain-faced and menacing, wielding bars, stones, and bloodied, broken swords.

Akosh took them all in, but it was Milli's feral bark that clinched the deal, freezing Kyira's blood with its ferocity.

The Banèman Akosh winked. "Until we meet again, Sami." Then vanished into thin air.

Diary entry

Holy Fighter Inn, Kyotho

Life used to be so simple, and now, I question every decision I make. Every day I look at my maps and think of how small Rengas is, and then when I look away I see only distant horizons in every direction.

The scars of numerous Bohr invasions stand stark and clear in Kyotho. From old blood stains near the Domst to the charred ruins of every outer city home. The residents of the citadel have obviously been able to repel the Bohr, but for what? They've got almost nothing to call their own, just a few inns and some sand dunes.

The refugees left me at the gates and continued their own journeys, assured and confident. I found a place to sleep and eat, but really, I'm just happy to be alive.

That Banèman Akosh almost had me. And that speed...

Holy Fighter Inn.

15

HOLY FIGHTER

The door of her inn room banged shut, making Kyira jump and sending her journal flopping to the ground.

She got up closed the door, placing a chair up against it. Milli stared up at her, cocking her head and Kyira realised her mistake. Cooking and baking smells were drifting up through the open window from the inn downstairs, promising full bellies and long sleeps.

"Sorry, girl. I know you're hungry."

Milli sighed and plopped her head back on her paws. Those eyes were so big, and any other day Kyira might have given in to them, but she had to finish recording. Her maps were laid out in front of her on the desk. Her life's work, a catalogue of Rengas, with detailed terrain that stretched all the way from the Outer Isles down through Sulitar and to the isle of Ge'Bat. Kemen was new, the empty shape only showing detail around the bay where the smuggler's boat had landed, but already she'd seen enough of the damned place to last a lifetime. Maybe she should go, but where? Nord was no longer her home, Ipiti never was, however hard she tried to make it so—this was her life now.

Who else would mind the paths of the world? She etched and scratched upon the thick parchment carefully, bringing form and structure where before there was nothing. A familiar feeling of completeness began to swell inside her as the town called Kamsin took shape upon the subtle line below the words Kyotho. She took great care in those shapes, drawing what she remembered from the place as a homage to the poor folks who were murdered there by the Bohr.

The window shook as new rain and wind blew in from the other side. Rain here in Kemen was not so vilified as it was in Nord, it brought life to a place that usually was dry and arid. Kyira had redefined what she considered to be a storm after the city of Tyr. Those holes, destroying so much and killing so many. Innocent lives lost, and yet there were those who still swore by the Great Mother, even after she almost obliterated the world. There was no other explanation to the devastation Rengas experienced. She had always known the Great Baeivi was behind it all. One day she would greet Kyira and own her, but not yet.

"Let go," she whispered to herself. The Great Mother's words still echoed in Kyira's mind, even twelve cycles on.

Milli's wet tongue made her jump. "Oh! Girl. I'm sorry, I shouldn't burden you with this." Kyira gave her a good scratch and Milli's breast rumbled in pleasure. "Come on, let's get something to eat."

The Holy Fighter Inn was as richly coloured as any other tavern in Kyotho, though perhaps not as well subscribed. Still, with its open fireplace and thick stone walls, it was comfortable enough to call home for a night or two.

A maid walked by and Kyira reached out and touched her arm. "Meat, and bones if you have them."

"We've nothing but the dregs of the leftovers," said the maid, dragging her forearm across her very large nostrils. She picked at the trails left there and sprinkled them on the floor next to Kyira's table. "We've a thick brew on though. It'll fill the gaps left over. Certainly nothing for the mutt though."

Milli growled and the maid's brow drew together into a scowl.

"It's fine. I'll take it. And the brew."

"And *you* better be quiet, mutt. Or you'll find yourself in a pie." The maid's eyes found Kyira's again, and she looked her over, as if really just noticing her. “You’ve been fighting.” The words seemed to catch the attention of the only other two patrons in the tiny room. The walls drew in as they both stood from their chairs.

“I have,” said Kyira. She brought her fist to her heart. “For freedom. And glory.”

“Good then.” said the maid, holding up her own hand. The two men sat back down and resumed their quiet drinking, and the maid sat down too. “Where were you?”

“On the outskirts,” said Kyira. “Near the border. The coast.”

The maid shook her head. “Not Kamsin? Hasn’t there been enough death already?”

The man closest to the fire looked up. His face was dirty, and the cuff of his jacket was pinned to his shoulder where presumably his right arm used to be. “Borders ain’t gunna yield ground.” He spoke with a thick Kyotho accent.

“They’ll just move em,” grunted the other man.

The maid looked disturbed. “And so Bakla gets smaller and bloody smaller.”

“Stretched thinner, or rather pushed inwards.” said the armless man

“They had a Banèman.” The news dropped like a foul-smelling carcass that had fallen down the chimney. Kyira almost regretted the words, but a hard truth was always better than an easy lie.

Another maid appeared by the inn door, standing listening.

“A Banèman?” said the armless man. “This far south?”

“They’re not all power-wielders,” said the other man.

“Is that right now, Sam? Then what are they doing here? It ain’t to spread joy and glee into the lives of strangers.”

“Piss off. I’m in this fight the same as any other. I fought them back in the Arcol wars. Where were you then?”

“Fighting as you were, Sam. Fighting for freedom and a free Kemen.”

“Well, alls Kyotho got then was the Northern Territories.”

The maid sitting with Kyira crossed her arms. “And look what that got us.”

“Excuse me,” said Kyira. “I hate to interrupt, “I just—”

“No, no,” said the maid, standing. “Come through the back with me, love. I'll see you fed and then some. And I'm sure we have a bone lying around somewhere for your friend here. Leave these two to their war of words. They'll be at it for the rest of the night."

Kyira and Milli followed the maid to a private room in the back of the inn, less a room and more of a cupboard with a single table. The maid brought her a plate of well-roasted goat and a shoulder bone for Milli. The goat was overcooked, but it was food and Kyira badly needed the energy. She was waking up tired most days, and everything took so much effort. Iqaluk would have moaned at her to see her so thin.

The second maid, a young girl with sleek dark hair, returned with some dry bread and pickles. "I hear you've been fighting?"

Kyira nodded, waiting, but the maid held the plate firm. "I have."

"What news have you? Of the fight? Where was it? Was it on the shores?"

"Off the shores," said Kyira, doing her best not to look at the bread. "Kamsin"

The maid bit her lip. The plate was shaking.

"You know someone out there?"

The maid nodded. "My partner." She sat down next to Kyira. "His name was...is Joris." Her far-away gaze pulled back and focused on Kyira. "He is very tall with dark hair like mine, but blue eyes."

"Sulitarian?"

The maid leaned in, her expression suddenly hopeful. "Does that sound familiar?"

It did sound familiar. Kyira thought of the bodies lying piled in the mud. The maid's stare was glassy. Kyira took the plate off her and set it down. "If he was on the shores then he was probably not involved in the main battle. It was short and intense. An ambush. I found myself there, but I was not there to fight."

The maid's lip wobbled. "His mother will be devastated if he..." Her hand wandered to her stomach.

"You are with child?"

She nodded. "He doesn't know, I only found out a few days ago. But if he's gone, if he's—" It was too much and she broke into a fit of sobbing.

Kyira wrapped her arms around her and held her tightly. She

wanted to comfort the girl and tell her everything would work out, stroke her hair and tell her that Joris was probably on his way back here to Kyotho right now.

"I killed one of them, you know."

The maid looked at her, chin wobbling. "Who? The Bohr? I don't believe you."

Kyira shook her head. "One of the Banèmen."

The maid's mouth hung open. "You? There's nothing to you. They're magical. Beasts who can change form and control fire! A Banèman would make short work of you. You'd not last—"

"They can be killed," said Kyira, sharply. "And anything that can die, has fear somewhere in them. You just have to find it." The maid stared at her and Kyira wondered if she had gone too far. She didn't care. "They should all be killed. Every last one of them." Kyira pulled her knife from her belt and placed it on the table. The shard of Duga's bluesteel sword was now a deep red, it had changed colour from the day she had used it to kill Jagar, even after it had been reforged. "I killed a Banèman with this weapon."

The maid reached out for it, her sobbing just a memory of the past. She snapped her hand back as if stung and stared at Kyira anew.

Before anything else could be said, the doors burst open as the chief maid backed into the room with two steaming bowls of soup. "Undermaid! You are not here to blub and annoy the customers." Her frown deepened so much her eyebrows became one. "And are you sitting down? Tell me, is there not pans to clean and floors to mop?"

Kyira held up her hands. "Please, no, it was my fault. I asked her to sit. She got upset that I didn't want the bread. I said it looked a little hard and to take it away." Her stomach growled in protest.

The maid sneered and took a long nasal breath. "Fine. Undermaid! Get back in the kitchens. Now."

The undermaid jumped up off the chair and scurried out of the room with the plate of bread. Kyira watched it leave hungrily.

"Where you off to next then freedom fighter?" asked the chief maid.

"I don't fight. I navigate. I capture the world we live in, but now I feel...lost once more." She shook her head. "Imagine it, a navigator lost within her own mind."

“All we see are the lost, here in the Holy Fighter Inn.” The chief maid frowned again. “And, there’s only two places a proper holy fighter should be.” She leaned forward and snatched up Kyira’s blade. “Either dead or in Bakla. And seeing as you are currently sitting in my lounge eating my soup, I might suggest Bakla. My guess is that the Republic army could use someone like you.”

Kyira blinked. “The republic? There’s another resistance in New Bakla?”

“The Republican army are the best of us, led by the best of us. They are a bastion of human hope who stand against all that the Bohr are, and upon the shores of their own homeland no less. If there was a last stand for our race, girl, it would be with the Republic.” With a causal flick of the wrist, the chief maid threw Kyira’s knife to stab into the table next to the soup bowl, where it stood, solid and true. “Now, eat up. Bakla is a good two week’s walk and you’ll need all the strength our good chef can get in you.” She stood. “Sit back, love. I’ll away and get the honeybread and another bone.”

16

A LEAF'S JOURNEY

Vasta dropped the last lump of mear'pid into its holding box and replaced it atop the stack, quelling the rising unease in his breast. He crossed the shop floor and stood over the guitar. It looked as forlorn as an instrument could look, all broken and unplayable. It had seen an exciting morning, dragged around by the White Dragon Guards and that curious little girl. The neck was still broken, but that could be fixed, now that the strings were off. Their tension had ripped the neck from the body, in essence the very purpose of the thing had been the undoing of it. The metaphor had a certain eloquence he supposed. His hand twitched, but he dared not pick it up. It had to stay there now.

He swallowed hard. The shop was clear, returned to its former, managed state, so there was nothing to remain uneasy about. There was also little work to do, and yet his mind would not give him peace.

His eye fell upon the singing dreamcatcher the girl had brought in. It was a well-made little thing. The subtly chamfered edges, the scored centres giving the metal blades a leaflike appearance. The music box was well chosen too, *A Leaf's Journey* if his recall of human folk songs served him well. He pulled the string and listened as the broken tune played.

"To this a new song, a leaf 's journey begins, flies high to the sky, and falls, falls, falls. To this a second—sec. Second leaf… Oh, no. Are you out of tune as well? That makes the fix a little harder." He hummed the tune again, trying to remember the correct key, not doing it justice. In fact, had a child heard the rendition of that famous tune, he imagined they would have run away to their mothers in tears. Of course, the words for the Kemen version of the same song were vastly different to that song in Ipiti, it being a battle cry, of all things. He didn't know much about children, or humans for that matter, outside of their peculiar need for aggression and violence. "More like us than they realise. B-flat. That's it."

The unease followed him as he rehung the dreamcatcher above his counter, but there was no greater gift than a task that needed to be completed. Besides, he knew himself better than this.

He padded back to the workshop corner and filled a glass from the sink. A few gulps were enough to tell him he was not so thirsty.

He pulled on his machinist's apron and gave it a slap at the belly. The shining, thick leather made such a lovely sound, but if he was being honest with himself, the slap was out of frustration.

The gloves went on next, then he stepped onto a faded spot on the floor in front of the lathe. Using mostly his toe, he pressed down on the pedal, giving it a heavy pump to get the velocity of the headstock up, before settling into a more rhythmical pumping. It was akin to a body, this machine, the way the pump fed the springs and cogs within, turning and sliding along the greased axles all so the spindle could spin at an easy thousand revolutions. "Hmm." He pumped a little faster. A thousand revolutions was probably a little slow for this more intricate work. Fifteen hundred would do it. He brought the drill in, sliding the tailstock along the feed rods until the bit barely touched the metal rod held within the spindle. He stopped pumping and waited for the spindle to slow before changing from a pilot bit to the bigger drill, then began anew. The larger drill bit ate into the rod, drawing out twisting metal smoking from the hole.

The mid-morning moved slowly even as his fingers and claws worked quickly over the metal, polishing, sanding and cleaning. Soon enough, he was holding the finished item in his hand. It was an elliptical spoon with internal threads. He took a cuboid of coalwood from a shelf of timber on the desk and changed the drill head once more. Soon the coalwood was turning at a very slow three hundred revolutions, spitting out dust darker even than his own skin, though flecks of the grain came close to the tone, creating the illusion that in places his forearm and the instrument were one. Were it not for the difference in the frequency of their atoms, they would be one. It was a wonder that, even in the face of the tiresome machinations of the world, the makeup of things still held his heart's interest. Imagine controlling the atoms of the world, deciding on the structure, not only of this lathe, this spinner, the coalwood, but of him and his body. Of his organs and his skin. The power to control was the power to make. Or the power to destroy. The spinner crunched as the cylinder strained, then snapped. Vasta snatched it out of the air as the white-hot metal bit exploded out of the lathe. He stopped pumping and held the smouldering metal on the thick skin of his palm.

"Concentrate, Vasta! You fool."

He reset the machine and finished the coalwood handle of his new tool, making an effort to banish intrusive thoughts. There was no need to check the thread spacing, he knew they would fit together.

Lifting his tool case from beneath the steel bench, Vasta placed it down on the steel worktop and opened it vertically like a tome. He ran a finger over the inside shelves, admiring the uniformity of it all, the way all of the items within sat nestled in their purpose-built holes. This new tool would need one too, but things were getting tight in there. He would have to create a new drawer beneath the two shallow bit-drawers already hidden within the brushed wood. He pulled the number-six die from the range hanging above the lockpicks and planes, screwed into the new piece he had just finished forming, then removed his apron and gloves and padded back into the main shop. The dreamcatcher took the new tool and Vasta tightened the screw held deep within the music box. He put the tool down and pulled the string. "Still out." It was sharp. He turned the screw once more with the new tool then tugged on the string and its sweet tune filled the shop.

"To this a new song, a leaf's journey begins, flies high to the sky, and falls, falls, falls. To this a new song, a leaf's journey ends, bringing life to flies, all, and all, and all. To this a third song, a leaf's journey's echo, bringing life to the world, grow, grow, and grow. To this a fine song, a leaf's journey's life. A new leaf lives, unfurls. And grows and flies. Ever more."

The tune lingered in Vasta's head, alongside thoughts of ruin, pain, and anxiety. He was distracting himself.

Blessedly, the door opened. A customer by the name of Al'Dan stepped in. "Good morning, Vasta," he said, in Iporitian.

"And hopefully it will be shall," smiled Vasta. "What is it I can help you with today?"

"Well," Al'Dan glanced around. "I came in to see you, my friend, and to warn you."

"Warn? Al'Dan, that seems a bit out of character for you. How long have we known each other?."

"Too long, dear Bohr. Too long." Al'Dan's usually expressive face became pallid. "The threat isn't from me, my friend, but rather the Guard of the—"

"White Dragon. Yes. They are busy this morning. What is it now?"

"They chased a girl from this district, Vasta. Ran her in through the market and cornered her. One of them jumped into the canal."

"The girl?" asked Vasta, concerned.

Al'Dan looked strange without a smile. "One of the Guards. They perished in the water. Great Mother rest their soul."

"I'm not sure the Guards of the White Dragon have souls, Al'Dan. That girl though, she had been here with me. I let them take her. Did she escape?"

Al'Dan looked all at once very uncomfortable. "See, that's the thing. There was a boy, I've seen him around. Sells pipeweed. But it was Al'Duong who helped them escape."

Vasta couldn't help but sigh long and hard. This was not good. "And..."

"And they killed him for it. Some young lads just found his body in a house above the market."

"The Guard of the White Dragon murdered Al'Duong?"

Al'Dan nodded. "Abetting a criminal."

The sunlight split as footsteps sounded outside, and Vasta felt his waters vibrate. It had been a long time since he had felt such a feeling. The footsteps carried on past his door and away.

"What is going on?" Al'Dan turned back to him, his face pale. "The Guards have never been so bold as to murder. And so blatantly."

"As all oppressors, Al'Dan. Little by little they encroach on our lives, until finally they step over the line. Believe me when I say I know the type. Where is the girl now?"

Al'Dan shrugged. "The citadel?"

Vasta held up the dreamcatcher. "Here, my friend. Take this. Give it to your son." Vasta stopped. "If I don't return, there is a spare key inside a hollowed chunk of mikronite at the back door. The shop deeds are rolled together with a stash of currency in a panel under the lathe."

Al'Dan frowned. "What? No, where are you going?"

Vasta placed a hand on Al'Dan's shoulder. "The citadel."

17

REBEL

Rebel. That's what Losa had called her. There were worse things to be called, although perhaps not within the jail cells of the citadel.

The dark stone of the prison walls smelled like old blood, amongst a host of other noxious scents Abika tried her best to ignore. Pale scratches marked the grime at all heights—apparently the Guard of the White Dragon didn't care how old their prisoners were.

She had stopped shouting for Lorith after the on-duty guards had come in and beat her. The sound probably didn't penetrate the dense walls anyway, not when all she could hear was the blood pounding in her veins. This was a tomb.

Squinting, she looked up. A square of pristine blue told her the new day had begun. It was a cruel thing to cut a window from the stone so far out of reach. The ceiling tapered smoothly towards the hole so there was no way to climb up, taunting even the most adept of climbers. Its purpose was to remind the occupant that this place was a punishment and that the freedom they took so easily for granted was now forfeit. A bird broke the shape of blue, peeking its head into the hole to look in.

"Get out of it!" She would have thrown a shoe if the Guard had let her keep them. The bird turned back and looked down the hole towards her, cocking its head. At least it was free, up there, in the calm vastness of it all. Her heart slowed, and her blinks became heavy. "What a place to be...Bloody...birds." Then music. A voice low like thunder.

To this a new song, a leaf's journey begins, flies high to the sky, and falls, falls, falls

The tune sounded familiar. She focused more, and spots of light came to life in front of her, floating in the air like jewels on strings. Reaching out, she tried to touch them but they passed through her hand as though they were not really there. The song became clearer, and it was as if the owner of the voice sat with her...

A new leaf lives, unfurls. And grows and flies. Ever more.

"Vasta?"

The iron door clanked as the lock was turned, and Abika cowered in the corner.

"It's me, Abika. I won't hurt you." Another voice, familiar, but unwelcome.

"Aki?"

The door shut behind him, and he squatted in front of her, below the window. "I told you to wait by the cart, Abika." Jekob took off his metal helmet, all polished and shiny.

"It's *rebel* now," said Abika. "My name has no meaning here." She couldn't have said what the man was feeling—he was practically unreadable—but she knew him even less now.

"This—" He stopped and lowered his voice. "This is what happens when you disregard us, Abika. You never listen to us, and you never have."

"Us?" spat Abika. "So, Freja knows you are a traitor too?"

"Freja knows what I tell her." Jekob's gaze dropped. "She's a shrewd woman, but she's no fool."

"Does she know you sneak into the town to command an army of thugs who work for the Bohr?"

Jekob squared his shoulders. "The Guard of the White Dragon are not thugs. We are here to police the city, we look after its inhabitants. Protect them."

"Protection against innocent people like me visiting the market?" Jekob opened his mouth but Abika hurried on. "Or against rebels?"

Jekob studied her, then when he spoke the words were measured. "The rebels oppose us, Abika. They oppose the White Dragon and all that we stand for. Losa shouldn't have cried rebel..."

"But she did, and she used it to trap me here. How many more like me have been called rebel in the name of *protection.* Did they die in these cells too? Innocents, whose only crime was walking through the market!"

Jekob's eyes narrowed, and Abika held her breath at the side of this man she might yet still see. "Your only crime?" he uttered. "Abika, your actions were foolish. More than one died by your hand. Including an innocent market seller. Al'Duong may have been old but his death was premature. His blood is on your hands. Because of your miscreant ways! If you'd just done as Losa had said—"

"I'd likely be dead!" roared Abika. "If Al'Duong hadn't helped us we'd be dead at the bottom of the canal!" She sneered at Jekob. "Like your friend. He got what he deserved."

Jekob adjusted his footing. "The man who drowned in the canal was Dolum. He had children. Two girls and a boy. A family who relied on his work to live and eat. Dolum's mother looked after his children because his wife died last cycle, meaning they will grow up with neither mother nor father."

"Then they deserve to die too for his wickedness." The words were poison, Abika knew it, but she spat them out anyway. This treacherous man deserved it and worse.

"You're going down a dark path, Abika."

She got up and started pacing the tiny cell, her feet bare on the cold, uneven slabs. "Dark? Who are you to judge me?" tears pricked Abika's eyes. "You're a liar, so what difference does *my* behaviour matter? Freja said it. I'm not yours, and neither is Lorith!"

Jekob swallowed, then studied his helmet. "I am yet to speak to Lorith."

"Of course, you came to see me first." She nodded. "I should have known you'd be too gutless to face up to a son. But a daughter is no problem, is it? Am I not the lucky one. Tell me, Jekob. What is to stop me telling the prison guards that you are actually my father and you lied to that Captain in Vasta's shop. What would happen?"

"I would likely be struck off and executed." His calm was beginning to grate on her. "Is that what you want?"

"It's what you deserve."

Jekob stood, ready to spar. "There is some truth in it. I raised you, but I am not your father. You know this."

Abika stopped. The words were almost too heavy to hear. "No, you're not. Isak is my father, isn't he? That was his name. You didn't just conjure the name from thin air while we were in Vasta's shop. You know him. His name really was Isak."

Jekob stood straighter. "I didn't know him."

"But you knew her, didn't you? My real mother."

"Abika, we should not—"

"Tell me the truth!" Tears had come, flowing freely, but Abika didn't care. "You owe me that for your lies."

"A woman named Kyira left you in our care."

The shock of the name hit Abika as hard as if he had crossed the room and punched her. Kyira.

Jekob's face was drawn. "Kyira walked along our road one day. She told us that she had come north after working the fields of the southern islands. You were slung to her back." He let out a long sigh and traced the reflection of the cell window in the helmet. "I had never seen such big eyes—" Jekob's brief smile melted away. "Kyira stayed with Freja and I for a spell, until one day she just left. She was the one who—" Jekob took a moment, a pause. A breath. An age. "She knew him, your father. She knew him."

Abika clenched her teeth, and tears found her pursed lips. "Where did she go?

"We don't know. She left me, us, without a word."

"Where was she from?"

Jekob turned the helmet over, studying the inside. He was ashamed at himself! Standing like a boy caught with his hand in the biscuit jar. "I shouldn't be telling you this. I should go."

"To leave me here and rot? No, Aki." Abika couldn't keep the waver from her words. "Please."

Jekob backed up until he touched the door. "Kyira...was from Nord."

"I am Nordun?"

Jekob looked conflicted, like he was forming a lie, Abika knew the look well. Defeated, Jekob let out another sigh. "You are part Kemenese, that is all...she told me."

"That was the truth, wasn't it? Kyira is my mother and she left me with you and Freja." Abika's stomach swirled. "But there's something else, the way you speak of her so fondly. You were lovers."

Jekob blinked and she knew she had caught him in his own lie. His lips parted as he struggled with the truth.When he spoke, his voice cracked. "Yes." Jekob pulled on his helmet and turned to leave.

Then something occurred to Abika like a bright flame flickering into life, lighting up the cell, the walls, her entire life. It was not a candle that held warmth though, this was a fire that would consume her. "That's why Freja hates me isn't it? Freja forgave you and took you back. That's why she tormented me, and—"

Jekob rushed towards her. "She loved you!" he hissed. "She loved you, and you, YOU tormented her! You pushed her and fought her at every corner. She wanted desperately for you to be hers. Don't dare drag Freja's name through the mud. You think she enjoyed watching as the children in the commune grew and left?" his voice cracked again. "A woman who could not bring life into this world herself, but who gave everything she had to other people's children." He stood back and shook his head at her. "Don't you dare."

Abika swallowed but stood her ground. "But you did betray her."

Jekob looked up at the blue sky above the cell, composing himself. "I did, Abika. You're right. I don't deserve Freja. I said as much. I told Freja to cast me out. I offered up my life to her, to take it or to leave it." His tone grew warm so that Abika felt an urge to comfort the man. This man, her father, no longer. "She let me keep it. And we grew stronger."

"I'm glad for you, Jekob, that one of us did well out of all of this." Her mouth tasted bitter. "What did it mean for me though? It meant being brought up by a mother who hated me. A mother who, every time she looked at me, saw a devil in disguise. You did that, Jekob. You did it. You and your lies. You should think on that as I lie here rotting. This is all because of you."

His flat expression returned, the emotion all gone. He had said and done enough. Say one thing for Jekob, he knew when to leave. He crossed the cell and grasped the long bar over the door.

"I know it was you."

Abika sneered and spat like a rabid dog. "Me? What was me? I am the one who—"

"Who sabotaged the pipes."

He didn't shout, or even raise his voice, but the words silenced her as if he had. She swallowed. "I don't know what you mean..."

"Now who is lying? You tormented Freja, but you also tormented me. Maybe not directly, but enough that it showed me who you really are. What type of person you would grow up to be. Freja would talk into the night about you, Abika. Our little Bee. She was adamant she could quell the daemon inside of you that made you so angry. Whatever gifts your parents had given by blood were hers to let shine. But you were rotten to the core, Abika. You tormented us like you tormented that poor sow. We tried everything to make you ours, but there is too much of your real mother and father in you for that." He leant against the wall. You are not of me, and you are not of Freja."

Footsteps rang outside, and a voice sounded through the iron. "You alright, Cap'n Jak?"

"Fine, Rivan."

"Tormenting the prisoners?" The jailer laughed and the footsteps carried on by. "Brilliant! Just bloody brilliant..."

"I talked Rivan and Stae into giving you this back. They would have sold it back to Vasta for ten times the price." The faint light of the room somehow found every face of that hanging shard. The chain, the crystal itself. It was the most beautiful thing Abika had ever seen, and it looked completely out of place dangling from Jekob's spiked gloves in this horrible place.

"I thought it belonged to Freja."

"It does. She stole it from the Bohr Vasta many moons ago, in the hope it might help her conceive. We tried everything to have a child. Rituals, magicka, shamans, soothsayers. Some lawful, others not so. Freja might not have been your mother, she might not have been able to make you hers, but she loved you regardless." He placed the shard on the floor beneath the blue canvas above, then pulled on his helmet.

"Time to see Lorith?" said Abika.

Jekob hauled the door open. Darkness lay on the other side, and Abika could just make out a hallway and another door across from hers, before the heavy iron door slammed shut, blowing wind into her face. The bird high above squawked and fluttered away, the echo of its twitters bouncing off the walls long after it had gone.

18

HEART OF THE ETHER

The darkness had eventually faded, but the Sami girl and the bundle of rags she protected were gone. Jagar was used to channelling the flows of the many realms, yet he couldn't do something simple like define his own being! How did he exist? The answer was not important.

If this place was a river, he was a boat. Or perhaps a fish. No. He was foreign here. The power he had once known, the Soulfire that had filled his mortal body, was gone, but he opened himself up to it anyway. The soft clouds of colour filling the ether began to shake violently in response. They jerked and spun, then sped towards him. Jagar broke the connection, and the lights immediately returned to their inert state. Soulfire was energy from other realms, and these drifting souls did not like it when he tried to call it.

The forces of the ether, like all things and places, had weakness, and anything that had weakness could be controlled. Jagar probed the ether, pushing aside ethereal mists until he found resistance. There was something here like him, but older. Much older.

Jagar pushed harder, driving all of his spite and malice into that single point against the barrier. He had to know what it was. He wanted inside, to penetrate it and infest it. It would become him and he it.

The surface yielded to his touch. Weakness. He pushed harder, pulling power from everything around him, absorbing the mists and using their strength to augment his own. The surface pushed back against him, repelling his touch. If there were forces in here acting upon him, then he, Jagar, the bringer of death, was a force unto himself. The being that pushed back at him was immensely strong, it was the heart of the ether, the central mass of which the souls of all things that had ever lived would spend eternity orbiting. So existence truly was for naught!

The heart of the ether screeched and screamed as the immovable object to the unstoppable force. Waves blew out from the surface, attacking him. Jagar reeled. The power of the mass was more terrible than the fire at Makril, stronger than the holes in that world he used to inhabit. It could level mountains and melt glaciers—it could undo the realms!

A great voice spoke. "You will not escape."

Jagar looked inward, and found that he too had a voice. "Who will stop me?"

"I am Baeivi."

"The Great Mother," thought Jagar. "Finally. I did so hope you would show up. This is your realm after all."

Baeivi attacked. Magnificent force pressed down upon Jagar. It should have ended him but he did something he had never done: he gave in, and it ceased.

"Why did you stop? I was enjoying that."

There came no answer. Perhaps the Great Mother was still in shock.

The force returned a thousandfold. It took all Jagar had to give in. To just let it crush him, and at the moment where it should have pulverised him, the pressure evaporated.

"Interesting. Now a little to the left, if you would..."

Again. The power of a thousand moons, a million storms, tore through him, but he was Jagar, and he gave in once more.

"You do not belong here," said Baeivi, finally.

"No. I don't. And what's more, there are not many people who can say they had an itch scratched by a God."

Baeivi released the full onslaught of her wrath at him, but the torrent of power, the stream of afterlife in which he swam, coursed through him as if were simply not there.

"You will not end me, Baeivi. You may be the creator, but you did not create this Banèman."

The torrent stopped.

Baeivi had left him. She too, had realised that negative force could still be a force. Infinite nothingness.

Was this where the rest of his existence would be, floating like jetsam amongst a sea of stars? A grain of sand stuck in the sandal of the Great Mother forever!

"There has to be a way out."

Then he saw her. A soul quite unlike the rest. It looked something like what he used to be. The puff of cloud was iridescent, beautiful, and ancient. As Jagar floated towards it, he could hear the heart and voice of the owner of that soul.

He smiled. "Kaliste? Is that you?"

KALISTE / MAE

19

EVESGIVING

The Banèman Kaliste grasped Soulfire, bringing the fire within to the surface as a raging torrent of power. It took the form of a serpent, and snapped at her naked body. Its fangs and mouth splashing apart against her skin like it was made of nothing but water. It could not hurt her, but like all Soulfire, it was pure energy stolen from another realm and would always fight to get back there.

Kaliste caressed the snake's head. "Even after so many cycles of being together you still treat me so?" The snake withdrew at her words. It was a game. "We need, each other, you and I. Can you even imagine it?"

Life without Soulfire was no life at all. The snake coiled its fiery body around Kaliste's forearm. "My Bohr ancestors would cut me down to see the decadence of this life. These curtains. This room. This palace." Kaliste pointed at the ornate curtains hanging across the huge bay windows and the snake leapt towards them. She felt a deep excitement as it snapped back to her. "And that hanging rug." She extended a hand towards the tapestry hanging across the fireplace. "Rugs belong on the floor."

The snake reached out, stretching to twenty times its own length and tore through the fabric, running down the length of that thousand-cycle-old threadbare, ancient carpet until it too was burning. Kaliste watched the flames spreading. The chairs, the tables, the desk, the papers. Maps, pens, quills. All of it burning.

If a queen could not burn down her own palace, then who could? Kaliste closed her eyes and willed the snake's shape flat, into a length of fiery material that folded and cut itself in front of her until it was the shape of a long swooping dress. Her imagination painted the lost images of that tapestry upon the flame, her fingers conducting the piece, and the material becoming a canvas of living fire depicting the Battle of Pulier's Pass. What a time that had been! She had been a lot younger back then, but she remembered every moment as if it were yesterday—the horse charge, the flaming dragons, the castle's war machines—and she had destroyed them all.

"Oh, to be young again!"

Kaliste stepped through the flaming backpiece of the sweeping dress and it momentarily vanished before reconnecting at her back. The flames were calm now, moving as though in slow motion, holding the dress form. The fire within would never hurt her, but should anyone venture too close...

Kaliste stepped in front of the mirror and admired herself. The Banèmen were the best of the Bohr, and she was the best of the Banèmen. Slayers and assassins bred for war, able to wield the power of the many realms. She was a god. And as her hands caressed down her own torso, waist and hips she marvelled at her strong frame and features, which echoed the strength inside. She could tear down Zunqai if she wanted. Burn it, and cast it away from Rengas and into oblivion. The fiery dress responded by flashing blue, then green, and purple.

Kaliste let a rare smile touch her lips. It was good to dress up occasionally. It did wonders for self-esteem, which can melt away without us even realising. "This Evesgiving is going to be special. I just know it."

Despite the incessant rain outside (it had been exceptionally stormy of late), the evesroom in Zunqai's Central Palace was already filled with Bohr and most of them had opted for satin, spidersilk and linen. It was not often the Bohr would get together for an event like this one, let alone even congregate for any length of time, but that was why tonight was special. It was why her Soulfire dress was showing off by flashing through as many colours as it could manage, and why Kaliste was happy for it to do so.

She stopped by a group of younger Bohr. "My Queen," they said, each in turn.

Kaliste nodded. Their auras spoke of fear but with respect. They smelled excited, apprehensive and youthful. "This is your first time at an Evesgiving?" It was a foolish thing to ask, seeing as they were all barely fifty cycles, but it was nice to be nice.

The first Bohr nodded, waiting for permission to speak. Kaliste gave it and the young male recounted his reasons for being here. In hindsight, Kaliste could not have remembered what those reasons were, because she was too busy considering the evening's events

"And what do you think of the framing of this Evesgiving? As a human *party*?"

The young Bohr looked nervous. He was standing a fair distance away because of the dress of burning power clinging to Kaliste's every curve, but he still looked like he would prefer to be anywhere else.

"Co-existence is one thing, my Queen. But abidance is something else entirely. Appropriation of human traditions is undesirable."

"Undesirable is a book answer," hissed Kaliste. "The Bohr pre-date the humans of Rengas by a thousand generations according to Doctrine." The words were bitter; Doctrine was as useless as the human infatuation with Baeivi. "And while my fellow Banèmen didn't appear until after that time, we are by far the...how do the humans say it? Cream of the crop?"

The young Bohr inclined his head in acquiescence, his aura turning from a storm of reds and greys to a calming green.

"But it was a thoughtful answer nonetheless, young..."

"V'olpar."

"You are V'Laerk's underling?"

"I am, my Queen."

"V'Laerk is an impressive specimen. I've been very much interested in what he has to say about Bohr rule in Sulitaria."

V'olpar nodded, his snout crinkling enough to show that his

nervousness was still present. "He talks of Bohr unification often, my Queen. He is very keen to please both you, my Queen, and this court."

"Good," said Kaliste. "Then let us hope he fights as well as debates." Kaliste turned to leave, then something else occurred to her. "Unification is the only way to create a pure kingdom. Remember that and you may yet find yourself deciding the fortunes of others, young V'olpar."

"I will, my Queen," said the Bohr, with a deep bow." Thank you for your generous words."

V'Laerk was one of the favourites of the evesmen, and probably Kaliste's preferred winner of the day. Even standing in the centre of the evesroom, its gaudy hangings draped across each side, the Bohr sigil of the White Dragon painted anywhere there was space, it was clear to everyone that Kaliste was running this show. The cycles had passed, leaving their marks on her, but she would still occasionally daydream. Perhaps it was the promise of the evening's rewards, that she found herself filling the fool room with fire, burning the eyes from every skull, turning all life to smouldering ash—all in her mind, of course, but it was so tempting to just do it anyway. She could find new chancellors, and evesmen and even their followers, but then that might just ruin the night.

"Well, I shall leave you to your circle, V'olpar. Wish your master good luck."

V'olpar squared his shoulders, his expression triumphant. "I will, my Queen."

Kaliste ambled over to the centre of the room, where the tiles of the floor came together in a huge, nine-pointed star made of gold, seasilver, and inlaid with the rarest charn from the cursed city of Tyr. Upon the star's centre stood an ornate dais made of ivory from the bones of Bohr long dead. This might be a more unusual framing of this century's Evesgiving, but civility had its price. The days of hot orgies and fighting to the death in mud baths were long gone. Zunqai was a city of gods, and a prime example of Bohr rule. And it had to stay that way.

She reached out, took the bell sitting on the dais and gave it a ring. The doors swung open as V'Laerk and seventeen other evesmen marched into the great evesroom. There were many different shapes and sizes: rams, wolves, bulls, even a Bohr with Ruffin scales that she'd heard could change colour at will to confuse his opponent, but it was V'Laerk that held her eye. She made no qualms about it either, watching as his shining hide rippled over hardened muscles. The soft markings in his fur were subtly dappled, like the beast himself, dark brown against black, almost invisible. He wasn't the biggest, the most beautiful, nor was he the strongest—that accolade was owned by the wolf—but what he lacked he made up for in keenness. Those dark eyes took in everything. Every inch of him, even those covered beneath the scant cloth at this groin, looked poised and ready. He was primed. He *was* prime.

The entire precession made its way around the room, padding, growling, snarling until the first nine stepped into one of nine large circles that surrounded the central star pattern. The second group circled Kaliste looking outward. She didn't need to study their auras to see their readiness, although it hung with some more than others. That was the thing about holding Soulfire, it impressed a byproduct of sorts upon the wielder, and while seeing an aura could give wonderful insight into a person's being, it could not be relied upon.

Kaliste gestured to V'Laerk. "YOU."

V'Laerk responded with a bow then pointed at the bull. The bull Bohr nodded and stalked over to V'Laerk's circle to stand at his side.

"YOU."

The Ruffin Bohr chose a wolf Bohr. And so the process repeated until each of the nine circles were filled with two Bohr, ready and waiting to fight.

Kaliste's belly started to warm, but it was not the thought of filling the evesroom with fire. The glow of new life was beginning within her. Her body was preparing for the seed that would help create a new generation.

Kaliste roared mightily, then begun her piece—She did not need to use Soulfire to help project her voice, not tonight. "Children of the Bohr, some call us. Banèmen. Slayer. We are capable of wielding unlimited power, control and strength, but yet we cannot create life by ourselves. A cruel twist of fate?" She paused, tonguing her own fangs. Her mouth was watering. "Or an opportunity for you, my evesmen to claim the unclaimable!" She raised her fist with the last and the room filled with noise as every Bohr roared and howled high into the domed ceiling above.

"READY."

The evesmen began circling, sizing each other up. It was necessary and prudent to gauge the room before beginning to fight—not everyone could be the biggest or strongest, although often that was not the most important factor in determining the victor. These Bohr had likely been watching each other for months before this day, but only the highest order of Bohr were chosen from each of the city's tribes.

The circles upon the floor were a cage that only one could leave alive. Kaliste turned on the spot, admiring her evesmen, ravenous for the blood about to be spilled, for the seed to be planted. She took a long breath, inhaling the musk of so many worthy fighters, of such strength, power and intelligence held in each of them. These evesmen were the biggest, best and most intelligent the Bohr of Zunqai had to offer.

"FIGHT!"

Nine pairs of Bohr launched at each other. Teeth bared, claws extended, horns lowered. Three hit the ground immediately, set upon by their opponents. Two of the evesmen wrestled with each other, tearing chunks of meat from each other's bodies, the iron within as unyielding as the iron of the earth.

The ram and a bull drew Kaliste's eye. They were well matched, butting heads with devastating force. But who had the hardest skull? Would it be one of them, or would intelligence seek to win the night?

Another fight, the wolf with inch-long claws cut across the face of the Ruffin Bohr, dragging long slashes, open and red. The Ruffin Bohr turned towards Kaliste, ducking low below another devastating swipe from the wolf's terrible claws.

Kaliste licked her lips. A Bohr hit the ground, a desert-dog who managed a strangled yelp before the bull he was fighting brought his fists down together in a fatal blow across his neck.

"ONE DOWN."

The crowd behind the fights gasped and Kaliste spun around to see another wolf, holding his opponent, a wolf like him but much bigger, above his head. He slammed the bigger wolf to the ground, and set upon him, biting and clawing and spraying blood everywhere. The tiles were already drenched in the night's spoils, and their patterns were channelling the blood towards her and the dais. As Kaliste watched, the smaller wolf found the larger wolf's throat and tore it out. The flow grew faster and as the first bloods touched her bare feet, a tingle of sensation rippled through her. The dress of fire shimmered and flushed through a rainbow of oranges, reds and blues.

"TWO DOWN."

The fighting wore on as each pair tried to outlast each other—taking a moment to breathe and regain composure was common after the first bloods. The thirds, fourths and fifths would take longer to reveal themselves. One pair, a hog and a goat, circled each other like boxers, jabbing, but keeping their distance. The crowd egged them on, booing them until the goat finally ran at the hog. The hog moved sideways at the last minute and the goat flew out of the circle, sliding across the ground. Kaliste drew deeply upon Soulfire, and her dress coiled onto her arm as the snake reappeared, waiting eagerly. She extended a hand and the fiery snake took the goat, setting him alight until there was nothing but charred bones remaining. The hog squealed in victory, but only for a moment. The snake's body growing thicker as Kaliste drew more and more Soulfire, and the snake pounced upon the hog, taking him as well. Kaliste's dress returned, glowing as brightly as before.

"FOUR DOWN," roared Kaliste. "NO DIRTY PLAY."

V'Laerk caught her eye next. He was ducking and diving beneath a bull's wild head thrusts, blocking, and fighting defensively. It was not always prudent to be so forward in the fight, but V'Laerk would not last long with such cowardly play.

Kaliste turned back to the Ruffin Bohr, who was pummelling the wolf, his lizard-like scales changing colour with each punch from his armoured fists. The wolf with the terrible claws had barely time to breathe, let alone reply. He found his moment, but the Ruffin Bohr was there, extending his long lizard mouth over the wolf's head, and both Bohr fell to the ground, then the Ruffin Bohr was rolling, and twisting. The wolf rolled with him, trying to avoid the inevitable, but tiredness slowed him. On the last spin the wolf's shoulders stayed locked to the floor, and as the Ruffin Bohr rolled again, the wolf's neck cracked. The

Ruffin Bohr stood, letting the wolf Bohr fall limp to the floor, then brought his hands together, bowing towards Kaliste.

"FIVE DOWN."

Four fights remaining. There were two more well-matched wolves, V'Laerk and the bull, a tigre and another feline, and the ram and the bull who continued to butt each other, unrelenting.

One of the two wolves took the other's arm in his mouth and twisted until the bone snapped, but it was ill-timed. The injured wolf had clearly sacrificed his arm in favour of the opening, and as the first wolf exalted, the injured wolf dove forward, jaws agape.

"SIX DOWN."

Kaliste wiggled her toes as the blood warmed them, growing deeper and deeper with each death. A horrendous crack filled the room, and Kaliste spun just in time to see the ram's head crack open like an egg, the bull covered in the ram's gore roared at the ceiling and then collapsed himself, breathing heavily.

"EIGHT DOWN."

The tigre and feline slashed and pounced around within the lines of their circle, they would jump twenty feet off the ground and still land delicately within the lines, tails whipping, sometimes on four legs, sometimes on two. The two very different fights continued, the tigre and feline easily the most entertaining for the crowd. The feline fell scratching to the tiles, hissing at the tigre as he inched forward, shoulders rolling. The feline slashed out with a claw on the end of his tail, beckoning the tigre forward, playing weak. The tigre leapt forward, and as its feet left the ground the feline's tail stiffened, each of those backbones lining up perfectly, extended like a sword. The tigre fell upon it, its weight dragging it slowly down, impaled. The feline whipped its tail back, leaving the tigre to fall to the tiles, and prowled around the circle on all fours.

"NINE DOWN. ONE FIGHT LEFT."

V'Laerk looked like he was trying to goad the bull into a charge like the hog had done. Oh, how the bull Bohr liked to charge, but if either of them left the circle Kaliste would burn them both, even if she would not take the greatest pleasure in it. The bull charged and V'Laerk stepped aside, but rather than letting the bull leave the ring, V'Laerk grabbed the bull's horns and using the Bohr's momentum, swung him up into the air. The bull Bohr hung high above V'Laerk's head before he came crashing down to land neck first in the circle. V'Laerk climbed onto the dead bull's large belly and sat there cross-legged, offering Kaliste a head-bow.

Kaliste bowed back. "TEN DOWN. ROUND ONE IS COMPLETE."

V'Laerk purred as Kaliste's fingers traced the Bohr's back, drawing patterns on his blood-soaked fur. The dress she had been wearing stood high above them as a flaming tent, its orange light giving the illusion of a dark green hue. "Congratulations on your win, V'Laerk."

V'Laerk swallowed, as well he might. There were very few beings who could claim to have mated with a Banèman. "Is this the end now? How should it be done?"

Kaliste sat up, the bloods still a good half-foot deep in the centre of the evesroom. "You expect to die?"

"That is tradition, my Queen. Is it not?"

Kaliste marvelled at how calm V'Laerk's aura was in the face of execution. "My Queen? No. You call me Kaliste now. No one else can. Not those who value life. You have sired a new Banèman within me today, V'Laerk. It grows in me, ready to take over and be free." Her lip trembled with the thought of it. "A sire is never killed, V'Laerk. You get to live. *That* is your prize, and it is my plan to keep you alive."

V'Laerk stretched out his hoofed feet and splayed them. "Then I am happy." He said simply. "What will you call it?"

"Him," said Kaliste correcting him, and stroking his muzzle. "A name is important. The act itself may take only a few hours, but it is not so easy assigning a name. A name holds power upon it. The saying of it will conjure and create, it will determine the flavour of the Soulfire that will fill the child. Imagine it. A new being, A Banèman like no other. He will live. He will rule." She took V'Laerk's hands and placed them on her stomach. "A flower. A fruit ripened. Seeded. These are all the same. The plush beginning of new life, ready to take over. And V'Laerk, your bloodline committed to the ages, moving onwards like a ship across the

Middle Sea, untouched by wave or wind." V'Laerk's hand ventured further, up to her breasts, to hold her neck, his claws digging into her pale skin.

He started to purr again. "I still do not understand why K'azar did not lunge."

Kaliste ran her finger along V'Laerk's snout, and along his lip, drawing a purr from within his massive chest. "Think no more of the Ruffin Bohr's inadequacies. His hesitance is what lost him the final battle, and won you your prize."

V'Laerk's teeth bared and he took Kaliste by her hips and, already engorged, pulled her on top of him. She took him in, feeling him from the inside, his raw strength but a shade of her own. She gave in to it anyway.

The daydreams and colours swirled in her mind, Soulfire burning the world. The pulsing canvas of fire overhead throbbing in time with V'Laerk, deep as he was within her, and all felt right. The stars were aligned, and all that was meant to be, was there.

Abruptly, Kaliste's mind was filled with white noise. She winced as something even deeper took over, and a voice filled her body and soul.

Kaliste? Is that you?

Kaliste went stiff.

V'Laerk growled, then howled in pain. "You're burning me!" He pushed Kaliste off.

"Jagar?"

The voice spoke again, this time it was unmistakable. *Speak from within.*

Kaliste sat back, holding up a hand to silence V'Laerk as he attended his burnt cock.

"Where are you?"

Not important. There's little time...

There was a pause, and Kaliste waited. Jagar's skill with Soulfire outranked hers.

The long battle is coming. We need to prepare. Fragment the Bohr.

"Fragment them?"

Trust me, Kaliste. His voice, already like a quill scratching paper, began to fade. *Spread our forces wide across Rengas. Play the game. Develop our pieces.* The voice vanished into the fog of her mind.

Kaliste drew on Soulfire so deeply the dome of fire fluttered and winked out leaving patterns upon her eyes. V'Laerk jumped back, leaving the Queen of all Banèmen sitting in a pool of evesblood and holding enough Soulfire to level the evesroom, a good deal of the armoury and the square beyond.

Licks of flame left her skin, taking form as the energy from other realms found a way through into Rengas.

The crowds of onlookers, councillors, all Bohr, stood waiting for their deaths, even as the underlings bolted, Kaliste took the Soulfire to the edge of her control, holding it on the precipice. Then she saw V'Laerk.

Once more he had stayed with her, waiting to meet a fate he had been prepared for, for many moons. He was ready, but Kaliste was not. She killed the fire, burying a thousand cycles worth of feeling, compressed into a single moment. It was better than anything her mortal body could have felt. And now it was gone.

She slammed her fists into the pool of evesblood, and she screamed and mourned for the loss of it all.

20

ESCAPE

The stars moved over the canvas of violet night, the opening of the prison cell above a colourful reminder of Abika's captivity. The guards had thrown in a rancid blanket, but it was barely large enough to cover her knees. Then there was the necklace and her own torn night shift, and what good would bloody jewellery do if she froze to death in the night? She pulled the blanket tight, and, dropped the necklace around her neck.

Jekob's words had stayed her with her until the birds were replaced with the fluttering of bats and moths. But as shocking as those words were, something didn't add up.

"A Nordun mother, and a Kemen father..." They sounded awkward in Abika's mouth. "Nord. Kemen. Mother. Father." At least she now had a name. Using Jekob's own guilt against him Abika had once emerged the victor. "Where are you, Kyira of Nord? My mother."

Absently she traced a finger through the dust, tracing the shapes of the world. Sulitar was the largest of the islands known as Sulitaria, with the Red Isles, Hauwi, Ipiti, Dor, and a few others scattered around it, but Nord? Kemen? She hesitated. Both places were far across the ocean, and a complete mystery to Abika. Maybe she should steal a boat? She drew a shapeless blob on the left side, trying to create a sort of ring shape. The Middle Sea couldn't be so big could it?

She had sailed before in the bay with Jekob. The memory drew disgust from her stomach, like she could sick the thing up and kick it into the dark corner of her cell. Everything that she knew was a lie, Jekob, Freya. Was Meorith in on it too? Did they all know that she was a Nordun cuckoo dropped into the wrong nest?

Abika clutched the necklace. The edges of the window above shone as the moon worked its way around the sky. Soon it would shine down upon her, and she would sit in a square of white moonlight. She crossed her legs and closed her eyes, waiting, emptying her mind of all distraction. It wasn't easy. Jekob's presence lingered like an echo through the hills, reverberating through her.

"They're not all power-wielders," rasped a voice.

Abika blinked, but the room was empty. Panic was there for the taking, but she closed her eyes instead and concentrated.

"Is that right now, Sam?" The second one was drinking something. There was the sound of a heavy glass being put down. "Then what are they doing here? It ain't to spread joy and glee into the lives of strangers."

Chairs scuffed. "Piss off. I'm in this fight the same as any other. I fought them back in the Arcol wars. Where were you then?"

"Fighting as you were, Sam. Fighting for our freedom and a free Kemen."

"Well, alls Kyotho got then was the Northern Territories."

A different voice now. A woman. "And look what that got us..."

The next words brought fear into Abika's heart. "Excuse me, I hate to interrupt—"

Abika pulled off the necklace in panic, jerking around. There was no one else here. "How? Those voices..." They were as clear as though she had been standing with them. Who were they?

The moon had long passed the zenith, the square of moonlight had crept back up the cell wall. Hours had passed since Abika put the necklace on.

She stood, trembling. "I need to get out of here."

"You hear about Dolum?" Rivan nodded, barely registering the words. Instead he concentrated, before throwing his dice. The wooden cube flew true, the power of the toss soaked up by the slight deviation in the outer walls of cell one. It was such a perfect throw that the dice practically crawled down the wall like a cave caterpillar, landing gently on top of Stae's red dice and sliding behind.

"Briš!" roared Rivan, elated. There really was none other that could match his skill at this game. "Briš, and then some. That's a bloody six there!"

Stae shook his head like the loser he was. "Briš literally means *end* you fool. It doesn't matter what the dice says. The game is done."

"Better to win twice, than not at all," Rivan paused whilst picking up both dice. "Wait. Dolum?"

Stae picked his teeth with a little knife. "Alright, alright," said Stae. "Just pick it up, you chunk of a man. I ain't done yet."

"No," said Rivan. "What happened to Dolum?"

"Died, didn't he? Drowned. Fell in the tearing canal."

Rivan shook his head. "By the Great bloody Mother. How?"

Stae nodded down the hallway. "The rebel."

"In cell three?"

"Aye. There was a chase, or something. Look are you going to let me win back my earnings or no?"

Rivan stepped back, then glanced at the dice in his hand. "I was talking to him just last week. Could've been me."

Stae shrugged. "How exactly could it have been you? Tell me that." The skinny bastard's gaze fell to Rivan's belt. "Your bloody keys, Rivan. You can't be a bloody jailer without keys. How many bloody times!"

Rivan checked his pockets. Nothing. He glanced down the dark hallway at the cells beyond the jailer's office and his eye caught a twinkling of a thing, hanging from the rebel's door. "Shit. I must have left them there when I threw in the blanket." He stepped into the hallway. The dark had always scared Rivan, but he never would have said it, not with his friends. He valued his life too much for that. If they found out he was afraid of the dark then that was it!

Rivan pulled his keys from the lock and clipped them to his belt. "Drowned. What a thing."

A scream sounded from the cells, a scream that would have emptied the bowels of even Rivan's father, and he was a tough nut.

"What the hell was that?" said Stae, his head appearing round the corner of the hallway.

Rivan stepped back from the cell door. "It sounded like her." Rivan took a deep breath and unclipped his keys. He found the key marked with a three but hesitated before putting it in the lock. Nothing. No sound. Maybe she'd had a heart attack. He'd heard that could happen. Surely she was too young for that?

"Stae, how old is this one again?"

"Just hurry it up, Rivan," came Stae's thin whine. "I'm aging over here."

"Oh, shut up," grumbled Rivan. "bloody bastard." The key slid into the hole, and he kicked the door open. "What are you about, girl—"

The shadows came to life, and a ghost flew towards him and over his head. Rivan had barely time to breathe let alone scream before something attacked him. Covered him, then swiftly kicked him in the nuts.

Abika ducked left out of the guard's way as he collapsed into Abika's cell. It couldn't have gone more perfectly, and the blanket covering his head had been more effective than she could have dreamed. She was out in the cell-block corridor. She grabbed the handle of cell three and yanked it shut.

"Come on, Rivan!" came a voice from the guardroom. "Stop pissing about! I want my bloody chits back."

"Thanks, Rivan," whispered Abika, turning the keys still in the lock. Lorith was in cell four. Rifling through the keys on the large ring she found the key and pushed it in. The door needed her full weight to move even slightly.

"Lorith?" she hissed. "Lorith, come on. We need to go!" The door moved slowly open and she stepped over the threshold. The smell made her gag.

"Euch! Lorith, are you in there?"

Something grabbed her, dragging her inward and the floor leapt up to meet her. Lorith held a ball of tightly knotted clothes above his head, his own clothes, ready to smash into Abika's face.

"Bee?"

"Yes," hissed Abika. "Yes, you idiot. It's me." Lorith slithered off her and held the ball in front of his groin.

"Oh, Lorith." She couldn't help but bring a hand up to her mouth. His naked bony frame was a tapestry of bruises, old and new, cuts, some healed some still weeping. His usual bright features were gaunt and tired.

"They look worse than they are," he croaked.

"Did Jekob do this?"

Lorith nodded, then winced. "Sometimes it was Jekob. Other times it was them." He motioned to the door, then he looked her up and down. "They didn't...hurt you, did they?"

Abika shook her head. "No. Just left me lying in my own filth."

"They're all afraid of you, Bee."

Abika ignored him, and looked over the dirty corner of his cell. "Look, just put your clothes on. We have to get out of here."

"I can't. They're too tightly bound."

An inpatient voice roared from beyond the cell door. "Rivan! Are we playing or not? Leave her be!"

"He's coming, Bee!" hissed Lorith.

"Quiet." Abika pulled the door just as the other jailer's footsteps sounded outside. "Lorith. Grab a pile of that and rush him!" She pointed to the corner of the cell. It was absolutely disgusting but Lorith just nodded and scooped up a handful of his own mess.

"Ready," Lorith nodded to the door.

The awful smell wafted by as Abika opened the door and, naked as a babe, Lorith slammed into the guard outside cell three. The man, still fumbling with his keys, turned but received no less than an entire handful of days-old shit in the face. Lorith followed it up with a blistering display of punches and knees into the poor guard's head. The guard was thankfully skinny, but taller and far more practised at fighting. After barely a second or two the guard had regained his bearing. He pushed the keys into Lorith's face, forcing him back.

"You little shit!" spat the guard.

"Get him, Stae!" roared the guard locked in Abika's cell. "Get the fucker!"

"You disgusting little—"

Lorith sent punch after punch into the man's head, more slapping than anything, trying to ward off the bear hug the guard was clearly aiming for—a wrestling match would end only one way.

Abika slipped behind them, and ran down the hallway, stopping in the guard room. The desk, strewn with papers, looked like it had been pushed against a wall. She rifled through looking for something. Anything. There. She grabbed a fountain pen and rushed back into the cell hallway. "Cutting meat."

"Rivan, get out here!" said the guard, standing above Lorith. He wiped his gauntlet over his face and spat.

"The door's locked!"

"I've unlocked it you fool!"

"Give it a kick!"

Abika had to leap on the guard's back to make it work, but oh did it work. The fountain pen was sharp, and she poked many a hole into the guard's neck before he managed to turn. By then though, it was too late. Abika stabbed the guard in the stomach and the man keeled forward, landing heavily and groaning in a foetal position. Abika recognised him as one of the guards she had met her first night in Ipor Dan. Pity swelled in her chest.

"Come on, Lorith. We have to get out of here. There will be more coming." Abika took Lorith's arm and they hobbled towards the light of the guard room. "Gods, Lorith." She placed a hand on his side, and he winced away. "I think your rib is broken."

"I can't breathe."

"He fair caught you. That'll be one hell of a bruise to show the girls."

Lorith managed a snigger then winced again.

Abika rummaged through the drawers and cupboards but they were all just filled with paper. "You need clothes. And a wipe down!"

In the last cupboard was an old towel. Only the Great Mother would know what it had been used for, but it was better than nothing. She threw it over to him without thinking, and Lorith watched it land on the floor.

"I can't, Bee. You'll have to do it."

Abika sighed. "Fine. But you owe me big time for this."

The skinny guard was just taller than Lorith, and while the bloodstains were still obvious, the height difference had been hidden easily enough with some turnups. She had taken the guard's knife too—a pitifully small thing but it's weight was reassuring in her shift pocket.

The hallways of the citadel were a warren of narrow passages and false ends. They had been hobbling around, peeking around corners, and hiding in nooks for what felt like an hour and were still no closer to finding a way out.

"This way."

"Bee, I..."

"Just come on, Lorith." Abika hurried him along, worrying at how long it would take for Lorith's cuts to become infected.

"It's meant to fool attackers."

Abika watched around the corner as a Guard of the White Dragon stepped out of a room and walked off down the corridor. "We should follow him."

"It's so if any enemy does get in, they can't get out."

"What? What are you talking about?"

"The layout. Of the citadel." Lorith slumped against the wall. "They'll find our dead bodies in a week or so, starved to death. Oh, what I would give for some fried dumplings. Or a steak. I could eat the thing raw." With the last word, he clenched his teeth and slid down the wall.

"No, Lorith. Come on get up. We've still got to get out of here."

"Bee, I need to tell you something—"

Abika slapped him hard, not so hard that she might kill him, but hard enough. The shock was like electric coursing through him. He stared up at her, eyes bright again. "Ow."

"Come on! We don't have long."

Half walking, half hobbling, they shuffled along the corridor in the direction the guard had gone. It led to a stone staircase, spiralling down. It wasn't until they were barely ten steps from the bottom that they heard the voices of those below.

Lorith used the central plinth to lean against, staring at her expectantly. "Abika, what if they come up here? I can't run back up."

Abika pulled the fountain pen from her pocket. "Then we'll just have to—"

"Write them to death?"

"If I have to. It worked with that other one, didn't it?"

"I just don't get why the guards didn't have any weapons. Not even a knife."

"Probably to stop people like us from overpowering them and using them to escape."

"Or maybe nobody's escaped from the citadel cells before." Lorith shrugged. "I've never heard of it."

"What, on the streets?"

Lorith grabbed her shift beneath the chin. "You have a strange sense of loyalty, Abika. Why are you even here? What are you running from?"

"From?" Abika shook her head. "To, Lorith. Running to. You were abandoned at the commune too, weren't you?"

"Is that it? A beef with your parents? Is that what all *this* is about?"

"It's much, much more than that."

"Whatever." Lorith pushed Abika on. "Well go on then! Lead us on, oh mighty leader. Your vengeance awaits."

Abika all but dragged Lorith onwards, down the passageway which led to a narrower hallway and down at least six sets of stairs before opening into a short, cobbled area with an archway that led outside. "That smells wonderful."

Abika couldn't agree more. Even the stink wafting up from the stolen prison guard's uniform was lost as a fresh breeze blew in through that archway. There were towels piled up in the corner next to a pillar holding up the arch, and the air held about it the feel of presence and joy. There were people nearby bathing.

"These are the baths." Lorith turned and pointed to the wall behind them. "There's two uniforms here, look."

Almost on cue, a naked woman walked along the path beyond the baths, completely uncaring.

Lorith followed her every step. "Bee, they'll see us, we can't sneak by them."

Of all the points to exit a bloody citadel, they had managed to find the only place where a guard uniform would look out of place. "We'll have to strip off too."

"I can't, Bee."

Abika went to pull off her stained shift. "We've no secrets now, Lorith."

Lorith shook his head. "No, that's not it. Look at the state of me. They'll know something is up the moment they lie eyes on me." He was right, and what's more, he was looking greyer and greyer with each passing moment.

Abika pressed her hand up against Lorith's side where the worse bruising had been, and Lorith hissed. "I'm bleeding inside. Bee, I need to tell you—"

"Shut up, Lorith."

Abika tip-toed over the cobbles and peered around the pillar. There were ten baths built into the ground, each big enough for five or six people, but only one was steaming.

"We can go," she whispered back to Lorith.

"What?"

"Trust me."

She helped Lorith along the cobbles and past the pillar and out into the bath courtyard. "Oh my."

Abika nodded, smiling to herself at the passion of the two men in the steaming bath. They weren't bad looking, but whereas one couldn't have been older than twenty, the other was easily in his sixties. She wanted to stop and watch them, rubbing and grasping at each other, kissing, touching and—

"Bee!" hissed Lorith, ahead of her. "Come on." He pointed to some stone steps leading to a garden.

The gardens were well kept, all green with colourful buds hanging about the place, the path led to an outdoor gate, but it was locked.

"How do we—"

Abika pulled the guard's keys from her pocket. "This is how."

"Why would a prison guard have keys to the gardens, Bee?"

Abika tried each key in turn, but Lorith was right. They were cell keys. "Maybe one of them has a key?"

Lorith shook his head. "Baeivi's blood, you better be quick then." He peered out past the gate into the street beyond. There wasn't much to look at other than an old alleyway, but the citadel was central in Ipor Dan, surrounded by streets on all sides, except for a small square at the front for daily worship.

Abika started back up the stairs, when a familiar rumbling voice caught her attention. "Child."

She turned to see a familiar shape appear out of the shadows half again as tall as either of them, dressed neatly in green and yellow leather, with silver buttons, but no shoes. "Vasta?"

The Bohr took them both in. "You are on the wrong side of this gate." Vasta pulled a thin tool from his sleeve and slipped it into the lock. It clicked open, but Abika placed a foot in front.

"Abika, what are you doing?"

"What are *you* doing, Bohr?"

"You still have my necklace, child." The Bohr's deep rumbling voice might have turned her legs to water, given half a chance. As it was, she held no trust for anyone. Especially him.

Lorith yanked the gate then fell into a fit of coughs. "Can we talk on this later?" Then they were pulling the handle and stepping out of the gardens.

"What are you doing?" said Abika, turning back to the gate.

Vasta slipped the tool back in through the hole and relocked the gate. "Covering our tracks. Being methodical. Call it what you like."

"*Our* tracks?" said Abika. "Where are *we* going?"

"Away," said Vasta. "Away from Ipor Dan. It is time to leave, again." He stopped. "Unless, child, you have more questions?"

Being given a choice to do anything had been one of the more unusual experiences of her life since leaving the commune, but she couldn't go back, and the Bohr knew it too. It unnerved her that he seemed to know her so well already.

Abika sneered. "Nothing that can't be answered on the road. Let's go."

PART II

CAPTAIN ATALFIA (Fia)

21

BORDERLANDS

Drizzle found its way into every fold and flap of Fia's clothes, so that even her undergarments were soaked through. What was it about Hatàr and rain? The borderlands were closer to the Half Line of the world, so why did it feel colder? It made no sense. League upon league of heavy sky, trapping the hills beneath it, holding them in suspense. It was an oppressive place where time stopped.

Tight in her fist was her union cross necklace. The unions were the five human rebel factions, symbolised by two oval loops of gold-plated iron as arranged in a cross. The cross sat over the top of a circle ring which represented Rengas.

In the long cycles since Tyr, four factions were born and unionised, working with the Bohr in the Kemen capital of Zunqai, but Fia had come along with the remainder of the Tsiorc army and claimed a fifth union. She had spent many cycles since solidifying their presence as a core union and she believed with everything she was that the Fifth Union were absolutely crucial to the success of the human resistance against the Bohr, even going so far as to change the name of her army. The central diamond of the Fifth Union cross existed where the loops of the cross overlapped, underpinning the entire resistance, regardless of what the Northerns, Easterns, Southerns and Westerns thought. It was more than just distance that separated the Fifth Union from the rest of them—the other union's ideals were so Bohr-like that they may as well have been Bohr themselves, council or no.

To hell with them all!

Fia studied the necklace, polishing it against the fur hood and blowing away the tiny hairs that stuck to the metal. It was battered and bent, but it was still holding together, for now at least.

The lake came into view beyond the last short hill before the flatlands, after which lay the border of Kemen, marked so by a long wall that stretched from one side of the continent to the other. A stone and iron sheer barrier built by the first Bohr builders, wrought of the hardest metal, and two hundred feet high. It was hard not to look at it. But Fia's aspirations were more than just looking or studying. She had ventured to the foot of it many times, looking for weakness, looking for some way in, but the Bohr knew their trade. The first builders had been gone for hundreds of cycles and still all of their creations lived on. If anything, that border wall looked even stronger than when she had first arrived with the remnants of the Tsiorc army twelve cycles ago. Once, the Fifth had tried sneaking around by the coast, only to find the wall extended to the seabed, and where it did end, the currents were too strong to circumnavigate. The Bohr wall was completely impenetrable.

"Home," said Jona.

The sounds of the lake's soft waves lapping upon the sandy shore did bring feelings of warmth and of home. That happened when you left a place for a spell, but Fia knew it would wear off, and they would soon be back to their colourless lives.

"Home," said Fia, sighing. Her boots slipped on the red clay for what felt like the thousandth time. She caught herself, thankfully before Jona reached her.

"You alright?"

Fia held up her stump. If she still had a hand there she might've slapped the fool with it, or given him the finger. It was strange the things you missed. "I'm fine."

Jona frowned, equally unsure what to do. "At least let me—"

"Don't play the gentleman with me, boy." Fia hefted the oilskin bag onto her shoulder. The blood pooling in the bottom of it made it awkward to keep in one place, but there were enough lumps in it that it eventually settled.

Jona stopped at the top of the hill ahead of her rubbing his neck like a man with all the troubles of the world hanging off him.

Fia placed a hand upon his shoulder. "Do you want to talk about it, dearest?"

"With you?" Jona grimaced. "Gods no."

Fia should have felt a little affronted, but truth was, she didn't care. Jona was a good fighter, and a charismatic man—his charming demeanour kept many a man laughing and many a woman weak at the knees—but Fia would rather spend the night sleeping inside a rotting sandshark than spend another day with him.

"You can see Anqamor from up here."

"See what happens when you get out of the camp?" Fia let the oilskin bag thud to the ground. The sea was a distant line on the horizon but there was no sign of the snake-shaped island of Anqamor. She looked at him. "Were it not for the cloud and mist you mean?"

Jona looked momentarily thoughtful. "I used to live in Anqamor's capital."

"You lived in Anake Bain? How did you get past the guards?"

"Charm and bribes." Jona pointed at the shifting smear of blue against the horizon. "It was a wonderful time. Long mornings, long evenings. And all thanks to one little bird."

Fia's breath caught. "Little Bird? What? What did you say?"

Jona stepped back. "Nests, boss. Bird's nests, to be precise."

Fia cleared her throat. "Nests?" It took some effort to switch off the anger that had so quickly appeared at hearing those two words.

"No," said Jona, continuing. " The local rich folk liked eating a soup made from the nests of these little birds. If you can believe it. They paid in harkko gold."

Fia took a snow apple from her pack and took a bite. It was an old one and the skin was shrivelled, but it was still a little sweet even if the moisture had long since left it. "It won't do you good to look back on such times of plenty. Although it's nice to know you were once an honest man."

"Far from it, boss," laughed Jona. "Far from it. We'd send the children up to collect the nests so we could sell them on. We promised them riches and then paid them a few marks each to keep them happy and fed. Then we pocketed the rest. Gods, I made more money in that single summer than I have in the rest of my life combined. All because of a little bird!"

Fia cringed. "Alright, thank you. Apparently I need no more confirmation that you are indeed a horrible, manipulative person."

"Just trying to keep things positive is all, boss."

"Lying is for cheats and thieves. Not the rebels." Fia rearranged her heavy jacket. "Besides, positivity is luxury, Jona. Don't waste your time on it."

"I guess you'd know all about living a life of luxury."

Fia stared at the back of Jona's head, waiting for him turn. "Look at me. You think I care about your opinion, Jona? I'd be alone if Eris hadn't recommended you to come, so don't you dare stand there and pretend—"

"Peace, boss, peace!" Jona held out his hands like he was taming a tigre. "Look, I meant nothing by it. Call it road humour. Call it anything you want." He brushed himself off. "Everything is hard. Layers and layers of hardness. There's no respite for us rebels. None at all. And why should there be? We chose this life." The smirk returned.

"Sarcasm doesn't suit you, Jona. I'm not in the mood for games."

Jona squatted down over the oilskin bag and popped the cork. "What I would give to just be sitting playing games right now, instead of traipsing over the bloody Hatàrian mountains." He wiped his nose, leaving a smear of red across his chiselled jaw.

"The bag's leaking."

"The butcher ain't going to be happy with this," said Jona. He looked the bag over, shaking his head all the while.

"No, he won't," said Fia. The butcher wouldn't tolerate Jona, nor anyone for that matter. "But you let me handle Derval. You know, I did use to like games," she said, absently. "Long ago."

"Chinaes?"

"Life was my game, and I was very good at it."

Jona eyed her sidelong. "Really? You and the game of life?"

"Don't pretend like Eris hasn't already told you everything about me, Jona. I'm no fool. I've seen you two gossiping like little girls." She backhanded him lightly across the shoulder. "Anyway, you're hardly one to bleat about gaming."

"I did alright back in the tavern."

"No you didn't, Jona. I know children with a better understanding of Chinaes than you. Even so, I'll yield. While it's a simple game to play, it's very tough to master. Impossible even." She gestured to her waist bag where she kept her little bag of character stones. "Strategy, tactics and a thousand levels of possibilities. Conquer one level, to find another, then you're dragged back deep, deep down."

Jona looked at Fia as though she had lost it. "Well, I'm not great with things I'm not immediately good at, boss. You oughta know that by now. But yeh, it looked simple enough. A stone here, a stone there. I've hustled with worse games." Jona stood. "There, it's not fixed but it should last us home."

Fia hauled the bag's strap over her shoulder. "Hustling. Womanising. If I didn't say it before Jona, you're a hell of a catch."

"Now who's being sarcastic?" Jona thumped Fia on the shoulder. "I tell you though, I could have married any one of those tavern girls in Raeven's Torr. I should have proposed right then." He shook his head. "You know they would have said yes."

"Yes?" Fia shook her head. "For a rake you don't know women much, do you, Jona."

"I know em better than you!"

"I highly doubt that. What would have been your play then? Sweep her off her feet and drag her down to the camp?"

"Point taken." Jona touched his eye tenderly. It was still bruised black, though not as swollen. "Raeven's Torr is—"

"Raeven's Torr is a dump. A relic of the old wars. It's a city of war vets with nothing left to fight for."

"That's almost exactly what I was going to say. That tower is impressive though."

"Typical man, impressed by the big long thing. The tower must be five hundred cycles old. It should have fallen long before now. And the people of Raeven's Torr? I've met nicer Bohr." She turned and prodded him in the chest with the stump of her wrist. "Your future wife would likely have knocked you out cold and left you with only your socks had those two fishmen not beat her to it."

"Well, that's one way to get her into my pants." Jona pulled some dried meat from his pocket, brushed off the fluff and tore off a piece.

"Uch."

Jona smiled, showing bits of black jerky stuck to his usually very white teeth. "Uch at the meat, or the pants?"

"Both. Men are disgusting. *You* are disgusting."

Jona's rich expression became serious. "No more games then. I hear you've got plans for more skirmishes." It wasn't phrased as a question, but it was. Jona did that a lot. Perhaps it was ego, men often tended towards telling rather than asking.

"Until we figure out how to conquer the wall." Fia drew a deep breath and turned towards the line of stone snaking its way through the valleys of borderlands away from the coast.

When Jona spoke he was unnervingly close. "Can we really call ourselves rebels, if we don't have anyone to fight?"

"There's plenty of Bohr waiting for us in Kemen, Jona." At least, that's what Fia wanted to say, but for some reason the words just wouldn't form.

22

THE FIFTH UNION

The camp was a mess. Huts and tents stuck out of the ground like clumps of crabgrass on an ugly lawn. The Fifth Union army were not builders—the best fighters never were—and how could you be when you spent all of your time thinking of how best to destroy?

Above the lake on the far side stood a rise that hid the border wall for a few leagues in each direction. From some angles it looked like you could simply leap across the wall, a place called the Pass, but the trick of perspective had long since been debunked, the very first time Fia had laid eyes on these flatlands, in fact.

A daily spyglass from the top of the Pass would confirm that the Bohr Pan guards who walked the wall would sometimes glance over their little camp. There were only two hundred souls here—the entirety of the Tsiorc resistance—the only humans willing to stand up and fight against the Bohr. The Fifth Union. Some would say Fia was crazy for rounding them up, crazy for staying and fighting when the world was moving on. One such man was Derval, the butcher.

"Captain Atalfia." Derval looked Fia up and down with that permanent squint of his, then brought a cleaver down through a slab of pig shoulder. He pulled two fillet knives out from underneath the bench and started trimming the fat, using both knives at the same time.

"Derval. We're using titles again. That's something."

Derval wiped his forehead with the back of his hand. He had a sharp widow's peak that was flecked with grey, and a double chin which seemed to hold all the fat he had on his entire body. Still, Fia was sure he might have been considered handsome by those beyond his wife.

"It pays to be polite now," said Derval. "Even if most days we leave as enemies."

"Enemies is a bit hard," said Fia. "How is little Alis?"

"Yewla has her the now."

That was all the small talk Fia was going to get. "Have you started the evening meal yet?"

"Aye." Derval's closed eye opened momentarily, and he gestured over his shoulder. "Ovens are on, as you can see. Meat is in, but we're running low."

"Again?" Fia placed the oilskin bag on the carvery table at the pig's head. "This should help."

"What's this now? Meat? You can't just be dragging any old—"

"It's Grace, Derval." She took a long breath to steel herself. "It's Grace."

"Not my Grace," breathed the butcher.

"I'm afraid so. Do what you can with her."

Derval slammed down the cleaver. "What I can? Now, you look here!"

"No!" snapped Fia. "You look here! You're a meat cutter. So cut. Prep. Serve."

Derval crossed his arms over his apron. Oh, but his forearms were huge. "I will not! I will not accommodate...this, any longer. It is ridiculous!"

"Derval, I have been riding for four days, and walking for six, I do not want to get into this now, I want to go to my hut and sleep until tomorrow. Maybe eat something that isn't dried. Or salted. Understand?"

Derval didn't understand. "When I signed up for the Union I had no intention of spending my days as a butcher!"

"You'd rather fight then? Butchering those with thinking minds."

He tore off his apron, which was extremely clean considering the collection of meat cuts on the carving table. “This fight began as a battle for what was right and has descended into a hunt. And now you kill my love, my Grace and just expect me to butcher her carcass? No. The line must be drawn here!”

“Alright,” said Fia. “You go on, Derval. But leave that apron, would you?” She circled around to his side of the table and pulled the cleaver from the wood.

“This is my—” He stopped. “Fine. You keep it. I have others.”

Fia pulled on the apron over her thick leather coat. She must have looked ridiculous. “On you go then, Derval. Just remember to leave your hut clean before you go.” She cut through the pig’s neck and moved the head to one side. “Jona mentioned he was after a bigger place.”

Derval watched, or rather studied Fia as each cleave reduced the pig to smaller pieces. “You’re better slicing along the muscle lines, not through. Wait. Jona? He is *not* taking my home!”

“Home…? Derval, you are no longer a rebel. You said it yourself. The line must be drawn somewhere. Why not here.” Fia brought the cleaver down with the last word, missing her stump by only a finger length. Had she still a hand on the left side, the cleaver would have just cut it off.

“Fine.” He placed a hand over Fia’s arm. “You’ve made your point.”

“There are no points being made here, butcher. We all must do our bit to survive. A captain who cuts meat. A squad leader who shoes horses.”

Derval’s anger had almost fully dissipated, replaced with sadness. Fia recognised it, because she had been through the very same process when Grace had died. Derval held the bag but couldn’t bring himself to lift the weight from the carving table.

Fia took a long breath to steal herself “Grace was beautiful, and strong. But ultimately, we can only do so much in the eyes of the Great Mother. Baeivi stands above, holding the strings to all of our lives.”

Derval fingered the oilskin bag. “Tell me what happened.”

“We had been riding all day, and Jona and I were just about to set up camp for the night. We spotted a clearing near some trees but didn’t see the rabbit hole until it was too late.”

"So, you just—"

"Her leg was snapped, Derval. There was nothing we could do. We stayed with her for the night and made her comfortable, but we had to put an end to her suffering before the shock killed her."

"She slipped a bloody shoe, didn't she?" The anger returned white and hot. "I'll bloody kill that farrier."

Fia shook her head slowly. "It wasn't Eris's fault. The shoes were tight on. It was luck. The Great Mother stood over us that night and welcomed Grace, in her name, into the next life. It was her moment."

Derval licked his teeth behind his lips, mastering his snarl. Misplaced anger was as dangerous within a closed camp as foot rot. "What about Tia?"

"We sold her in Raeven's Torr."

"Sold her." Derval nodded, slowly.

Fia had to end this now. "Derval, you listen to me, and listen well because I will not say it again. Grace meant a lot to me, and still I cut the best of her and carried it across the borderlands to feed my army. Understand that your emotions are not the only ones that matter. You live with us here, providing a valuable service to the resistance. But make no mistake, I will not hesitate to remove you from rank. We need as many fighters as we can, but I will not abide—"

"Yes, yes." Derval turned away, leaving Fia speechless.

"Derval—"

"You've made your point, Captain." Derval's eyes were full of tears. One dropped across his cheek into his beard. "Please go, and take my apologies with you. I won't thank you for it. But I'm glad Grace was with a friend when she greeted the earth."

"Good," said Fia, feeling a mighty sting behind her eyes. "Now, prepare what is left of her and we shall honour her name properly. You said it yourself, there's nothing fresher, tastier and better for the men than horse meat." She finished by letting the cleaver drop into the table, tip down, and swallowed the lump in her throat—she had to be strong.

"So it is, Captain. Grace will feed us all tonight. I'll do her proud." Derval shook his head and the tears fell freely, splashing upon the bloodied chopping board. "It's not you, Captain. It's...Yewla and I. We're calling it a day."

"Oh," said Fia. "I'm sorry to hear that."

Derval nodded. "Just one of those things." He took up the knife and started cutting again.

"Captain?" came a voice from behind.

Fia shut her eyes. "What is it now?" A young soldier stood there expectantly.

"It's Haral."

"Haral. What is it?"

"Well..." he glanced at Derval. "It's best if we discuss it in private."

"Fine. Then let us go find somewhere private." Fia turned to leave, then stopped. There was one last thing to leave the butcher with. "Oh, and Derval. I wouldn't go laying any blame at Eris's feet. She may be but a simple farrier, but I'm quite certain she would cut your head off before you got within two feet of her."

23

PRISONER

Fia's stomach felt like it might try and eat its way out of her. A prisoner? It had been twelve cycles since she herself had been captured by the Kin an imprisoned. She had often wondered about her torturer, Gorm, and what had become of him after Tyr. So many had died that day. Hopefully his lifeless, broken corpse had been washed down the Way with the rest of the city.

"Thank you for telling me, Haral, and for insisting on privacy." She nodded to the entrance of her tent. "Not to be rude, soldier, but I need some privacy of my own. Please return to the brig for now and mind the prisoner for me. I'll be along shortly."

The young soldier nodded and left. Someone else came in as he was leaving. She ducked in and gave Fia a strange smile. "Hi."

"Eris." Fia grabbed her bag from the floor and began rummaging through it.

"That's all I get?"

"That's all you get." Fia put down the bag.

Eris wasn't the most beautiful woman Fia had ever seen, but she might have been the most striking. Her usual auburn hair was bleach-white this week, but her hook nose and high cheekbones were the same as ever. Her powerful frame made Fia feel small; she didn't hate it.

"You heard."

"I did."

"Have you seen him yet?"

Fia stretched her pained back, trying to ease some of the knots out. "I have not. I am barely back myself."

"Jona told me."

"You've spoken to Jona already?" She locked eyes with her. "That was quick."

"Was it?"

"You're good friends then?"

Eris tilted her head, but her expression barely changed. "Good enough. I'm going to see him. If you want to..."

"I've just spent the last month with Jona, I really don't want to—"

"The prisoner, Atalfia."

"Oh." Fia dropped the bag and ran her hand through her hair. Lord gods of all she needed a bath. "Yes. Yes, I'll come. Just give me a few minutes." Eris just stared at her, those slanted eyes hiding a fool's fortune of hidden emotion. "A few minutes, Eris. Please?"

Eris pressed her lips together and nodded. "I'll wait outside."

Then Fia was alone again. It should have felt wondrous to have her own space, to be able to think and do as she wanted without Jona's eyes falling upon her. He was still not quite old enough to have learned when best to hide his leers, which were as obvious as the man himself. Even in Raeven's Torr, sharing a room, changing her clothes in a tiny space that was almost out of their budget to afford. He had been right though, the rebels had coasted for far too long. Money, food and morale were all low in supply.

Fia stripped off and wiped herself down, then threw on some fresh clothes and stepped out. "The bath will have to wait."

Eris stood outside on alert, as though she were guarding the tent from invaders. "Shall we?"

The walk was silent, but they knew each other well enough to not have to fill every waking moment with useless words. "How have things been here?" asked Fia, trying to keep her tone light.

"The same." Silence could be useful to those not used to it. Still, it took almost half of the journey to the brig before Eris elaborated. "The horses are in a low mood. They will feel the loss of Grace and Tia keenly."

"Jona filled you in then?"

"What?"

"He told you what happened? At Raeven's Torr?"

Eris nodded. "Oh, yes." She coughed. "I sympathise. It must have been awful."

The problem with Eris, was that everything was delivered so plainly that discerning sarcasm from reality was almost impossible. Fia wondered if it was she who had changed rather than Eris. She used to be so good at reading people, which was a very necessary part of being Kumpani, but like so many of her other skills, it too had dulled over the last decade.

"It was awful." Fia stopped near to where she had spoken to Derval; he was chopping away in the background.

"Are you ok, Atalfia? You seem different."

Fia's eyes betrayed her, finding the butcher.

Eris shook her head. "Derval?"

"I can handle him, Eris. He was just a little upset is all."

Eris bristled. "I'll throttle the man! Then I'll—"

Fia lay her hand on Eris's. "You'll do nothing, you hear?"

"He only acts tough," said Eris. "I have it on good authority that inside he's as soft and gentle as a baby rabbit."

"Well, that's no rabbit I ever want to meet." Fia swallowed. "He and Yewla have split."

"They have not."

Fia nodded. "He just told me."

"I knew something was up. He's been sleeping on his own with the single men." Eris glanced back at the butcher's stall, an unreadable expression on her face. "Supplies *are* tight."

"Yes," said Fia, "but the man feeds the entire camp. You'd have to pry it from his cold, dead fingers. And besides, he could demand favours from any man with a handful of dried goat."

Eris raised her eyebrows. "Or horse."

"Stop it!" Guilt stole Fia's smile away. "I just feel bad for his daughter."

"Alis?"

"She's only three, but oh so bright."

Eris rolled her eyes. "A miracle itself with such dim parents."

Fia glanced over at Derval, hacking away, and he was staring back at her. "In all the excitement I forgot to ask how the raids went."

"About as well as you would expect," said Eris, taking a long breath.

"Did we lose anyone?"

Eris shook her head. "No, and neither did the Bohr, but, the soldiers are not happy. They're asking questions I don't have answers to. Like why the captain of the rebellion is leaving them to go to some northern city and returning with no more fighters and minus two of our best horses."

"Raeven's Torr has become a cesspool after the trade wars. There are gangs there, and they're organised."

"Oh, Fia. We've been down this road." Eris stepped closer, lowering her voice. "We need *good* people. When the Bohr are not knocking down the door, or taking the families we care so much for, the humans who are left to fight are not trustworthy. They fight only for glory or coin. Mercenaries would only seek to destroy what we have here."

Fia wanted to disagree, but Eris was right and she hated her for it. "It might be a cesspool, but I refuse to believe that there was not a single person who might still have hope in their hearts. Who might join us."

"And how many of those people did you find?"

Fia shook her head in resignation. "Eris, I had to be sure. This can't be the last of the rebellion here, hiding against the enemy's wall like an injured spider."

Eris shrugged. "I told you, Atalfia. There's rumblings of a force to the east of Kemen."

"New Bakla?" A feeling of warmth spread through Fia's insides at thought of her old home upon the beach flats.

"Maybe the Northern Territories have finally unionised." Eris spread her palms. "With your experience and their numbers..."

"We've been here so long though." Fia swallowed. "Too long." It was hard to talk about; she'd gone so long without having to address these questions, and now they all wanted answering simultaneously. "Come on, Eris. Let's get this over with. Maybe this prisoner knows a way into Kemen that doesn't involve trying to scale a two-hundred foot sheer wall with Bohr Pan Guards marching along the top."

Eris put an arm over Fia's shoulder. "And don't forget, once we've beaten the Pans, then all we have to do is cross the entire Kemen Empire with two hundred people, families, children and equipment to find a ghost army, who may or may not exist, to help us finally defeat the Bohr scourge once and for all."

Fia felt sick. "That's not helping."

"Oh, and don't forget the Banèman. Magical assassins who—"

"Shut up, Eris."

"Captain." Haral offered Fia and Eris a salute, and Fia reciprocated before they ducked into the brig. Immediately her stomach turned to ice, not just from the smell of blood and sweat, but from the memory of the Kin's torture.

"Let's keep this brief," she said, swallowing.

"Captain." Jona stood abruptly from the prisoner's side. "He says his name is Zular."

"Zular? So, you've even taken a Bohr name?

The half-naked man sat cross-legged upon a desk. A chain around his ankle disappeared into the corner of the room. "It is a name I earned."

"And your accent. You are not Kemen." Now it was Fia who was hiding questions in statements.

"Ge'Bat." Fia moved to speak, but Zular beat her to it. "And no, we are not all as rich as your sources would say we are. It seems that those who spread news of eastern promise are often the ones who partake in it. The rest of us, my friend, live on a menial wage."

"But a wage nonetheless," said Eris.

Zular held up his hands. "So you say."

Fia nodded at Zular's scars. Most were old, but a new one near his collar bone disappeared over his shoulder. It had recently been sewn. "You are enjoying our hospitality then."

"Your surgeon is very well practised."

"You know, when not fighting, Derval is actually our butcher, not a surgeon. We are all forced to take on professions to ensure the running of this camp. We run it because we must, because without it, we would have nowhere else to call our home. Not since Tyr."

Zular followed each word, retaining a dismissive air, as though all that Fia said was inconsequential. "So, these are peaceful times for you?"

"We are at war."

"With the Banèmen?"

Fia blinked. "What an odd thing to say. We are at war with the Bohr." She took a step forward. "And all those who aid them. How long have you been watching us?"

"Long enough."

"From the wall?"

"Near it, at least."

"Do you know a way through?"

Zular smiled. "There is none."

"Is that so?" Fia glanced at Eris, her eyes clearly saying *this man is dangerous.* Eris gave the slightest of nods, imperceptible to anyone else. Eris was strong, dependable, but with a mind of her own. She followed Fia, but still retained that lawless streak, the very same streak that had urged her to raise a rebel faction of her own in Tyr that helped end the Bohr occupation there.

Fia turned back to Zular. "Well, if you have been watching us, me, for so long, then you know that everything I say is the truth."

"My friend. You are hard-working and were it not for the shadow of the wall, I am sure it would appear to anyone else you are simply settling here. Looking for a new home to call your own. I know that to be untrue. Not in the time I have observed your army." He placed an accent on the word *army* as though the word were not fitting of the people that lived here. "I know your quandary."

Fia knew his type. It was all an act, drawn out of fear. "Do you?"

"What do you do with a man such as me? Do you kill him? Do you torture him for information? Do you set him free?"

Fia smiled. It came easily. "You think those are my only options? You know, Zular. I used to be a spy. Like you. I know the games very well." Eris's stare must have been burning through the back of her head. "I also know that the words of a spy drip with untruth. The way you speak, the words you choose, the order in which you put them. Everything, from balls to bones, is designed to do one thing and one thing only." She stepped close to the man. "Manipulate."

Zular tensed, then visibly loosened himself off. His guard was back up. "Have you heard of Chinaes? You strike me as player of games." When Fia didn't answer he made a noise like he was amused then continued. "You should. I think you'd be good at it. Chinaes is all about—"

"I know the tearing game!"

"Good. Someone taught you? Someone you knew?"

Fia opened her mouth to speak, but the words stuck.

Zular's lopsided smile flashed once more. "I see. They are dead now. Sorry. Hopefully your comrade taught you that the trick to Chinaes, as with most games, is misdirection. Do something here, but really your focus is over there." A coin appeared briefly in his cuffed hands, before promptly vanishing. "I am a master player. I play Chinaes, not for enjoyment, but to win. I have beaten grand masters all over the world, played in King's halls, and as such, I know strength when I see it." His eyes flicked to her sword, almost imperceptibly. "Most games of Chinaes have the same openings. Did you know that? But it is our choices in the middlegame that determine the end. The Bohr are the strongest side, and so they have my money. My bet resides firmly with them. Your little camp here will be short-lived."

Fia shook her head and sighed. "Honestly, I thought you were more than that, Zular. But it's just money. Isn't it? Currency? Chance. You want to win."

"The honour of bastards," said Eris, from behind.

"That is the essence of the game," said Zular, shrugging. He flicked the coin towards Fia.

Fia snatched it out of the air. "More games."

"Surely a player of games would know?"

Fia licked her lips but did not take her eyes from him. Before she could speak, the tent flaps were yanked aside.

"Captain?" Haral stopped and looked around as each bemused face beheld him.

"What is it, Haral?"

"The flour has gone off. Weevils, I think. Thousands of the little buggers. Sir."

Fia shrugged to Zular. "Well, I'm afraid, duty calls. Eris. Let us leave this prisoner to himself for a spell." She stepped away and stopped at Haral's side. "Haral, you stay here."

"Captain?"

"Watch our prisoner. For every second of every hour until you are relieved. Then tomorrow, you can come back and do the same thing again."

"Of course, Captain."

"Good day, Zular."

The prisoner smiled warmly, sending a chill down Fia's spine. "Good day to you, my friend."

24

FRAGMENTS

Kaliste neither understood nor could fathom the ether that connected the worlds. Realities, some called them, but she preferred *realms*, for that's what they were, places of intrigue, encapsulated in their own rights, capable of holding and destroying life. Energy could not pass from other realms to this one, the so-called *Common Realm*, which was a fact that even Bohr children were aware of, and yet harnessing Soulfire and wielding it was a direct violation of that rule. Baeivi was a benevolent God, but it was clear that there were holes in her design.

The echoes of Jagar's lifeforce still reverberated through Kaliste, unsettling and unbalancing her every thought, yet even with as much energy as she could draw from the other realms, she could not understand why. Perhaps it was the new life growing inside of her amplifying the effects, or perhaps *he* still had a hold of her. Jagar's body was gone, but his being must still exist in Baeivi's realm, trapped in the ether, tangible, present and yet wholly incomplete.

"It should not be," she muttered to herself. Her voice carried too far in the council chambers and a group of Bohr lords nearby glanced sidelong in her direction. Their curious, beady Bohr eyes didn't linger long though.

"Since the Bohr King's demise in Tyr, we have yet to even..."

Kaliste ignored the councillor's voices once more and focused inwards. Every problem could be picked apart, she knew that as she knew the thousand cycles that she wore, and this was just another problem. There was just no solution yet. "Or perhaps I am simply unable to see it, surrounded by such distraction!" The circular chambers fell quiet. She didn't need Jagar's powers to hear the heartbeats of those fearful beings standing around the podium upon the chamber floor. She cleared her head and let her voice ring out like the peal of a bell. "Chancellor." She directed her words to a wolf Bohr wearing red robes and holding a wide book. "Seeing as the ongoing Bohr fight with the human rebels is as important a potential victory as the Dreki Wars was to our forebears, tell me exactly, what does recalling our roaming Bohr factions to the motherlands actually achieve?" It was a potent question, and enough to throw off even the most experienced of Bohr Councillors.

The Kemen Chancellor's ear twitched. "It will allow us to present a unified force, my Queen."

At a height of barely eight feet, and a mixed blood heritage, the Chancellor was an odious man, but times had changed drastically. No Bohr could just attack another anymore. It wasn't kill or be killed. If you want civility, everyone, Bohr and Banèman alike, had to act like civilians. And the very worst part of this civilisation was navigating a maze of political machination before getting close to anything resembling a solution. The good old days were truly far behind them.

Kaliste shook her head in disappointment. "A unified force does nothing but create a backlog of problems for everyone." A wave of nausea swept over her. Were these her words or Jagar's? She couldn't tell, but the distraction was long enough for another lord to seize the floor.

"It's what we have always done!" growled a large goat Bohr from higher up. "We explore the lands, we conquer and we return! Unification is the last step each generation must undertake. I ask, how is something so fundamental suddenly being called into question? We must live and die by tradition." He tugged at his white beard and sat down, shaking his head.

The Kemen Chancellor rubbed his snout in satisfaction. "Exactly. It is what we have always done. Surely there is more reason to conquer than a simple need for supremacy? And there is." He left his seating circle and dropped to the walkway, pacing on floors that had seen many pacers and as many straw points. "Kemen is a stronghold, with access to ports on all sides, but we're separated by leagues and leagues of treacherous lands. Lands like the Cracked Wastes that would kill even the hardest of us."

The goat Bohr stood up again. "Hardest of us. I agree with my honourable friend, that unification will help keep the Bohr together and resolute, but the humans are here for us! They will not revolt in any serious way! So, there is time yet before we even need to consider unification in my opinion." He tilted his head and folded his arms, indicating plainly he'd rather be somewhere else. Even so, the murmurs or agreement from the council were loud and many.

Kaliste had heard every argument countless times from countless lords. Even the rebukes. She was tired of it all. "And again the councillors of this chamber sew the same tapestry." Kaliste sighed. "Bohr rule. Unified forces!" She held out a mocking fist. "Strength."

"My Queen," said the Chancellor, pleadingly. "With all due respect, why the sudden change of tact? You have always been a furtive follower of unification—"

Kaliste opened her mouth in outrage, but sickness closed it again. She swallowed and the Chancellor seized the floor once more.

"Our motivations must be visited and renewed! Doctrine insists upon it, but not our traditions! Every day we must renew the vows that—"

"That bind us," said Kaliste, taking the floor by finishing the goat's statement. "Next, you will talk of the ports, the threat the humans can pose if left to breed. How we must let our heritage lead us, and our blood. We will pray, and snarl and howl, but the question still stands! What advantages will unification of our armies bring to the Bohr?" The question said out loud brought stars across her vision. She held the podium for support. "What benefits will Zunqai...as...as...the great capital of the Kemen Empire, receive from drawing every Bohr home to the motherlands?" Kaliste plucked a paper from the podium. "There are reports of resistance fighters to the west along the border, north of Koroeil."

"Yes," said the Chancellor, the wind very much removed from his sails. He adjusted his robes as he spoke. "Resistance fighters. There's a settlement near the wall at the Hatàrian border. They call themselves the *Fifth Union*. The Pans regularly walk by and inform me they are harmless."

"Harmless?" said Kaliste. "You see, Chancellor, our enemy are fragmented. Unification brings us nothing. Would we send out an entire force to remove this scourge? No. A small force should be enough." She swallowed, feeling woozy. "We shall send some of our forces in...into Kroth to meet them." Kaliste examined the Chancellor's aura for clues as to his next argument, but something blocked her, and the more she tried, the more ill she felt.

The Chancellor noticed. His wolf eyes squinted, and the corners of his snout lifted in something resembling a smile. Or was it a snarl? "Communication lines between the great cities of the Empire, Kroth, Koroeil, Kopema, even Zunqai, are slow. It will take time for our word to reach Kroth."

"And what...what of our raevens? Are they suddenly unable to fly?"

"Raevens are susceptible to interception..."

"And our forces," continued the Chancellor, "being so fragmented. Well, it makes communication very difficult. We have no recourse any longer."

"Our recourse, Chancellor, is to fight. To win. To conquer. This is our goal. It has been the way of the Bohr for a thousand generations, long before even I was brought into existence. It troubles me greatly that I must remind you of this incontrovertible fact. It is true that our forces are fragmented, although perhaps a new angle is required to understand the opportunities that affords us." Feeling stronger, Kaliste turned, talking now to all one hundred council members. "You say our forces are fragmented? I say that those same forces are spread amongst the human populace of Rengas spreading the word of the Bohr, conjuring fear within the hearts of men. If one Bohr is worth a hundred men, then the thousands of Bohr that are out there are capable of grand feats indeed!

Pushing, pulling, sabotaging and moulding the world into a place that suits us! Rengas is ours!" It felt wondrous to unleash again, to stand amongst those who required her council and deliver unto them her rage. She wished she could smite them all, pulverise this hall, and reduce it to rubble. She took a long breath, savouring the silence and fear that permeated the air, clutching the podium. "The power of Zunqai resides within this room. The decisions we make create waves around Rengas that are felt by all. It is our duty then, to act not only with absolute affirmation, but with justice to our ancestral lines. How would the great Bohr of old feel about our actions within the circular walls of this chamber? Would they quail and hide, cheer and applaud, or would they condemn us? Would they reach down from the heavens and annihilate us? Turning us to dust. We are all dust in their eyes." The room fell utterly quiet, and somehow the podium moved. She caught herself, but pushed the podium crashing to the central floor below. "It can be argued..." The room was swimming. "That by fragmenting the Bohr we are actually enabling Doctrine. We are enabling...enabling the Bohr to be...to..."

"Kaliste." V'Laerk blinked, standing assuredly, hands folded patiently in front of him, snarling softly to quiet the rows around him. The fresh scars from the Evesgiving, most of which were drawn from Kaliste's own hand, still stood proudly upon his skin. "The Bohr stand at a crossroads," said V'Laerk, "where lies three choices. One. We stand against the humans as a fragmented force. Our forces are stronger, but history teaches us that we *will* be overrun by the many, as we were at Tyr. All it takes is a resolute commander who understands this and suddenly we will find ourselves picked off one at a time. Two. We unite our forces. Bring every Bohr home to the city of cities, Zunqai, and we build our army ready to roll over the lands. Three." V'Laerk hesitated, and while there was ample opportunity to take over his speech according to Bohr Hall of Council law, none dared to speak. "We join the humans."

"You can't be serious!"

"We should kill them all!"

"They are less than us. Less! They deserve nothing from the Bohr!"

Kaliste considered a moment, then held up her hand, bringing silence to the hall. "V'Laerk. Your words had their desired reaction. The wick of your firestick is lit. Please conclude before the old masters return to this hall and find you guilty of treason."

V'Laerk moved slowly. He licked his lips, savouring the moment. "Joining with the humans..."

The hall erupted, and Kaliste was once again forced to raise her hand.

"Joining with the humans is ridiculous. We are Bohr, after all." He slapped the White Dragon painted upon his wide chestplate. "We. Are. Bohr. And yet, there are factions out there who are doing our job for us. We all want to live more simply, but it seems even this very council is a human construct. This great hall was a byproduct of humans, but it has helped forge justice since that day. Of course though, it is not who the Bohr *are*." He snarled again, showing off the whites of his canines. "We are Bohr."

"Factions?" asked Kaliste, her mouth-watering.

"In Sulitaria, there is an island, and news has reached me of a faction there called the Order of the White Dragon." He let the words lie for a moment. "They walk the streets, command curfews, and imprison those who rebel against them. Against us. I've even heard of executions taking place, all in the name of White Dragon." He banged his chest. "The sigil of the Bohr. Let the Order of the White Dragon support us, let them be our arm, a sword upon which we command. Let them do the work of rounding up the humans for us. Because if we are to stay a fragmented force, let's at least be clever about it. Let us infiltrate the humans and poison them from within."

"We tried that in Tyr!" roared someone near the back of the hall.

"And look what happened to the cursed city!"

V'Laerk shook his head. "Tyr this, and Tyr that. Yes, we learned our lessons in the Cursed City, but look at us now. We stand upon the homeland again, the great capital city of Zunqai, the soil of our forefathers. A place that belongs to us. Kemen is pure once again."

"What about Rathe?" asked Kaliste. "Did he learn his lesson?"

V'Laerk looked troubled. "The Way tides turned, disrupting trade, and the city sank under the soft foundations upon which it had been built. Only Zuveri knows for sure what happened there." The hall was abruptly filled with Bohr touching their foreheads, and the sound of snarls rumbled all around, but V'Laerk was still in danger of losing them. Only rarely did the Bohr Council result in actual violence, but some subjects almost demanded it. The death of the Bohr King was one of those subjects.

Kaliste knew what happened in Tyr. She knew that Baeivi became too powerful. The Great Mother drank deep from every world, soaking in their power, and drawing energy from them. The result was so many holes that the great tapestry of existence began to fray. The tragedy at Tyr was inconsequential to what might have happened should Baeivi have been released.

Despite the rising sickness, Kaliste looked for Soulfire. It would make things right. She could sense the flavour of it, the vibration always present, but that block was still there. She didn't need that much, not so much that it might burn her from existence—such a thing would undo the very world, considering how many waves she had caused in her long life—but there was barely a trickle of Soulfire available to her, but she took it nonetheless. Just enough to create a soft blanket of compulsion. A soft white mist that only Kaliste could see filled the council chambers, drifting down as particles of light, each one finding a Bohr and disappearing into them. The air in the room lightened as everyone but V'Laerk suddenly became very receptive to his and Kaliste's word.

"V'Laerk, you shall go forth from this council to discover more about this Order of the White Dragon. You will travel to this island of Ipiti and meet with them. You are correct, that a faction acting for the Bohr must be also governed by one. If an accord can be struck with the humans, then you shall be the one to do it." She moved to step down, then caught herself. "Oh, and the Bohr *will* remain fragmented. There will be no unification. No return to the motherland."

The council all murmured happily in agreement. V'Laerk bared his teeth, and Kaliste bared her own back at him.

Never before had Kaliste felt so conflicted. She'd found a quiet corner outside the great halls to lick her wounds. "Is this your doing?" she said, clutching her stomach. "Is this the price I must pay for your existence?"

If it had been up to Kaliste she would have brought every single Bohr back to Zunqai, but even now, the pressure upon her mind at simply entertaining that reality was almost too much to bear. It was as though her own desires were being phased out of existence. "The Bohr must... uni..."

Abruptly, she could sense that Soulfire was waiting, and she let it in. The power filled her from head to toe, feeding her soul, brightening her senses. She drew more, pulling the fire even deeper into herself, and there, on the fringes floated a light.

"Jagar. I have done as you wished."

Good. They accepted it?

"Reluctantly."

I knew they would.

"Jagar, why do you wish our forces fragmented so?"

Kaliste, you must trust me. I will be released soon, and the long fight will come soon after.

"Then why would we purposefully spread the Bohr? Unification gives us our best—"

Fragmentation gives a broader spread. Then, when the time is right, we bring them together. Your task, Kaliste is to build an army. An army of men.

"To crush the rebels?"

The biggest army in Rengas. Every soul in Zunqai and beyond drafted to fight. Every ssssoul under our control.

"So shall it be." Kaliste felt fear ripple down the link. *"Jagar? Where are you?"*

I don't have much time. Go to the fifth street past the twelfth statue of Zuveri. Go there and you will see.

"What is there?"

Search low and you will see. You will see. You...will...

"Jagar—"

"Jagar!" Kaliste was thrust back into her waking life. A hallway, long shadows, satin drapes with servants milling around. They knew enough not to look at her, but it was clear from the echo still bouncing around the high ceilings that she had shouted something. Screwing her eyes shut, she tried to remember what, but there were no memories there, just the remnants of a lurking task.

25

BONDS

V'Laerk stalked through the crowded streets of Zunqai. Even the larger Bohr stepped aside for him, and not least because of his ties to the Queen.

Following in his shadow, Kaliste felt more whole again at least, as though this task of hers was enough to bring balance to her mind. A crisp shell of Soulfire shrouded her—a form of illusion that literally changed her entire being into someone else's. A human female. A timid princess of old with flowered garments of spidersilk and wheat. Her hand strayed to her stomach once more, and almost absently she started counting the ways she could kill those around them. Even V'Laerk himself.

"Fifty-four."

V'Laerk rounded on her. "What did you say human?"

Kaliste raised a hand and cowered until V'Laerk turned back to his stalking. "Apparently motherhood already has its trials," she uttered, rushing back close behind.

As V'Laerk led her on, occasionally pulling at her shackles for realism, she considered all of those mortal ways. The simplest was to burn them all from existence with the power of Soulfire, but there was little challenge in that. She could certainly outfight them, even in this human form Kaliste possessed some speed. It was not to the depth of ability as

Akosh perhaps, but she could still outmanoeuvre V'Laerk if she had to. Akosh had been known to move so fast that time practically stopped; there was little any being could do against such monumental power.

And if not the physical, then perhaps the emotional. She could ply V'Laerk's mind with riddles designed to unhinge, or perhaps she would just beat him down until he snapped—not all attacks had to be seen. There had been many instances in her long life where she had seen leaders brought to their knees with but a simple statement delivered at exactly the right time. Some would say that was the very essence of the game Chinaes, where one plays to win by trying not to win. Lateral thinking and accuracy spoke far more than speed and strength.

"The river that is diverted with but a stone."

"Quiet!" growled V'Laerk.

Kaliste whimpered, playing up the role, until finally they stepped out onto the main street.

"Have you a name yet?" asked V'Laerk when the road narrowed.

"No," hissed Kaliste. "V'Laerk. And don't ask again."

V'Laerk didn't look at her, yet somehow still managed to knock over some poor youngling's cart of briknuts. The spikes of aura hanging around him spoke of not just a clever mind, but a tactical one too. He was a fine specimen, and now the father-to-be of a Banèman.

"Must you wear that face?" He grumbled, leaving the owners of the cart behind.

"Ah. So, that's it." Annoyance crept into Kaliste's tone. "Must it all be about the Bohr?"

V'Laerk's clouds of colour became dark and red. "You want us to blend in? Then lose the human face. Zunqai is the capital of Kemen, where Bohr roam the streets and humans clean up after us. Walking together on equal terms is just wrong."

"So deep, V'Laerk," said Kaliste, amused. "I wouldn't have thought such a depth of fire could come from so pretty a head." Kaliste smirked. "I took this face from a princess I met over five hundred cycles ago. She was very beautiful and had jawbones that...well you can see yourself." Kaliste tilted her head just so. "You see?"

V'Laerk frowned. "No."

"Fine. Well, get used to it, V'Laerk. I am not removing this face."

"Just consider that there are reasons for my choices that even you might not be aware of. Now, unless you want some real trouble..."

V'Laerk stared at her. Confusion, fear, excitement all melted together in the aura cloud above his head. "You spoke to my mind. I didn't know you could do that."

Kaliste felt the shock too, and while she had spoken the words, they had reverberated from her mind to her stomach and out to V'Laerk through some unknown connection. "Neither did I. Interfacing is a skill that only one of the Banèman have ever possessed." The realisation caught her completely off guard. "It has to be the child."

A Ruffin Bohr leaning on a post nearby was watching them. She was not quite as tall as V'Laerk but she had the same iridescent scales as the one who had lost at Evesgiving. The Ruffin Bohr leapt forwards, claws extended towards Kaliste. Kaliste reached for Soulfire, but she wasn't quick enough. The Ruffin Bohr was on her, pinning her down. "Show some respect, human, or I will make you!"

Kaliste bared her teeth back at the Ruffin Bohr, but it was V'Laerk who was the quickest. The Ruffin Bohr was abruptly airborne, lifted high above V'Laerk's head, before crashing down heavily onto the cobbles. V'Laerk pounced as the Ruffin Bohr had done, slashing across the Bohr's stomach, then holding her by the neck. "She is mine to discipline!"

The Ruffin Bohr bared her teeth, but did not retaliate. V'Laerk stepped away, letting her retreat quietly to the alcove of the building she had come from.

"Hit me."

V'Laerk looked confused. "What?"

"We are being watched."

Kaliste felt V'Laerk's bewilderment melt into comprehension before he swiped a hand across her face, knocking her to the ground. She held her stomach, crying, holding out a hand to protect herself. *"Good. Now, roar. Stake your claim."*

V'Laerk let out an almighty roar, so loud that it made Kaliste's human ears ring. He dragged her up by the shackles and pulled her down an alleyway. "What was that?"

"We are connected," said Kaliste. "The Evesgiving has drawn us together closer than I—"

"Is it normal?"

Kaliste blinked. *"I've heard of it before."* She bowed her head as more curious eyes began to glance in from the main street. *"Let's keep moving. I suggest we carry on with the ruse for now. At least until we reach the fifth street."* She started off again and V'Laerk followed quickly, making sure to keep ahead of her.

She let a trickle of Soulfire touch V'Laerk's left shoulder, indicating a turn at the monument of Zuveri, and he did so without question. The huge stone rendering of the Bohr King, killed in Tyr a decade ago, loomed over her. Zuveri was an original, there was no mixing of blood within any of her blood lines—she was as pure as they came. Kaliste had considered breeding with Zuveri on more than one occasion. A female Banèman and a female Bohr king. It was fortunate then that not all magical conceptions of this world required male and female. Now, that would have been an Evesgiving for the ages!

"One more left turn, V'Laerk, at the fountains of Kalcoon, and you will see a small archway."

V'Laerk gave no indication he had heard until they rounded the monument and passed through the square, then he made straight for the archway. They slipped on through and closed the gate behind them. Kaliste readied invisible flames of Soulfire ready to engulf anyone foolish enough to follow. She preferred the more obvious methods, but there was no denying the thrill of watching someone melt into dust without a lick of visible flame. She held her stomach again, wondering if the violent thoughts were coming from the child or from her.

"It is safe. Move on."

There was only one property on the street that could have held anything below ground. Look low, Jagar has said. It had to be the one. This time V'Laerk didn't need instruction. Walking practically sideways along the narrow lane due to his massive bare shoulders he opened the red door and heedless, ducked in through the hanging beads of the hidden house.

"You should look next time, V'Laerk. I do not know what awaits here."

Kaliste pulled the door shut behind them plunging them into darkness. "But we do make a good team."

"That we do," rumbled V'Laerk, showing his teeth. He padded to the end of the corridor and back checking the rooms. "Whoever used to live here, has long gone. We are alone."

Kaliste clapped her hands together. "Well, shall we move on downstairs, or should we stand here in this tiny hallway until the walls become sand?"

V'Laerk growled. "I still do not know why you have brought me here. I should be on a boat on the way to Ipiti to find this Order of the White Dragon."

"And how long would that take you?"

"Two months," said V'Laerk. "On a good ship with good seas."

"War is coming, V'Laerk. In two months, I suspect the face of it will have changed more than this woman's face you see before you.

The narrow hallway led to a broken stone staircase, which took them down into a basement. It was storage for an old pawn shop, with knick-knacks and rubbish strewn everywhere. Ahead, in the centre of the basement there was hole, cut perfectly round through the floorboards and layers of earth beneath.

"What is it?" asked V'Laerk, hesitating. "Is it safe?"

Kaliste squinted at him. "Don't patronise—" She stopped as V'Laerk reached out and placed his huge claw almost completely over her abdomen. "You are worried for me." She placed a tiny human hand atop his. "For us. I will be careful."

Kaliste peered over the edge but it was too dark to see, so she dropped down and sat upon the floor, her legs dangling over the edge. There was a tunnel, bored from beneath.

There was no denying the feeling now. Even cloaked as she was Kaliste could feel something in here beckoning her forwards. The tunnel widened out into a completely spherical space, carved out to the sharpest of tolerances. and as her human eyes adjusted, she saw it!

A perfect sphere of glass sat nestled in the ground, the curve as perfect as a rain drop, the surface as still as a tropical Kemen sea—green and inviting.

"You smell excited," said V'Laerk, from behind.

"I am," said Kaliste.

Kaliste didn't need to look at V'Laerk's aura to see his surprise. There was no denying the purpose of the thing. Even from above, the green flora from the other side could be seen moving as wind from some other place gusted this way and that. It was a window to somewhere else. Was it bound to the common realm or did it go beyond?

V'Laerk landed heavily beside her, ducking low. "Is it safe?"

"You are afraid?"

V'Laerk frowned deeply. "Who would not be?"

"It is a doorway," said Kaliste, lost in its beauty.

"Doorways lead to places. Where does this lead?"

"I don't know, but I think we ought to find out."

Kaliste strengthened her threads of light and coated them. Soulfire was similar to fire only in appearance, otherwise it was an extension of herself, and just as easily as she might reach up with her hand and pull the doorway closer to the floor, she did so with Soulfire, the flames of light surrounding it like rope, following her will and way.

The doorway resisted. It was clear from the tunnel that it could move, but only upon its own volition. Kaliste's Soulfire would not move it, nor compel it. Closing her eyes, she strengthened the strands of fire further, the rope was thicker now, thick enough to pull down a building, and still the doorway refused.

"It is stuck," said V'Laerk.

Kaliste snarled, and one of the strands of Soulfire whipped the wall beside V'Laerk, cutting a hole from the smooth rock walls. She mastered herself. "Like a ball in a whistle." Kaliste delved deeper, drawing more power. "*How dare you deny me!*"

The strands of Soulfire that surrounded the spherical doorway hanging above glowed brightly as Kaliste's well of power grew. Unleashed all at once, the Soulfire within would level most of the city block. Heat radiated from her eyes, and even the walls began to glow. V'Laerk struggled as his awkward footing slipped, the smooth rock melting beneath him. If she was not careful, the room would become a ring of dripping molten rock, and she still held human form. A single drop would end her life and unleash all of this Soulfire at once.

"I have to be quick." It was easier to communicate to V'Laerk via their link.

Kaliste raised her arms, and willed the strands of Soulfire to pull the doorway lower. At first, the sphere resisted, but then, like an immensely heavy object, it began to move. Kaliste urged it on, drawing deep from the well within her, urging the Soulfire to drag the doorway down lower.

"V'Laerk. Get ready. You must go in."

"My Queen, no!"

"When...I say. You will...Jump in."

V'Laerk's eyes were wide. His snout twitching, his teeth bared. He was nervous, as well he should be, but he did as he was told. He stepped down into the lowest point of the chamber and waited below the doorway. "Where does it lead?"

"There is only one place in Rengas in which the flora grows so thick, and the rain falls so heavily. It is Dor."

"The Outer Isles?" V'Laerk marvelled at the sphere above him. "I can travel to Dor? Through this?"

"It is a hole in our reality, into which you will step, and if you step out, you will be in Dor."

"If I step out?"

"Are you afraid?"

"No."

"Good."

The Soulfire coursing through Kaliste required no effort to push out now, it was self-sustaining. Layer upon layer of fire and energy stolen from Baeivi herself, until all at once there was something different. The frequency changed. The doorway began to interact with her strands, and she could feel the intentions of it. "It's alive," she said, her human voice cracking. Tears rolled down her cheek, warmth spread through every fibre of her human muscles.

V'Laerk turned towards her, caressing her human cheek. "Then, if I am to leave," began V'Laerk, "I should tell you, I know you cheated."

Kaliste was caught off guard, but she held on. "Cheated?"

"You killed the Ruffin. I know it. He was about to beat me, everything was there, and he had the advantage, then he took a wrong step, faltered and I was able to best him. But I think it was you, Kaliste, who made him falter."

"Sometimes, dearest V'Laerk, our efforts pay off far more than we ever hoped. Place your pieces, move and try not to hang, and you will be rewarded. To err is human. As they say. The Ruffin died because you beat him. I did not intervene. You were the evesmen. You are my evesman."

The sphere dropped, following over the top of V'Laerk and swallowing him. The huge Bohr was far taller than the doorway, but Kaliste knew she would not see his head pop out of the top of it. It was a doorway. A hole. A tear in this world.

Stepping carefully down the steaming cavern wall, she studied the surface of it and the way it reflected all and everything in the room but her. Greenery flashed once more across the surface. A band of green jungle sat within the slash of reflected light. The image moved with her, but it was very real. There was some movement as a figure stepped out from the blurry bushes. A Bohr she knew well. He turned towards her, staring at the doorway from which he had just emerged, studying the doorway in Dor, as Kaliste did herself in Zunqai, on the other side of Rengas.

"Can you hear me?"

V'Laerk's distorted head nodded. He spoke, but there was no sound.

"I used Soulfire to knock the Ruffin."

V'Laerk didn't move. It was almost impossible to tell if the words had landed, and the doorway masked his aura, so she carried on.

"The peoples of Dor are crude and simple, but from there you can cross the water to Ipiti. The cities of Ipor Dan and Iporiti are much more likely to yield answers on your quest for the Order of the White Dragon. Find them. Organise them. You are my eyes and ears. Our connection should stay open for as long as our child lives."

The blurry shape nodded once more and then disappeared into the flora.

26

SHADOWS OF ANGER

In the beginning, Baeivi would call upon Jagar, but no more. Perhaps the Great Mother had realised that to respond was to give him an enemy. It was rather clever. Let him exist, let him fight, let him vanish into nothing. Let the realms crash atop one another. Let existence fail, for her moronic, cosmic self-indulgence.

With every moment, Jagar could feel the shift of power. Just his presence here, in her realm, the afterlife, the space between, call it what you will, was enough to cause unbalance. Unbalanced forces broke the rules, created chaos and unpredictability, and Jagar stood in the middle conducting that maelstrom. He was a storm running its course, growing stronger with every gust of wind. Even his form was more solid, the essence of the ether that surrounded him, clouds of ethereal mass, the fine particles of other souls, less corporeal than he, bolstered Jagar's own substantial being and he drank deeply from their wells.

The souls of those others had taken to attacking him out of some misplaced sense of loyalty. Loyalty to the creator? Or were they simply bound by the design of the realm, sworn forever to protect the Great Mother, like drone bees protecting the queen? Either way, it made no odds—each attack only succeeded in making him stronger.

The ether hardened, souls in all colours swirling like liquid, ready to drown him. Jagar laughed, or at least, he imagined he was laughing. The power of a god. The God. The Great Mother, trying to wear him down with showers of cosmic rain! Clouds of dust tore through him like cannon fire, always leaving some of themselves behind for him. The clouds, a mixture of the souls of humans, of Bohr, of animals and insects, clumped together like dumplings in a stew pot, growing harder, and more massive with every second, hovering in front ready to strike him down once more.

Resistance meant annihilation, but rewards awaited those who could manipulate the creator of all things. What power would be bestowed, and how would it come?

The ball shone brightly now, burgeoning with power. Was this her best shot? Shining and golden, the rays of some unseen sun shining upon it, points of light twinkling around it, feeding it, drawing from it in a cycle of self-relenting and defeating power. It quivered with anticipation.

The attack came much faster than it had any right to. The atoms that made Jagar urged him to resist, to fight and claw back like an animal, but resistance was what Baeivi wanted. Jagar had to let go. That was his power. To fight the unfightable. To float as specs of conscious dust in front of the wrath of a God and simply blink it away. He stood upon the rocks of a shore in front of a wave that was higher than any mountain. The ocean loomed, ready to fall and drown and pulverise him until there was nothing left.

But it all passed right through him. The wave parted, destroyed the rocks, turning them to sand, and then smaller and smaller still, but he still stood upon a mantel of his own creation.

The core of his being had warmed as the cloud had passed through him, imbuing him power. He ignored that too. It was inconsequential when viewed against the power that Baeivi, the Great Mother held. So, he waited. The next attack would be along soon, a hundredfold more powerful, leaving him with more remnants of power against his soul.

Jagar imagined himself kicking back, putting his feet up. Perhaps he might imagine the Smoking Wench back in Rengas, the real world, and sure enough its slimy walls flashed into existence. A table, a plate, and an unlit candle.

A question.

Then a fireplace, the details shimmering like an unfinished painting, but it was slowly growing sharper. The more he could see in Maell's shitty little tavern, the more powerful he was becoming. He stood up from his chair, and he saw it vanish. He dared not look behind either, because deep down he knew that the walls behind him were not there. The stone fireplace felt real beneath his fingertips, he pushed in and it caved in like chalk, like it had no substance. Inside was blackness. So black, so dark that even light couldn't escape. The darkness called to him, so he tore away the fireplace of the Smoking Wench's lounge and stood back to admire the hole. It was deep, dark and infinite. A place beyond this place. A place of sorrow, of anguish and end. Tendrils of black crept out towards him, urging him in, and he felt the realm shiver.

"Baeivi," he said. His voice was crystalline. "What is this new place?"

"Nothing," came the response. "You defile me."

"So, you are there, dear mother." He let the tendrils drift around his fingers. "You are afraid."

The Great Mother moaned and the walls of Maell's tavern shook so hard the bricks began to break and crack. "All is mine."

Jagar shook his head. "Even the creator must have come from somewhere." He blinked at the hole. "What crack of the world did you crawl out of?"

The room shook again, and a swirling mass of ether took form in front of his eyes. It wasn't Maell though. Pinks, purples, blues, reds into white. A dress. A woman. She stood there, the most fair, the most terrifying. The most. And where everything else was but an implication of life, she was as solid as though he were back standing in that town of Makril.

"Jagar." A voice, like a bell ringing drifted towards him. "Harvesting the souls of others is an act against nature. You must stop."

"Bargaining?" scoffed Jagar. "Already? You must be worried, truly. The maker of all the realms. The creator herself. The Great Mother." He spat at her feet. "Although you do give me an idea. What if I choose to take more souls? Would this warmth inside me grow? Would I become a Mortal God?"

"What do you want?" said Baeivi, flatly.

"Do not offer me anything, dear mother. You cannot pay the price."

The room shook again, but the Great Mother Baeivi did not move. Neither did she repeat herself.

Jagar roared his demand. The questions that burned hot within him. "You know why I am here! Don't you? You know why I did not die when that Sami girl stabbed me in the temple. Tell me, dear mother, why it is that I exist still?"

"No."

Jagar laughed, the mirth bursting out of him like hot lava. She was dampening the room somehow, but he could sense the tension outside in the ether.

The dead souls of the world were watching them. She had an audience. Then the candle on the table flickered into life as Jagar realised the truth.

"You do not know! You have no idea why I am here!" He walked around the black hole in front of Baeivi. "I had always thought of this as a god's realm, and yet clearly it is not. It existed before you." He stared at her. "You are no god. You are an invader. You...are like me." The candle burned brightly now. "I...am like you." For the first time, the Great Mother's features changed. She became unreal. "You are projecting yourself here." He laughed again. "You are not here, because you are not real. None of this is real, which can only mean one thing." He strolled up to her and poked her in the chest. She was more solid than the fireplace, but he felt her give. Just a little.

Baeivi grabbed his hand, and the smell of her appeared in his nostrils. He had a nose! She smelled like roses and truffles. Awful.

The walls of Maell's inn crumbled, and the souls waiting and watching beyond readied themselves to attack him, and penetrate him. Baeivi was getting angry, impatient at this foreign body within her realm that she couldn't extricate, but that would be her downfall. The Great Mother, brought down by her own crushing will!

The souls arranged themselves into a needle, impossibly thin, and it shot towards him as a javelin through his heart. Jagar shook his head as the ether tore through him. A thousand, million times stronger than the first, second or hundredth attack. The core of him shone brightly.

"Now, I have what I need. A gift from a God! Dear mother." Jagar reached inside himself, and sure enough, the flame was waiting. The remnants of Rengas's long dead had finally given him a spark all of his own. He would never again need a talisman to see Soulfire. He took hold of it in his mind, ready to wield. "I have a gift for you too." The fire poured forth from him. It burned everything, heedless of structure or of being. The ether evaporated, the souls of the million, billion dead gone, reduced to nothing. The walls of the tavern disappeared. The stars, the lights, all gone in an eyeblink. Finally, time meant something. Jagar had control.

Baeivi stumbled back as the flames spun around her, exactly like the fire tornado in Makril. It may have been Jagar who started that fire, but it was the power of the realms that took the fire and wielded it that day, destroying the fishing town. He had watched from the hill as that power took his creation and used it on an unfathomable scale, but now he was in charge. He held the power of the realms within his hands, he could call on it at a moment's notice, decide whether to create or destroy. He glared at Baeivi. "Or whether to burn a God to cinder."

The flames pulled in, surrounding Baeivi in a fiery cage becoming solid, cracking like orange charcoal and falling about her feet. Her eyes were lightning blue, and she was floating off of the inn floor that Jagar had conjured. The attack came without hesitation, and she melted through his fire like it was not there, her hands grasping his throat, the very same throat he had just created for himself.

Her voice was no longer the sweet syrup of a fair lady, but a monstrous growl that echoed around her realm. "If you will not bow before me, child. Then you will die before me."

Jagar reached up channelling the flame along his arms, concentrating it where Baeivi held until they were both glowing with heat. Baeivi held on, tightening her grip. The smell of burning meat filled the air around them, and Jagar felt his newly created stomach churning with hunger.

Baeivi smiled, her mouth was full of pointed teeth. "You have succeeded in remaking yourself, child. You are mortal again."

For the first time since that girl had killed him, Jagar felt fear. He let it come. It was not an emotion that often lay claim to him, and here it was knocking at his door. He gave himself over to it because that was all he could do. He focused the fear inward, feeding it into the flame, and that fear evaporated in the shadow of his anger. It paled in comparison to his hatred of her.

The fire intensified, and Jagar finally felt the tides turn. Baeivi looked back at him, her fair features inches away holding the same look of fear.

"Let go," she said, her voice returning to sweetness. "Let go."

Jagar growled. "Dieeeee."

"I cannot die here."

Jagar wanted to tear her to pieces. He wanted his wrath to overtake her and her entire existence.

She stared at him, a helpless young woman. "If you do it. You will undo everything I have done. All will end, child. All."

Jagar snarled and spat. He was an animal. "Then I will do it!" he spat. "I will fucking do it."

Baeivi started to glow with the same blue that had once been in her eyes. It surrounded her body as a soothing, healing light.

Jagar felt his resolve and anger change form, his head was filled with peace, and had he been anyone else, he might have let it come. It wasn't that Baeivi could not die. This woman was the avatar of God, a messenger sent to hold him, and drain him, and she smiled at him as meek as a little bird.

"Let go," said Jagar

Jagar imagined the Smoking Wench once more and it returned, swirling into form again, but minus the fireplace. The hole he had made, the darkness itself, was still there. Waiting. Jagar seized Soulfire, but now he was calm. The fire took his order, then he stopped feeding it so it became self-sustaining. He let it surround Baeivi once more, solidifying and encasing her in a shell. It wouldn't hold her for long, but he didn't need long.

Jagar got on his belly and crawled into the fireplace, towards the darkness. The tendrils of black reached up to embrace him like an old friend, and as he left the realm of the Great Mother, the God of all, he heard her muffled scream fill his waking ears.

Diary entry

The Road to Bakla

Bakla is almost as far from Kyotho, as Soporia Din is from Costra'Dae. I had always thought of Sulitar as far, but the vastness in Kemen is undisputed. It is a desert, with a few very busy cities. Even so, I still had to hide to write this. With the exception of Ge'Bat, there seems to be a fear of the written word in the far east. Even fishmen navigate the many islands of Sulitaria by memory alone. Ringlanders refer to Sulitaria as the Outer Isles, but they are all part of the same fragmented world.

My dreams still haunt me. Darkness swallowing, and never-ending roads that I walk alone. I don't dream of Milli, or my father, nor even my brother Hasaan. The only real feeling is a force which beckons and pulls at me, dragging me on like it did in the portal above Tyr. Is the Great Mother coming for me? A Forbringr, once more obsessed with claiming me for her own? I swear I can feel it, her, them...and it terrifies me. I fear that should I not sleep properly soon, I might descend into delirium.

27

MADNESS, DUST, WHEEL AND BONE

The *road of bones* some called it, but it was the only way to get to Bakla. Ten carts could have easily fit edge-to-edge, but animals wandered loose everywhere, breaking wheels and bones. Camels forged their own lines through the traffic, whipped by cowled masters throwing obscenities and sand at anyone foolish enough to protest.

Those without wheels, like Kyira, were consigned to the outer edges of the road, where it was less busy, but no less safe. Embankments on both sides were piled with broken carts, but none stopped to check for injured or dead—the pace of the road just wouldn't allow it.

Kyira pulled her hak over her face and tried to breathe the air closest to her chest. "Oh, Milli. This dust will be my end."

Milli's usual white and grey fur was now a murky orange. She shook herself, leaving a cloud hanging in the air and the walker behind them muttered for them to hurry up—this was no place to hang about.

"How far to Bakla?" asked Kyira back over her shoulder, in Kemenese.

The man held up three fingers and gestured her on. Kyira nodded, scratching Milli's ear to soothe her growl, but not missing a step either.

Three more leagues. At least the worst of was behind her. What she would give for an icy breeze and a glacier to run over. The sisters of

Nord would be a welcome departure from this hot, dusty, southern land. She was not built for this place, but then like everyone here, she was just a product of her own choices.

"Come on girl."

Bakla was not the oasis Kyira had been expecting either. The boundary between road and city was non-existent, and the traffic drove on through the centre of the city. Kyira stayed close to the sandy walls that lined the east side, but as the road split into hundreds of streets, so did the buildings that followed them. All logic was lost in clouds of blinding dust that clung to skin, clothes and stone.

Vendors and sellers grabbed, probed and pushed in the middle of every street, splitting foot traffic like boulders in streams.

Kyira ducked away into an alcove to catch her breath. "I'm sorry, girl. I'd rather not be dragging you along by the scruff, but I'll lose you in that...throng." Lines of people milled past the alcove, ceaseless. "I want to stop. My feet hurt. This walking, it's not like running. It's like wading. I've never seen so many people in one place. Not even Costra Dae was as busy as this and that's a capital city! Girl, we have to find a place to sleep. Then we can eat." She squatted down to Milli's side and buried her face in the dog's neck. Milli groaned with pleasure, her foot bouncing as Kyira scratched her ear. A shuffling noise caught her attention and abruptly she realised they were not alone.

Milli lurched forward, snarling like a rabid wolf.

"Ath'all ma deratlchioo!" urged a man, lifting himself off the ground. Kyira jumped back as the man rushed over. His skin was the same caramel colour as most of Bakla, but large pockets of white had broken out like hives all over this man's face like a map of the world. His family, a woman and three children, sat behind him in the shadows of the alcove around a steaming pot on a burner. They all stared at her.

"Go! Go!" The map man grabbed a broom, and all at once Kyira had a face full of bristles.

"I'm going!" The kerb came quickly, and Kyira stumbled out and onto the road, the broom jumping between her and Milli, driving them out. Feet stomped around her, and she was lost in a forest of stumbling legs. "Stop it, you fool! We'll be killed!"

"Go, go!" shouted map face.

Two llamas emerged from the street cloud, heading straight at her. Kyira pushed back against the broom, grabbing it, using it to pull herself out of the road.

"No!" She pushed map face hard. She was taller than him, but he may have been a tree for all that he moved. Kyira shoved a fist into the man's multi-coloured face.

"What are you doing you fool?" shouted Kyira, pulling the broom form the man and wielding it like a sword. She wanted to snap the thing in two. Two children appeared behind him, little hands covering their father's face as though they could protect him from their mysterious invader. The mother came next looking just as terrified.

Kyira took a step back. "You can't just go attacking someone in the street!" Discomfort blossomed on her cheek and she felt tenderly where the stiff bristles had scratched her. "Perhaps if you are nicer to those who are just catching their breath—"

Behind the family lay blankets, rags, old cushions. The alcove was their home and it was all they had.

They all had dark skin, and their eyes were so big and wide and brown, with hair a deep dark red. Kyira was Nordun, Sami. A traveller, with tanned skin and slanted eyes. All gifts from her mother and father to help weather the bright, snowy lands of Nord. Yet here she stood a monster, invading the home of this Baklian family. Had they ever met a Nordun before?

"I'm sorry." Kyira put down the brush and dug into her bag, pulling out some of the dried fish she'd been saving. "Here."

The family stared at her in fear. Map face picked himself up off the ground and brushed himself off, gesturing for Kyira to leave.

"Go, go!"

"Fine. Come Milli, let's go—Milli? Milli!" Kyira jerked around frantically, but there was no sign of her anywhere. Kyira forced her way out of the alcove back to the road-edge, heedless of the shouts that followed. "Milli!" Dust filled her mouth with as she searched the road. "Milli! Where are you?" She threw herself back, feet slipping on the loose surface as another cart hurtled towards her. Then she was up and searching again, using her feet to feel for Milli's broken body. Her bloodied, broken—

Tears blurred her vision, then another shadow loomed at her side. Kyira prepared for the impact. It was too close!

Map face appeared, his blurry outline directing traffic by waving his broom. Oxen, llamas and camels, all trotted by her, jingling with beads of silver and wood, giving her space to run back and forth safely.

And she did, checking every square foot of road until she stood on the other side of the street.

"Milli!" she said her name, hoping that the world would take pity on her, on her beautiful friend. "Come back!" Perhaps the Great Mother might hear her plea and grant her wish. The kerbside came up to meet her as she stumbled over. "Milli." Already she missed her white fur, her eyes, one blue, one white.

"Do not let the darkness overtake you, girl, said map face, appearing at her side. For the first time, Kyira noticed more alcoves, the same beautiful ornate archways and in each one there were families who lived there. The smell of people, and waste and food mingled together, and Kyira's heart ached. Ached for her loss, ached for this place, ached for it all.

Map face helped her to her feet and stood awkwardly in front of her. He was as unsure as she was. Two strangers, connected by an awful circumstance. "Flior mere saath aaie Florr. Come with me. Your dog, we will find."

They crossed the street together, back to where she had met him, but Kyira was in a daze. The man's family had left, probably in fear of her, but he just sat down at the pot and began slurping. After a long minute he gestured to the cushion opposite and Kyira sat down.

"I am Darc."

"Hello Darc."

The more she looked at him, the more strange he became. Balding, with forgettable features that would shift to become expressive and deep in an eyeblink. He lifted a piece of flat bread. "It's the peppercorn," said Darc. "In Bakla they have an oil inside that helps the bread to be crunchy. You look hungry. Here."

Kyira refused the offer, and instead studied the alcove. "You live here?"

"I do." Darc licked his lips. "You speak Baklin well for a Sami."

Kyira blinked. "You know my kind?"

"I've had run ins with the Sami once or twice. Bakla is a big city, with lots to offer travellers. The world's gates. That's what Neubakla means." He smiled. "I imagine you thought it meant New and Bakla. In the wake of the wars of the Northern Territories?"

Kyira nodded. "I did." Sadness gripped her heart, stealing the meaning of Darc's words.

Darc leant over the pot and took her hand. "Sami, don't worry. Your friend will be found, of that I am sure. Your loss is written all over your face." He dipped his flat bread into the pot and pulled it out, soaked in red with flecks of green. "Or at least it may as well be." He sucked the bread dry and repeated the process until the bread was falling to pieces in the pot. "Or perhaps that is just the scratches from my brush. I am sorry."

Kyira swallowed and stared out at the road. "It was my fault, Darc. I am the invader. I did not mean to scare away your family."

Darc's sparse eyebrows raised. "They will be back." He smiled and Kyira felt brighter, far happier than she should have, having just met him. She almost felt like she had always known him.

"Once we have eaten," he said, "we will walk down the street." Darc pointed north. "The streets split and come back together near the beach. So, we can sweep the area. If Milli is alive, we will find her."

Darc offered Kyira some tea in a tiny cup, and she sipped some. It was bitter sweet, and felt as foreign to her as she did in this place.

"You don't have to come," she said, standing. "I can find Milli myself." More images of Milli's broken corpse in the gutter filled her head, the sorrow as keen as a blade in her guts.

"No," said Darc. "You have the look of someone who always knows where they are, but Bakla is new for you. I will come with you, and I will help you. I will introduce you to the world's gates and guide you."

It took everything Kyira had to not crumple to the ground in a fit of sobs. She clenched her jaw shut. "I can do it myself, Darc. But thank you."

"Then here," said Darc. "Take the fish back. I do not need it. There are many little birds here in Bakla. They keep me well fed." Kyira took the dried fish, fingering the patterns of their scales.

Kyira stood, wiping the wetness from her face against her dusty coat. "Be well, Darc."

"And you, Sami." Darc offered her a simple nod. "Godspeed."

28

WITHOUT ME

Kyira left the main roads behind, and as the dust settled, the inner city revealed a maze of long wide roads that cut through each other at odd angles. The blocks were single buildings four floors high with a courtyard beyond—it was astonishing to consider so many people living together!

With its tall buildings and maze of streets it felt like Tyr, but instead of hard stone, Bakla was wrought of clay and wood. Everything was a shade of gold from the layers of sand blown day after day against every surface. It grit got everywhere: crunching between her teeth, rubbing between the webbings of her fingers, the crooks of her elbows, and down her shirt.

Kyira adjusted her cowl. The Laich in Nord would have washed it all away. Cold, blue and deep with a crust of ice, the water would envelope her, cleanse and refresh her, but Nord was as far away as—

Her elbow caught someone heavily in the shoulder, but before she could speak the dark-dressed man had melted into a sea of gold cloth and skin.

"Ignore them all, daughter." Iqaluk's words echoed in her head. *"You owe them nothing."*

"Ignore them, like they ignore me?" That was what she would have said to the man if he still was alive. "What did you ever know of crowds?

Of cities? Hiding in a cave in Nord." Her anger rose like hot tsampa bread.

"You lost Milli like you lost Vlada."

The thought caught her like a punch to the face. A thought she had conjured herself, against herself. More people filed around her, jostling past, irritated grumbles meant only for her and her selfishness.

"Milli was born in a box," thought Kyira. "She would have been sold as nara meat in a market in Dor! Without me." Kyira shuddered as someone forced their way by her. "Without me...Milli would have died. Without me..."

"You are Sami."

Iqaluk's words hung in her head as though her father truly had spoken them himself.

"Without me—"

"Without you, Milli would have lived. Someone else would have taken her, and what's more they would have kept her alive and well."

"I am Sami. Don't tell me—" A golden face turned and beheld Kyira, a woman, with a look like thunder, and sand upon her brown eyelashes. Kyira had spoken out loud.

The woman replied with something unintelligible, a curse probably, then she too melted away into the crowd.

Kyira carried on, trying to mingle back in. "There," she uttered to herself. "Are you happy? Now half of Bakla thinks I've lost my mind." She sighed long and hard. "Maybe I have. I don't see anyone else standing in the street talking to their dead father."

The wide roads gave way to smaller streets, one of which was full of children playing happily, unaware that they lived in a tiny box of the world. They paused as Kyira dropped her cowl, gawking at her foreign face.

"Hi, have you seen a dog around here?"

The youngest girl laughed and reached up to Kyira's face. Her little hands were as grubby as the road but Kyira knelt down anyway. The rest of the group did the same, dirty fingers and nails pulling and poking at Kyira's cheeks and eyes.

"What these?" said the girl, touching Kyira's chin.

"Tattoos," replied Kyira in broken Baklian. "They're called them Lines where I am from."

"What mean?"

"They are my aspirations," said Kyira. "They guide me." She looked around. "Is your mother here?"

A tall girl, and the oldest by the look of her, spoke up. "No mother. No father."

"You have no parents?" A chorus of *no* and shaking heads. "Then who looks after you?" Before she had even said the words she knew the answer.

"We look after ourselves," said the older girl.

Kyira swallowed and stood up. "I've lost my dog. Her name is Milli."

"No. We've not seen your dog." More laughing, and then they were all running away. Bright little lives, shouting and barking like dogs, pretending and playing in the streets on all fours like animals themselves.

Kyira turned to leave and the older girl padded over. "Ishmal took this from you." In her hands was Kyira's belt knife. "It is yours." The girl nodded to a young boy standing sheepishly.

"Thank you." Kyira handed her the fish from her pocket. "It's all I have."

The girl looked perplexed but took the dried fillets. "They sell dogs on the beach," she said. "For meat."

Kyira's grasp of Baklian was poor at best, but she had still been able to extract the meaning of the girl's words. Fear drove her on like the fire that chased her in Makril, until finally she rounded a corner and met some sand dunes.

The beach was a mudflat that stretched on for miles in both directions. Kyira ran from stall to stall trying her best to work with the language which was quite unlike her own, or even Sulitarian. "Dog." Kyira thought back to what Darc had said. "Um, florr? Have you seen a florr." Panic filled every attempt to communicate, and the vendors just pointed along the beach, urging her along.

There was not the shouting or din of a live market because they didn't need to shout, not when queues of hungry soldiers stood in line at each stall, waiting patiently for cooking food. An actual army of men and women wearing deep green uniforms, sparring, eating and ready to fight. Some held their weapons with them, but most stood quietly waiting to break their fast. When they were served the would walk back towards the east side of the beach, where instead of water there was a sea of tents. Thousands of them. This was no beach. The sand was too fine. The shore was too far away, so far that the line of the Middle Sea and the horizon were one, with just the odd matchstick-sized figure cutting through the haze.

Keeping her distance from the stalls at the top of the beach, Kyira casually studied each area, listening for barks. She still couldn't fathom why dogs were so coveted as food. They were too clever and friendly to be eaten, but even in Nord it was a common practice. Cows had far more meat on them, but they were sacred creatures in Kemen, and could usually be found covered in colourful beads and beautiful crafted crochet, while their owners whispered sweet nothings in their ears.

"Iqaluk," she uttered. "Why is it you never come when I need you?"

The smell of food was intoxicating, and her eyes followed each steaming wrapped package carried past her, but still her stomach groaned with nerves rather than hunger. Acid hung in her breast, burning. "What am I to do, Iqaluk? Where is she? I can't...lose her."

A boy jumped out in front of her. "Worms?"

"What?"

He looked in his eighth, and had a large cast-iron bowl of water. He bent over and pulled up a huge plate of dried mud, beckoning Kyira down. "Worms."

Beneath the slab of mud were thick worms wriggling away from the heat of the sun, burying themselves in the wetter mud beneath the ground. The boy picked a handful up and dropped them in the wide bowl. Then without hesitation lifted the longest out and sucked it into his mouth, grinning as he chewed. "Very creamy. You try." He passed her one and Kyira copied the boy by sucking it in.

"Huh," she said, chewing. "They're good." The boy smiled, then took a handful more and added them to the bowl. "Thank you," said Kyira. "Have you seen a dog?"

The boy cocked his head. "Dog?"

"Florr?"

The boy nodded and shook his behind. "Florr! Yes. Ruff!" He nodded past her, down the long beach into the distance. "Florr."

Kyira shook her head, "Alive."

The boy shook his head mournfully. "Food."

Kyira watched him wander away. Tears pricked her eyes, and a dark pit of despair opened up inside of her. In her mind's eye she fell into that darkness, falling forever into her own sadness. How could she live without Milli? It was like losing Vlada all over again, except Milli had been with her for so long. Kyira turned, this way and that, but all she saw was darkness, dragging her deeper and deeper.

Breathe.

A light, bright and blue...It was beautiful and soothing and—

"Sami!"

Darc was standing there as though he had just appeared out of thin air. At his feet was a familiar bedraggled animal.

"Milli!" Darc let the leash go and Milli raced towards her. "Oh, Milli! It is good to see you!" Milli set about trying to lick Kyira to death. She had a bandage upon her hind leg.

"I told you she would be fine." Darc smiled widely, but it looked strange on him. Perhaps it was the light patches upon his skin.

"Darc, thank you. I owe you so much! Where was she?"

"Some children had found her." He adjusted his shirt against the sun. "The girl had the same fish you offered me. It is not a fish you would find in these waters. They sent me here."

"It's called a skate," said Kyira, feeling the fresh sting of tears prickling. She laughed instead. "They like the coastal waters, but cliffs and rocks." Milli sat, tongue hanging out as Kyira stroked and petted her. "I doubt there's a skate for a hundred leagues. A thousand!"

"Then where did you get it, Sami?"

"Ge'Bat. I travelled through on the way to Kyotho."

"And you have not eaten properly since then?"

Kyira wanted to lie, to hide from Darc, but she couldn't say why. His eyes were so kindly, his demeanour so charming. "Just that flatbread."

Darc smiled. "A hunk of flatbread? Kyira, come on. Bakla has some of the finest food in Rengas. Food good enough even for this hound of yours."

"I'm just glad she's not in a bowl herself," laughed Kyira, burying her face in Milli's fur.

"Then let us eat and rejoice. I may live upon the street, but that is where the best food is!" He held out a hand. "Come and let's begin your introduction to the fine city of Bakla anew."

29

ORIGINS

Vasta left the road as soon as the gates of Ipor Dan were behind them. The weather stayed dry, which was a blessing—an Ipiti monsoon was nothing to shirk at—but the wind still had a bite to it. More than once Abika had to hold her shift tightly between her knees, not that the great Bohr would have cared. Maybe if she died of the cold, he might notice her pale blue corpse, lolling about the cart. Earlier, she had asked where they were going and Vasta had snapped at her. He might've been a Bohr, but he was just like Jekob, preoccupied and staring off into the middle distance ignoring all else. Now she thought on it, Jekob must have always been a liar. Not just to her, but Freja and Meorith too. He lied about the pipes so he could come to Ipor Dan, and he lied about his past. How much did Freja truly know?

Their cart had some modifications like springs that allowed it to move more smoothly over the ancient, long-dried bogs around the city, and a wheel that the Bohr used for steering. There were some spring buckles on the yoke too, so Vasta's nara seemed less bothered by the rough terrain, which was probably a good thing considering how bloody old the creature looked. She leant forward and stroked the nara's head, careful not to go too high. The nara snorted, indicating that the petting was not welcome—most nara would only let their masters get near their antlers.

Defeated, Abika turned on the cart's seat, and climbed into the trailer where Lorith was lying. The redness at his side was now a shade of midnight, and worse, the bruise was gradually moving up into his chest.

She smoothed Lorith's long hair and began to sing. "To this a new song, a leaf's journey begins, flies high to the sky, and falls, falls, falls. To this a new song, a leaf's journey ends, bringing life to flies, all, and all, and all. To this a third song, a leaf's journey's echo, bringing life to the world, grow, grow, and grow. To this a fine song, a leaf's journey's life. A new leaf lives, unfurls. And grows and flies. Ever more."

The cart stopped, Vasta was staring at her. "Where did you hear that? Those words."

Abika shook her head. "In the citadel."

"Someone was playing them?"

"Must have been," shrugged Abika. "I heard them as clear as day within the cell walls, as though the person was singing—" She paused as the memory returned bright and clear. "It was you. I heard you singing it." She sat up. "How did I hear you singing?"

Vasta stared off into the distance again. It would have been easier to guess what a sheep was thinking. "Do you still have the necklace?"

Abika pulled it out from beneath her shift. "What's the shard got to do with anything?"

This time she saw an emotion she recognised. Fear.

"I'm sure it's nothing," said the Bohr. He nodded to Lorith. "What about him? Is he dead?"

Abika stared at Vasta in disbelief. "No, he's not dead, you bloody fool."

Vasta flicked the reins urging the nara forward. The animal tossed its head and dragged them on.

"No," said Abika. "Stop the cart."

"Why?"

"Oh, I don't know. Maybe because my commune brother is near death, my commune father is a secret guard of the Order of the White Dragon, a band of humans who actually want the Bohr to oppress them, and because I am sitting in a cart with an actual Bohr, who apart from smelling like a dead horse, is spiriting me away from jail. Why the hell do you think I asked you to stop, you great fool." She whacked him on his arm as hard he she could, but the Bohr was solid muscle all over. She would have doubted he even felt it had he not slowly rubbed the spot with his animal claw. "Vasta, where are we going?"

"Away from Ipor Dan, girl." He pointed slowly towards the hilltops in the distance. "The long sisters of Ipiti should offer us some prote—"

"The hills?" said Abika. "No. We're not going there. We need to go to the commune. The place I live. We need to go there, and we need to go there now." Abika doubted herself as she always did, but something deep was drawing her home. She told herself that it was because Lorith needed help, but in truth she knew there was a chance she could drive a dagger into Freja's heart.

"Where is it?"

"On the bay. The west side."

Vasta shook his head. "No."

"What do you mean, *no*!" snapped Abika. "I've just discovered my mother's name!"

"Freja?"

Abika shook her head. "My real mother is called Kyira." Saying her name turned Abika's stomach. "I need to find her, Vasta. She has the answers I need. Freja knows who she is, Vasta. I have to speak with her."

"What if finding Kyira only raises more questions?"

Abika scanned Ipor Dan in the distance, the hills beyond, the flatlands, but no inspiration came. There were no answers anywhere but for the ones she created herself, and those thoughts already felt as though they were cast in iron, hanging around her neck ready to drown her. "My mother left me to rot in the hands of two strangers on an island halfway across the world. Imagine leaving a baby, Vasta! Just leaving her on a doorstep. I *need* to find...Kyira, Vasta." She closed her eyes, composing herself. "Give me a better reason than that. You great oaf."

Vasta studied her unblinking. "I am leaving Ipor Dan because the Order wants me to join them. You saw them. That was their last warning. The next time they come they will bring fire and weapons and I will likely be killed."

"Then why did you come back for us?"

This time it was Vasta who hesitated. "I...I thought some company... I do not know." His eyes drifted to the shard necklace. "You needed help."

"Are you afraid of them? The Order?"

Vasta nodded. "I am Bohr, but I can still be hurt. Like your friend here."

Abika placed a hand on Lorith's side and he winced. "What about all of your stuff? All of those tiny boxes filled with gems, the tools, and machines?"

"I might collect in the name of science, but once I have my answers, girl, they become empty trinkets."

"You just left?"

"I had to," shrugged Vasta. "For the good of my existence."

Abika swallowed. "Then for the good of my existence, we're going to the commune, Vasta. Take us back to the road. Now."

Once more, Vasta studied her like she was a piece of fossilised cow shit. "You are a capable one, Abika."

This time it was Abika's time to frown. "Capable?"

"You drive forward, moulding the world to your will. You are truly a pillar of the fates."

Abika had heard such things before, but never directed at a person. Let alone herself. "I am no pillar of the fates. You think I create the waves upon which the world sits? That is what it means isn't it?"

"In a way, yes. In other ways..." Vasta stepped off the cart, and it looked normal sized once again. He held a hand up to the sky like a painter might have. "The worlds move according to a pattern. Some can see the pattern, others cannot." He picked up a rock and dropped it in a puddle. "You see the waves that rock makes? The effects of an event carry on beyond our sight. Those waves come to meet the shore soon, and they are bigger and stronger. I have been puzzling over it since first we met. It is why I am here."

"What of the Order."

"I meet conflict wherever I go. The Bohr shun me for my human ways, and the humans for my Bohr ways. I have no place."

"I didn't ask you to do this, Vasta."

"Oh, but you did. The moment you entered my store the fates of the worlds rippled. You are an unbalanced force, Abika. I did not say anything, because...well it's not good for custom, is it? What I find fascinating though is how a pillar of fate does not recognise that she is one. Escaping the Order of the White Dragon, not once but twice, and now here you are, directing our course like a shipmaster travelling home."

Abika shook her head in confusion. "The commune is not my home."

Vasta continued as if he hadn't heard her. "...Everyone underestimates you. It's fascinating." He turned to her. "Not your home? Then where is your home?"

Abika drew a ragged breath. "Only my real mother can tell me that."

"Then we ought to find this Kyira," said Vasta, as if it were the most obvious and simple statement ever spoken. "And ask her."

Diary entry

Bakla

Darc knows the streets of Bakla well, which makes sense for someone who seemingly grew up here. Did he, though? I don't know much about him, other than the kindness he has showed me.

I remember a time not too long ago when kindness might have been enough, but I left that childish girl back in Ipiti with Abika and Jekob.

I have no appetite, but worse are my dreams, which are plagued with crystal towers that split the sky. Pillars of light that hold my heart and mind prisoner.

30

WE ARE MANY

Kyira marvelled at the Domsts and other places of worship within Bakla. There was not just one religion in the city, based on the many rituals she had witnessed throughout the day. Watching monks chanting on one street, and then seeing reams of bright young things dancing on another was exhilarating. The colours, the noise. It was as though she weas back in Makril watching the Sulitarians mingling with the stiff-necked townspeople.

Darc was an enigma. The more she looked at him, the more detail she noticed. He'd seemed weedy and thin in the shadows of that alcove, but he was very trim, with wiry muscle. The same sinewy strength Hasaan and Iqaluk used to have. She placed a hand over her heart and muttered a prayer in their names.

Darc turned. "For whom do you pray?"

Kyira blinked. "For souls that are no longer with me."

"I see." Darc moved a wisp of hair from his burnt-wood eyes. "What gods have you in Nord?"

"The Forbringr, the Great Mother Baeivi."

Darc gestured upwards. "In Bakla we celebrate a range of gods. The god of the sun, she is called Klhi, the god of the earth, an old man named Reold, and the god of the people, Greava." Like most Domsts in

Rengas, it dwarfed all other buildings around it, but for all its grandness, the carvings in the stone were graphic and terrible.

"Why are they all so—"

"Violent?" said Darc. "Reold betrayed Klhi and Breava was the result. A love-child born out of lies. Like most gods."

"You have no love for the gods of Bakla?"

Darc shook his head. "No, I do not. Of any god." He ran his hand over a stone bust. A weathered man with an expression of intense pain. "Gods do nothing for those below them."

"And that is why you hate them?" asked Kyira, feeling that she'd had this exact conversation before. "Isn't that just the irony of belief?"

"The irony of belief." Darc smiled. "Indeed, Sami. Indeed. You are wiser than you look."

"My brother and I would spend hours considering our existence."

"My guess is that many Sami do so, when you sleep under a sea of stars."

Kyira nodded. "I may have wisdom but you are perceptive, Darc." The words were spoken lightly, but Darc stared at her, expressionless. Kyira continued on past the awkwardness. "In Nord we talk of the gods of the land, but they don't have names. They sometimes find themselves as characters in books." She laughed. "But that's it. Elders take them more seriously than others."

"The old see death," said Darc, with a half shrug. "And they see it more keenly than the rest of us. Sami, I have shown you much of Bakla today, but many of those areas have escaped the war. Bakla is a fresh fish, yet to decay. But it will." He beckoned her to the Domst doors.

"We can't. It is not prayer time."

"No one comes here to pray, Sami. Not this Domst." He opened the doors, but instead of a dark hall lit with the sparkling rays of sun through coloured windows, there was ruin. The roof and walls were rubble and charred wood exposed like a broken skeleton.

"What happened here?"

"The Bohr snuck into the city. We've had our fair share of leaders since the war of the northern territories, and they have each expanded the city in their own unique way. Some call the layout a mess, I call it progress. Even so, a Bohr raiding party was still able to find their way to one of our most precious Domsts, and they burned it down during an evening prayer time, murdering the families praying inside."

"I saw the same in Kamsin." Kyira ran her hand over the bell lying on its side near the door. It was almost as big as her. "They are inhuman. A scourge."

"You've have had dealings with them before. I can see it in your eyes."

Darc's overfamiliarity was making Kyira uncomfortable. "I fought them once. Long ago."

Darc stepped beside her, rapping the bell with white knuckles. "The bells should have rung across the city that day, but in the dead of night, a small squad of Bohr can move around without being noticed. As hard as that is to believe. They locked the doors, then slaughtered anyone who got close or tried to help. My own brother was there. Unable to help, as his friends and neighbours were burned alive."

"Lands—"

"Don't!" snapped Darc, his quiet demeanour shifting in a heartbeat. "Don't blame the Gods for this. Not the Gods of the lands or the gods of the sky. This was the Bohr. They are free beings like you or I. They came here and they killed upon their own will." He let the door swing shut. "The war between humans and Bohr is not dead. It is here. The Bohr have not struck in a few months, but that does not mean it is over."

Kyira's skin tingled as though insects were crawling over her. Milli too, stood erect, her eyes trained on Darc. "Tell me, what of your family, Darc? Should you not get back to them?"

Darc shook his head. "The children you saw me with in the alcove are not mine, but my brother's."

"Oh. I thought—"

"I have no children."

Kyira nodded slowly, but a noise caught her attention. A cheer from a crowd echoed along the high walls.

"Ah!" said Darc, suddenly excited. "It's started!"

"What—"

Darc took Kyira's hand. "Come, follow me, Sami. Trust me. I promise you will enjoy this."

The short street quickly gave way to another square, much like the one they had left, but surrounded by houses and taverns. In the centre was a crowd of over a hundred people, cheering and nodding along with the words of a man who stood high in their midst.

"Republicans, your resolve is harder than Bohr steel. Your resolve is harder than even the flaming stone hurled by their war machines!" The speaker had tied-up dark hair rather than the usual auburn hair of the rest of Bakla, and those eyes were most assuredly blue. A tight-fitting shirt clung to a muscled torso—a man of war, plainly. "With every strike, we shall resist." He thumped a fist into his palm. "With every hunting party that sneaks into the walls of our fair city, we will fight. Hunt them! Ring the bells!" The crowd erupted in cheers again. "The Bohr are nothing. We are stronger. We are many."

Proclamations burst from every window as those watching from the homes of the square shouted in support of the speaker, banging the ledges upon which the green, red and white flags of the Republic hung.

"BUT THOSE BELLS RING TOO OFTEN." The crowds quieted immediately at that. Sombre heads bowing in unison. "Today I am addressing you, Republicans. The honest, the brave, the rational, the freedom-loving peoples that you are. How do we stop the Bohr? News reaches us of war from Sulitaria, from Nord and Hatàr. The Ringland of Rengas is teeming with Bohr bent on war, bent on killing us! They invade our lands. They kill our people, our children, our livestock." The speaker licked his lips, letting the silence linger. When he continued, he was much quieter. "But they will fail. We have been here longer than they. Humans have bred ourselves into every corner of the circle of the world, because IT IS OURS!" He waited as the crowd cheered with him, hanging on his words. "Humans are too broadly spread to fight with a single force. We would overrun them in an instant. They know our strength is their weakness, and they are AFRAID!"

The crowd erupted again, and even Kyira felt the pulse of positivity running through them all. The inspiration, and most importantly the resistance, of a leader speaking the truth felt like it did at Tyr, when Laeb spoke to the Tsiorc fighters, when he commanded them to strike at the heart of the Bohr stronghold. It brought warmth to her heart to see how united the human race could be in the face of tyranny.

"He's good, isn't he?" said Darc.

Kyira cleared her throat. "Yes. He is."

"His name is Fiskal."

"He is Republican?"

Darc shook his head. "No. He is from somewhere else. Some say Ge'Bat. Others say Sulitar."

"A foreign captain?" Kyira scoffed. "I've heard that one before."

"What do we have left?" shouted Fiskal, as the chorus died down. "Our values? Unity? The determination to defend our freedoms? All of that. Sign up to join the Republic army. Sign up to protect your freedoms against tyranny. The fight begins here!"

"You should talk to him," shouting Darc, over the din. "I imagine you would have much to offer the Republic."

Kyira felt a pang of guilt, and this time it was overcast with something darker. Disgust. She looked Darc in the eye, studied his unreadable features, looking for something more. "What are your intentions, Darc?"

"What do you mean?"

"What I say."

Darc swallowed. His expression shifted like a grey mackerel whose shining side had caught the sun. He was deciding what information to give her. "I am...not..." He rubbed a finger over his eyebrows. "I am a convict. There are those in Bakla who would see me killed given the chance."

And there it was. "What did you do?"

"I killed a man." The line was delivered so matter-of-factly he could have been recounting what he'd eaten for breakfast. "And his wife." He watched Kyira as the words settled in. "You've probably wondered why I stick to the shadows, and why I might disappear without explanation."

Kyira glanced around at the men and women forming lines at Fiskal's table, waiting to sign their lives away. "Only fools believe the lesser of two lies. Is that what's happening here, Darc? You show me the Domst, sympathise with me and bring me here to join your army?"

"You are wise, Kyira." Darc held his hands together in pleading prayer. "And I can see it plainly, but you mistake me. I am a simple being. This is not my army. I only know Fiskal through his words here. I swear it. Don't let my past colour your impression of me."

"I don't care what you've done, Darc. Just what you will do."

The corners of Darc's mouth raised in a slight smile. "Isn't that what life is? Who we can and cannot trust? Well, Kyira. You can trust me. My intentions are not to harm you, but to use you. I make no qualms or excuses for it. I wish to leave Bakla. You are Sami. A nomad. The Sami are well known for their understanding on the lands, and you strike me as no different." Darc bowed his head low, showing more of those light patches, like maps across his bronze skin. "With you, I saw an opportunity. Accept my sincerest apologies for the deception."

Kyira pulled her blade from her belt, and as she did Milli growled. "I do not take kindly to deception, Darc. Never deceive me. I do not mind the company, but I will not abide a liar. If you try to cheat me again, I will kill you."

Darc looked up, his eyes wide in servitude. "And I believe it, Sami."

"My name is Kyira." She held for a moment, studying his patchy face, but it had returned to its usual pallidness. "Good." She scratched Milli behind the ear, and her growl faded. "Let us see what Fiskal has to say about his Republican army." She tapped her map bag. "Perhaps there is something I can offer after all."

FISKAL

31

WHISPERS OF WAR

"Numbers are not everything." The commander of the Republic army spoke in a thick Baklian accent.

"No, Commander. But they matter." Kyira glanced at Darc, who stood by the inn door slowly stroking Milli's head, looking like a proud father. "They matter a great deal. In Tyr—"

"Tyr?" Fiskal looked up from his bowl. "You were in the cursed city?"

"Yes. I saw it all."

Fiskal stood up, noodles half-eaten, and broth dripping from his chin. "I heard the Tsiorc tore down the city with power, and they were led by a man who was stronger than a Banèman!"

Darc sniggered, but Kyira ignored it. Everyone, even the two heavily armed guards standing in the empty tavern, ignored it. "Laeb was definitely not a Banèman. He was just a man."

"You *knew* him?" Fiskal's face lit up. For every expression Darc did not have, Fiskal had about ten. The man was in constant motion and spoke with heartfelt enthusiasm on every subject. Unfortunately, Kyira had met his type before. Excitable, but prone to boredom. Ready to cast away the old for the sake of the new. And here she stood, the new.

"Yes," said Kyira. "I knew Laeb. I saved his life. I drew maps for him. For this honour he made me the chief navigator for the Tsiorc."

"Chief Navigator? And now here you stand!" Fiskal starting pacing back and forth. "I can't believe you were actually there! Laeb was an artist. The siege at Soporia Din, the battle of Lumael, and his movements at Mataasca Din are legendary. Then of course Drakemyre." He stopped. "Wait, you said he wasn't a Banèman, but how can that be?"

"He was a man," said Kyira. "As you. But better looking."

"A man?" Fiskal frowned but let it go. He strolled over to the bar and grabbed a bottle standing upon it. "You know, Bakla creates some of the finest wines in Rengas. Do you know why? No? Then I shall tell you. The sea air caresses the wild grape vines that grow along the dunes of our beaches, imbuing the wine with a unique saltiness." He grinned and tapped his temple. "Salt, I hear you think? Salt indeed. Wine is sweet, everyone knows that. So the introduction of salt creates a new dimension to the flavour that transcends it." He paced back and forth in front of the bar, examining the bottle. "My father was a winemaker. Many on the other side of the world knew his name. In fact I still have two of his very best bottles down in the cellar. The twenty-nine. As invaluable and rare as someone claiming to have been an original member of the Tsiorc!" He let the comment sit a while. "The twenty-nine, if you ask me, is probably the best combination of flavours to be found in the circle of the world." He put the bottle down on the table and stared at it. "The Tsiorc are long disbanded. Some say there are none left at all, even in the long cycles since Tyr. They have all faded away along with their fight. There is talk of a fifth union, but I feel this to be just more conjecture. The four unions of Zunqai are so powerless, that a fifth could no more for us if they wanted to." Fiskal looked over at the two guards, and they nodded with him. "Humans governed by Bohr will never be free. And so the unions are as toothless as their slimy words. Powerless. And Kyira we need power against the Bohr." Fiskal turned on Kyira. "If Laeb truly was a man like me, then tell me, how did he conjure an earthquake to destroy an entire Bohr army?"

Kyira shrugged. "I don't know. I wasn't there."

"It was the holes," said Darc.

"The holes?" repeated Kyira. Milli blinked at her.

"No," snapped Fiskal. "No. The holes cannot just explain away everything! These mysterious tunnels that tore Rengas apart. I don't believe in them."

Kyira tilted her head. "You don't *believe* in them?"

"There are two camps, Kyira of Nord. Two. Those who believe the Forbringrs came down and tore holes in reality, and those who firmly believe that they were all just whispers of war, moving from mouth to mouth, each time losing a sense of itself."

Darc scoffed.

"I assume then," said Kyira, "that you are in the latter camp, Fiskal."

"You assume correctly. I would pay a lot of money to find out how a man like Laeb could wield so much power. Imagine it Rolla!" He strolled over to the doorman. "Imagine having the power to lift the very earth and send your enemies plummeting into the depths of Rengas!"

The doorman Rolla nodded. "Such a thing would make a man a Forbringr," boomed the man.

Fiskal pointed emphatically. "Exactly! A god. Power like that is unknown even to the Banèmen!" Fiskal pulled some tabac from a tin of the table, rolled it into a square piece of paper, then placed between his lips. "What was Laeb like? Did you *know* him" He dropped low to light the end against the candle flame, then took a long draw.

Kyira rolled her eyes. "No. I didn't *know* him. Not like that. He was a private man, although I heard that he loved someone. A Kumpani."

Fiskal punched Rolla in the arm. "A Kumpani. Taming the unlovable! Of course."

"Laeb lived and breathed the Tsiorc. He was a hero. I have no doubt that without him, the humans would have lost tragically at Tyr."

"But they did. Or so I hear. I mean we're talking of a battle that is over ten cycles old now."

"Twelve."

"Twelve." Fiskal took another draw from tabac. "Indeed it is twelve. A lot has happened since then. The Bohr have fragmented, they are much harder to fight. Their unified force at Tyr was at least something that could be seen and heard, but now they have split. Groups of guerrilla fighters who roam the countryside striking at supply chains or sneaking into cities and burning domsts full of praying people." He slammed a fist down on the table. The tabac tube went flying and landed on the floor. He stared at it for a moment. "At least before we knew what we were fighting! Now it is impossible. And *we* are as fragmented as they!" He punched his chest for emphasis. "The Bohr have cells all over Rengas, raiding human settlements that still resist them, which is basically everyone. The only thing we can be thankful for is they have no one to bring the Bohr together, the distance between them and us is too great. Our world too large. As a map reader, you know I speak the truth."

"They will come eventually," said Darc, quietly.

When Fiskal didn't respond or even acknowledge Darc's presence, Kyira repeated the words.

Fiskal swallowed. "If they do, we will lose. Kemen is a land I do not want to fight on. It cannot be done. It is too hot, too dusty. We need the elements on our side. Laeb used the world to help him fight. I need to do the same."

Kyira nodded. "You are right. You cannot fight the Bohr in Kemen. They are stronger, and they have Banèmen, who alone, could crush Bakla. Any human city would fall like the tidal wave that almost wiped out our fleet on the Way channel. The water swallowed that ship whole, without hesitation." Fiskal was with her now, listening intently. Darc nodded along, urging her forward. "You need help, Fiskal. My help." She swung her map bag off her shoulder. "Take the fight to them." She unravelled the map of Rengas on the inn table, the heavy parchment knocking the noodle bowl to the floor. Nobody took heed of that though, not when their world sat laid out in front of them. "That is what Laeb did, and *that* is why he won. He chose his own game to play."

Fiskal's bright face was colourless as he poured over the shapes and words Kyira had drawn. The only sound in the inn was of her finger moving over the canvas, starting from the Határian borderlands and moving down and through Kemen to the capital city of Zunqai. "The Bohr's stronghold was never Tyr, Fiskal. It is Zunqai. Their birthplace.

I know of Zunqai, Kyira! "I know that in the wake of the death of the Bohr King in Tyr, that Queen Kaliste took over. Zunqai is her city, and she owns everything from the youngest babe to the oldest servant!" Fiskal started pacing once more. "I know that they have a navy there. The Bohr care not for ship life of course, but there are humans there who do their bidding. Imagine a human, working willingly for the Bohr. The unions do nothing. That is why the Republic exists! What else are we to do in the face of such power?" He leaned on the map, and Kyira felt an uncontrollable urge to hit him for doing so. "What would you do in face of such power?"

Kyira took her knife out once more, she placed it upon the middle sea and spun it. "I used to have two blades. One which was gifted to me from my father, and another that belonged to a man named Duga, who was one of the fastest men I ever saw fight. I had them reforged together into this, a new blade. One of which I used to stab my own brother upon the Waybridge, and the other I used to kill a Banèman."

Rollo's laugh boomed, but Fiskal's face held firm. His eyes widened as they fell upon the blade, and it stopped in front of him, pointing at his heart. "You killed a Banèman?"

Kyira nodded. "I killed Jagar as he killed my father. He is gone forever because of my actions that day." Darc was watching her intently as she spoke, watching every word leave her lips. "He was the strongest Banèman, and I killed him. But I almost didn't leave with my life that day. Of the six people who entered that tent, only three left alive. Duga was reduced to ash, Eoin's heart was willed to stop beating and Iqaluk, my father, had his chest burned through with a bar of pure fire. Soulfire. The fire within. The camp caught fire afterwards, and many people died in their tents asleep. Others were badly burned. That was his legacy. I decided there and then that I would end the Banèmen, or that I would find a way to end them. To bring their unnatural strength to an end. The Bohr are one thing, but the Banèmen are pure evil. And there are many still out there. I met another at Kamsin. Akosh. A being who can move faster than the wings of a humbird."

Fiskal's eyes had gone wide. He resumed his pacing back and forth behind the table, muttering to himself. The midday sun behind burned the thick air in the tavern. The bar, which should have been bustling with people, was empty because they were all outside, signing up to the Republican army.

"Kyira. I want you to join us. My day today started as any other, but I fear I cannot carry on past the night without you by my side. If we are to succeed, we will need all the help and all the experience we can get. I cannot turn down the opportunity to stand alongside someone like you." Fiskal placed a hand on Kyira's side and Milli growled. "Come with me, Kyira. Come see what I have built." He let go but stayed close enough that she could smell the sweet odour of his sweat. "The Republican army is my legacy. I must know what you think about all I have created here upon the beaches of Bakla."

"You think a unified force will oust the Bohr once and for all?"

Fiskal ambled over to the table and picked up the wine bottle. He pulled the cork and took a long drink. "Yes. I do." A knowing smile spread across his face, and he lifted his shirt to reveal hundreds of Lines painted upon his chest and stomach, depicting battles, lands, lovers, all wound together by a master Liner. Kyira's breath had seemingly stuck in her throat, and without thinking she brought her hand to her face.

"You are Sami?" she said, aghast.

Fiskal's grin widened even further. "Not Sami, not like you, Kyira. But I am from Nord. And that is why we will win. We will triumph over the Bohr because they have never met our likes before. They have never met the intelligence nor the honour and pride of our people. We are unconquerable. We are many. We are Nord."

32

KEEPSAKE

If Abika's head was a jug of water, then it was overflowing, her thoughts spilling over so that all she could think about was *her*.

What did she look like? Was she soft or hard? Would she love Abika? The last thought caught her off-guard, and conjured a sick feeling in her stomach. Perhaps it was the blur of the road trundling by beyond her vision, or Vasta's sidelong glances in her direction; the very air felt close enough to strangle her.

"I recognise this road..."

Abika jerked around to the back of the cart. "Lorith? You're awake!"

"Why have we come to the commune?"

"Because this is your home." She climbed over the back panel and tried to sit alongside him, inadvertently bumping Lorith's side.

"Ah!" Lorith screwed his eyes shut. "Watch it Bee!" His face was flushed and beaded with sweat. His eyelids fluttered as he spoke. "You were always all knees and elbows..."

"Lorith, try not to talk." She whacked Vasta in the back and the Bohr nodded and urged the nara on. "We're almost home. Tell me that story again."

Lorith's breaths came shallow. "Which one. The one where you killed that...that fucking pig for no reason?"

"Whichever one you want Lorith. Just keep talking." She stroked his hair and Vasta's song filled her head. "I didn't just kill it for no reason, brother."

"No? It looked like you did."

The trees hurtled by, but they were still three field lengths away from the bay and the commune. "I did it...because the sow was sick."

"She wasn't sick, Abika. But you are."

"What? No, I—"

Lorith sat up, in pain and shaking, and looked her in the eye. "It's not a bad thing. This world is cruel. It doesn't let up. Not ever. You think I chose to leave?"

"Jekob told us—"

"He lied, Bee. So did Freja, but it was Jekob who forced her hand. He is the biggest liar of them all. Freja was always kind to me." He licked his dry lips and turned his head towards the water appearing through the trees. "I was so sad to leave."

"Why didn't you come back?"

Lorith began to cry, tears falling from his red-rimmed eyes. "Pride? I was determined to do better than they thought of me. Than *he* thought of me."

"You did do better Lorith." Abika wiped her face. "You took me in. You took in Alar and his brother. You looked after the hidden and homeless when no one else would."

Lorith's eyes were rolling. "Do you think he would have been proud?"

Abika bit her lip, urging the anger bubbling up from her stomach to stay where it was. She swallowed hard, but the words still came out all cracked. "Jekob would have been so proud."

Lorith leaned back and Abika helped him down. "He knew where I was, Bee. All the time. I was no stranger to the citadel cells. Although, I never broke out of them before!" He laughed, but it caught and became a ragged cough.

Abika lifted his shirt. His stomach and ribs were black. "Oh, Lorith."

"Bee. Listen to me. You have to keep fighting. You were always stronger than me. Always. Some...might call it a sickness. I call it strength." He smiled over Abika's shoulder as the bay came into view. "You never belonged here."

Abika began to cry. “No, I didn’t.”

Lorith grabbed her wrist. “They’re afraid of you, Bee. They all are. Do what you must, but don’t lose that. Fear keeps people in check. If they fear you, they respect you...Being feared is everything.”

Vasta made a noise and they pulled to a stop near where Abika and Meorith used to smoke. The bay lapped behind them expectantly. It sounded like home, but it wasn’t.

“You stay here,” said Abika, turning to Vasta. “I’ll ride him up.”

Vasta stepped down from the cart and Abika took the reins. “Ya!” The old nara surged forwards, galloping past the crater at the bottom of the commune path, past the still-broken pipes jutting out of the ground like spindly roots, before skidding to a stop where the path became narrow. Everything was different—smaller somehow. The commune itself was half the size she remembered, but nothing had changed. It was still the same place, the same paths she’d run down to meet Jekob coming back from the fields.

The commune doors flung open, and Freja ran towards her, then Meorith appeared from the kitchen entrances, a similar look of fear and concern upon her face.

“Jekob!” shouted Freja, long before she reached the cart. “Jekob, my heart!”

“It’s not him!” shouted Abika.

“Lorith? Gods!” Freja looked Abika dead in the eye. “What have you done with Jekob?”

“What have I done with him? That piece of shit?”

Stars exploded in Abika’s eyes, as the force of Freja’s slap almost threw her clean out of the cart.

“You dare speak of your father in such a way.”

Abika yawned off the pain in her jaw. “He is not my father. And you, Freja, you are not my mother.”

“Oh, not this again, Abika. Meorith, come help me with Lorith.”

“Lorith?” Meorith sped up and skidded to a stop by the cart. “Oh no!” Meorith sobbed as she lifted Lorith’s shirt. “Lorith! Can you hear me?”

“Abika!” snapped Freja. “What happened?”

Abika glared back. “The Order of the White Dragon happened. You want to know how our brother came to be knocking upon death's door? Jekob did this. That's who."

Freja's hand came up again, but Abika was ready, she blocked the slap and delivered one of her own. There wasn't room to put real strength behind it, but she was higher up than Freja and it served its purpose.

Freja stared at her, mouth agape. "You dare—"

There was no turning back now. "I dare like you dared to drive out my real mother, forcing her to leave me behind with you!"

"Jekob told you of her?"

"Yes, he told me of *her*! You drove Kyira out like a dog. My own mother!"

Freja snarled. "I did no such thing! Kyira disappeared, and left you with us! Meorith take him into the house."

Meorith had lifted Lorith off the cart. Say one thing for Meorith, but she was as strong as an ox. "He needs attention, Mother. He's not well."

"I can see that, girl! Take him inside."

Meorith offered Abika a pitiful glance before hauling Lorith up the path to the commune. "I could have taken him up."

"No," said Freja. "Abika. You will not come up to the house, because I forbid it. You will go and never come back here."

Abika swallowed. "You think I want to go back in there? With you? Maybe we can play happy families?"

Freja's expression turned sour. "How many cycles I wasted trying to get through to you, Abika. How much of my life did I waste forgiving your sins?"

"And my mother's sins?"

"What?"

"Jekob told me. Or at least, he told me some of it. I put the rest together myself. You see I had the time available to me, sitting in a jail cell in the citadel." Freja's mock look of concern sickened Abika to the bone. "He told me everything. You drove my mother out after Jekob slept with her." The silence was wondrous. The effect of the words settling on Freja like water to drown her in. She deserved this and far more, and Abika was savouring it all. She leapt down off the cart, standing as tall as she could. "He slept with her, and you took him back.

What sort of woman does that? What of your self-respect? What of your—"

"Of what?" Freja's eyes were welling up. "Of my hurt, of my pain at such a betrayal? Well, seeing as you're apparently old enough to have this conversation with me, Abika, let me tell you the truth. Jekob, my heart, didn't just sleep with Kyira. He *loved* her. He loved us both."

Abiak swallowed. "Jekob loved my mother?"

"What?" scoffed Freja. "Are you imagining a life where Jekob was your father? Kyira your mother?" She smirked through the tears. "None of it would have been true."

"More lies!" growled Abika, through sobs of her own.

"Oh, Abika, you should know by now that I don't lie." She leant against the cart, stroking the nara between his two antlers. The nara lifted his head in pleasure. "In fact, Abika, seeing as we're being completely honest, I have some gifts for you. That is what your name means isn't it? God's gift? Well, child you were no gift to me."

"What do you—"

"Kyira isn't your mother."

Abika's legs felt like they were going to collapse beneath her. Everything, the trees, the path, the house, the nara tossing its head. Reality was crumbling... "Kyira is not—"

"You heard me." The real Red Isles was coming out in Freja now. She was channelling her words like they were spears, each with a sharp tip aiming at Abika's heart. "I'll say it again. Kyira is not your mother."

"You lie..." The words were more a whimper.

"The little fairytale you have in your mind of a perfect world where my Jekob is your father and Kyira is your mother is false. They would have been just two more parents that you couldn't call your own."

Abika tried to speak, but nothing came out. Her throat was too dry.

"Kyira came here with you," said Freja. "But she looked nothing like you. Nothing at all."

"But, my father..."

"No, no. Your real father was not from Kemen either." A light flickered in Freja's eyes. "Kyira would know who your real father was though. And I say *was* because he is dead. How might Kyira know that? Because she told Jekob what she did. And Jekob told me. Yes, he might have slept with her, he might have loved her, Abika. My own husband in love with another woman, making love to her under my own roof! He felt the guilt of that shame as keen as a knife! But he told me everything there was to know about Kyira. Everything!" She bit off the last word like it was a bitter fruit.

"No," said Abika, barely able to breathe. "It can't be...It can't—"

"Kyira is not your mother. And she killed, she murdered, your real father, Abika. That was why she brought you to us. She held you in a mother's embrace, but not for life, but for guilt. For shame. For fear."

Abika wanted to vomit. Her mind was a turbulent mass of anger and fear, burning her away and leaving her with nothing. "You're lying."

Freja took Abika's hand. "You know I do not lie, for I know your father's name was Isak, and Kyira murdered him. She cut his throat in the night. You'll know how that feels now, won't you? The feel of a blade as it slices through the throat of a being that deserves better." Freja was close now, talking to her like she was a child again. "What's the matter little one? Can't you talk? Well, let us leave it there, shall we? This is the gift I leave with you, Abika. Take it, take them all. They belong to you now."

She held on for another second and then let go and Abika's hand flopped to the side, banging against the cart wheel. The pain didn't register because her body was numb to the core. She had nothing left. She was no one.

33

SOMETHING FROM NOTHING

Abika clenched her fist. She had no idea what was inside, yet it was still hers, and hers alone to wield. Freja had been right, it was a gift. The animals she had killed that had been chopped up for food were full of muscle, sinew and bone.

"We all look the same on the inside." Her voice cracked.

Tears fell freely as she watched Vasta pick up a round rock the size of a dinner plate, studying it like it was a thousand cycles old. The urge to snatch it from the fool Bohr and crack it over his head was so strong. Violence was always the easy answer to a question asked. Even in Abika's short life, it had never bothered her to see others suffer. We are all equal, we are all capable. Look after yourself. Maybe it was a lesson she had learned from Jekob because it certainly hadn't been taught to her. Not that she remembered. But then, if you didn't know what was inside, how could you claim to really *know* anything?

Vasta launched the rock low and fast over the bay. It skipped and skipped and skipped until it was almost out of sight.

"Good one," murmured Abika.

The Bohr looked at her thoughtfully. Was it sympathy? Perhaps she was finally getting better at understanding his expressions. "It did not go as you expected," he said, flatly. Everything he said was flat.

Abika wiped her eyes. "I am not sure what I expected, Vasta. I have no expectations. I have nothing." She picked up a skimmer herself. "I am nothing."

"If I have learned anything, child, it is that we are all nothing. The most common belief in the universe is that our lives are governed or are parts of larger designs. But the truth of it is that we are but a by-product of the stars. A side effect."

"A side effect?" Abika shook her head. "That does not make me feel better."

"It is the truth though."

"You truly believe there are no Gods?"

"I do. We must carve our own path in this life. Look at you. You brought your brother back to his home. That is something at least to be proud of."

Abika couldn't help but feel sick. "I brought him home to die." She picked at the pockmarks on the stone. "And Lorith is not my brother."

"We are all of us, siblings. Brothers and sisters. Besides, I'd rather die surrounded by loved ones than in a stinking prison cell covered in my own muck." Vasta folded his great arms. "What did you learn from your—"

"Don't call her my mother, Vasta." Abika turned on him. "That's what you were going to say, wasn't it?"

"For lack of a better word."

"Her name is Freja." It was strange ordering around a being so much stronger than she, but by the bloody gods (or whatever the bloody hell was out there) she would do it anyway. "I don't know what hurts more, the lies, or that Jekob was right."

Vasta frowned. "Right about what?"

She swallowed and let out a long sigh. "Isak, my real father, is dead."

"Isak. That is the name that Guard of the White Dragon mentioned in my shop. I do not know what happened there, but that guard appeared to know you."

"The man in your shop, the leader, he is Jekob, and he is as dead to me as his wife, Freja. They grew me. Raised me like one of their pigs." Abika turned towards the commune. The house sat nestled amongst a band of trees on both sides, as it had been every time she had looked at it from this part of the bay. It stood proudly, familiar and yet unfamiliar. "My time here is up, Vasta."

"What will you do?"

"What?"

Vasta shrugged. "We all must have a thing to do, and a place to go."

"I have nothing!" shouted Abika. "I am...nothing."

"Perhaps not. You still have the shard."

Abika yanked the stone from her neck and went to throw the thing in the bay.

"No!" said Vasta, grabbing her arm.

"Get off me!" New tears fell. "Just get off."

"No," growled Vasta. "First of all, it is not yours to cast aside. It is mine. Even if I gifted it to you. Secondly, if it is all that you have, then why throw it away. There might not be any Gods, but that does not mean there are not rules that bind us. Your mo—Freja, stole that from me, as you stole it from her."

"You talk in riddles." Abika tried to pull away from his iron grip. "Let go of me, Bohr." Vasta let go but stepped in front of her, his vast bulk blocking any notions she might have had of throwing the shard in the water.

"I did not want to tell you yet," said Vasta, " because you are not ready, but that shard will give you power."

Abika opened her palm. "Power?"

"The power of the worlds." His big eyebrows leapt upwards. "It amplifies what you have."

Abika stared at him, confused.

"You did not know this?" Then abruptly he was scrutinising her like a spider in a jar. "I am sorry, I thought you knew about your gifts. The shard enhances you. I am not quite sure why yet, but I have a feeling I will know very soon." He pushed a clawed finger into her chest at her heart. "It amplifies everything you have inside, Abika. It is why you heard me sing, while you were imprisoned in the citadel. It is, in part, why I am here. I am a scholar, and you and that stone shard are the most interesting things I have come across in my long life thus far."

The fog in Abika's head parted for a moment. "What I have inside?" She closed her fingertips together. The calmness wouldn't come now, she was too emotional, and her thoughts too erratic. She focused her thoughts on Jekob, Freja and Kyira and the anger sparked inside of her like a fire starting. She stood above it, stoking it with her will. Drawing it into herself.

"The power is called Soulfire," said Vasta, his bushy eyebrows coming together. "It is energy stolen from other worlds."

The words didn't make sense. "I am a weapon?"

Vasta hesitated, then shook his head. "No. Soulfire is a tool."

"A weapon is a tool," said Abika, feeling a familiar warmth at her fingertips. "For killing. I just need a target." She shook her head, then scoffed. "And I have a target, Vasta."

Vasta stepped back. "Kyira?"

Kyira killed her father. Isak was his name. Why did he have to die? Why couldn't she have met him, or better still, loved him and been grown by him? The heat grew. Who was Kyira, and how dare she? She blinked at Vasta, unsure if she had spoken or not. "Some people deserve to die."

Heat blossomed at Abika's chest. She pulled it inward stoking the flame, and it spread through her limbs. At first it was like stepping into a warm bath, growing hotter until every muscle, bone, and sinew was burning. Quickly it became a light she could no longer control. Fed by her rage the heat became too much to bear.

She opened her eyes. Vasta had backed off; he had a boulder in his hand, as though Abika could suddenly hurt him. The thought took flight like a morning bird, and exhilaration replaced rage. A bright light burned forth, so white she couldn't see.

"Not here!" growled Vasta. "You will kill us both!"

She wanted to unleash it against the Bohr, but a torrent of fatigue washed over her. The light extinguished and the ground came up to meet her. Mud, dirt and dried seaweed cracked against her face.

"Uhhh." Abika felt nauseous. Numbness had spread throughout her body, and her limbs were dead weight.

Vasta snarled like an angry goril. "Did you not hear me, stupid girl!"

She tried to argue with this fool of a Bohr, but the words wouldn't form. Fatigue sat upon her like a heavy blanket, suffocating her. "Pick me up!" The words were unintelligible, like she had smoked too much. "Pick me up!"

Vasta dropped the boulder and lifted her like a doll, sitting her up.

"What was that?"

"I...you're not ready, yet."

"Tell me!"

"Abika. You are special in ways you cannot possibly realise. But no. I will not tell you. My thoughts are incomplete. It would be wrong to guess as to the nature of your power."

Abika's head lolled to the side. She couldn't lift it, not even to look Vasta in his stupid face. "What are you talking about."

The world suddenly moved, colours rushing by, and then she was being set down on Vasta's tiny stupid cart.

The Bohr looked down at her, nodding. "Like this shard, you are special, Abika. For now though, child, sleep."

Abika wanted to hit him, to fight him and shout at him. Even as the cart began to move, and they joined the path towards the main road, and the commune became smaller and smaller, she still wanted to hurt Vasta. She wanted to hurt him in ways he had never known, until he screamed in pain and begged for death. The anger persisted long after the place she had once called home vanished behind the trees. The commune was all that she had ever known and ever loved. But now she was cast out into the unknown. She had nothing. She was nothing. And as that final thought in her head began to fade and draw her into a warm and familiar darkness, she took Freja's shard necklace in her hand and held it tight. She did have something. She had power, and she would use it to deliver justice to the woman who killed her parents.

34

THE RIDDLE OF THE ESCAPED CHILD

Jekob reached over and raised his glass, lifting it up to the midday sun and enjoying the glow of the amber liquid sloshing around inside. The clay signet ring Kyira had given him so long ago clanked against the glass. It must have been ten cycles old now. Freja had asked him where he had gotten it the day Kyira had left, and of course Jekob had lied. The affair had been short, but it had burned bright, and she still haunted his soul. He had spent most of his life lying, playing roles to suit the situation. It was partly why he sat now in the stronghold of the Order of the White Dragon, confident about who he was and what he was doing. Freja knew that he lied, but she never spoke of it and so he carried on. What else was there to do?

The baths were one of his favourite places, but they were popular with everyone. Perhaps it was the emergence of spring flowers that brought out the freshness in people. The baths were full of the bouncy, springy flesh of new adults. Young folk who were adamant that the Order of the White Dragon was the only way the Bohr and humanity could live harmoniously. It didn't take much to convince impressionable minds to join the Order's cause, especially under the pretence of regular food and sleep. Ipor Dan slums were only getting bigger, and all to the benefit of the Order.

He drank in the naked bodies, basking in the sunlight. Today, sadly, it was only Vard and him in this bath. The other baths had at least five people in each one, with soft, wandering hands and feet. He glanced at Vard, who looked blissfully unaware of all that was going on, or he was just enjoying the fruits of his hard-earned promotion.

"Penny for your thoughts?"

Vard blinked. "Huh?"

"You're frowning, but a moment ago you looked as smug as a mouse who had found the cheese."

Vard tapped his lips. He was unable to think unless literally drawing the thoughts from his head. "Well, I was just thinking." He took a slurp of his beer. "You know Vasta? Well, how did the Bohr know about Zular?"

"He didn't know."

Vard looked taken aback. "I could have sworn—"

Jekob shook his head. "No, Vard. The Bohr knows Zular, but he doesn't know about what has happened to Zular. That was why Losa stared you down."

"So I would keep my mouth shut?"

Jekob inclined his head a little. "Exactly. Because you talk too much."

"Right." Vard frowned again. "So, where is Zular? It's been an age since I laid eyes on that fellow."

"He's in Koroeil, I believe."

"Kemen?"

Jekob held up his beer glass. "This is us on this side," he said pointing to the right side of the glass near the handle. "Koroeil is about here, in the exact opposite side of the circle of the world."

"So, quite far."

"Yes," said Jekob, amused. "Very far. But we've got to get the word out somehow. Don't we? The Order of the White Dragon will find every corner of the world."

"Well, the Circle of the World, doesn't really have corners thought does it?" Vasta smirked. "I take your point though, Captain. So, Vasta was right then? We are recruiting for the Order of the White Dragon in Kemen?"

"Closer to Hatàr, but yes." Jekob held up the glass again. "The

Speaker knows about it. In fact, it was Ohalo's idea." The reflections bounced around, and the mirrored image of Losa's breasts filled the glass. "Mostly." He held it a second longer, before putting it down.

Losa scowled at him as she settled into the bubbling water. "There are other baths."

"Yes," said Jekob, "and I...We were here first, Losa."

"I know." She shot him a sickly smile. "But I like this one. The sun hits it full on, and besides, the others all sit below the blossom trees."

"They're not shaded," said Jekob. "They get the sun too."

Losa sneered, it was the only expression he really ever saw on her. "They drop needles and seeds into the water, and I don't like it. They get everywhere." Jekob gave her his best dead-eyed glare in the hope she would just get up and leave.

"So, nothing to do with the young tits and ass filling each one?" said Jekob.

"She's afraid she won't fit in." Vard sniggered.

Losa leaned back and sighed. "This is the best bath, and you know it."

Vard nudged Jekob, winking as Losa's breasts lifted above the surface of the water. "This *is* the best bath."

The water sloshed as Losa's toe kicked up between Vard's legs. "Stop it, you pig!"

Vard turned away, holding his bare knees to his chest. "You bitch!"

Losa stood up in front of him, in all her glory. "You want a look, you snivelling weasel? Next time it won't be a toe that finds that saggy nutsack, but a knife!"

Vard raised a hand. "Alright, Losa. Alright."

"She can demote you too, you know."

Losa sat back down. "Shut up, Jekob. You looked as well. And you are worse. You have a wife. And children."

Jekob ground his teeth. "They're not my children."

Losa stretched her arms back out over the back of the sunken bath. "It seems strange that you would insist on being so clear about such a detail, Jekob. Are you not proud of your children?"

Jekob suppressed the anger bubbling up inside. "It's just a matter of terminology, Losa."

"I doubt that, Jekob." She regarded him, her gaze sharp. "A pragmatic man such as you does not strike me as one who cares for labels over his family. The substance of things. Well, what has more substance than family?"

"Is that a rhetorical question, Losa?"

Losa sneered. "Is that a label? No? Let me elaborate on my line of thinking. The girl who escaped this very citadel, Abika, I think her name was. Did you know her?"

"I did," said Jekob. "I do. What of her?"

"Abika is not your daughter?"

"She is most definitely not my daughter, Losa. Freja is barren."

Losa shook her head. "Barren? You're disgusting, Jekob. If I didn't say it before, she's a lucky lady."

Vard reached to the bottom of the bath, soaking his ginger beard in the process. He held up the glass towards Losa now very much devoid of beer. "I'm just getting the glass! Calm thyself."

Losa eyed him suspiciously then turned back to Jekob. "So, if she is not yours," she said, loudly. "Whose is she? Who are the parents of this girl in her twelfth who was able to escape the royal citadel of Ipor Dan. Tell me, Jekob. Please." She sat up arms folded.

Jekob was fuming, but he couldn't let Losa see that. It was exactly what she was after. He glanced around to find that others were listening, the baths were full of blinking eyes waiting for an answer to the riddle of the escaped child.

"Abika is very resourceful, but tell me, Losa, do you think it was the actions of the twelve-cycle-old child who masterminded that escape and injured poor Staegrim, or was it the tom'ra dealer who escaped with her? I'm hearing a lot of accusations for someone who is running on second-hand information."

Losa's eye twitched. She was trapped in a hole of Jekob's making. He had put her there, and now she had only one option, and she took it.

"I guess we'll never know the real truth will we." She stood up and stepped out of the bath, turning to the other officers. "The Bohr rule us all. We were created by the Great Mother as subordinates, and for that we must be grateful. We might be the lesser species in the eyes of the Bohr, but that doesn't mean we cannot coexist! It is our duty to preserve the natural order of Rengas. That is our manifesto." Just as Jekob was wondering where she was going with this, she turned and pointed directly at him. "And the truth is something we hold especially dear here at the Order of the White Dragon. It is what sets us free from the dark, maintains the bond of our oath to create a world where a true, natural hierarchy reigns. Truth is life." She smiled glumly. "Life. Is. Truth. Those who lie will all be ousted." She stood there, a martyr, a statue to the cause of the Order, without covering, and behind her the heads of those officers Jekob had come to know so well over the past fifteen cycles of service nodded with her. Even the young folk were nodding in agreement. Fresh in the door, without a clue supporting whatever cause happened to be loudest.

Jekob held her stare. He could do nothing else until finally she walked away and the unceasing sun reappeared bright and blinding in her wake.

Vard leaned in. "Losa is beating you down, Jekob."

"Yes!" snapped Jekob. He took a long breath, composing himself. "Yes, Vard. I know. The problem, is that she's very good at it."

"She's doing it to everyone." Vard, once again, studied his glass like a man who had lost everything. "Some fuck their way to the top, others climb."

"Using their associates as footholds."

Vard bit his lip. "She knows how to captivate an audience and make no mistake! It's hard not to pay attention to those curves when they're all out there in front of you. And that skin. She's a fucking dragon in human form." Vard shuffled a bit closer, creating waves in the warm water. "Ohalo is next. I'm certain of it. She wants to be Speaker, and if you're not careful Jekob, she'll get it too. Then we'll be bound to her. She could have you killed in the street and there wouldn't be a damned thing you could do about it. Hell, she'd probably be there holding the blade."

"Speaker Ohalo isn't that old."

Vard scoffed. "He's long since checked out, Jekob. Checked out and ready for the Great Mother. Losa could just walk into his chambers and flash him, and he'd be dining with the Gods, discussing the shapeliest breasts ever seen on any woman since Baeivi herself." He shook his head. "She's way ahead of you."

Jekob leaned back, closing his eyes against the sunlight. "I do have some semblance of a plan, Vard. It's just been put on hold while I try and figure out what to do with Abika and Lorith. I can't believe I let them escape!"

"Don't beat yourself up, Jekob. You taught her well." Vard scratched his forehead and lowered his voice. "I'll support you. You know that, right? But you have to play the game! Get this plan of yours back on its legs, otherwise Losa will beat you to Speaker. I'd much rather you were the one standing above us all, but I will follow her if I have to."

Jekob stared down those inquisitive eyes in the other baths. "There's only one way to deal with someone like Losa," he uttered.

Vard nodded, then caught himself. Frowning, he moved his lips as if to conjure the answer, trying it on for size. "Murder?" He hissed. "You can't be serious? That's your play?"

"I am serious." Jekob studied every micro-movement of Vard's face. Losa was not well liked amongst the Order of the White Dragon, and her uncouthness and competitive nature would make it easy for her to be lifted out of the ranks, but he couldn't do it alone. "Can I count on you, Vard?" The man didn't realise it, but his own life depended on the next words to leave his mouth. Jekob had a vial of spidro in his quarters that he'd found in Lorith's room after Losa had finished with it. It was a potent mixture, spidro, and like its name suggests, is retrieved from a special spider that lives in the sea-ice holes between Nord and Ipiti. They're small, only the size of a thumbnail, but their venom delivers a quick death that looks like a heart attack.

"Of course, Jekob. Of course I am with you." Vard nodded. "It seems a shame though, to rid the world of those curves." He sighed, and took a swig of bathwater from his glass.

"Captain Jekob!"

Jekob turned to the porter. "What?"

The porter took a hurried breath. "There's a Bohr here!"

"What?" Jekob leapt out of the bath. "Where?"

Vard jumped out standing dripping on the warm flags at Jekob's side. "A Bohr? Are you sure?"

"Very sure, Captain. He's waiting at the front of the citadel now."

It had to be Vasta, and if Vasta was here, so Abika might be. But there was something in the porter's eye, news he had yet to give. "What else? What's he done?"

"The Bohr killed the gate guard."

Vard blinked. "Jekob, Vasta would never—"

Jekob grabbed his tunic. "Vard get dressed. Armour. If it isn't Vasta, then we need to be prepared. Understand? We'll need a full fist of men, no less."

Vard nodded and they both sprinted naked and soaking towards the armoury.

V'Laerk tasted the human's blood. It was coppery, and very unlike Bohr blood. Like it was made from iron. Ironic then that their bodies were so weak. He smeared the rest above his eyebrows and growled. "Tell me about the Order."

The three guards stared at each other dumbly. They had no idea because they were just idiots with swords standing all day in front of the Citadel in case trouble decided to arrive. Well, trouble was here. V'Laerk picked up the gate guard he had killed and threw his body at the other guards' feet. The sound of their friend hitting cobbles like a sack of meat drew winces and fear.

"Stand back!" came their uncertain chorus.

"Is this the Order or is it not?" growled V'Laerk.

The man in the middle, an aged warrior who smelt like cheese and wine, stepped forward to speak. "We are the Order of the White Dragon."

"The White Dragon is the sigil of the Bohr. How can you be the Order of the White Dragon if there are no Bohr here?"

The guards looked between themselves. "We are the Order of the White Dragon."

"Who is in charge?"

"The Speaker."

"And where is he—"

V'Laerk stepped aside as a spear flew past him. It had a good speed on it, but it would never have pierced his hide. He followed the trajectory back to the thrower, another man, clad in white armour. He stood there legs apart, and even from this distance V'Laerk could see he was prepared to die.

"You are the Speaker?"

"No, I am Leader Jekob."

V'Laerk shook his head. "A Leader who speaks, but not a Speaker who leads?"

The man seemed to hesitate, but it wasn't the foolish inner workings of a henchman, this was a thinking man. Thinking humans were dangerous. More guards appeared behind him, all dressed in white, running in from the great doors of the citadel. They stood behind Leader Jekob in a line.

"Ah now," said V'Laerk with great pleasure. "This is more fitting for a Bohr such as I."

"Why did you kill the guard?" demanded Leader Jekob.

"Why?" growled V'Laerk. "Because it was his time. His family will exalt when they find out a Bohr killed him. They will celebrate him for cycles to come. I have done his bloodline a favour of unspeakable purity. Not all get to die by the hands of a Bohr, not least this Bohr, Right Hand to the Queen of Zunqai herself." There was some murmuring in the background, as well there should be.

The thinking human blinked at him but said nothing.

"Leader Jekob, I suggest you escort me to your actual leader, this *Speaker* of yours so that we may speak on leadership." V'Laerk couldn't help but smirk at the joke. It was a good one indeed, and one he'd been itching to let out.

"He's an idiot," whispered Vard. "But he's got a point."

Jekob raised his chin, inside he felt a riotous mess of emotion and fear, and as much as he tried to hold it back, he was sure this Bohr would smell it on him. But what choice did he have? "What is your name, Bohr?"

"You and no other may ask my name," said the Bohr. "V'Laerk,"

"Then V'Laerk, I suggest you follow me. The Speaker will be anxious to meet you."

35

TALK AND TEACUPS

Speaker Ohalo was poring over a map of Ipiti when Jekob walked in with V'Laerk. Ohalo peered over his eyeglasses, pausing for a moment. Perhaps he was counting the inches V'Laerk's head stood below the high ceiling, which wouldn't have taken long, or perhaps he was simply trying to understand what, or who, had stumbled into his domain so unannounced. Regardless, he dropped his eyes back to the map, drawing a line with a right angle between two points somewhere in the north.

In Jekob's experience, and when faced conflict, people could be summed up into a number of categories. There were those who faked their emotions, those who pretended to be busy, and those who plain forgot who or what they were. The latter was usually the most unpredictable and dangerous. Jekob himself was very much amongst the first, and adept at it too. Speaker Ohalo, however, was the exception to the rule. The man had simply reached an age where the only thing that mattered to him was the Order of the White Dragon and its success. If a conversation he was a part of veered away from the topic, he would walk away. The fact a Bohr stood in front of him now seemed to him as interesting as the colour of the drapes covering his office window.

After a long minute, Losa coughed and Ohalo looked up. "Yes," was all he said.

"You may give my name," said V'Laerk to Jekob. "And only you."

"This is V'Laerk," said Jekob, "Right Hand to Queen Kaliste."

Ohalo blinked slowly. "Kaliste? The Banèman?"

"The same," said V'Laerk, his voice as soft as a rug being torn. "Unless you know of another?"

"Which boat did you take?" asked Ohalo.

Jekob wished he could have turned to look at him, to see what was going on with that angry, animal face. He doubted he'd have been able to work it out anyway.

"I came through Dor. A Dor...way you might even say."

"Dor?" Ohalo took off his glasses. "Your boat landed in Dor?"

"You doubt me?"

"No. Of course not." Ohalo shuffled some papers around. "Dor is past Ipiti, so as a natural question I would wonder what brought you there before coming south. Such answers are not necessarily needed."

"And none shall be given." V'Laerk casually took Jekob and Losa by the throat.

Jekob swallowed his panic down, then glanced sidelong at Losa, trying his best to convince her not to protest. She stared back at him equally as panicked, but kept her cool.

"Let us put how I got here aside, Speaker Ohalo. Tell me about the Order of the White Dragon, and if I like the answer, I may let these two live. If not, then their families will talk of their deaths here today for the next fifty generations."

Ohalo nodded, and the tanned folds and wrinkles of his hairless head wobbled with him. "I may use your name?"

"You may," said V'Laerk, flashing his canines.

Ohalo looked to Jekob, and spoke quickly. "Leader Jekob, the honour of name falls to me now. Understand?"

Jekob gave a quick nod, trying to avoid swallowing past V'Laerk's crushing grip.

"The Order of the White Dragon," began Ohalo, "run Ipor Dan. We look after its citizens and police the streets." He started to pace back and forth behind his desk. "We have set our allegiances to the Bohr and their rule, blessed be the shadows of any Bohr who walk these halls, and so, as you are here, Bohr, you undoubtedly stand above us. I am Speaker Ohalo. I speak for all humans in this great city."

"You wish to be ruled by the Bohr, and yet you have no Bohr within the city to rule you?"

"Inconsequential," said Ohalo. "Bohr rule is the natural order."

"How many of you are there?"

"Nearly one thousand."

"A thousand?" Jekob abruptly found himself released. He resisted the urge to rub his neck.

Jekob listened as the words Losa had so eloquently spoken at the baths came from Ohalo. The speech went on for some time, covering everything from how humans were only here to be governed, all the way to the quest for truth under doctrine. Jekob was no liberalist, nor was he a rebel, but the old ways were getting boring. Jekob had joined the Order for the same reason most did, to provide security for Freja and the commune, and to build a better life for himself. After so many cycles of working within the citadel's walls and studying Bohr lore he had come around to the Rightful Order as it was known. Humans could either work with the Bohr, or they would die trying to fight them. It was as simple as that.

"My mouth is dry," said V'Laerk.

Ohalo nodded. "Mine too. Leaders Losa and Jekob. Between you could you please arrange some tea for the room. It seems Vard has snuck out."

Jekob turned to see that Vard had indeed left the room, though he couldn't have said when.

"Of course, Speaker," said Losa, quickly. "Come with me, Jekob."

Jekob ground his teeth at the lack of a correct title, but followed silently behind her. After the doors closed behind them, she rounded on him. "You can go."

"Really, can I?"

"Of course," Losa caught herself. "You're being sarcastic."

Jekob shook his head. "Losa, the Great Mother just dropped a fucking Bohr into our laps. If you think I am going anywhere else, you are sorely mistaken." He flagged down a passing servant. "Now, you get the tea, I'll mind the room."

With one hand on the door handle behind him, he pulled, silencing Losa's retort, and then he was back in the lion's den.

Ohalo and V'Laerk bounced around strategy, resources and the landscape of Ipiti while Jekob stood in the back listening.

"The land of Ipiti is largely flat," said Ohalo. "We are not volcanic like some of the islands of Sulitaria, but there are some places where deep fissures create high cliffs. We are centrally bound and are easily the most powerful and richest of the islands." Ohalo sounded like a salesman trying to sell fruit at the market, but for an entire island of people. "Our soldiers are all very well trained, coming from all walks of life."

A knock at the door announced Losa had returned with a tray of tea, plus an array of raw meats. "I took the liberty—"

"And how quickly can the Order mobilise?" said V'Laerk. "What are the plans for expanding the Order to other islands. Sulitar for instance."

Losa put the tray down carefully in front of the now seated Bohr and Ohalo. V'Laerk took the bigger cup, drained it, then grabbed a handful of raw meat while Ohalo answered.

"Sulitar is an island with many different denominations. In people, religion and even currency. We can't just—"

"I want you to expand into Sulitar immediately," growled V'Laerk. "Leave a small force here in Ipiti, perhaps twenty percent, under my proxy rule, and I will take the rest of you over sea to Sulitar."

Ohalo was pouring himself a tea when he was interrupted. He set the charn kettle down, leaving his cup only half full. "Proxy rule? And eighty percent of our forces? For what?"

V'Laerk smiled. There was no other word for it. His teeth bared, and his lips curled upward. "To bring the message of the Bohr to the heathens of Sulitar, of course. You will stay here, Speaker Ohalo. But I will command the rest myself, with the help of Leader Losa here."

Jekob swallowed hard. He had to focus otherwise his legs would collapse beneath him.

"Of course, V'Laerk. I would be—"

The Bohr stood, knocking the chair back. "You dare speak my name! You have broken my honour!"

Ohalo, as brittle and old as he was, somehow managed to cross the room just as V'Laerk's hand took Losa by the throat.

There was nothing Ohalo could do, but he stepped in the way of the towering Bohr anyway. "V'Laerk, please. As much as Leader Losa would like to be honoured by you in this way, she has much yet to do here. She is demoted of course, but she is still very inexperienced."

V'Laerk seemed to think on it, then dropped Losa in a heap to the polished floorboards. "Fine. But your life is mine now, and I will choose at some point to take it. When I call, you will come. And if anyone else should take it before me, they will feel the wrath of the Kemen Empire fall upon their heads!"

Losa was ghostly pale, but somehow she found the courage to stand. She glanced at Jekob, her lip wobbling. "How am I to stand below *him*?" she uttered. "He who let his own daughter escape the citadel?"

"A girl escaped your fortress, Speaker Ohalo?"

Ohalo pounced on the change of subject. "Leader Jekob, care to explain?"

"The guards were afraid of her!"

"Losa!"

V'Laerk's red eyes turned slowly from Losa to Jekob. "Why would your guards be afraid of a little human girl?"

Jekob felt the pinch of Ohalo's speech keenly. He could not lie. "She is special."

"Special?" repeated V'Laerk.

"I wish I could tell you, Bohr. I helped grow her from a child, left by one who claimed to know her real mother, but she was always different. There is a darkness about her, and she kept secrets from us."

"Where is she now?" said V'Laerk.

"I don't know."

"In the hands of another Bohr," added Ohalo, "called Vasta. He owned a shop nearby."

V'Laerk nodded. "And why wasn't this Vasta the ruler your Order so craves?"

Jekob spoke first. "Vasta is not a ruler. He claims he is a scholar."

"There is no such thing inside of Zunqai," said V'Laerk. "Let alone out *here*."

"He may be Bohr by name," continued Jekob, "but he holds nothing to the traditions of Bohrkind. He is an enigma who has ignored our requests, and our kind, ever since he first arrived here."

V'Laerk stood. "Good. Then the plan holds. We leave tomorrow for Sulitar. Leader Jekob you will be my First and I again grant you use of my name." He bared his teeth in something resembling a smile. "If we are going to spread the good word of the Rightful Order across Sulitar then we may as well meet this heretic scholar Vasta of yours and hold him to account too."

———

The stench of fear was almost intolerable. Each human in the room seemed to be exhibiting a different flavour of it. Perhaps the strange new power that Kaliste has bestowed upon him also included a heightened understanding of those around him, because V'Laerk felt more attuned to his prey than ever before.

He left the humans to their talk and teacups and after being led through their pithy palace, closed his room door in the human woman Losa's face. He looked inward, and as his thoughts encircled Kaliste's there was a stirring in his groin.

"Kaliste."

"V'Laerk." The voice of the Queen sang in his mind as though she were standing in the quarters with him and not a thousand leagues away across the Middle Sea. *"What news?"*

"I am with the Order of the White Dragon. The finally have a Bohr who will show them the way."

Waves of pleasure returned to V'Laerk's groin, deep and caressing as the power of Kaliste took over his body. *"Good. Well done."*

V'Laerk smiled widely. *"They have a thousand here I can make use of. They will augment our own forces well."*

"No! They will not." The pleasure came to an abrupt halt. *"I cannot see why this doorway leads to Dor. There is no explanation for it, and I refuse to send the Queen's army, the strongest army the world has known, through to Dor. There is simply no use in it—"*

"Kaliste? Are you there?" The connection became warm once more.

The pleasure returning to V'Laerk's groin tenfold. He growled. And then as quickly as it came, the pleasure once more ground to a halt. He snarled.

"Be still, V'Laerk. I must go. It seems I have some work to do."

The connection winked out and V'Laerk howled long and hard into the low ceiling of his Citadel rooms.

36

THE RED ISLES

The Red Isles were two islands, the only residents of the mountainous northern island being a few thousand sheep. Both islands were twisting green hills and craggy coastlines, with hints of purple daubed in large patches all around. But, of course, it didn't matter what the bloody island looked like. It could have been floating in the sky for all Abika cared.

Jekob had told her that Kyira had come from the north heading south, and so Abika was going south. The woman who had killed Isak and perhaps even her real mother, must have left a trail somewhere. That's why Abika had trudged all the way through Ipiti to the southern towns, and it was why she was sitting on this gods-awful boat studying the Red Isles.

"Did you land here, Kyira?" Just saying her name was bitterness in Abika's mouth, astringent and chewy. Or was that just the salt air blasting her face. She hated boats.

The Myathar lurched and Abika grasped at the rickety guard rail of the boat's side, hoping to all the gods that it held. She felt worse than she ever had in her life. Once she had caught a cold from the children at the commune that had given her uncontrollable shivers and flashing lights in her eyes, and it paled in comparison to sea travel. After this journey, Abika resolved never to again set foot on another boat.

Vasta was sitting across from her, making awkward conversation with a woman who kept touching his arm whenever he spoke. Most had given them a wide berth, until Vasta opened his mouth and they all realised that the stories of Bohr who would kill them in their sleep were indeed just stories, and everyone knew that stories were just lies made up by the unkind.

After that it was open season; everyone wanted to know what a Bohr thought of every subject that could be probed. Vasta stared over at her, his eyes screaming.

"You got yourself in the mess, Bohr," she uttured. "You get yourself out." The woman with the blonde hair threw it over her shoulder and fell into Vasta's arms, laughing.

Vasta had given Abika his long coat, but underneath she had only her stinking shift, and no shoes. She drew the coat tighter, against the fresh sea breeze. At least her arms and legs were working again.

"Why did you leave me?" asked Vasta, easing down at her side. The boat creaked as his weight settled

"She let you away then?"

The woman had struck up a conversation with the man sitting next to her, presumably her husband. "She is persistent. Any question I asked her was immediately rebuked." He frowned down at her. "You are cold?"

"Yes, I am."

"You are withdrawing."

Abika shook her head in annoyance. "Withdrawing from what, Vasta?"

"The efforts involved with touching the power are significant." Vasta studied the Red Isles sliding along beside them. "Add to that your reliance on pipegreen—"

"Tom'ra?"

"It is a scourge on the streets, Abika, and if it doesn't kill you, you will fight and steal and lower yourself to anything just get more of it." He placed a huge hand upon her, a hand big enough to crush her head like an apple. "I've seen it happen. It is rife in parts of Ipor Dan and Iporiti."

Abika thought of Lorith lying dead at the commune. "Perhaps not for much longer."

Vasta studied her but said nothing. He probably knew Lorith was the cause of most of the ills within the slums of Ipor Dan.

"It helps me stay calm." When Vasta shook his head in apparent disgust, she turned on him. "What? You disagree?"

"Of course I disagree."

"Then what would you have me do? You wanted—" She lowered her voice. "You wanted to learn more about me *and* my power. Well, this is me. I am unbalanced. I cause chaos wherever I go. I am—"

"You are an unbalanced force, Abika. But that does not mean you are unbalanced. There is much you can learn about Soulfire and its place in the world."

But this Bohr was a fool! "Say it out loud, why don't you."

Vasta leaned towards her. "If I can maintain calm, so can you."

Abika balked. "You? Why do you need calm? You can't touch Soulfire."

"Not calm in the way you mean it. Meditation feeds the soul, Abika. But in my case, it helps cage the beast inside me. Equilibrium with my environment provides me with a peace that wraps itself tightly around my inner self."

Abika might have frowned, but she understood. Vasta was hiding his inner Bohr from the world, not because he was afraid of what others would do to him, but rather what he would do to others. She tilted her head, trying to see past the scholar to the beast within. "Is that why you are like you are, Vasta? Why you speak in riddles?"

"Why is anything like it is?"

Abika shook her head, irritated. "Whatever."

The Bohr took a long breath. "It is who I am, to question everything."

"Questioning everything and yet not offering up any answers of your own?"

"You are one to talk, Abika." Vasta probably thought he was lowering his voice and yet Abika was under no doubt that every other passenger on the Myathar could hear what he was saying. "I wanted to go north, and yet here we are travelling south. Explain to me why that is. South is Bohr territory. I do not wish to go there."

"You're just sore, Vasta, because you had to let the nara go."

"And my cart!" He sighed. "I modified that cart myself. That pawnbroker had no idea what he was buying, hence the paltry price he gave me. We should have taken it out of town, to a farm, or smithy."

"Once we've found where Kyira came from, we can return. Kyira holds the key to it all. We'll likely be heading north after that anyway. Then you can buy the damned nara back."

The blonde woman's husband appeared at Vasta's side, an awkward looking man with black hair. "Excuse me, um, Vasta. I, that is...My wife said that you worked with minerals. I do too. Is that why you're travelling to the Red Isles?"

"Minerals?" scoffed Vasta. "The Red Isles have no minerals I am interested in. I have catalogued all minerals on the east side of Rengas. I doubt much has changed in the twenty cycles since I was last here. Minerals take thousands of—"

"What about the tower?"

"The tower?" Vasta moved back over to the opposite side and once more the boat listed with him.

"Must be nice travelling with your own personal Bohr friend."

Abika turned to the man at her side. "He's not my friend." She had tried to put some timbre behind the words, but her stomach had protested and threatened instead to soak everyone, all ten of them, in vomit. She swallowed it back. "We have an...arrangement."

"Well, arrangement or no, you'll need to be careful. The Bohr are no much liked in Minerva, or really anywhere in the Red Isles." The shipman surveyed the sea around him. "First time out of Ipiti?"

"Yup."

"The Red Isles are beautiful, but wild. Don't let the countryside fool you into thinking the folks are the same."

"My mother is from the Red Isles." The words were out before she could stop them.

"What's her name?"

"Look, do you mind if I just..."

The shipman shrugged. "Course. Course. I'm Rothmarr"

Abika gave a half smile. "Itraeka."

"Nice to meet you, Itraeka." Something in Rothmarr's tone suggested he knew it wasn't her real name, but then he must meet many people who give false names. Convicts, murderers. Bastards.

"What does that mean?"

Rothmarr held up his hand and traced the inked symbol. "It's the sigil of the Tsiorc. We were the victors at the battle of Tyr. Tore the city to pieces with magic. The gods stood at our sides and we beat the Bohr King to the ground." He fingered the tattoo. "I always thought the triangle symbolised a shield."

"And the cross within it?"

"The beating heart of the resistance!"

Abika sighed. It seemed everywhere she went, people wanted to preach to her about the past. She nodded to the hazy purple hills growing larger on the horizon. "That heather growing there. Is that where the name comes from?"

Rothmarr shook his head. "What a world it would be if the Red Isles took its name solely from the heather. No, the Red Isles takes its name from the old wars. Before then it was called Earla."

Abika didn't care about old battles. At all. But she still needed to keep Rothmarr sweet, at least until they landed at the southern island so she let him blab about the fights, the deaths and the blood that stained the once green grasses of Sulitaria's crown jewel, Earla.

The hills rolled by as Rothmarr talked, Abika only really half-listening, until a fast-flowing gap opened slowly up as they drew alongside the channel between the two islands.

"What about that?"

Rothmarr nodded slowly but looked grim. "The midpass used to be almost completely still. No currents, until about a decade ago, when it all changed. Many people died trying to travel between the two islands. Currents that not only go forwards and backwards, but sideways. The channel literally turned on its side, going deep into the seabed. A lot of Red Islanders think the two islands grew, but the channel is the same width. I've sailed by it more times than any other. It hasn't changed. The real cause is a mystery to all if you ask me. The Red Isles are...not what they used to be." Rothmarr shook his head as Vasta leaned back with the two passengers. "Your companion was listening intently there. To think, an actual Bohr on my boat! I never thought I'd see the day. If my papa were here, he'd fall over hisself to speak to him. He used to run this very route back when I was a boy."

Abika frowned. "Your papa, is he dead?"

Rothmarr laughed. "No, he'll outlive us all. He has some memory, my papa. He remembers every single person who ever set foot on his boat...But the cycles have not been kind to him, his mind is all in pieces now."

Abika stared at the man as a thought took shape. "And you take people in both directions? From the Red Isles to Ipiti and back?"

"Course."

"Would he remember a female passenger? With a baby? Fleeing from the Red Isles."

Rothmarr nodded but gave her an awkward look. "Hard to say without a name or description. But, like I said, my papa was good with faces. And names too, come by it. If they rode on his boat, he'd remember them." He raised his eyebrows. "Do you have a name?"

Abika swallowed. The cold wind whipping about her, the incessant chatter around Vasta, the fresh smell of sea, and the gentle lapping of waves as the Myathar cut its way through the deep blue sea, yet none of it mattered. All Abika could see was vengeance. "Her name was Kyira and she travelled with a babe called Abika."

37

FORGOTTEN FRUITS

"Minerva," said Vasta. Abika was getting better at understanding the Bohr's true meanings when he spoke, but still this one seemed cloaked in something new. It sounded almost like fear. Before she could ask, he pulled her off the dock away from the Myathar. "Minerva holds a danger that you will never have encountered anywhere else. The people here do not give second chances. Rothmarr seems friendly, because he has to be, but did you see his blade?"

Abika shook her head, glancing over at the man as he tied his boat to the dock. "He doesn't look lethal to me, Vasta. He looks like a shipman."

"And therein lies the danger. He was a member of the Tsiorc, and has likely killed many people. Trust no one." He stood to his full height. A crowd of people were walking along the dock's jetty towards them, and even from here Abika could see they were not friendly. Vasta drew a ragged breath. "A Bohr is an unusual sight throughout Sulitaria. Our kind have not been native to these lands for a thousand generations. Not since before the old wars. You are best to leave me."

"Leave you?" Vasta's fear spread through Abika like a contagious disease. "I don't know this place, Vasta!"

"The Red Isles are quite simple to navigate. Just find the orange groves."

Abika's jaw dropped. "The orange groves? Why are *you* trying to get to the orange groves?"

"Because of that." Vasta nodded to the shard around Abika's neck.

"Get him!" The angry crowd began to run towards them.

Vasta pulled Abika off and bounded away down the jetty's far side on all fours like a wolf. The crowd all turned back on themselves to head him off, their pace quickening. As they turned, all manner of sharp things were revealed: knives, poles, spears and they were all held up high in the air.

"It won't be long until they realise that you were with him."

Abika jerked around to see Rothmarr standing nearby. She stepped away. "What will they do to him?"

Rothmarr shrugged. "If a Bohr's hand will be passed down from generation to generation, then imagine what price they would get for a head."

The shipman had known exactly what awaited them here in the port. Everything here was false, just like the thick trees behind the docks that hid the city—the land was so flat that beyond the treeline there could have been anything waiting. If not for the sound of bustling traffic, bells ringing and livestock mewing, she might well have been standing at the commune or on the bay.

"You lied," she said through gritted teeth.

Rothmarr shook his head. "I warned you, Itraeka. I told you the people of Earla would not play nice."

Abika nodded to a pile of boxes behind her. "Are those the famous Red Isles oranges?"

As Rothmarr turned, Abika slipped the jailor's knife out of her shift pocket. Meorith had once told Abika that no matter what, a man's most prized possessions were the fruits between his legs, and they controlled everything he said and did. Abika pressed the sharp side of her blade against Rothmarr's groin.

"What are you—"

Abika stepped forward with Rothmarr as he backed away until he met the edge of the jetty. "I lost something precious, once." She gestured down. Not so far down, as she was still a good foot and a half shorter than Rothmarr. "Unless you want to lose something too, I suggest you help me. No tricks."

"Course," breathed Rothmarr. "Course. What do you need?"

"Your father," said Abika.

"He won't—"

Abika ran the blade higher up Rothmarr's tight breeches. "And neither will you if you don't take me to him."

Rothmarr's eyes darted back and forth, but there was no way out. "Fine, but let's lose the knife, shall we? Unless you plan on walking like that the whole way."

———

Threat lurked around every corner, or at least that's how it felt in the pit of Abika's stomach. The island was so flat that all she could see were granite buildings in all directions. The city was a contrast of high walls and flared roofs. Old temples stood on every street, almost outnumbering the homes, but all were in the same state of disrepair. A heavy air of lethargy hung about the city, where even the animals moved slowly. The air was warmer and thicker than Ipiti but not so that it could be blamed for the slowness of life that marked every living being Abika saw. The clothes people wore were much like Ipitians, except here they were all drab and tired, as though the Red Isles were a cursed shade of Abika's home.

"Your papa, does he still work?"

Rothmarr shot her a look over his shoulder. "No longer." His glance flicked to the long arms of Abika's jacket where the knife lay hidden. "He will not appreciate his son being threatened so."

Abika nodded. "You still have your balls, don't you?"

"And here, I thought the people of Earla were bad."

"Explain it to me then. What is wrong in this city?"

Rothmarr stopped by a side street, but after a second look didn't venture in. Mounds of stinking dirt and rubbish were piled up blocking the way. "It's not just Minerva. I see it, and am somewhat immune to it, because I leave every day on a boat and return. But in the past decade the people have changed. My old school friends no longer acknowledge me, my own father even. Their souls have turned sour." He nodded at the heavy-lidded eyes of those passing by. "They all have, Itraeka. Whatever it is you want to find out from my father, you better do it quickly and leave. It only takes one person to single you out, and before you know it, they'll be cutting your hands off for trophies."

"I'm twelve, Rothmarr."

Rothmarr raised an eyebrow. "Truly? You think that matters?" He lowered his head as someone passed close by. Rothmarr turned back to the road, leading them off the beaten path, walking down streets that seemed to get narrower with each turn, the sense of danger following behind like a creature unseen. Abika thought about reaching for the power as she had in Ipiti, but even the thought of it delivered a wave of fatigue that threatened to buckle her knees and send her reeling to the cobbles. Besides, she wouldn't know what to do with it anyway.

"Still feeling sick?" Rothmarr had stopped and was facing her. "The sea can do that to those who are not so well-travelled."

"I'm fine. Is this the way? To your home?"

Rothmarr gestured forwards to an old green door, the paint peeling all over. Abika didn't wait, and banged it twice with her fist. Something rattled against the wood on the other side and as the door opened a noxious smell filled the air.

"Rothmarr? That you?"

"Papa, we have a guest. This is Itraeka, she wanted to meet you."

Rothmarr's father looked browbeaten, as though he were a corpse already. The old man's milky eyes took her in. "This shrew?" He sneered. "You fix that boom pole yet?"

"Course, Papa."

"Liar!" The man slammed the door shut.

Abika kicked the door as hard she could knocking flakes and curls to the steps.

"Piss off," came a muffled shout. "The both of you! And you Rothmarr, you bloody liar. That boom pole is as broken now as it was yesterday."

"Let me in, old man," "snapped Abika. "I have a question for you. About one of your passengers."

The door opened a crack. "If you can answer mine first, only then will I let you ask."

"I'll answer it," said Abika.

"No, no, shrew," said Rothmarr's father. "Not just answer, you need to get it right, then maybe I'll answer *your* question."

Abika couldn't tell if his expression was a smile or frown. "Alright. Go on then."

Speaking through the crack in the door the old man recited his riddle. "I have cities, but no houses. I have mountains, but no rocks. I have water, but no fish. What am I?"

Abika racked her brain, but no answers appeared. She thought of the stories she had read, the tales Jekob and Freja had told her. Images popped into her mind, but then..."You are a story."

"Wrong." The door shut.

"Please! I'm looking for someone, a woman who travelled with a baby about eleven or twelve cycles ago. She was on your boat, I know it! Rothmarr told me you could help." Rothmarr opened his mouth to speak and Abika quieted him with a glare.

The door opened fully, and the old man stepped out onto the doorstep. He was more round than any man had a right to be. His distended stomach peeking out above poorly fitting and stained trousers. Worse though were his feet, which were host to the most disgusting toenails Abika had ever seen.

"Shrew," he said, voice crackling. "I pride myself on remembering all who travelled on my boat. What did this woman look like?"

Abika shrugged. "I don't know. She had a baby."

"I've shipped a lot of folk over the cycles, Shrew. Families, mothers, children. You'll need to give me more than that."

Abika racked her brain. "I...She was...I don't know! I just need to find her. Her name was Kyira."

Rothmarr's father shook his head and a shower of dry skin fell from his grey beard onto a threadbare woollen top. "Name doesn't ring a bell. Oh wait! Was she travelling with her husband?"

Abika took a long breath. "No. She was by herself, just her and a baby."

"Baby was you then, I take it?"

“She was Nordun.”

The man’s eyes lit up. “Oh yes. Striking face, she had. Slanted eyes like all Norduns. And a babe slung to her chest.”

Abika heart leapt. “Did she speak to you?”

Rothmarr’s father showed off his yellow teeth. “She did that.”

Abika’s heart leapt. “What did she say?”

“Not until you answer the riddle, Shrew.”

Abika let the knife drop into her hand. “Listen, old man. I need to find her, and if you knew where she came from, then you’d better tell me. Or—”

Quick as a blink, the old man’s hand snapped out, knocking Abika’s blade clattering to the cobbles. He snatched it up before she even knew what was happening. “Or what, Shrew?” Rothmarr’s father stepped up to her. “You don’t think I spent a lifetime’s shipping people around Sulitaria and didn’t learn a thing or two about danger?” His mass took up the entire alleyway so that even Rothmarr was forced back a few steps along the narrow road. Abika’s back pressed hard up the opposite wall. His hot breath filled Abika’s head. “All people are scum. All people. You, him, me. We all fight for ourselves and do nothing to help others. Everything we do is for the self. Even now, here I stand as an old man, a life that will soon end that could have been something! Spent watching others. Well, now, Shrew, I hold the lashings, ropes and all!” He slid Abika’s blade into a crack in the wall behind and snapped the metal with a ping.

“Hey!”

“I steer where I need to,” said Rothmarr’s father. “And I regret not a single thing.” He glanced up at Rothmarr. “Although, you boy are a bigger disappointment than the day that Earla lost its fruit!”

“The only one who’s lost his fruit here is you.” Abika felt entirely justified in the words. The old man was a fool and deserved more besides. Still, it did nothing to help her when he rounded on her and grabbed her by the collar. And just like that, the answer came as clear as day. “A map!” said Abika, her feet off the ground. “You have cities, but no houses. You have mountains, but no rocks. You have water, but no fish. You are a map.” The old man put her down. His eyes wide and unreadable. He turned and pottered back to the door and stepped inside. Abika ran forward and dropped a foot in to stop the door closing. "So, you really do have nothing left, boat master. Not even your word."

Rothmarr's father turned towards her. "This Kyira of yours, she was sad. That's all I remember."

"No, wait!" said Abika. "Please. Where did she come from?"

The old man frowned at her. "From the groves. *The* grove." The door shut with finality and this time Abika knew it wouldn't open again.

It was Rothmarr who spoke first. "Well, Abika. This is where we part. You're on your own now." He turned towards the door.

"Please, Rothmarr. Please. I have to find Kyira. Please. Where is the grove?"

Rothmarr stopped, his hand upon the doorknob. "The grove is the largest of all the orange groves on the Red Isles, but you won't find anything there. It's been dead for cycles."

"What about the famous Red Isles oranges? I tasted them myself."

Rothmarr shook his head. "The Red Isles buy their oranges from Costra Dae, across the water in Sulitar, they arrive here and we rebrand the boxes and sell them out across the islands for ten times the price. There are no oranges left on the Red Isles. Whatever happened on the Red Isles, the island never recovered. It rots from the inside, like forgotten fruit." He sighed. "As do we all. See you in another life, Abika."

38

SHOES

The water was clear, blue and cold, and it filled Atalfia's lungs. A bold darkness like the sky after dusk, seeping into her, spreading through her, reaching into her veins, stretching into her mind, seeking her out. It was a violation, not only of her body, but of her soul, and that was hers. Her soul could not be taken away. Not by anyone.

Her body retched as the water engulfed her, until bright, broken light cracked through. A pair of arms burst through the mirror surface of the water and grabbed her, and she gave in like a child being picked up by its mother.

"Janike? Is that you?"

"It is me."

Atalfia had to ask, because Janike's features were not hers but of another. Patched skin, all white and black like a map—Atalfia could walk those borders, so distinct they were.

The water's surface was no longer around her waist, but a hundred leagues below her, churning and frothy and muddy. Even from this distance she could see the huge logs of broken ships being tossed around like matchsticks upon the Way.

A shadow rose up from the depths, breaking the surface. Rock, shining and iridescent flashed as the sun's rays found it, then it was ascending up and up, a mountain of black glass growing out of the seabed where Tyr once stood.

Fia turned to Janike, and her friend snarled. "We are not one." Blood sprayed from her beautiful lips. "We are not one!" She opened her mouth and screamed, a horrible sound that filled the air and the clouds and sky with anger and pity. It carried long, moving like shadow, changing key and pitch. Then all at once, Janike snapped her head back towards Atalfia. Her face was evil incarnate, with eyes of fire and pointed teeth. "Goodbye, Little Bird," it said. "May we meet again."

"No!"

It was too late. Atalfia fell. She knew that the fall would wake her, The wind was rushing. The surface drew closer and closer with every second. She had to wake, and yet the fall seemed to go on forever. The surface warping and getting further away. Atalfia willed herself down, wishing for death. Hoping for it.

The water reached up and took her, waves greeting and grabbing at her. Her feet tangled in fingers of kelp. Huge logs of wood smashed into each other. Flaming debris and bodies drifted by, breaking into pieces by falling rock and stone. Of fear and fortune those ships had sailed, and now they were scattered and broken and sinking. Muddy water enveloped Atalfia's face. She grabbed at clothes. A person, and a bloated face lolled over to meet her. It was Seb, his glasses still clinging somehow to his pulverised head. There were screams. People like her, lost in the maelstrom. Hasaan, her captor, struggled against the water, grasping as she did, eyes wild with fear. The side of the broken hillside above the Way groaned as a new landslide loosened. A million tons of dirt, rocks bigger than houses, fell into the already churning waters, birthing a monstrous wave. Hasaan swam towards the centre of the Way, where the currents were strongest, and Atalfia followed, swimming as hard as she could. Hasaan managed a final shout before he was sucked below.

The cold reached up, urging her to let go and let the water in then the wave took her. Pulling her down. She gritted her teeth, willing her sleeping body to wake and leave this nightmare!

Slimy fingers once again crawled up her skin, pulling her deeper, while her breath reached its zenith. Pushing away, she reached for the surface, and her fingers broke it. Cold air, and hot fire was there waiting, but she couldn't get higher. The fingers below held tighter, their mucus crawling upon her bare skin up her legs, around her waist, over her shoulders. She screamed and the water rushed in.

"Atalfia!" Fia felt herself being rocked, was it the ships? The water?

"Janike?"

"Wake up, girl!"

Fia opened her eyes, and fell against Eris, sobbing uncontrollably.

"Oh, Atalfia, you fool." Eris stroked her hair. "You utter, utter fool."

Eris's warmth began to register against Fia's wet skin. Were they tears? Sweat? Blood? She pushed Eris away and sat up towards the lamp. Shaking, then turned the wick. The tent filled with light. Fia stood up, mastering her body. Breathing through her nose, and calming the sobs that refused to abate.

"Atalfia."

"I'm fine, Eris."

Eris was usually so beautiful, until anger touched her expression. Like now. Her face contorted into a mash of disbelief and rage, but somehow her words came out all soft. "Atalfia." Eris adjusted her position and moved the blanket, revealing her naked chest. "Do not lie to me. Lies might come easy to the Kumpani, but do not lie to me! I know what torments you."

Fia swallowed. "Do you?"

Eris held out her hands. "Alright, alright. Peace."

"Peace?" said Fia. "You sound like Jona."

Erin rolled her eyes. "What? Look, you know what you must do with the prisoner."

Fia blinked. Was that what had prompted such a vivid dream? Responsibility and the urge to keep balance when they sat upon the knife edge about to fall.

She swallowed. "What do *you* think I should do?"

"Don't do that."

"Do what?"

Eris crossed her arms beneath her breasts. "Replay the question back to me. I might not be completely immune to your Kumpani *ways*, but I still recognise them when I see them!"

Fia felt a refreshing surge of anger. "I am not Kumpani, Eris! Those days are long behind me."

"Yes, but the tricks remain." Eris threw up her hands. "And now look, we're arguing about something else. Well done." She leaned forward. "Atalfia, you know what you have to do. And you'd be right to do it."

"You mean I should kill him?" said Fia. "That's what you're saying isn't it?" Fia started pacing. "At least call it what it is. We're talking of someone's life here."

"What is that supposed to mean?" spat Eris. "Atalfia, what are we talking about here? One minute you seem as soft as a baby rabbit, then the next as hard as rock."

"As soft as a baby rabbit? That's a new one Eris."

Eris blinked. "Is it?"

Fia waited, but Eris's expression was too placid, and too beautiful. Fia wanted to run a finger over her sharp jawline, to kiss along her collar bones and down upon her breasts, down and down to her stomach and beyond. What a way to spend the rest of this shitty day, between the legs of her lover.

"Ok then," said Fia, pulling on her shirt and breaches. "Well, I have things to get about. So, I guess I'll see you around."

"Will I see you tonight?"

"Leave me be." Fia threw the tent flap aside and stepped outside.

"Will I see you—"

"YES!"

Fia stomped away, immediately regretting the decision. The churned, stinking mud that marked the lines of soldier's tents squelched between her bare toes.

"Shit." Literally.

The walk back to her tent had been supremely unpleasant but at least the camp porters had thought ahead enough to leave her some hot water in Fia's tent. Warm? Not even. The water in the reconditioned pig's trough was tepid at best, but was still wondrous, nonetheless. Pressing her feet against each other she sighed in pleasure as the cracks eased from her bones. She might have missed out on her chance for a steaming foot bath but warm bodies held close brought so much more, and the afternoon's memories were still fresh in her mind, keeping her warm still.

"I would kill for a foot masseuse," she said to herself. She brought the stump of her missing hand to her mouth and bit it gently. The strangeness of that missing hand still fascinated her, losing a piece of herself. No metaphors. A real piece of her, gone. Had it fed some fish beneath the torrent of waters at Tyr, or was it still there, her favourite rings still attached to a bleached white skeletal hand? It didn't matter. Having a stump instead of a hand still had its uses. She grinned to herself.

"Argh! What a stupid fight!"

And all her fault no less. She snorted, and the laugh brought tears to her eyes, and suddenly she was crying. Sadness, despair. It was all there, jostling for attention, filling her up, taking her over. And she let it. The river had to run dry or the rest of the evening would be a total loss. A full ten minutes passed before she could regain control of herself.

Fia lifted her bag and dug inside, but her fingers found the neck of a glass bottle before anything else. Fyrevin, they called it in the west, less a liquor and more a boot cleaner. She held it up to the light, watching as the dark green liquid sloshed around. Eris could drink most under the table and that was a fact, but a Kumpani spent a lifetime learning how to drink and stay sober. Perhaps that was one Kumpani skill she did not miss any longer.

Buried inside her dirty clothes was a circle of wood, a tree cutting with some carved and coloured lines to any untrained eye. She pulled the Chinaes board that she'd had made in Raeven's Torr. It was not hewn from a stoytree like Laeb's had been but still it reminded her of him, and that made it precious. Her stray thoughts lingered on Laeb as she pulled the rest of her stinking clothes from the bag, folding them neatly and dropping them in the basket beneath her mattress for the porters.

They had never been compatible, she and Laeb. No matter how much he felt for her, and yet still she found that she compared herself to him almost daily. *Would Laeb have done it this way? Would Laeb approve of her?* That is what happened when two people spent so much time together, they synchronised, their thoughts becoming one, so that sub-consciously they copied each other in language and movement. It was a tale as old as time.

It was one of the Kumpani's highest lessons, preying upon the kindness of the soul and our need to be near and feel accepted by others. Like a pair of shoes, everyone wanted to feel *part of something*. Her lost love, Janike, was a perfect illustration of it, being so like her father as to fall out constantly on a regular basis, and yet she had always been distant with Fia, no matter how close she had wanted them to be.

Fia sighed and frowned at the board. Jona and she had played Chinaes most nights in Raeven's Torr—there was little else to do in that dung heap—but that wasn't why she was frowning. She closed her eyes, racking her mind, replaying the conversation.

"And what's the point of this one?"

Atalfia held the piece out. "Are you joking? I just told you." She snatched the character stone from Jona's hand. "This is a keystone."

"Ah, the keystone. The one that..." He scratched his head, then subconsciously flicked the fringe back up over his forehead.

Anger filled Atalfia's stomach. "I'm not telling you again. If you spent more time listening than ogling, then you might find that you have some ability to play. You know what, let's just play. You can pick it up along the way."

Jona's eyes darted between the serving girls. When he wasn't rubbernecking he was drinking. He'd already had three times what Atalfia had drunk, but those big, friendly doe-eyes were finally beginning to droop a little.

"The board starts neutral. Each stone owes a point." She looked up at him.

"I'm with you," he said, nodding hastily.

"I doubt that. Chinaes sharpens the analytical side of your brain. Helps you understand strategy. It helps see below the surface where things are hidden."

Jona's eyes darted behind Atalfia's right ear and followed the rear end of a passing serving girl. "I understand just fine," he said. "But a little extra clarity never hurt anyone."

"Speaking of clarity, you remembered to knot Grace's reins this time, didn't you? Derval will kill me if we lose her."

Jona shook his head. "Derval? Grace is his?"

"Don't do that. You know she is." Atalfia sighed as Jona's attention once again slipped away. "Did you tie her?"

He rolled his eyes. "Of course. Why do you continue to think so poorly of..."

Atalfia snapped her fingers in front of his face. "Jona! Derval is a man with many, many knives. Don't piss him off."

Jona leaned in. "Derval is as a soft as a baby rabbit..." He reached out and groped the serving girl's behind, forcing her to turn and back away against the chairs. Beer and wine spilled over laps and shoes. Then shouting filled the air as the two bearded fishmen at the table she was serving both stood tall...Steel flashed, hostility filled the air, and words were forgotten.

The Chinaes gameboard clattered to the ground as the realisation hit Fia, the sound of wood splintering. She'd sacrificed two bags of rice and a ring to get that board, but that was the farthest thing from her mind now.

"As soft as a baby rabbit..." Tears fell freely again. "When two people are together for long enough, they synchronise." Her own words were acid. "She's betraying me." Fia grabbed the fyrevin, tore off the wax lid and drank deep.

39

PURITY AND IRONY

Kaliste wrenched the red door closed behind her. The alleyway sheltered her from the worst of the wind, but the rain was incessant. Even so, she lingered there. To anyone foolish enough to try and enter, the trap she had painstakingly conjured and revisioned would appear as hanging beads. Simple beads that any soul could walk through—a soul destined for destruction.

The thrumming Soulfire trap was not why she had hesitated, however wonderfully built it was. It was the secret that lay below the hidden house. A doorway to another place, less than a quarter-league from the bed she slept in. It was so very difficult to imagine, travelling in an instant from one part of Rengas to another, and yet the fact that the Bohr now had the ability to cross vast distances in a heartbeat was a power too great to share.

The first phase was to fragment the Bohr forces. This was easily done; the mess of Tyr had created huge division amongst the Bohr clans, but where some sought to unite the Bohr, Jagar had urged her to spread them apart. In the beginning the reasons had been unclear, but as soon as she'd found this doorway, it all made sense. If there was one doorway, there were many. The laws of life told her this was the truth, and if she could find one, she could find them all. And that was the second phase. The war against humans could be won, but it was a war that needed to be brought to their doorsteps and that was impossible with a single unified force when they too were so broadly scattered. It was a ridiculous irony. As useful as the doorway could be, they were still so limited in their usage. What good would an allied army be stationed on the island of Dor? What was the Great Mother thinking when she opened a doorway between Zunqai, the most powerful city in Rengas, and some sparsely populated island in Sulitaria? The word of God? The word of a mad woman, more like.

"Now is not the time to try and fix this." Her voice became human midway through the sentence as she willed her human form to take over. "The answer to that question lies outwith this house, and I need help if I am to change the exit." Saying the words and hearing them in the Princess's sing-song tones seemed to help quell the side of Kaliste that constantly longed for answers, a side of herself that she had learned to live with over the generations. It had brought her great power and great joy, but also unimaginable horrors. The truths of this world were always harder than the lies that lurked beneath the surface.

She set off, and before long she was thinking again. Analysing the facts in front of her and looking for some angle that she was yet to see, or a dimension yet to reveal itself. The fragmented force that she had lobbied for in the council made no sense when there was no earthly way of bringing them back together. The doorways, properly controlled, could act as corridors. They could give the Bohr back the power they so sought—secret ways that one, ten or a hundred thousand could travel through. Imagine! An army appearing on the beach of Bakla without notice. The slaughter would end the human rebellion once and for all.

The alleyway opened out into the square, and the fountains of Kalcoon, their many stone figures mid-battle, Bohr fighting Bohr. Ridiculous. The Bohr hadn't fought each other in millennia Those were times long since passed. She shook her head in distaste and carried on by, hopping over the splashes trickling over the flagstones, her bare human feet as deft as a ballerina.

The streets of Zunqai were not a place for the faint of heart. Humans could walk them relatively unscathed, but the Bohr were the masters here. Kaliste's disguise afforded her great opportunities to see how both sides conducted themselves, and had, in the past, provided her with incredible insight. Humans, for example, were just as egotistical as Bohr—a particularly negative trait considering they had not the power to back it up.

Today, however, was not a day for reflecting on the inadequacies of human or Bohrkind. Kaliste's human head was full of calculations and questions. The doorway was not power itself but rather a proxy to power. She rubbed her stomach. "A side-effect of something greater."

A Bohr, not as large as V'Laerk but much wider than her, stalked around the corner. His aura was red, and she didn't need Jagar's gifts to see that he would try to kill her should she get in his way. Sidestepping to the left, she played the meek human female, waiting for the wind of the Bohr to come rushing by. When it didn't, she lifted her head.

"You are with child," croaked the Bohr.

Kaliste looked up and fluttered her big human eyes. "I am. Please forgive—"

The Bohr grabbed her, pulling her over, and dragged her back the way he had come. Kaliste looked around, but no one cared as this lowly human female was dragged away to certain death.

The Bohr threw her down again, and she fell heavily on her front. The child inside moved, and a deep unsettling feeling of discomfort filled her mind.

"Don't do that again."

The Bohr kept lifting his lips, a snarl of sorts. A smile. "You will sate me." He moved to lift his loincloth, then jerked back in pain. He held up his hand, first of all confused, then a mask of pain drew over his face as Kaliste trickled Soulfire into his body.

Kaliste started breaking at the fingers, the joints snapping back against themselves. A simple trick of reversal, deep and natural. The Bohr watched in surprise as the bones in his hands twisted and cracked, seemingly by themselves. Kaliste brushed herself off. "You were saying something about a desire to be satisfied? Now, you will—" Abruptly, the Soulfire tricking out of her became a torrent and the breaking resumed, first with the Bohr's hands, then his wrists, right up to the forearms, snapping back upon themselves. The Bohr grit his teeth so hard they burst from his mouth like yellow pearls, pattering to the stone.

It took shattered bones all the way up to the shoulder until finally the Bohr began to protest. "Sshtop!"

The life inside her was wielding Kaliste's Soulfire like a sword, threads of light protruding out of her body like spiderwebs into the Bohr's muscles and limbs. The Bohr's shoulder cracked backwards with a satisfying apple-bite crunch, and it howled its dog-head up at the archway above them. The legs went next: feet, ankles, shins, femurs to hips, all curling backwards like a dying spider. Then the ribcage, popping as the Bohr's spine pulled it backwards and finally the Bohr fell twitching to the street, a broken bundle of Bohrflesh.

Kaliste turned at a noise to find a child standing there. "Hello."

The boy frowned, leaning past her to the broken and bleeding Bohr lying there groaning. "Did he fall?"

Kaliste's human form quivered, but not in pain. Where the Bohr had experienced the worst pain, she had experienced waves after wave of pleasure. She tried to talk, but her skin was alive with sensation. Did she still hold her human form? She didn't know.

"I just...found him like this," she uttered to the little boy leading him away. "Wretched soul. Tell me, what is your name?"

"It's Vitz. What's yours?"

"I have many names," Kaliste's breath still shook, "but at the moment it is Mae." With difficulty she added a smile and wiped a tear from her eye.

"Mae? That's pretty."

"She was a princess you know. A long time ago. She ruled over a vast empire, bigger than the Kemen empire..." Kaliste was having trouble concentrating. The boy's outline was growing fuzzy. "She...She ruled with an iron fist...until I came along and...and...took her..."

"Took her where?"

Kaliste tried to steady herself against a wall, dragging poor Vitz with her. Her human reflection flashed in front of her then all she could hear was him. That echoing voice, cutting through Kaliste's soul.

Kaliste.

"Jagar."

Vitz's hand tried to pull away, but she squeezed harder with every word that came.

Kaliste, where is my army?

"Jagar! It is being built. It takes time to recruit over—"

I DO NOT HAVE TIME.

Jagar was touching her with his mind, which was as clear as her feet upon the cobbles. But there was no Soulfire. When Soulfire was near, it drew excitement in the bodies of those who could wield it. Gooseflesh, pleasure and even orgasms all driven by the power that ran through the lines of reality. Jagar was not using Soulfire. His presence in her mind was something else entirely, and it terrified her.

"The army will be ready, Jagar. I said I would do it, and I do not lie."

No, you do not lie. But we are judged upon our actions in the face of the Great Father.

"The Great Father..." Kaliste closed her human eyes, she couldn't bear to see the world so dimly any longer. *"The army, the Ruffin, the Banèmen will be ready to fight."* She felt Jagar's unhappiness before he spoke.

No Ruffin. No creatures, nor Soulfire. And no Bohr.

"What sort of army are you raising?"

A human army. Every human slave and human citizen in Zunqai will augment the Republican rebels in Bakla.

Outrage burst out of Kaliste like a boiling kettle. *"Bakla!? You want to hand my army over to the resistance?"*

Your army? If this is to be the last stand of the humans, then doesn't it make sense to add more humans to fight so that we finally cleanse Rengas for good?

"Jagar, it is our right as governors to control the Queen's army. To control humans. Wiping them out—"

Is my ultimate goal.

"How on earth does sending our human forces to the rebels help us, Jagar?"

You need not worry about my intentions.

Confusion rocked Kaliste to her very core. *"I TRUSTED YOU." The shock of the words reverberated through the space in her mind that Jagar was currently occupying. "And I will not betray the Bohr! They are the best chance Rengas has for a pure kingdom."*

Whether under duress or by your own free will, you will help me Kaliste.

Kaliste tried to contain the madness; the sheer audacity of him! *"The humans outnumber us, you fool! A thousand to one. We need unity, not fragmentation. You are setting us up for failure."*

The Bohr and the Banèmen will prevail. I will prevail.

All at once the world became grey. Bohr and human alike still wandered by the end of the short street that her and Vitz stood in—it had not changed—and yet she was suddenly alone.

"What...What have you done?"

I have taken your fire.

"But I am still human."

Yes. And so you will be. Forever.

Panic set Kaliste's breast alight, and not a thousand, nor a million generations of lives could have prepared her for the loss. *"How dare you violate me!"* The child in her womb had stopped moving. *"Give it back!"*

What should concern you more, Kaliste, is the ease in which I took your fire. There is much more yet I can take from you.

Kaliste drew a long breath, and the voice she wielded in her mind took on a sterner tone. *"Then how exactly do you intend to send the army to the rebels? Ships? It will take months to move so many. Plenty of time for the rebels to inflate their forces beyond ours. Or marching them perhaps? Should we walk them through the Cracked Wastes and deserts of the Kemen Empire? Not to mention the resources involved. You are talking about moving the biggest army ever conjured from Zunqai to Bakla."*

That is why I brought you into the Council, Kaliste. Fortitude and fervour. Did it ever pass you by at all to perhaps question where I am at this moment?

"It did."

And?

"You are not using Soulfire to touch me."

No. I'm not. Soulfire energy doesn't exist here, because energy does not exist here. Energy is a worldly construct, and I am between realms. This is the domain of the gods. The Great Mother. She tried to stop me you know and failed. I banished her, and now this is my kingdom!

Even connected as she was to Jagar, Kaliste could still feel her body, in human form, still clutching the boy's hand. In a revision she could usually split her focus between the real world and the channel she was inducing, but Jagar was not using Soulfire, so she had absolutely no control. The stream of vision was coming from him, wherever he was. Her physical self was shivering.

Kaliste. As a Queen and leader of the Banèmen, you understand better than most that the order of things must be maintained. There must be structure, and in this version of the world I have decreed that the humans will all die. Every. Single. One of them. And to do that, they must be banded together. Akosh is on his way to Bakla to oversee this very task.

Kaliste ground her teeth. *"Akosh? That stuck-up—"*

Akosh knows himself. Better than most, granted, but his power is comparable to yours, Kaliste.

"Speed is not comparable to what I can do with Soulfire, Jagar. Akosh is a circus performer."

He has his ways. Amusement coloured the connection between them, amusement and then annoyance. *I have humoured you, because I respect you, Kaliste, but no more. You will raise an army of human soldiers and you will send them to Bakla.*

"How?"

As quickly as Jagar had touched Kaliste, he had left her standing in the street clutching Vitz's hand. The light was always so bright when returning to oneself. She took a long and deep breath, and as the world slowed, she realised she was being watched. She turned her head to see her own reflection staring back at her from a dark window. Her human form had left her completely, thanks to the energy Jagar had been channelling.

She admired herself for a moment—those strong legs and shoulders, and those eyes she had inherited from her feline mother. Set upon a human face they gave her a sultry yet feminine look, even with her greying hair and stretched skin, it had helped her fit in with humans. It had taken her many cycles to become proud of who she was. She was a Child of the Bohr, she was a Banèman. She was a Queen.

Still holding the child's hand, she smiled and opened her eyes. "Vitz, my dear, have you ever met a royal?" Vitz's looked up at her, shock turning his eyes red until tears were cascading down his cheeks. "What is it?" growled Kaliste. "Do you not know the difference between a Bohr and a human?!"

Vitz pulled his hand away, slicing his skin on Kaliste's claws. Pure driven anger burned through Kaliste's veins. She wanted to punish him. But it was not the boy's fault. He was an innocent. So when he started backing off, Kaliste chose not to hurt him. Instead, she snarled, snapped and spat until little Vitz tore off back down the alleyway.

"Alright, Jagar. You want an army of humans? Then I will create the biggest army Rengas has ever seen, humans. Bohr. Banèmen and Ruffin, and they will fight and they will destroy the human rebellion once and for all! I swear that I will undo everything you have done!"

Jagar glanced over at the dark window. Shapes of black and white swam over his skin like flotsam upon silken waves. It was remarkable, the way this new body was both his and yet not his, but while he might not have chosen this form it was not without its beauty. It was ironic then beauty only mattered to the corporeal. Infesting a mind was one thing, but it couldn't be understated how important it was to be seen by everyone.

He watched as Kaliste stumbled around the corner at the end of the street, then bent down to the broken Bohr she had left behind.

"You are truly more powerful than you realise, Kaliste."

The Bohr's eyes focused on Jagar as though the words were meant for him. It was the last effort the fool creature would ever make and the realisation that Jagar was not there to help was too much. The Bohr managed a groan then died.

"Another life. Another soul. I shall make sure to look out for you, dear Bohr."

Jagar stood and brought his hands together, accessing Baeivi's power just *felt* easier with a bit of bravado. He looked inward and, beginning at the fringes of his vision, the cobbles, walls and windows grew dim until they were all replaced with yellow stalks of grass and hills as far as he could see. Hatàr wasn't so far from Zunqai but the sun had already set here, leaving a murky light that washed the colour from everything. Even so, it still looked wonderful so close to the Kemen wall.

"Now," said Jagar, turning and placing a hand on the great wall. "This is a place I have not been in a while." He looked towards the camp of the Fifth Union, its shanty-town huts and tents a smear against an otherwise beautiful Kemen landscape. "It's about time I dropped by, wouldn't you say, Little Bird?"

40

A THOUSAND PIECES

The drum thumped with a deep roll that drew something primal within Fia. Music had always been a love of hers for as long as she could remember. Her papa would tell her to savour every moment, to follow and enjoy the journey before it was pulled from under her feet, and so she had. It was her papa's advice that convinced her to join the Kumpani, even if it had been Laeb that presented her with the need so long ago. He'd coerced and manipulated her. It was masterful, really. She said she would never be manipulated again, and yet here she was, betrayed by her closest friend.

At the back of the makeshift tavern, the drummer thumped the bass drum before turning on his stool towards the bodhran hanging behind him. His name was Althios, and he was as deft with a double-ended beater as he was with an ongaxe. An ongaxe was of course much longer and heavier, (being that it was mostly used for killing people), and yet Althios was somehow able to make it look light, whipping that double axe around his body as easily as he flicked that beater across the surface of the bodhran drum. The beat was infectious, and it took hold of Fia's foot and lifted it up and down in time, forming a little puddle beneath the sole of her flats.

"He's good, isn't he?"

"No," said Fia. "He's incredible."

Eris leant against the heavy wooden pole at Fia's side. "Where did you find them?"

"I didn't find them. They came to us, and as with all musicians of the world they found each other at the bottom of an empty glass. I saw Althios tapping one day, no drums. Just his ongaxe and his shield. Even that was incredible. My father played, you know."

"Drums?"

"The fiddle." Fia raised her voice a little over the tunes now filling the air, louder even than the shouting of conversation and raucous laughter. "He used to play to me, back home."

Eris nodded slowly, and for a few minutes they both just stood, watching and listening to the tune roll over keys and bars as naturally as a story written. The skill of musicians never ceased to amaze Fia. To build and create such wonderful landscapes with rhythm and melody —it was like dreaming, building worlds inhabiting simultaneously. These players did the same, forging paths through a landscape they wrought with their own fingers and hands. Ebbing. Flowing… Forbringr's Blood, Althios was good.

"You're staring, Atalfia. Maybe I can set up something between you."

Fia mulled on it a moment. "Perhaps. But then, probably not. He's a little old for me. What's he in? His sixtieth?"

"Then do me a favour and tear your gaze from the man!" Eris nodded to a group of women sitting near the makeshift stage. "It is not going unnoticed."

Fia glanced over at the group. She knew them well. Cooks, cleaners and gossipers. "Beauty comes in many forms, Eris. There is nothing wrong with admiring a man caught up in the throes of his own creation. Althios is a wonderful player and…well, very, very easy on the eye." Fia winked at the leader of the little gossip group, a woman named Raliyah, and she turned away whispering and hissing. "It is perhaps one of the better parts of being who I am, that what lies between the legs doesn't matter so much as to what lies in the heart." She turned on Eris. "Wouldn't you say?"

Eris took a half step back. "I suppose." Eris adjusted her leather armour. "Anyway." She gestured back over to the group. "I think the idea of losing one of the better prospects of our little settlement to one such as yourself scares them a little."

"As it should." Fia shook her head. "Raliyah thinks that because she's a doctor, she somehow has some kind of hold over the lower ranks."

"Well," said Eris. "She does."

"Yes, but that doesn't give her freedom to outrank her captain." She said the last much louder than she should have, so Raliyah would hear. They frowned in Fia's direction and resumed their titters.

"Are you sure you're alright, Atalfia?"

"Eris, leave me be." Fia lifted a drink from the table at her side. The man sitting there looked up with a deep frown, until his realisation that it was his captain who had relieved him.

"Evening, Captain."

"Thank you, Soldier Slocrate." She dropped the tankard, empty, back in front of him. "Good job."

"On what?" said the soldier, with a confused smile. He was a young one, but like the rest of them, so very, very talented.

"On the gin. You make it don't you?"

Slocrate nodded modestly. "Yes, but it was just the first batch. I've never tried the method of—" he caught himself. "I'm sorry, you don't want to hear this. Thank you for the kind words, Captain Atalfia."

Fia shook her head and tried to move; the room spun and her feet appeared to be intent on tripping her up. "No, no. You performed a dutiful task, dear Slocrate. Dutiful. And important. Without gin, we wouldn't be here, forgetting our worries and enjoying ourselves. It is people like you who make our task here...our duty...here..." She searched for the word. "Worthwhile."

Eris put a hand on Fia's shoulder. "Atalfia, you are drunk."

"So?"

Eris smiled, but her eyes bounced around the tavern. "And yet you still know everyone's names? You are truly a noble leader."

The rage Fia was barely holding back suddenly tipped over the edge of her cup. "Of course I know his name!" she hissed. "I know everyone here, Soldier Eris. Everyone. Because they are my people." She slapped a hand on Slocrate's shoulder.

Eris bristled. "I am more than just a soldier."

It wasn't only the group of gossipers who had turned around now, the whole tavern was watching. Every eye was on them, each stare a slimy finger searching over her skin. Fia drew a long breath, but the damage had already been done. The seed of doubt was planted. Their leader was a fool. "But of course you are, Eris." Fia stared at her. "You're much, much more than just a soldier."

Fia turned to leave and Eris followed. The short distance to the door felt like a long walk, as though it was she who was the main attraction for the evening and not the band thrumming and beating away the troubles of a sad and depressed army sitting about waiting for death.

The cool night washed over Fia's skin, bringing with it a stark reminder of the fyrevin currently dissolving her stomach lining. The taste was still on her tongue, even after Slocrate's sloeberry concoction. Fia looked up at the stars. "The lamplights of Tyr were usually so bright that I would never see so many stars."

Eris cleared her throat. "I remember it well."

"But of course you do."

"I thought you might like your shoes back Captain." she pulled Fia's boots from a bag somewhere behind her and held them out. "It must have been an interesting walk back to your tent in bare feet." She chuckled softly, trying to make light of it all. Of everything. It might have worked any other time. "And those flats you have on will not last long in this camp."

"Eris," said Fia, taking her boots. "This afternoon, I—"

"It's fine, don't think on it. We will fall out with each other, it's bound to happen. The main thing is that we make up." She touched Fia's face.

"I know about you and Jona." The words were out, delivered. A fizzing nightlight waiting to explode in her hands.

Eris's beautiful face crumpled into one of sorrow, but she didn't cry. She never cried. "How..."

"As soft as a baby rabbit?" said Fia. "They say that those who spend too long in each other's company, synchronise. They begin to sound like one another. You are a couple." She nodded, like it was the most simple statement in the world. "You are two, we are three."

"Atalfia, yes. Jona and I. We..." she took a moment, swallowing the guilt down like Slocrate's disgusting gin. "We slept together. It was before you and I...Well, before I knew you liked me."

"I've seen you together, Eris. I know chemistry when I see it. Trust me."

"No, it's not like that."

"I wish you both well," Fia turned. She willed her legs forward.

"Atalfia, please. It's not like that at all."

"Leave me alone, Eris."

Eris reached out and grabbed Fia's shoulder. As she spun, something bright and gold fell from her open shirt and landed at their feet. Fia bent low and picked it up. Her union cross necklace had broken. The loops of the cross had fallen apart leaving only the ring hanging on the chain around her neck. She shook her head at the remains of the necklace in her fist, then offered Eris a thin smile. "Good timing."

"It's broken?" said Eris?

"*We* are broken."

Eris swallowed, her eyes glistening. "I know you, Fia. This can't be the end. You'll walk away and we'll never talk again."

"You don't know me!" The words came out as a scream, so loud that she felt as though the force of the air alone might knock her over. She steadied herself against the inn wall, shrugging off Eris's hand as she sought to help.

"Please, Fia. Please, let's not let this be the end."

Fia couldn't help a little laugh. "It's kind of beautiful really. Our time is up, Eris. The time of the Fifth Union is up—"

Eris's eyes grew wide. "We are not done here—"

"Oh, yes we are, Eris." Fia yanked the chain off her neck, then let the ring of the union cross drop into her hand. "Don't look so shocked. It was bound to happen."

"Fia, no. The rebellion...We must keep fighting."

"Didn't you ever wonder why, in full view of the tearing wall, they didn't come and finish us off?" Eris looked like she was searching for the words, but Fia's anger was bright and real and present. "You think the Bohr consider us any more than an annoyance?" she growled. "I doubt the Fifth Union are even that! We are flies, insects that the Bohr are too busy to swat away. And you talk of rebellion? We can't even beat their wall! The other unions were right all along. We are broken."

Eris began to sob. "No..."

"You wanted to know if this war with the Bohr would beat us down. Well, here it is. We've found it. We're there. It is no war. There is no rebellion. And to top it all, Eris, you've successfully beaten this Captain down too. Congratulations."

"You...You said Laeb once told you to keep fighting."

Fia almost collapsed at hearing Laeb's name. "Don't you dare drag up his name to suit you!"

"What did he say, Fia? What were his words?"

"May you always fight." It came out as a whisper, but the shock of it still reverberated around her insides, crumbling her bones and breaking her heart.

"May you always fight." Eris stepped closer. "May you always fight, Fia."

Hearing it from Eris, after her betrayal, was too much. The fine line between them had snapped. The memory of Laeb hardened, shattering into a thousand pieces.

"NO!" screamed Fia. "No." She pushed Eris away. "The fight is over! It is beaten. *I* am beaten. Laeb might've won the battle but he couldn't beat the Bohr. And neither can I." Fia took a long breath and closed her eyes. When she opened them, Eris awaited her judgement the only way she knew how, as a soldier, and as a fighter of freedom. "We are over, Eris. I have no more fight in me." Fia took Eris's hand and placed the pieces of the broken union cross on her palm before closing her fist. "Not for us, nor the rebels. I'm done. We...are done."

41

JUDGEMENT OF THE STARS

The stars followed Fia like forever candles, twinkling, and spinning and watching her every move. They had always felt comforting, but tonight they judged her. Was it always this way when you made such a final choice? She mulled the consequences. Families reunited, relocated, lovers separated by the promise of war and death coming together to begin anew. New life. New seasons.

The wall that separated Kemen and Hatàr stood high, a silhouette that stole the night. Still, the wall could go to hell. It was not her problem anymore. The alcohol was taking hold now. Gin always had the effect on her, which was why she usually chose not to drink it.

She stumbled to a stop at the officer's quadrant, her tent was in view, but there was a bog of stinking mud in the way. She dropped down heavily on a nearby stool, and nearly fell right off. Eventually she was able to exchange the right flat shoe for a boot.

As Fia fumbled with the laces something beckoned her to look up, and in the dark a man stood watching her. As soon as she caught his eye, he turned away and hurried off through the tents. With only one boot, Fia up and was following after. The gin in her legs forgotten, she ducked in and out of the tents, avoiding the guidelines and pegs, between sleeping families and soldiers. The world became a spinning blur of nausea, the stars stretching into long bright lines that swung every which way, but she scuttled after the shadow in front of her as it flew through her camp. Fia knew everyone who fought and worked for the Fifth Union, but this man's face was unknown to her.

The edge of the camp was surrounded by a fence that had seen better days. The man would easily have been able to escape and disappear into the night, or even travel all the way to the shadow of the Kemen wall, and she would lose him. Bending low, she pulled a tent peg and it slid out of the mud, sending the guidelines pinging away.

"Stop!" The shadow immediately obeyed. The cloaked man stood in front of Fia, his back to her. "Who are you?"

"Names are not important." His voice was like dry paper.

Fia held the peg out. "Turn around."

The cloaked man turned. His hood hiding everything but the tip of a pale nose.

"Drop the hood."

The man complied, and Fia swallowed. It was Derval, except the butcher that Fia knew so well had smoother features, looking almost ageless. Most striking though were the patches of white and dark skin fighting for control of his face.

"Derval?"

The man shook his head.

"No, you're not the butcher," said Fia. "I'd know that hairline anywhere. In fact, I know everyone in my camp. You are not from here, even if you wear Derval's face."

"No," said the cloaked man, amused. "I am not Derval."

"Then, why are you here?"

"Intention is so important. Isn't it?"

Fia swallowed. "What are your intentions?"

"To help." The cloaked man held out an arm towards the wall. "How long have you searched for a way into Kemen?" The man flourished his cloak like a bad actor in a worse play. "What if I told you there was a way through it?"

"*Through*?" Fia balked at the idea, but by the blood of Baeivi herself she wanted to know. "How—"

The man smiled. "There is a section a few leagues from here that is designed to look like the rest, but is actually an illusion. There is a narrow panel that can be walked through. Narrow for a Bohr at least." He chuckled softly.

Unease clutched at Fia. "Tell me who you are, or I shall introduce you to my friend."

The man cackled, throwing his head back and laughing, showing perfect teeth. His expression turned abruptly sour. "Fia, you stand upon a road with many forks, and the fates of the worlds sit upon the ends of those roads. The decisions you make will shape every realm for many cycles to come. The ways of those who shape the worlds. Shape us all."

"Who are you?"

"Don't worry about who I am." The man came closer, standing so the bright moon was just behind him. "I am a friend, but my time here is limited. I have enemies everywhere. Enemies that would smite me down in an instant if they could. Take my information and check out the gap in the wall." He gestured to the tents around him. "The people here need you, Atalfia."

"You know me."

"Oh yes," said the man, teeth flashing. "Better than you think. Just heed my words, you are not done here. There is still much to do. And you, Captain Atalfia, are the one to do it. What would your friends do if they were in your shoes?" The man's eyes drifted to Fia's feet.

One boot, and one flat shoe, both covered in mud. Fia couldn't have said why it was, just that it was. She frowned and looked up, abruptly remembering the mysterious man, but there was only the moon staring back at her. It waited, like the stars, for her decision. Waited for her to decide the fates of those around her, the people she was charged to protect. She had to beat the Bohr down and end their reign of terror.

And as bright and clear as the spring sky Fia knew what to do. "We need to invade Kemen," she said to the moon, and the moon smiled back.

42

THE CRYSTAL TOWER

The road out of Minerva was as dark and unsettling as the town itself, and remained so all the way to the orange grove. Vasta would have kept her safe had he not ran off into the bloody night. Still, what were you supposed to do when chased by an angry mob?

Abika had stolen some old moccasins from a drunkard lying on the outskirts. He wouldn't miss them, besides it served him right for having such ridiculously small feet.

The old orange grove was not easy to get to. The trees, wilted and long dead, surrounded the grove house on all sides. A smell of sweet decay hung about the air; the stiff breeze of Rothmarr's vessel was just a distant memory. The house looked like her commune, even if it had once held workers rather than children. Abika tracked the long lines of the old groves, padding carefully up the stone path, stepping over the rotting bushes and thorny branches that lay across it. A gust of wind found the bottom of her shift and lifted it up, filling her with cold. She held it down and cursed. Maybe there were some clothes in the house.

The front door was boarded up, and the wooden walls looked like they might collapse inwards at any moment. Through the first floor she could see the upstairs had already fallen through to become a new downstairs, and the thorny creepers blanketing the steps up to the front door.

"Not this way then."

Winding her way through the orange trees, she found the house's corner and tried to follow it as best she could, avoiding the bushes that filled every space large enough to walk through. Eventually she found her way to a clearing at the rear of the house, and spied a window where the boards had fallen. As carefully as she could, she worked her way towards it, her new shoes crunching on old leaves and the occasional rotten orange. The smell of citrus and mould drifted up from the fruit flesh covering her boot. There were still some oranges clinging to life higher up, it had been some time since she had eaten. If she could reach the top floor, perhaps she could reach them.

The ground at the window was covered in broken glass and the boards were not quite loose enough to pull off, so began climbing the tree. The leaves were already in show, masking the world as she climbed upwards, the house's wall barely a few feet away. The corner wall and window were open to the world as part of her tree had fallen in, crashing through the house. With barely a thought on it, Abika tiptoed across the limb and into the room.

As soon as her feet touched the floorboards she grabbed a handful of oranges from the hanging tree and began tearing them to pieces.

"Oh, gods," she said, devouring the fruit, flesh, skin and all. Sticky-fingered and covered in orange peel she stood and padded over the floor, resolving to pick as many as she could before leaving. The shadow of the trees made the room dark, but not so dark it hid the old bed, the hay mattress still covered in a yellow bed sheet. At the front of the room the floor had given way completely, but there were enough joists still in place that she could tip toe around. The cupboards were empty in all but two of the rooms, which yielded a pair of dark fielder's breeches, a man's work shirt and a pair of old leather shoes which looked like they would fit someone twice Jekob's height let alone Abika. She tied the laces together and let them dangle from her neck.

There was a ladder up to the attic in the hallway, its rungs still intact, so she made her way up. The loft space was easily the lightest part of the house, and as she pulled herself up several birds panicked and flew out of the hole in the gable end, squawking their threats at this new intruder.

"Eggs!"

A clutch of beautiful, blue eggs sat in a nest of twigs and orange leaves. She held them up to the light. "Oh, you'll do! Shoes that don't fit and dinner. I knew it was worth coming in here!" Abika stripped off again, removed her shift and wrapped the eggs carefully, before pulling on the shirt and breeches. She turned to leave, and her breath caught. On the other side of the grove, stood a tower of blue crystal. Stepping as far as she dared along the loose joists Abika leant out and peered over the tops of the orange trees, trying to make sense of the shape of it. The light bounced off the crystal in ways her mind couldn't understand.

A bird swooped in at her, pecking and flapping. "Argh, get off!" Then all of the birds were swooping, attacking and diving. She threw an arm out and her balance shifted. She fumbled for the side of the hole. Her hand found rotten wood and grabbed hold, but it came away splintering a dusty in her fist. Twisting, Abika tipped back, and the world tumbled with her. Leaves, branches thorns and—

"Woah!" Vasta's arms were hardly the softest landing she could have hoped for, but they stopped her fall.

She stared up at him, dazed. "Vasta!"

"You are the luckiest—"

"What are you doing following me about?" she raged as he put her down delicately. "You bloody fool!"

"You saw the tower."

"Are you trying to kill me?" she snapped. She couldn't stop herself.

"I saved you."

"I don't need to be saved!" She spun around and whipped her soaking wet shift at him, covering his clothes in eggs and shell as it unravelled. "That was food. Now it's all gone!"

"Abika. I will get more food."

She stormed off through the trees, and Vasta followed. The grove opened out, but the field was empty. Everything that had been alive was reduced to grey ash.

"A perfect circle." Abika reached down and picked up a grey-looking orange. It was light, as though it had no body or flesh inside. She squeezed, and it crumbled to dust. Abika focused on the tower in the centre of it all. It was barely a field away, looking five times as high as the house. It was as though a shard of diamond had been pushed through the underside of the earth, grown like a tree from the ground.

"The house has been abandoned for at least ten cycles." He looked at her with those animal eyes. "Or twelve."

Abika frowned. "What? You think this has something to do with *me*?"

"I think it has everything to do with you." Vasta stepped by her and padded on over the dead ground. Each step left a footprint that seemed to spread, growing in size, reducing what was left of the dead vegetation to dust. The soft crackle of death followed behind them, turning the tower's field to dust and filling the air with the putrid smell of decay, until finally the tower stood majestically above them. A rock of light that shone with every beam of the sun at once. It was the most beautiful thing Abika had ever seen.

"You are right to be afraid of it," said Vasta.

"You're afraid."

"I am."

They stopped at the base, which was a full ten metres around. "It must be very dense to remain standing." Abruptly Vasta turned and shouted. "Abika, no. You don't know—"

It was too late. Abika's fingers found the surface of the crystal tower. It was impossibly smooth and somehow warm. The world around her grew dark. The trees, the sky, even Vasta disappeared. The crystal tower shone bright, pulsing with the energy of the sun. It knew her, and it would fall this day. First, there was an echo, then two words, softly spoken.

Let go.

Abika wanted to step away and leave. But her fingertips were not there, her arm was inside the crystal, joined to it seamlessly, the crystal moving like liquid over her skin.

"No!" She pulled away, but a force inside the crystal tower pulled her closer. The liquid crystal reached her shoulder, and she gasped as it went cold.

She couldn't die here.

Let go.

She would not die here.

Let go.

Abika reached within, and Soulfire was there, waiting. She grasped hold and it filled her up, coursing through her veins bringing warmth and strength. Nausea followed, like with the tom'ra leaf that Lorith had given her. Power surged through her like fire itself. The tower was alive, and this was a fight for her life. She could give up and it would take her now. Then that would be it. She would be gone, burned away as though she never existed. The sky was replaced with red and black clouds that rolled and burgeoned. The bright crystal filled with darkness, black clouds of blood filling the insides and taking over. A woman's hooded face materialised, a reflection that replaced her own on the black glass, staring back at her. Her panicked expression mimicked Abika's own.

"Kyira?" Abika couldn't say how she knew it, but it was her. The tower wanted her to see.

The woman's expression twisted into anger. Her mouth open in anguish, her eyes alive with the same fire that filled Abika's veins. Abika directed her will at that reflection, and it bounced back at her. Fire and warmth, too hot to imagine.

Abika drew Soulfire through the necklace around her neck, and the power inside became a torrent of fire filling every fibre of muscle, every sinew and bone with strength. She funnelled the power along her arm like a conduit, pushing the flame into the crystal, filling it with her anger and pain and fear. The woman in the tower screamed in pain, her skin burning as the whirling flames within found her skin, tearing it from her flesh. Abika pushed harder, forcing the power in, and the blackness inside the crystal parted, as her flames consumed the inside. The woman's face, now a skull of white, turned black, then grey and vanished into a haze of dust.

The crystal tower had tried to confuse her, had looked inside her and thought it could fool her but Abika would not simply allow the gods of this wretched world to just take her! The tower pushed back against her, and Abika felt emotion pouring through. It was afraid.

43

SULPHUR, ASH AND ICE

The girl was frozen.

The moment Abika's fingers touched the crystal tower, her body shifted out of phase, her outline pulsing in and out of reality. Vasta knew there might be a reaction, but not one so strong!

He ran over, pulling at her as hard as he dared, but she was both here and not here and she repelled his vast bulk like two kin lodestones being forced together. The lightning crackling over Abika's body found its way onto Vasta's fingers, coursing up his arms, dragging at him as though trying to take control. He threw his arm around Abika's chest, ignoring the fizzing and burning of own hair and with every ounce of strength, tried to pull Abika way from the crystal tower.

The compound effect was immediate. Vasta's attempted interruptions of the force holding her, resulted in an explosive release of energy that catapulted him awkwardly away. The world was a blur of colour until the ground reclaimed him, shoulders, neck and the rest, bundled in a heap. The pile of ash that partially cushioned his fall lifted up into the air and hung about him like flies, taunting him for his foolishness.

"Vasta, you fool!" he growled. "Trying to move the immovable." He leapt up, and started to run. Abika's outline flickered. She was drawing energy from another world and was locked in. Like all forms of energy transference, the stream of power would continue until there was nothing left.

"LET GO, ABIKA! LET GO!" he roared.

He stopped short of her, looking this way and that for something he could use… But she wasn't moving, and her form was growing fuzzy. A soft blue glow surrounded her. And then a smile, forming slowly. Her expressions changed, bouncing then jerking back as though time had become inconsistent for her. Anguish then fear, then delight. Anger. Hatred. Resolve. "This is bad. Abika you have to let go! There's too much power!"

The shard necklace she wore shone and pulsed through the same rainbow as the crystal tower. It alone had enough power to amplify Abika's gifts a thousand-fold, with the current running through her, she could sink the whole of the Red Isles!

Abika twitched, shimmering through impossible colours, the flashing auras of energy pulsing with her as she drew more and more of the force from that other world.

He had to reach her somehow. "I don't know if you can hear me, but you must let go. Do not try and control it. Please. You'll kill us both."

Through the hundreds of expressions Abika's eyes began to move of their own volition. Her irises rolled towards him, giving her an unhinged appearance as the rest of features snapped back and forth between anger, fear, happiness. Abika blinked and Vasta knew she could hear him.

"*You* are the maker of ways, Abika. There is still much for you to do. That is why I am here with you now. To guide you on this journey. To open your mind the world and stretch the possibilities of your power." The air around her thrummed with danger, and against his better judgement, he stepped forward. "Abika you have the power to stop this. Deny the tower." The vibrations were so loud Vasta couldn't even hear the words he spoke, but he said them anyway. "Deny it."

Abika's eyes welled, she blinked and the crystal tower cracked like ice, beginning at the end of Abika's outstretched fingers. With each pulse, the crack grew, spidering into fractals that travelled away in all directions.

The hairs on Vasta's arms stood up. Even if Abika had successfully stopped the flow, so much energy had been drawn already that it would cause an imbalance. That reality's lifeblood had no business being here in this world. The crystal tower was going to fall and the release would only kill both he and Abika if they were lucky. There was nothing more he could do. Vasta spared Abika a final glance then turned and ran as fast as he could towards the house.

The nara he had borrowed from Minerva was still tethered to the cart, stomping and snorting.

She whinnied as Vasta mounted her. "Run, Brenax. Run!" He slapped her rump and the nara took off down the old path away from the house, the cart bouncing around behind. Vasta slammed a fist down onto the connecting rods, splintering the yoke and sending the cart spinning away into the lines of old orange trees. The pulsing from behind was so loud the very air was blistering.

It was foolish to do it, but Vasta looked behind him. He had to see it for himself. It was as though the sun had fallen to the earth and was burning bright at the tower, the old house silhouetted against it. A sphere of crackling energy burst out of the base of the tower. This was as far as they would get.

"Stop, Brenax!" Leaning forward, Vasta held her antlers to stop her turning her head and the shockwave came.

The pulse tore through wood, air and both of their insignificant bodies. The misplaced energy was out, it was an imbalance of opposing frequencies, seeking equilibrium. Not conscious, but by design. The reality of one godly body penetrating another. Those caught between would be annihilated.

Fire.

Heat blossomed against Vasta's back as the very air around them set alight. The smell of sulphur, ash and ice filled Vasta's head.

Wind and sound.

The air groaned as the explosion pulled it back then forth, the sound of two realities battling for dominance in a small space. There must always be balance. Vasta threw himself forward and covered Brenax's ears with his elbows while holding his hands over his own. Brenax was strong, but he was stronger. The sound still found a way in, and he felt his eardrums straining against an explosion that would wake the dead.

The battle ceased as quickly as it had commenced. Silence won out, but Vasta held. Waiting for the bright light behind his eyelids to dim before daring to look.

It was the blurry light of close fires that appeared first, the trees around him were alight. Hesitantly, he turned back towards the orange grove.

A crater was all that was left. Even the earth had been victim to the fight. The tower was gone. The house was gone. Of the grove, the remaining orange trees had been flattened. Aside from the eerie silence, a soft blue light was all that lingered, an echo of the shard and the girl that had been.

Diary entry

Bakla Beach

Fiskal's army is impressive. From what Darc and I have seen so far anyway. Darc looks tired and drawn. The man is an enigma, but he helped me find Milli, so I must give him the benefit of the doubt, at least for a little longer. We've been taken to a waiting area while the commander performs his duties, which has given me some time to digest what I've seen. Bakla is the home of the republic, where once again I find my path leads me to the fight against the Bohr.

Fiskal is a Nordun warrior who talks of Sami ideals, and still I feel as though I am being pushed and pulled according to everyone else's will. I walk, I run. And still I end up dancing to someone else's tune. The same fight. Different characters. And yet, ironically, I do not feel like myself. Something dark lingers within.

spice

44

A GIRL CALLED ABIKA

Darc paced back and forth like an animal in a cage. He had become increasingly agitated since Kyira's tour of the city and for no reason.

"Where are we?" He snapped. "A holding pen?"

"It's a tent," replied Kyira, sliding her journal away into her bag. "He's the commander of an army, Darc. He's in demand. He'll come for us when he's ready." She frowned at the man. "Why did they ignore you? The two guards."

"Rolla?" Darc turned to the wide tent's entrance. "Why did you ignore me, Rolla?" The doorman stood just outside the canvas and so must had heard Darc's shout, but the big man's shadow didn't even twitch.

"In Bakla, there is a culture of need," said Darc, spinning around. "And when someone is not needed they are ignored." He held out his hands. "Especially from someone who looks like I do."

"What happened to your face, Dara?"

"My face?" said Darc. He lifted his shirt to show a muscled stomach covered in patches of white. "My whole body."

Kyira traced the lines. "You look like a map."

"Yes," he said impatiently. "And I imagine one day I will change colour completely. Metamorphosing into a new being! Like the green beetle into the moth, the tern or perhaps the winter rabbit." He dropped his shirt, then after a long breath seemed to master himself. When he spoke again his voice was calm. "You and Fiskal both have Lines do you not? Illustrating where the paths of your life lead and how they get there." He sat next to her on old bench. "With whom we take with us."

"Perhaps you will change completely." Kyira pulled off her map tube and rummaged inside. "But you will not be a Nordun tern, because unlike other birds, they do not migrate."

"What are you doing?" asked Darc.

"Looking for something." Kyira have gone straight to the map, but she wanted to gauge Darc's reaction, and sure enough the man's interest was piqued. Those small dark eyes followed every movement like a dog waiting for supper. Kyira rolled out the map so its corners hung over the round table.

Darc touched the parchment and pulled away as if it burned him. "This isn't the map you showed Fiskal."

"I've made many maps."

"Kyira. My dear. This is utterly incredible. What an achievement."

Kyira flushed, she knew it was good, she'd spent a lot of time drawing it. The map was probably the only true and accurate representation of Rengas that had ever been produced. Her mind dragged up the image of its original source, Kai's ship the Celsathar, its grand decks and stinking, rotten rooms filled with treasures and of course the map of the world Kai had spent a lifetime carving into wood.

Darc's finger hovered above each inlet tracing it along Nord's sister peaks to the Bone Coast, across the ice to Ipiti and Sulitaria. He stopped at the Red Isles. "What's this?"

"An orange."

"Yes, I can see that," said Darc. "What does it mean?"

"That's the thing with maps," said Kyira, reaching by him and pulling the corners back. She rolled the thick parchment back up slid it gently into map tube with the others. "Symbols can mean anything."

"Yes, but every symbol has a meaning. Landmarks help us navigate life, so when I see one on a map such as that, I know it must be important."

"It is important."

"A grove?"

Kyira's breath caught. "That is where oranges grow."

"A grove in the Red Isles." Darc mused on it as a maid returned to the front room. He watched her like a hawk watching a mouse. "I highly doubt that your interests are import–export related. Maybe you are here in Bakla simply to sell us all oranges?"

"I don't think so," laughed Kyira. "I'm not so good at selling things. I am good at making things. Seeing things others do not." The words sat heavy and oppressive between them.

Darc laughed. "A mighty skill for a mapmaker. From what I understand it's all in the detail."

"It's *all* about detail, said Kyira, leaning forward. "We perceive these things as they are thrown at us, but in reality we all stand upon the knife's edge, doubting all that we do. Troubling over every choice." Kyira took a ragged breath. "Darc, I must apologise. Before, you told me your truth..."

"Of the man I killed?"

Kyira nodded. "And I repaid you with a threat. In rebalance, I need to tell you something." Kyira took a steeled herself—truth was never easy. "I also killed someone. An innocent named Isak. He deserved much better than what I did to him. I tried so hard to make it up to his partner, Lyla. Until she too fell."

Darc covered his mouth in feign shock. "You killed the partner too?"

Kyira shook her head. "My brother killed Lyla. They were fighting on opposite sides, and he realised too late who she was. Who I was. I couldn't save her." She swallowed. "Unfortunately, my shame does not end there. Lyla had a child, a girl called Abika, and I took her in and made her my own...For a time."

"For a time? You gave her away."

Hearing the words from someone else was too much and Kyira's chin wobbled. It took a minute for her to be able to speak. "I've been trying to make up for it ever since."

Darc took Kyira's hand. "Thank you, Kyira. For all that it means, I forgive you and shall always remember your words today. We are the same you and I."

Kyira pulled her hand away. She hadn't intended to be so...honest, but something about Darc drew it out of her. "Please, Darc. Don't repeat my shame."

"Kyira, when you can see the details as plain as a clear night sky as I do, you find there is much to look at. Not all can understand what they see though, my dear." Darc leant forward. "And that is what sets you apart, mapmaker." He tapped the map. "It is what Fiskal sees too. It is why he wants you."

"He wants to use me," snapped Kyira. "I know his type."

Darc sat back a little. "One thing that has struck me, bright and clear, is that you seem totally at ease here, Kyira. I sense that you have been in the midst of an army before." Before Kyira could respond Darc pointed at her. "Not just that though, there's something else. You've been a *part* of an army. An active participant."

"How can you possibly know that?"

"You have rubbed the shoulders of army seniors before. You are comfortable with Fiskal, but it's not just your common heritage. Anyone with eyes can see it."

Kyira scratched Milli behind the ear and gave her head a good rub, Milli pressed into her hand, relishing the attention. "You are right. I have. And it is why I will be telling Fiskal I will not be aiding him in his fight. I might stay for a spell and—"

"You mean to leave Bakla?" Darc inclined his head.

Kyira shook her head. "Not right away."

"You are a unique person, Kyira. Fiskal sees it too. And it's not just because of your skill. I see it as plain as if it were written on your faces. You need each other."

"I don't need anyone." Even as she said the words, Kyira could her hear her own hesitation dripping off them.

"Didn't you ever question why you came here? What purpose led you to cross from Ge'Bat and walk all the way through New Bakla to the republic's capital city, deep in the heart of Bohr territory. Was it the desire to understand the land, or the desire to understand yourself?"

Kyira swallowed. "You think I am running from something."

"Everyone runs from something." Darc took her hand. "The fates of our lives lead us to paths we may not be ready to take. But we must take them anyway."

Kyira pulled her hand back. "You talk like a Culdè. My aspirations are written upon my skin! I am a Pathwatcher. I mind the paths. I do not walk them."

"Every choice is a new dimension, girl. As we walk, we see. As we experience so do we grow. Your Lines may be your aspirations, but it would seem that this world has other plans for you. Walk the path and become who you are destined to be."

New light burst into the tent and Kyira shielded her eyes. Fiskal stood silhouetted against the bright beach of Bakla behind. "Kyira! Why did they put in here? Nevermind, come! I have much to show you."

45

CULDÈ

The walk through Fiskal's camp was all too familiar. The Tsiorc, the Republic—every army was the same—it was just men and women sitting around fires until it was their turn to practise fighting each other.

"I know what you're thinking," said Fiskal, hopping over a rock.

"Do you?" said Kyira.

"Why would I build an army so close to the city?"

"That's exactly what I was thinking."

Fiskal nodded to himself. "I have a way with people you see, I can see inside their heads. It is a true gift, no? For the commander of a great army?"

"Indeed." Kyira glanced at Darc, who raised his eyebrows.

They stopped by a group of sparring fighters, clad in shiny steel with red and blue feathers protruding from every crease. "Thing is, Kyira. I must ask you. I am...curious. When you fought with Laeb. Did he prefer to set out his men in a grid? Like I do? Or was it some other pattern? Something that would be easier to mobilise in the event of say...a surprise attack?"

"A grid. More or less."

Fiskal's face lit up. He was so expressive that Kyira almost smiled with him. "Excellent!" he said, clapping his hands. "Excellent. Then your Laeb and I are on the same page it would seem. We are kindred spirits. Separated at birth."

"Is this all he wanted to show us?" Fiskal ignored Darc's comment, in-fact the commander had yet to even acknowledge Darc at all.

Kyira spoke up. "Commander, I thought you wanted to—"

"Show you something," said Fiskal. "Yes. Come. Come!"

They carried on along the beach, and Kyira couldn't help but think about how well-suited the flats would be for a battle. Kamsin had been kill box, a valley sat upon a craggy coast, with nowhere wide or flat enough to contain an army, let alone two. Bakla was a bustling, thriving city where people were used to the throng and pressures of living in each other's pockets, rushing around from one place to another, shouting and bellowing—the chaos of a battle would be as familiar to them as walking the streets. Ironically, the Republic army, waiting on the red sands seemed more content. They sat by their fires, cooking spicy stews in huge flat pots wider than Kyira herself, filling the warm air with intoxicating smells.

Fiskal steered into the centre of a large community of soldiers. "Careful. The light sand may look solid but it is a trick. Watch." The commander lifted a stone and threw it. It landed in the middle of the light patch and sank within a few seconds. "You see why we are careful where we camp?"

Kyira shook her head. The idea that she couldn't trust even the ground dredged up frightful memories of Tyr. "How do you even live here, Fiskal? There are such dangers."

Fiskal brushed the sand from his hands. "Some say the same about Nord, with its steep cliffs and high mountains. The beach flats have always been safe, and a great source of food for all. But of late, these areas of light sand have been appearing, and they're getting larger. There are places now where there are no mudplates upon which to walk, and the light sand is all there is. My worry is that soon this beach will become uninhabitable. And on that day, Bakla will cease to be the powerhouse of the republic." Fiskal shrugged. "It may very well cease to exist. The Republican army will need somewhere else to call home." He took Kyira's arm. "So, if you find yourself out there, be careful. I do not mean to patronise, but when the very earth beneath us is suddenly untrustworthy then—"

Kyira pulled away. "Leave me be, Commander. I have been walking long enough to know where not to put my feet."

Fiskal studied her for a long moment. "Forgive me. Once a leader… Ah. This is why I asked you here. Look!" He beckoned her over to a group of soldiers sat around a large steel cooking bowl filled with dark red meat. A fire below kept the food sizzling.

Fiskal embraced each soldier in turn, asking them of their wellbeing, their equipment, even going as far as to comment on one young man's scruffy hair.

"They like him," said Darc. "A lot."

Fiskal returned, shoving a cremated chicken wing at her. "Take it. You are hungry I can tell."

Kyira took the meat and sniffed it. "It is burnt."

Fiskal shook his head. "It is spice. Eat. Eat."

"On your own head be it," said Darc.

Kyira shoved the chicken in her mouth. There was an explosion of flavour, followed by an intense feeling of panic. "Hot!" The spice on the outside was a sort of charred coating over deliciously moist meat.

Fiskal burst into laughter. "We use a spice called gharam in much of our food. In stews it is a little lost but coated on meat it is potent and strong! Much like our people, no?"

"I told you," murmured Darc, peering into the pot. The soldiers ignored him completely.

Kyira's lips were on fire, her throat and tongue felt like they were swelling. Just as her eyes started streaming, she gestured down at the soldier sitting at the fire. "Give me your water!"

"Milk," said Fiskal. "Trust me."

The soldier nodded and pulled a ladleful of steaming milk from another pot, cupped it and handed it up to Kyira. "It's hot?"

"Trust me," said Fiskal.

Kyira drank deep. At first the two heats battled one another, spice and temperature, until abruptly they cancelled each other out, and all that was left was a pleasant sweetness lingering in her mouth. She opened her mouth to breathe some air in, and it too became sweet as it touched her tongue.

"Mother's milk," said Fiskal. "The clams here in the shallows produce a thick milk when threatened, which is common when you are cooking them, no?! A little water and this is what we have. A drink that can cure most pained stomachs. And as one seasoned veteran to another, you will know that gut rot can make soldiering a tedious exercise. Don't let the red sands fool you. The soils of Bakla yield some of the richest roots of the world. The seafoods of the mud flats hide well, but they are juicy and number in their millions. Bakla is truly the jewel in Kemen's Crown."

"Is this what you wanted me to do?" said Kyira, licking her lips. "Eat some chicken?"

Fiskal smiled. "Of course not. But I wanted to give you a flavour of the Republican army, no? You see my choice of words? Flavour..."

Kyira nodded slowly. "I see. Very clever, commander."

"Call me Fiskal. But you see, Kyira. All here is not what it seems. I see it on your face, the doubt and scepticism. You are unsure. A lost lamb. I can help give you purpose."

Kyira turned to find Darc had once again disappeared. Fiskal steered her on, until they were beyond the grid of soldiers and onto an open section of beach. They walked up into the longer grass behind.

"Kyira. I have a secret. You have dropped into my lap, and I cannot let you go. I will do anything, say anything to have to stay here. To join our ranks and fight with us against the Bohr. I will not lie, your experience in Tyr, your relationship with Laeb—"

Kyira laughed. "Relationship? No. Laeb and I were..." What had they been? She pictured him undressing, he had been beautiful. Handsome. Had she loved him? She didn't know.

Fiskal tilted his head to the side. "Either way. I am so sure that you must join us. I am so sure that this must be the way. For I truly believe that we can and will win this war."

Kyira swallowed. The mother's milk was not doing its job properly, and this subterfuge was not helping. "How, exactly?"

Fiskal took her hand. "Kyira, I want you to fight with us. Give me your assurance that you will join the great Republican army and stand against the Bohr."

Kyira looked down at Fiskal's hands. They were rough but strong. And was that flour or some other powder pressed into his fingertips? She looked up at him. A baker? A man who bakes, who creates things, leading an army was better than one who sought to destroy. Yet Laeb had been neither of those things.

"I cannot give you that assurance," said Kyira. Fiskal's bright eyes grew dim, and Kyira wanted to change her answer. Change who she was for him and join him and fight with him for a cause as true as any. "It took me a long time to discover who I am." He tried to pull away, but she held tighter. "And I must honour it and the people who helped me by forging my own path."

Fiskal reached up and held Kyira's chin lightly. "I understand, Kyira. I too am Culdè."

Kyira blinked. "Culdè? You know this word?"

"Of course. The point of which one chooses not to follow the aspirations painted upon their skin. You may think my Nordun heritage is hidden beneath layers of Kemenese, and you would be right, to some degree. But my Nordun grandmother, taught me many things before leaving us to dine with the Great Mother. My path was due to take me into a family. A happy life with a happy wife. A musician, travelling as, how do you westerners call it? Ringlanders? Travelling with our children." He stared out towards the distant shore, towards the Republican army.

"How do you know this was not your path?" Before the words had even left Kyira's mouth she wanted to retrieve them. Hearing Darc's words was hard enough, but now she was replaying them to another! What a fool she was.

Fiskal sighed. "Perhaps you are right." He spread his arms. "All of this is but a charge of my own making. Some six cycles ago, I met a man who convinced me to hang up my apron. To leave a life spent providing for others, and instead ask them to follow me."

"A man?"

"A strange man with strange skin."

"Strange skin? Like Darc?"

Fiskal frowned. "Like Darc? I don't know. This man was bullish, strong and insistent. He talked all night about the Bohr, about the importance of the fight for life, for pride. For humans. He plied me with drink, and I agreed with him. In only a few hours, I moved my path to follow his."

"That does not make you Culdè, Fiskal. That makes you human. You changed your world. There are not many who can."

"Yes! But Kyira, the horrors I have seen since that day haunt me. Children dying in places where they should be safe. Worshippers cut to pieces in their local Domsts, places where they grew up. The Bohr infiltrated Bakla like they did in Cursed City. Tyr had money and resource. Bakla is a city whose only real wealth comes from its people. From the sands. The sea. So far away. The Bohr come to us and they kill us, and conquer us. They do not wish to rule here, they wish to scrub us from existence!"

Kyira had stepped back from Fiskal. Culdè or not. When she didn't respond, he looked up. Tears stood in his eyes, ready to fall.

He smiled. "But none of that matters now. The horrors of war, or the losses of one's people are just part of the role. Part of my role here, however awful."

Kyira's head swam with colour, her legs threatened to give way and a hard pulsing took over her senses.

"Kyira?" said Fiskal, holding a deep look of concern. "Are you alright? You don't look well."

The air felt queer, like it was not real. Her breaths came shallow, as her body fought the urge to drag it into her lungs. "Give...Give...me...a moment, comman—"

Breathe.

Breathe.

The tainted air felt like poison, and the urge to vomit took hold. The blood in her head pounded in time with her breathing but the pulsing was out of phase. Her body shook as though in the throes of feverblood, as though she were lying upon her death bed. Kyira opened her eyes but saw only intense blue light.

The man at her side spoke but the words were slow and distorted. Colour and substance floated between them. Kyira's own face stamped upon the air, reflected in blue crystal. Those eyes burned, the expression aguish itself. She opened her mouth to scream and everything went black.

46

THE BLADE THAT WAS

The clouds above the grove coalesced, creating new shapes, no two the same, swelling like the sea. Abika took long, relaxed breaths. The cloud broke in the middle creating new shapes, rimmed with rainbow colours that waned against the power of the sun, cutting the light. Blinking, she expected pain, but found strength instead. The grove, or rather, what was left of it, came into focus. The trees were all flat, but the flora beyond was blooming. New leaves filled every branch and twig, oranges dotted each and every tree as though they had been there all along. The Great Mother had reclaimed this grove, and it had grown wild and free.

Abika sat up. The tower was gone, but she knew it would be. She felt at her neck. The chain that had held Freja's shard was still there, but the housing was empty. All that remained was a red rash where the little shard had been hanging.

A haze hung about her, clinging to the bracken like the very sky had descended, settling around her. Inside the mist were bright points of light that frisked and frolicked like tiny firebugs. They sped up as she moved closer, joining together, getting bigger. They wouldn't hurt her because they were hers.

She opened herself up to them, and the lights combined and drew close. She should have been terrified, but she wasn't, not even when the light passed through her chest and into her heart. Warming her body and filling every piece of her with joy and light. The tom'ra Lorith had given her paled in comparison to this wonderful new feeling, which was so raw and real, like she was always meant to have it. She rubbed her fingers together, and heat blossomed there. Lifting her hand she conjured the light from within, like she did every time she had sat with Meorith smoking down by the bay. More tiny particles of light came to be, floating above her palm, coming together into a single light.

"Where do I go?"

The light leapt away into the trees.

"Wait!"

Abika leapt up, laughing, skipping over the broken ground to the edge of the forest. A thick jungle of leafy branches awaited her, and noise from hundreds of insects that called this new place home, thanking her in unison for the greatest of gifts. The light shone, hovering in place, waiting until she approached before shooting off again, searching for an explanation to it all. She must have walked for almost half a league before it finally stopped in clearing, where the leaves were sparse, changing through the autumnal colours of, reds, golds and oranges. The light sunk slowly to the ground at her feet, where it touched a shard of blue crystal, before fading gently away.

The blade's bottom half was scorched and rounded, but the top was as bright and blue as the sky. Abika went to touch it, then stopped herself. That edge was too keen. It would never blunt, and any wound it opened would never heal, but it had come from her. Abika ran her thumb along the blade's edge. It should have cut her, but it had refused, as though it had a choice. It was a soulblade—the remnants of an ancient relic returned to the ages. The blade that was.

47

MISTAKES

Time had no meaning when you were asleep—you could live a lifetime in the dreamworld but when you awoke, barely an hour had passed.

Kyira felt as though she had lived through a thousand lifetimes. The room was pale and blurry, punctuated only by a dark shape at her side. Vomit threatened to burst out of her, and her head pounded like she had been beaten into unconsciousness.

"It is night?" she croaked.

"Kyira, it's me. You're safe." Fiskal's warm voice resonated deeply, as though she was talking to another part of herself.

"What happened?" she said. She tried to squint, but her eyes refused to focus.

The commander's silhouette bounced. "You've been dreaming," he said with a chuckle. "Eyes of fire. Daemons, gods. All fighting over a gift.

"A gift?" croaked Kyira.

"That's what you said."

"Abika?" Kyira squinted, trying to focus. "I...No. I ate something. Forbringrs be damned, my head is so sore...All I remember is light. A shining tower of blue light."

"You collapsed," said the commander. "Here, take some water. We can't have the navigator of the Republican army falling to pieces now, can we?"

Kyira rolled her eyes. "I told you, Commander, I am not joining any army."

"Commander? No, Kyira, it's me. It's Darc."

Kyira rubbed her eyes and the commander's silhouette resolved into Darc's gangly dimensions, patchy skin and all. "Darc? What are you doing here?"

"I should ask you the same thing! Fiskal told me you almost died." His teeth flashed, then he was touching her head, pressing it down against the pillow. "Kyira, come, you should rest."

She tried to push against him, but his grip was like iron. "Get off me, Darc. Remove your hand. Now."

Darc sat back looking hurt. "I am just trying to help, Kyira."

"Are you?" Kyira leaned back. "Tell me what happened. From the beginning."

"You and Fiskal were walking—"

"No," said Kyira. "I didn't mean that. I mean you, Darc. Tell me of your family again. Your brother. Where you came from. Why you are here in Bakla."

Darc's expression hardened. "My life is dull Kyira, I am here to fight for the people of Bakla. We've been over this."

He was difficult to read, but was it due to the disease upon his tanned skin or because Kyira still felt groggy? She wanted the truth, but Darc was clever. "Please. I am just so...overwhelmed with everything. I just...I just need something other than armies, weapons, and Bohr."

"Kyira, you need strength. Regardless of your plans. You are skinny from months on the road. Is it any wonder that you keeled over at the first real taste of meat?"

"It wasn't the meat, Darc." Kyira sat up. The tent was like every other she had ever sat in, except this one was all white bed sheets, and a curtain hanging between her bed and presumably some other poor soul beside her."

"It's empty," said Darc, twitching the curtain. "I checked."

Kyira fell back to the pillow exasperated. "How do you know what

I'm thinking Darc? How is it that we meet and you know so much about me, and yet when I ask you about your life, you are so closed off?"

Darc sat up, his expression a mask of concern. "Kyira, I am a passerby. I helped you retrieve your belongings, I found Milli." He took her hand, but it felt awkward. "She's safe, don't worry. And now I sit for an entire night, waiting for you to wake! What sort of monster am I? One who cares." He let her hand go, and it flopped to the bed. "Or is there no way a man can care for a woman who is not his wife? Should we get married, Kyira and then perhaps you would believe me?"

"Don't be ridiculous." Something crept into Kyira's mind. "Your brother had children. And a wife. Why didn't you ever settle down Darc?"

Darc stood and sighed. "I did. For a while. Her name was Aashvi and we had grand plans, like every human does. We planned to start a family, but it didn't work out. She loved another and so our paths went in different directions."

Kyira nodded slowly, then swung her legs around to the side of the bed. Nausea swept over her.

"Kyira, I don't think—"

"I'm fine."

"You are not fine."

And then it came. The meagre contents of Kyira's stomach rushed upwards and she heaved, with no time to do anything but let it come.

Darc was suddenly by her side, a bucket beneath her. "It's alright, just let it out."

Kyira tried to tell him to leave her alone, but the illness was relentless. When it finally abated, her back ached and her throat was raw. She looked down to see milk in the bucket.

"I fed you more of the mother's milk in the night," said Darc. "To get some strength into you."

"You fed me?" Kyira wiped her face against a bandage on her arm. "And what's this? She lifted it to look beneath and found fresh cuts on her skin.

Darc shook his head. "I don't know, you must have landed on glass, or stone."

Kyira moved the blankets off the bed, and then snapped them back over. "Darc, did you undress me?"

"Kyira, you were covered in sand and blood!"

"Get out!"

Darc jumped back from the bed, pulling down the curtain. "Kyira, I—"

"Milli!" A distant bark sounded, and Kyira let fly a whistle loud enough to wake the dead. Milli tore into the tent standing between Darc and Kyira growling.

"Get out, Darc." Milli enforced the words with a vicious bark.

The man gave her a hurt look, then ducked out of the tent, leaving her and Milli to themselves. Doubt immediately washed over Kyira like a wave. How could she be so nasty to someone who had helped her so much? Darc was selfless and kind!

Yet Kyira of Nord had learned that nothing was free in this life, not food, nor money, nor friendship. Everything had a price, and the cost of your mistakes would haunt you to your grave.

48

THE IMPORTANCE OF DEATH

Abika stepped on a stick and stopped. It should've hurt. Perhaps the crystal tower had given her something that could numb pain, or perhaps the soles of her feet were becoming so thick the pain just barely registered.

She wanted to feel different (she always had) but the same doubts plagued her mind, and now the euphoria had left, it felt as though the shard knife was all that she had that she did not have before. She picked up the broken twig and prodded Vasta with it. The great Bohr offered her a sidelong glance, but kept his eyes on Brenax and the road.

"Vasta, what does it mean to be *good*?"

"*Goodness* is a human construct."

"That's such a scholar's answer. You mean it's made up?"

"Perhaps," said Vasta. "A construct is something you build to protect yourself. Like the belief in a deity, for example. An overseer, who forgives your ills and promises eternal life. Or in the case of your question, goodness. The act of being good."

"So you believe that being good does not result in goodness returned?" For the first time, Abika saw it all from Vasta's viewpoint. A scholar and a beast. A liar.

"Goodness as a construct is just a state of mind. Like anything. If you believe in something, you see it in places. If you believe you are good, you see goodness…"

"Even when there is none…" Abika examined her hand, the lines, the dirt. "If you are bad, you see badness." Vasta seemed to catch the meaning of the question now. Seemed to understand her hesitation. They had not spoken at all about the crystal tower yet, but she knew he must have sorely wanted to. "Why are you not like the other Bohr?"

"Because of death."

"Death? You mean you kill for sport? Or for money?"

Vasta shook his great head. "No."

Abika chuckled. "Maybe that's not such a bad idea. It would be a noble way to live, being an assassin."

"To live by death is no life."

"But it would be a life." Abika swallowed away the lump in her throat. "And with so much uncertainty why wouldn't you look to what can keep you?" Vasta didn't answer this time. He would do that, just be quiet, like he hadn't heard her. But he heard everything she said. "What do you mean then, *because of death*?"

Vasta stopped the cart then lowered a branch from a nearby tree. The leaves on the end were huge and thick and full of water. Meorith and Abika used to build tents with them back when they were younger. Vasta ran a claw along the thick fibrous stem, slicing it open. "You see this plant? It stores water."

"So?"

"So…How does it know how to do that?"

"That's just how it is built?" said Abika.

"And who built it?"

Abika opened her mouth. "It is just there, as it has always been. The Gods? The Ringlanders call her the Great Mother."

"Ah, the Forbringr. The Great Mother Baeivi." Vasta shook his head. "Now who is unsure how to answer? This plant is like it is because of death. The ancestors of this plant did not store water, and they died. Until one day, one stored a very small amount of water and it lived a little longer than the rest. Whether by accident, or by design. My bet, though, is that it was quite by accident. A mutation deep within the makeup of the plant. Being the only plant left alive, it went on to seed more plants like itself, encouraged by the soil of its less fortunate fallen friends." He held the leaf closer as if smelling it. "A new species is born."

"Plants don't think."

"No, they don't. But they are products of their environment. As we all are. And when the environment changed, this plant changed with it, and so was the one that survived. You see? The rest had to die for this one to survive. And as the cycles wore on, so the effects grew stronger, until today when you and I stopped here and sliced one open." Vasta put his hairy lips to the stem and sucked it dry. "And now, I am sated and can continue on my journey." He pulled another down and snapped it off then handed it to Abika.

As the cart trundled forward, Abika turned the stem over in her hands. She must have held a thousand of these things over cycles past, and yet it was like she was seeing it from a different angle. Everything was different. Not just the plants, the trees or the cartful of oranges bouncing around as Vasta's nara led them back to the road, but everything. Abika couldn't fathom it, she felt the same. She looked the same, although probably a little worse for wear, but the insides of her head had been rearranged.

"You're wondering why you feel different," asked Vasta.

Abika blinked. "I'm wondering how you found me."

"I do not mind telling you I hid when the tower fell."

"You were afraid." Abika was at once disgusted with the Bohr. "A giant like you should be afraid of no one. Perhaps it's the scholar in you, Vasta. Your insistence on acting like someone you're not."

"I *was* afraid, Abika. Fear does strange things to us all, Bohr and human alike. The fear of loss, pain, of fear itself can cause us all to act like we've been taken over." Vasta took a long breath. "Fear leads even the best of us to do awful things, but there is nothing wrong with *being* afraid. It kept me alive today. The energy the tower released when it fell would have killed me." He frowned. "It should have killed you."

"Well, it didn't." Abika tore the little stem to pieces and threw it to the ground. "Nor did I find any sign of Kyira. She was there though. I was so sure of it." She said the last so quietly, she doubted the Bohr heard her.

Vasta shrugged. "Then we will continue south until we do find her. We'll find another port, and if we can't find one, we can hire a boat to take us to Sulitar."

"No," said Abika. "Minerva. The town folk will chase you down and kill you if we go into town. There must be another way around. I don't even know how you managed to get away from them before."

"Who said I did?"

Abika blinked at him. "We'll go and see Rothmarr's father again, and if the old man gives us nothing, we'll burn his boat to the ground."

Vasta stopped the cart. "You are more focused than before, and yet, you still think of destruction and death."

"You said it yourself, Vasta. Death haunts us all. Standing above us like a nosy mother, dictating our lives. It would be unnatural of me not to think about it."

Vasta's eyes narrowed. "You twist my words into something new." He moved the nara on. "You fight me at every turn, but at least you are mastering your anger. Perhaps when you finally meet Kyira, you will be amicable."

Abika rolled her eyes. In truth, she still felt the anger, like hot soup swallowed, but Vasta would never reciprocate it. She wanted to make him angry, because she wanted to see him as he was. A Bohr. But he refused to embrace himself, instead lecturing her on how she should act, or on the ways of the world. What more could she do to reveal the monster within? The scholar was a thick hide that she doubted words could penetrate.

Reaching back, she plucked an orange from the pile behind her and tore it open with her teeth. It was the best, juiciest morsel of food she had ever tasted. If she hadn't known better, she might have said that this very orange had been grown by the Forbringrs just for her. She licked her lips to stop the juice from escaping, savouring each segment, and marvelling at the deep colour. "You know, death might have helped create this orange, Vasta. Like me. The death of one side of me, and the birth of another, but by the blood of the Great Mother herself if it didn't create just the most beautiful damned food I've ever tasted."

Vasta chuckled. "Very good." The mirth vanished in an instant. "It troubles me though. The transference of power from the tower to you is very obvious. From today, your power will grow to something never seen before. Not in the Red Isles, nor even Rengas, for a millennia." Vasta steered the nara onto the road. "It is why I stand by you."

"To study me?" Abika fingered the shard dagger in her pocket. Vasta had graciously let her keep his long jacket, with its myriad of secret pockets. "You know—"

"Shh!" growled Vasta. "Listen."

Screams. Torment. The sounds of death was all around. A low hum of tortuous intent, that every being on this earth would try and escape from. Abika's heart quickened, thumping harder with every noise. "It's Minerva," she uttered.

Vasta's face had gone unusually pale too. He squinted through the trees ahead, patting the nara to quiet her stomping feet. "It's not Minerva. We are too far out. It's the farm from which I took this cart and Brenax here."

"A farm?" The screaming quieted Abika. Tormented howls of pain rose up from behind the treeline where the road forked. She swallowed. "There's too many people for a farm, Vasta." She ducked below the edge of the cart. "What's going on?"

Brenax snorted. "I don't know." He pulled the nara and cart to the opposite side of the road, away from the noise, and Abika followed, tiptoeing for fear of being heard by whatever it was.

The fork for the farm approached, and they both couldn't help but stare down it as Brenax padded by. The curve stole away most of the view, but the corner of the farmhouse was still visible, its rough walls jutting out between blackened trees and grey leaves.

Abruptly a singular voice cut through the rest. "No! No! Leave it! Leave me!"

Abika's blood was frozen in her veins. She fumbled in her pocket for the shard blade and rang a finger along its length, feeling some strength in its presence. "Should we...help"

The scream was cut off suddenly, then growls, inhumane and monstrous. The sound of furniture being upturned, and then the beginnings of smoke drifting up and out of the farmhouse windows.

Vasta looked grimly at Abika, his animal eyes flicking to her pocket. "They are beyond help."

49

MINERVA

The screams faded as the road back to Minerva wore on, but the memory lingered like old spiderwebs clinging and crawling over Abika's skin. Even when the city's outskirts began to break through the flora, Vasta and Abika stayed silent.

Objects flashed between outbuildings and rows of dead crops, things that lay just outside of Abika's peripherals. She jerked around to catch them, trying to see if something was stalking them, but there was always nothing there. She shook her head at her own fear—it *was* playing tricks on her!

"Something is following us."

Abika's heart hammered. "Something?"

Vasta nodded ruefully. "We must try and find a way through to the dock that avoids the main streets."

Abika placed a hand on Vasta's arm and the cart stopped outside a red-brick, boxy building with cartwheels leaning against every inch of its wall.

Vasta hopped off of the cart. "Come down, Abika."

"No Vasta—"

All at once his hand was around her mouth, his hairy palms pressed up against her lips. He lifted her out of the cart like she was a doll, then dragged her around the corner of the building, and behind a wall away from Brenax.

"Put me down!" she mumbled through his hands. Vasta put her down, but kept looking back. "Vasta, your fool what are you—"Brenax's squeal silenced her.

The nara, which had but a few seconds ago been at their side, was now squealing for her life. Guttural pants and growls filled the air, and scuffling of feet on gravel, barely a few yards away! They sounded like voices, but without words. Then scrabbling and the sound of Brenax being dragged over onto her side. The cart followed and just over the tip of the wall Abika saw the spinning cart wheel and Vasta's clever springs being torn apart. Abika was just stepping back to get get a better look when Vasta grabbed her once more and carried her bodily around the back of the building, rushing through a yard filled with long grey grass and rusty anchors.

"Vasta—" said Abika, fighting the Bohr's grip.

"Quiet, Abika. They will hear you."

The squeals stopped, and were replaced with the sounds of tearing and ripping. Juicy noises too awful to think about.

Abika held her breath as Vasta moved through the long grass like a stalking cat. The sound of grass rubbing against her bare legs was impossibly loud. The Bohr stopped near a line of trees, which in any other place would have been the start of a forest, here, though, they just lined the back of the cart factory's boundary.

"Vasta—" It was only now she saw his tears. "Vasta, are...are you alright? You're crying."

"Brenax deserved more than that," he said, pressing his lips together.

"Well, you're a bloody Bohr! Go and fight them. Go and pull them to pieces with these." She held up the hand that had been at her mouth, claws and all. "You would make short work of them."

Vasta just shook his head. "Don't you see? Of course you don't. You are too preoccupied. Your mind has been through so much. The change within you is cloaking you from the obvious."

"Vasta—"

"Abika. The people of Minerva are—"

Screams. Abika's blood froze, and Vasta dragged her down, low into the grass. The back corner of the building was still visible, and beyond it the oranges from the cart fell upon the street, rolling away as something upturned the cart. There was no sign of Brenax, and no other sign anything was wrong at all, until the first one appeared.

It was a person. Abika knew that much because it walked. The face of it, though, was contorted and lacerated, so that his human features were lost amongst blood and red. As she watched, the daemon brought a shard of metal to its face and cut deep into its own skin, slicing a piece off like a butcher preparing steak.

"Oh, gods!" said Abika, moving just enough to look back at Vasta. The great Bohr's muscles twitched before the leap came. Vasta leapt thirty feet in a single bound, landing softly behind the daemon who was prodding at a cartwheel with its weapon. Vasta threw his great arms around the daemon's neck. The daemon twisted at impossible angles, against the flow of its own joints, working its way around to face Vasta, bloody jaws snapping and splashing blood all over him. Vasta held the creature back but it was slipping out of his grasp.

"Just end it!" hissed Abika.

Vasta hesitated and the daemon snapped its arm, bending it backwards, fingers strained and reached for Vasta's face.

"Kill it!" The Bohr would die! "Why don't you just kill the fucking—"

Vasta's face contorted. Wrinkled, as his upper lip lifted revealing animal teeth. Then his mouth was open like a striking tigre, biting at the daemon's neck, tearing out veins and skin and muscles and blood. The daemon didn't seem to notice, even when Vasta threw it to the ground and began clawing and mauling the thing's face and body. Abika watched, half in terror, half in fascination as Vasta tore the daemon limb from limb. Even without arms or legs, the daemon rolled towards Vasta, growling and spitting and gurgling. Bones and cartilage cracked and tore.

Abika stepped back, her mouth dry. "Is it dead?"

"It is." Vasta walked towards her, his chest heaving with the effort.

Abika swallowed back her fear, and nodded to the daemon's severed head. "It's human!"

Vasta shook his head. "It used to be." Each word was like a bite, and those teeth were out, still armed and ready to attack. "I have never in my life met any human so strong." Vasta looked taller, as though he had been stooping for the entire time Abika had known him. "We need to leave the Red Isles as soon as possible. We need to get to Rothmarr's boat."

Abika swallowed, tasting bile. "The boats were all tied up, but we might get lucky."

"We *have* to get lucky." Vasta's grim tone curdled Abika's stomach.

The street beyond the yard looked much like Rothmarr's father's street. He had lived on the other side of the city, but it meant that there was a discernable pattern to the place.

"We can't go down there," said Vasta.

"Why not?"

"Stick to the shadows. The dark places. It is the only way."

"Vasta, you are Bohr, I am quite sure—"

She was abruptly off her feet again, and Vasta was snarling in her face. "Don't you see, silly little girl? Minerva is dead. The people are dead walking! How many people did you see when Rothmarr led you through the city? Hundreds? Thousands? Tens of thousands? They are our enemy now, and they wish to kill us. Or worse."

Brenax's dying mews were still fresh in Abika's head, as fresh as whatever remained of the old nara barely two blocks away. If it could be, Vasta's expressions softened as he set Abika down. "Trust me now, child. I have spent a lifetime hiding in dark places."

Abika found herself nodding. "Where did they come from?"

"The darkness was already here, lurking in wait. But I think it was you, Abika, who did this."

"Me?" A shining blue diamond appeared in Abika's mind. "The tower."

Vasta blinked at her. "Just follow me, and stay close. And I mean it. Follow my each and every footstep." He moved to walk, then stopped. "And don't use Soulfire. If I am right, then they will sense it, if it is that they do not sense you already."

———

The smell of the sea was strong, but the stench of death and decay was stronger. Vasta's words buzzed around the inside of Abika's head as he led them through more overgrown gardens and yards. How could she have caused this? Was she a bad person? Was that why?

Vasta turned a corner, then stumbled back, but it was too late to hide the group of daemons gnawing on something dead. Fifteen of them, their clothes as human as when Abika had arrived here. They might have been praying, and thanking the Great Mother for their wonderful existence were it not for the grotesque sounds of chewing. They were animals working over carrion. Abika balked to think of what that dead thing might be.

"Back," hissed Vasta.

Abika backed off but was now in front, guided by Vasta's clawed hand into the shadows, and along the many overgrown yards behind the lines of red-bricked houses. They wove in and out of narrow streets, over walls, avoiding movement and sound, until the distinctive line of trees near the docks appeared. She shuffled low, trying to see past the rows of shacks sitting between them and the marina.

Vasta kept as low as he could but was clearly getting nervous. "There is danger lurking."

"What choice do we have, Vasta?" Abika burst out from their hiding spot, sprinting out from underneath the trees to a path that ran alongside, and immediately regretted the decision. "It's too far!" she yelled over her shoulder.

Vasta sped up to run alongside her, and then there were screams from behind, chasing them. Inhuman growls and shouts from a pack of daemon hunters. Abika turned to look and Vasta growled. "FORWARD! DON"T LOOK BACK!"

The marina sat bobbing calmly, as though today was just another day. Abika ran as fast as her legs would carry her, fighting Vasta's heavy coat to stop it from bundling at her knees and tripping her. "It's there! There's the Myathar!"

Their footsteps thudded loudly as they tore long the jetty, Vasta almost skidding off of the slimy wood. There were a few boats and a long catamaran but Rothmarr's boat was right there. Abika remembered how he had ducked below the boom, and how he unfurled the sail just so. She was sure she could do it herself.

Vasta's eyes widened and jerked Abika to a halt. An army of daemons red-faced and bloody, were sprinting towards the marina.

"Untie the hawser," ordered Vasta, reaching the Myathar first. It rocked with his weight. "Get the hawser, child. The rope. Untie the rope!"

Abika took the thick rope in her hand. It had a loop of some kind but was wound tightly around a metal knob on the jetty. "Vasta!"

"Pull it!" shouted Vasta, flapping out the sail. He ducked low as the boom flew over his head, but it still caught him with a *thunk* sound. He paid no mind to it though. "Quick, Abika! They're almost at the jetty!"

Abika grabbed the loop and pulled it with all her might, but if anything, the knot just got tighter. "It's stuck! Vasta it's—"

The first she saw of the daemon next to her was his pale and grey hand. Abika fell back, her mind racing, but it was Rothmarr himself stood there. His skin was pallid and were it not for the tattoo, she would not have believed it was him. Vasta was suddenly at her side, an oar held high above his head.

"Stop!" said Abika. "It's Rothmarr."

Vasta shook his head. "It's not Rothmarr. He is not—"

The ground boomed, shaking with a hundred footfalls as the daemons reached the floating marina. The wide group thinned as the bottleneck forced many off the sides, but the core of them found a way through, clawing and screaming and growling.

Abika turned to Rothmarr. "Run Rothmarr, Run!"

Rothmarr moved his mouth, his lips belonged on a corpse, then he reached low and pulled the hawser free. The boat's thick rope slid into the water, and the world tumbled as Vasta scooped up Abika and jumped aboard the Myathar. Holding Abika under his arm like a petulant child, Vasta pushed the boat away with the oar.

"No!" cried Abika

"He's gone."

"He's not gone you fool! Rothmarr jump aboard! Please!"

Rothmarr stared dumbly as the first of the daemons sped around the corner and slid straight into the water. Then the group were there, growling and snarling and screaming. The Myathar slid away from Rothmarr, and he just watched, disinterested and slack-jawed.

"What's wrong with him, Vasta?!" yelled Abika. "RUN! Why won't you run?"

Rothmarr turned his head slowly to the daemon crowd and then they were on him. He disappeared below as the daemons descended on him, tearing with their bare hands, and the shipman did nothing to stop them. It was only when they started eating that Abika had to turn away.

50

A WAY IN

The children's laughs filled the air like the sweet aroma of melting sugar. Fia lifted her stump. "Look!" she said, balancing the empty glove over her wrist. A little boy, barely even walking, stood and made a chopping motion with his hand and Fia dropped the glove off of her wrist. "Ouch! My hand is gone!" The little boy roared with such genuine mirth that Fia's heart could have poured right out of her chest. "Alright, children. Alright, that's enough hilarity. Let's get back to the story." She took up the book she'd put down and cleared her throat.

"Captim?"

"Yes, little one?"

The little girl near the back stepped boldly away from her mother, using the children in front of her to lean on. "Captim, what did happened to your hand?"

"You mean, what *really* happened?" said Fia. The little girl nodded, and the mother moved to pull her back. "No, it's ok, Yewla. I don't mind." Fia reached behind her and pulled out a cloth bear. "What's back here?" She held the bear up in front of her face, making funny eyes over the top. "Would you like to look after me, Alis?"

Alis pouted at her. "That's you making it speak!"

"Look, girl, do you want the bear or not. I could give it to Marcun instead."

"No! Me." Alis stumbled through the other children, lunging for the bear.

Fia smiled at Yewla's embarrassment. "It's alright. It's good to have a mind of your own. Isn't that right, Alis."

Alis squeezed the poor bear flat against her chest, then looking up, brushed the brown fringe out of her eyes. "Where is your hand?"

"Alis..."

Fia held up her stump. "Yewla. The girl wants to know, and by the Great Mother I'm going to tell her. The story goes like this." The children held their breaths, and Fia suddenly felt the best she had in weeks. "I was in Tyr the day the gods came to the earth. They opened up holes all around."

"In the ground?"

"No, Alis," said Fia. "Holes in the very air!" Fia spread her arms to make it joyful and the children gasped in delight. "I was very near one of those holes when it opened. The city of Tyr fell away from my feet, leaving me hanging in the air. Some people who were with me got pulled into the hole, and afterwards the hole vanished. Poof. Gone!" The children hung on her words. "The force that kept us floating vanished too, and I fell very far into the water below, which was full of sharp things and danger. Somehow, I managed to escape, but my poor hand got snipped right off. Snip!"

They were all stunned into silence, all except Alis. "Was it sore?"

"Of course, Alis. But I was able to get away with my life and so I was grateful. Grateful the gods spared the rest of me!"

"What about your friends?" said a boy.

Fia shook her head. "I've often wondered, but in truth I don't know. They vanished." Fia swallowed. "A very good friend of mine used to say that we will encounter moments in our life, where you have to choose whether to live or to die. Not all decisions are made for us." Yewla looked on the verge of tears herself. She nodded and Fia nodded back. "It's a lesson for all of you, dear children. That sometimes life will throw everything it has at you, and it may seem that you have no recourse, and that there is no way to keep fighting. But fight you must." She sat up.

"We have a saying here in the Fifth Union, coined by the bravest person I've ever met, a man called Laeb."

"What was his last name?" came a little voice.

"He didn't have one," said Fia. "But one thing he always said was *May you always fight*, which means just how it sounds. You must keep fighting because life will try and beat you down and take what is yours because life *is* a struggle." With every gaze sitting upon her, Fia felt the guilt sharply, but it had to be said because no one else would. "Alright children, remember my words today, and I want you all to read your books for tomorrow. Get to page six if you can."

The children disbanded in their usual chaotic and noisy way. It was only then that Fia's gaze found Eris by the tent entrance. Blessedly she waited until the last parent had ushered their child out of the tent before popping Fia's bubble.

"Your sewing still hasn't improved then. The cloth bear, I mean. I thought that was one of the skills—"

"They taught Kumpani? I must have been off that day."

"Off playing games?" Eris nodded to Fia's boots. "You remembered them this time. Well done."

"Yes, well..." Fia began cleaning up the discarded wooden bowls and cups the children had left lying on the floor.

"Heavy words for such small minds."

"I'd say it's better that they know what awaits them. Wouldn't you?"

"Or maybe they should be left to be children."

Fia turned towards her. "Since when have you ever been maternal, Eris? You think it was wrong to tell them of the horrors of Tyr? They asked."

Eris adjusted her armour, under the breasts. It was too tight, but she wouldn't be told. "If I was a parent—"

"Well, you're not. Are you?" Fia's irritation spiked. "Eris, what do you want? I don't have time for these—"

"We lost someone."

Fia closed her eyes. It was never nice to hear of someone's death, but worse was the guilt for how cold she felt about losing another of their dwindling numbers. "Who?"

"Althios."

"Well, at least it wasn't one of the young ones." Fia brushed a wisp of hair from her eyes. "What happened to him?"

Eris cleared her throat. "It was just a skirmish against the wall, we were searching for a way in and as usual not finding any, but the Pans were waiting for us. They grouped together near the camp and one managed a lucky spear."

"Maybe they're reading our attack patterns."

"I don't think it's that," said Eris. "They *knew*. They were ready."

"That doesn't mean anything, Eris. It just means they're organising. Did Althios suffer?"

Eris shook her head. "He was the last of his line."

"The nights in the inn will be slower without him," said Fia. "And quieter. He really had no one else?"

"No. He never settled as far as I know."

Fia motioned towards the tent door. "Well, thanks for telling me. If that's all—"

"No," said Eris standing straighter, "it's not all. I received a raeven from Kavik this morning. The Bohr are recruiting for a new army."

Fia shook her head. "What? How?"

Eris straightened her back. "The palace in Zunqai is rounding up all the humans in the city and conscripting them into an army at the request of the Queen."

"Kaliste."

Eris nodded. "The Queen of the Banèmen herself. I've drafted a reply, saying that he should try and disrupt them as much as possible."

"You think he has it in him?" asked Fia. "He's not as young as he used to be." Kavik had become their eyes and ears in the great Kemen city since Tyr. Janike's death had changed him, so much so that he'd given up everything to help the Fifth Union rebuild. All whilst keeping an eye on the other four unions, living with the enemy in their stronghold and spying. Kavik was probably one of the few humans Fia knew who could take on a Bohr in hand-to-hand combat and not immediately be killed.

"None of us are as young as we used to be," uttered Eris, "yet here we are. I also said he should go see Danna and the union."

"Danna? Forbringrs be with the man. She'll tear him to pieces."

"Danna knows herself."

"A little too well, if you ask me."

Eris looked troubled. "Captain, the Queen's army is barely a few weeks away from first assignments."

The news that Zunqai was building an army was not welcome, but also not unexpected. It should have been much sooner, but Fia knew cities, and she knew councils, and they were usually as ponderous as a parade of elephants.

"I'm sorry, Atalfia."

Fia dropped the bowls clattering to the floor. "What?"

Eris rushed over and picked up the still-spinning bowls. "I should have told you about Jona. It's over now. Long over."

"Is it?"

"Of course it is." Eris took the last few bowls from Fia's arms and dropped them in a basket near the entrance. She paused, her back to Fia. "You speak of moments all the time. Well, that was a moment of weakness. I am weak. You are so strong. You know yourself and all that you are, but I fight what I am. Jona offered me something else." She turned. "And I'm ashamed to say that I took it." Eris leant forward and took Fia's stump in her hand. She kissed it gently. "Please don't let this be it."

"It's not it, Eris." Fia pulled her arm back. "I just need some space. Some time."

"I dropped by your tent this morning. Was that your new Chinaes gameboard lying broken on the floor."

Fia nodded. "I...dropped it. Last night I was visited by a stranger."

"An intruder?" Eris's mouth fell agape. "In the camp?"

"The stranger," continued Fia, "told me that there is a gap in the wall." Fia had seen Eris's lip quiver just so many times and for many different reasons, but it was always the same emotion. Excitement and anticipation.

"A gap?" Eris blinked, trying to comprehend. "But we...we looked. We've been up and down that wall a hundred times. A thousand! There's no way into Kemen from Hatàr. The borders are closed. Where?"

"The Pass."

Eris shook her head in disbelief. "The pass? It must..." She took a long breath. "Did we ignore that place because...No!" Her mood shifted suddenly. "Who is this man? Why did he tell you this?"

"I couldn't see his face. He reminded me of Derval, but his voice wasn't the same." Fia rubbed her temples. "Or maybe it was. I'm so tired."

Eris was pacing. "You know, Haral was complaining this morning that he hadn't seen any meat. Derval should have been up and cutting well before sunrise."

"He doesn't have to, Eris. That's what he chooses to do. Besides, it's after a tavern night. He's probably just sleeping it off."

"Derval doesn't drink."

"He looks like he does." Fia shook her head. "Eris, it wasn't Derval. He was just on my mind. We had a bit of a...misunderstanding over Grace."

"Oh, Atalfia, but he did love that horse more than his wife and child!"

"Eris!"

"I'm just repeating his very words." Eris unclipped her sword pommel. "I say we go see him."

"You're being ridiculous." Fia shook her head. "Even if it was Derval—"

"Then something else was speaking for him." Eris shook her head. "And who are the only people we know who can change shape?"

"What?" scoffed Fia. "A Banèman? It couldn't be."

"They change shape." She poked Fia's chest. "All those nights you spent telling me of Jagar. What was it he referred to you to as?"

"Little Bird."

"You are anything but a little bird, Atalfia. You are fierce. You are Captain of the Fifth Union!"

"Thank you, Eris. It is true I am no longer the woman I was." Fia held up her stump. "But, still, if half of what you say is true, then a Banèman would have killed me at first sight."

Eris nodded. "And who wouldn't jump at the chance to wipe the Fifth Union from the circle of the world. Humour me, Captain, please.

Let us go see Derval. Then, when all is well, we can finish what needs finishing."

"A day in the life of a rebel leader without a cause."

"I meant Zular."

"I know what you meant, Eris."

"He's a prisoner, Atalfia. This is wartime."

"This isn't wartime. Not really."

"It is." When Fia didn't reply, Eris carried on regardless. "You know, Haral really has taken to the role of managing Zular. He watches him day and night. You left him in charge of him, remember. Well, he took the job and made it his own. He rotates the shifts, sees the man fed, supervises his exercise time. Nothing gets past Haral. Eyes like a raeven that boy. He's impressed me."

Fia undid her hair and went to retie it. Eris stopped her and took the needle from between Fia's lips. Eris must have tied Fia's hair a hundred times, and yet this time, it felt strange. Surrounded by toys in the school tent, it felt as though Fia was a little girl again, and Eris the teacher. It was a dynamic Fia did not enjoy.

"You still don't know what you're going to do with him do you?" said Eris, her breath hot on Fia's neck.

Fia waited until Eris had finished tying, then pulled on her coat and stood silently by the tent entrance.

Eris nodded slowly. "You still don't know. Ok, well, in the meantime let us find this bloody butcher. We work hard. We deserve our meat. Lazy bastard that he is."

"Fine," said Fia, "but you can explain that to him. I'll have no part in it. I'm already in his bad books for killing his prized horse."

The morning was damp, and dew hung about the air as Fia and Eris approached Derval's meat stand behind the west quarter. It marked the centre of the main section of the Fifth Union camp.

Eris scraped the worn dirt around the stand with her boot. "He's popular, I'll give him that."

Fia frowned. There had been no preparation work for the day.

Derval, for all of his annoying attributes, was always first awake in the camp. Morning meat, he called it.

"It's clean," she said, dragging a finger over the scored bench.

"So, at least we know he finished up last night."

Fia knelt down at the stall's cupboards, slid them open and took out a cleaver. "Was he in the tavern last night?"

"I didn't see him, but you saw how many people were there."

Fia tapped the cleaver. "You said he had moved in with all the single men?"

Eris nodded. "It's over there...Raliyah told me."

Fia held Eris's gaze. Jona's tent was in this direction. She would bet her life on it. "Then lead the way."

Before long they were standing outside a tent larger than any other. Fia leaned towards the entrance. "Derval? Derval, are you there?"

"Derval, you lazy prick. You've slept in!"

Fia shot Eris a look.

Eris shrugged. "What? If he's in there, that will be sure to rouse him."

Fia nodded to a pair of boots sitting neatly outside the tent. "Oh, he's in there." Using the cleaver, Fia pulled the tent flaps aside. Light spilled in through the entrance. Derval had modified his tent with panels of thick canvas sewn into the walls, so as to be completely black, even during the day. Many of those who worked early slept in the afternoon.

"Is he asleep?" whispered Eris, from behind her.

"Soldier Derval. The camp is needing fed!" That should have enraged the man, but the lump lying beneath the covers didn't move. "Derval?" Fia pulled the sheets away in one quick motion, holding the cleaver ready. She heard Eris pull her sword too, but Derval didn't move. He was lying on his side facing them, curled up like a baby, and a bloodied fillet knife held tightly in both hands.

"Forbringr's ashes," gasped Eris. "His eyes, look at his eyes!"

The butcher's eyes were solid white, and his lips were moving like he was talking quietly, but the rest of him was frozen solid.

"He's cold," said Fia, touching his head. "Cold as the dead. Eris, go and find Raliyah! He needs a doctor!"

The medical tent had always been neglected. Raliyah was lazy, and due to slow times of late, she'd been apparently spending her time performing other tasks. Fia and Eris, along with the help of Slocrate, were able to drag the butcher from his tent. Some others had tried to help on the way, but something deeply unsettling had taken seed in Fia's guts, and she had ordered them away.

Eris pulled aside the bed sheet they'd used to cover Derval revealing his lacerated chest. Shapes had been scored into his skin, and while most of the blood had dried, the wounds looked fresh. "Slocrate, tell Yewla and Alis to come now!"

"Eris, no!" snapped Fia. "They can't see him like this."

Raliyah appeared, and at her hands came up to her mouth. "Oh, no, not Derval. What happened?"

"You tell us," yelled Eris. "You're the expert!"

All at once, Raliyah's whole demeanour changed. She became efficient, tidy and authoritative all in the space of a heartbeat. "Slocrate, leave. There are too many people in here. The doctor licked her dry lips, unable to pull her stare away from the wounds. "Careful with sheet, Eris. You'll take the skin off. In fact, go and get me some warm water."

"Who would do this to him?" asked Fia. "To anyone?"

Raliyah's cold hand upon Fia's arm awoke her senses like a dose of smelling salts. Raliyah took the fillet knife from Fia and studied the tip. "He did it himself."

Fia shook her head. "How? How do you know that?"

"Derval is the only butcher I know who can use both hands, and the wounds here." She drew a light finger across the sides of Derval's chest. "And here, are shallower. Someone doing this to him would have gone in straight down. He did this to himself."

"What about his eyes?"

Raliyah shook her head. "It's like a coma, but with induced blindness. Except, it takes many months for the eyes to mist up like this, and I saw him last night." She covered her mouth with a shaking hand. "I spoke to him!"

Fia embraced Raliyah, feuds forgotten in an instant. Raliyah sobbed hard. "Raliyah. We have to fix him. We have to draw him out of this... this coma."

Eris burst into the tent. "Water."

Raliyah took the bucket and the sponge from within and began to dab Derval's chest.

"Those shapes," said Eris. "Are they...Is that a map?"

Fia watched as the sponge gently removed the dried blood on Derval's chest, revealing the shapes, islands, coasts...

Raliyah shook her head as she dabbed the wounds. "Why would he cut a map into his skin? Why!"

Fia traced the lines. "It's not a map. It's a disease. The man I met last night that looked like Derval. It wasn't him, but it wore his face. He had these shapes on his skin. Shapes of colour." She pointed to Derval's chest, and her curiosity got the better of her. She felt the scored flesh, the heat of it. "It stood like a man, it wore Derval's face, all the while Derval lay asleep in his bed. It wore his soul."

Both women had gone pale.

Fia placed her palm over the butcher's forehead. "And Derval did the only thing he knew how, he cut."

"What are you saying?" spat Eris. "That he...that he isn't..."

Fia nodded. "He's a shell, Eris." Derval was an empty being with no soul. Whatever it was she had spoken to after the tavern, whatever it was that had told her to keep fighting, whatever it was that had taken Derval's face had also taken the butcher's life force away from him.

Eris shook her head. "Atalfia, he's talking." She knelt down at Derval's head, his misted eyes rolled, and his mouth moved, but he was no more alive than a blade of grass blowing in the wind.

"What's he saying?" whispered Raliyah.

"It's nonsense," said Eris.

"Eris, he's gone." Fia let the tears come.

"Then what do we do now?"

"Keep him comfortable," said Fia.

"About the intruder!"

"The only thing we can," said Fia. "The being that stole Derval's likeness, be him a Banèman or something else, spoke of a gap in the wall."

Raliyah gasped. She also knew the importance of what that meant for the Fifth Union.

"We can't trust those words," said Eris. "A gap in the wall? Is it guarded? Is it a trap?"

Fia nodded weakly, she felt drained and sick. "It is probably a trap, but what other option do we have? We are the forgotten fighters."

"We have many enemies!" growled Eris. "Too many to count."

"Perhaps, but in the end what does it matter if never fight, and we must always fight."

Raliyah nodded with Fia. "Eris. She's right. We're just sitting here upon the borderlands, waiting for a Bohr raiding party to finish us off. How long must we wait for our deaths?"

Eris looked conflicted, but the truth was out, and saying it felt cathartic, it drew new energy over Fia's skin like beams of sunlight. "Gather a raiding part, Eris. And let us go see what our intruder wants us to see."

51

THE LAST SOLDIER

The Bohr wall was a feat of engineering that stood above Fia and her squad like the side of a mountain, wrought from earth, stone and iron. Fia ran her hand along the smooth, flat surface, shaking her head. "The Bohr know how to make a wall."

"It's immense," said Eris.

"You a sympathiser now?" Slocrate didn't see the backhand until it was too late. He fell back against the wall, grasping awkwardly for something to stop his fall, which, of course, just delayed it.

Eris stepped over to him, one foot either side. "See. If this wall had been more poorly made, maybe you wouldn't have fallen on your ass." She sat down on his chest heavily.

"Get off me!"

Eris whacked Slocrate about the head. "What, and miss the opportunity to teach you something? Never."

"Captain?!"

Fia rolled her eyes, but kept her mouth shut. "Don't look at me, Slocrate. This is your own doing. Own it."

Eris twisted Slocrate's face by the nose. "Let us talk some more on respecting our enemies..."

Fia left Eris, Slocrate and the thirty other men and women to their frowns and peering chuckles, and instead focused on the wall. It was all she saw, and it filled her head as much as it filled her eyes. The smooth mixture of rock and metal carried on for leagues in both directions—a mental block as well as a physical one.

"A gap?" she said to herself. "Or an illusion?" Illusions were a luxury, performed by street-hands and watched by those who had nothing better to do with their time. Her life was so plain, and so literal, that the idea of an illusion so close to them this whole time made her feel sick. She placed an ear to the wall, not to listen, but to look down its length. The mist and hills stole it before the horizon did. Hatàr was a borderland that stretched from the west coast to the east, with the wall cutting all the way through it. It was so high, only the birds could get over it.

"Maybe we should just try and climb it." Eris said from behind. She was holding a spyglass to her eye.

"We tried that, remember. It's too fucking high."

Eris's eyes went wide, and Fia blushed. The curse had been wholly unnecessary. "Alright. Well, Captain Atalfia, we've just spent two days walking along this wall, and found nothing of merit. Your imposter was lying."

"We will find this gap, Eris." Fia turned, holding the words as daggers. "We do not leave here, until we find it. We *will* travel south into Kemen, whether it is today, tomorrow or next month. Understand?"

Eris gave a single nod and turned on her heels. Fia shook her head. Once, she had been the master of her emotions. Using them as tools as a woodworker might fashion a jewellery box.

"Give me your spyglass."

Eris pulled the brass tube from her belt. "Don't break it. I only have one."

Fia nodded. "Thank you. Eris, it was—"

Eris shook her head. "Don't. Just find it. You said it yourself, if this is the final act, then it's up to you."

"It's too much, Eris." Tears threatened to fall from Fia's stinging eyes. "This expectation. I...I..."

"You will lead us," said Eris, steeling herself. "And you will lead us well, as you always have done."

"Eris. I love you. You know that don't you? Whatever you've done."

Fia might've laughed any other time, the pair of them standing like awkward teenagers unable to say what was truly in their hearts. "Whatever it is, we can fix it together."

Eris shook her head, then turned towards the wall, insurmountable, immovable. "Fia..." She turned and her emerald eyes shone. "I...I can't do it. Not now. Not...not here. I don't want *them* to see this."

"Then when, Eris?" Fia let the emotions come, filling her like water to a well. "Never? Because if you don't love me then...then you should just leave."

Eris bit her top lip. "You wish me to leave?"

Fia closed her eyes. "Yes." She wanted to add, "if you don't love me." But the words never came. Fia opened her eyes ready to explain, but Eris was already walking away.

The evening fire's smoke still clung stubbornly to the mossy earth. Stars had appeared, flickering behind a rolling, green blanket of aurora. The night animals were out taking full advantage of the mild spring evening. Crickets chirruped, bats dived after moths, there was even a wild raeven checking them out—a smear of darkness on the wall above.

Despite the cacophony, Fia was lonely. She needed a *real* embrace. There had been many conquests in her life, men, women and those who stood between, experiences that drew warmth to her nethers like a cup of hot seete. They used to flower in her mind unexpectedly, but now there was always something else that needed to be done or thought on. The line stopped at her feet, and so she carried the weight of its expectation and responsibility upon her shoulders like an overladen pack full of horse meat.

Closing her eyes, Fia let her mind wander. Eris was there waiting, but that was too easy—she knew the curves and nooks of Eris like she knew the camp, each valley and rise as familiar to her fingertips as home. Fia didn't want familiar.

Danna.

Danna's hair, her attitude. It had to be Danna. When they had first met, Fia had been barely seventeen, and Danna had seemed so exciting.

A real freedom fighter, like Fia's father and mother, and standing in the Fiskar in front of her, as bold as you like. It hadn't taken much that day to talk Fia into sleeping with her. Danna's practised hands made short work of her, whereas she fumbled and prodded and poked, but by the blood of Forbringrs, it had been good.

Fia's physical self began to connect with her mind in preparation, and she took a long breath. Before she could stop the images, she was tracing her fingertips over her stomach, relishing the gooseflesh that stiffened her skin. The night air kissed her lightly. Danna's hands that night seemed to know Fia's body better than she knew herself. They searched over her, as Fia's own hands did now, discovering, daring. It had been in the Den, and what's more, there had been others in there. Had they seen Danna's lips kissing, moving down her neck? Had they heard Fia's soft moans? You better believe they did, and Fia hadn't cared a jot. Danna's fingers found her, teasing, testing, sliding along her inner thigh towards Fia's knees, but Fia willed them back, and so they came, moving delicately, an echo of a touch, and then her own fingers were pulling her, sliding along her lips.

The night with Danna had taught her more about herself than any other since, but as well as her mind was, Fia's body refused to get on board. She was cold and stiff.

Fia sighed long and hard. An orgasm would set her free and bring sleep, but the connection was too broken to repair. She could have spent the entire night working on it, but when it came it would be but a shade of what she wanted.

She dropped her head back to her pack. "Oh, Fia," she said to herself. "You're hard up. Danna? One of the cruellest and most shrewd people you've ever met?" She should have laughed, but tears came first.

The wild raeven's call woke Fia. It must have sat there all night, high up on the wall, watching her toss and turn in fitful sleep, her dreams full of things she could not quite reach, and dangers that she could not quite escape. So when Slocrate appeared, his dirty, unshaven face stealing the morning sky, Fia was grumpy.

"Captain Eris is asking what the next steps are, Cap—"

"Go away, Slocrate."

Fia stood, letting her sleeping blanket fall, realising too late that she was naked.

Slocrate looked down. "Umm."

Fia shook her head and squatted down near her pack. "Tell Eris..." Fia glanced past the soldier to the group beyond. Some had noticed and were unashamedly glancing in her direction. Eris was nowhere to be seen. "Tell her that she knows where I am."

"Put some clothes on Captain!" A shout came from within the group of soldiers. Slocrate's shoulders began to bounce as he tried to keep his shit together.

"Slocrate," said Fia, clicking her fingers. "You will bloody look at me when I'm talking. Tell Eris that she knows where I am. Do you understand?"

"Yes, Captain." Slocrate gave her one last sidelong glance over his shoulder before speeding off, stumbling over the deep moss.

Fia frowned as she pulled on her breeches and shirt. Oh, how she missed dresses. Or even a nice hak. She shook her head at it all, slightly bemused, but mostly pissed off with everything.

She picked up a stone and with a scream, threw it up at the damned raeven. It barely got half way up the wall, but the raeven launched, its huge leathery wings opening like sails, then it glided straight through the wall as though it wasn't even there.

Fia was so shocked that she brought a hand up to her mouth. Then she was running, her bare feet squelching over the moss, not taking her eyes from the place the raeven had disappeared. It was barely a hundred paces from where she had slept. A hundred bloody paces!

Jagar watched as the Tsiorc began to file in through the gap in the Bohr wall. It had taken Little Bird some time to find, but that was typical of any and all human endeavour, so bogged down by emotion and attachment were they. He pondered their inadequacies for a moment longer, fighting a deep urge to cock his head.

Little Bird's partner galloped away back to the rebel camp in the distance. She held Jagar's bird's eye for a moment longer before he extended the raeven's leathery wings, admiring how the shapes of pale and dark skin worked with and against one another. He willed the creature around to face south to watch as the last of the rebel soldiers filed in through the gap in the wall and into the lands of Kemen. The Bohr liked to refer to it as an empire, but in truth Kemen was a united country. A single land. A Kingdom. But then, "The Kemen Kingdom" sounded a little strange. He tried it on for size and it came out as a squawk.

The last soldier was Little Bird herself, and she stepped on through the gap below, then paused and looked up at Jagar. She stared at him. Through him, as she had every right to. The rebels would not be welcome in Kemen, because the Bohr did not welcome humans or outsiders, and her little resistance was both. It was a challenge his Little Bird would have to overcome. She would lose much, but the gains would be greater than she could ever imagine! Jagar watched as she heeled her horse forward and followed the rest of the soldiers.

She had come far since their first meeting upon the roof of the Domst, another life ago, and she would go further still. This crossing here, today, was a turning point, and Jagar exalted to witness the beginning of a new chapter in Rengas's history. His Little Bird would help him ascend into ranks unseen by any being before him, and in a time not too far forwards, she would come to know him very well indeed.

Jagar gave another squawk, caught up in the thrill of it all, and dived off the wall to cheer the Fifth Union on their way. They deserved it. She deserved it.

52

A NEW ENEMY

Jona dipped the dry bread in some butter, making sure each side was covered and soaked before placing it on the plate next to the horse meat.

"Alis?"

The little girl hiding behind the door poked her head around. "Jona?"

Stupid child. "You are funny, with that," said Jona, feigning a smile. "So very funny." He squatted down to her height, and pulled the door a touch. "It's alright! I don't bite. Now, do you want to hear the end of the story or not?"

"Not," said Alis, hiding beneath her fringe. She hugged a lump of wool, tied roughly with twine in the shape of a bear. It had two lop-sided buttons, needled poorly into the head.

"You're a cheeky one. Now, should I just tell your mother you're here and not in school?" He glanced around the inn kitchen, the only building on camp. "This is not a place for children."

Alis seemed to wrestle with her own mind until finally she nodded. "Tell your story."

"How old are you?"

"Four."

"I don't believe you."

Alis pressed her lips together. "How old are you?"

"It is disrespectful to—"

"Then why ask me?"

Jona shook his head in disbelief. "There is no way you are four."

Raliyah wandered in behind him. "Jona." Jona glanced up, and he knew without any words what had happened. He stood to meet Raliyah's gaze. "Is he gone?"

"A few minutes ago," said Raliyah. "He just rotted away. There's nothing left of..."

Jona followed Raliyah's eyes to Alis who was watching them intently. "Alis. You see what happens with little girls who are cheeky? You were cheeky and now your father is dead. That's right. Dead." He lifted the plate of food. "Dead as this horse. Maybe now you'll respect your elders."

Alis's face went bright red and then she ran out of the inn and out into the muddy camp beyond. Jona shut the inn door. "Let all the heat out, why don't you. It's not like I've been stoking that bloody fire all morning."

Raliyah folded her arms beneath her more than ample breasts. By the blood of the Great Mother, he'd fall over himself to get a shot at those! "Was that really necessary?"

Jona took up a log and whittled it with his belt blade before throwing it on the low fire. "Of course not, but that's what made it so delicious. Did he suffer?"

"What is wrong with you?" said Raliyah, in mock disgust. It had to be mock. She hated the bloody butcher as much as Jona did.

"I never really liked Derval, so hearing that he had a painful death..."

"I didn't said it was painful. I said he rotted away. He was a shell, Jona. There was nothing left of the man."

Jona nodded. "Good. Grumpy bastard thought he was the owner of this camp. He won't deny me meat any longer!" He marched over to the inn's bar and lifted the plate of food and brought it to his nose. "Lovely. I'll need to get this over before it gets too cold."

"Is that for—"

"Indeed it is." He ogled Raliyah once more before hastening out of the inn. It was yet another shitty, grey morning.

Jona couldn't have said the last time he saw the sun, probably in Raeven's Torr of all places. Or perhaps the morning after when he had played Atalfia at Chinaes. She wasn't very good, despite what she thought, but then neither was she a good tactician, or a good commander.

He stopped at the brig and nodded to Haral. "Alright?"

"That's not for him, is it?"

Jona forced his eyes not to roll and instead chose mock outrage. "Are you serious? The man in there is a Bohr spy and very possibly a murderer! Why would I waste the last of our good meat on him? No, my friend, this is mine. I'm going to torture that bastard."

Haral smiled. "Damn right. Good on you Jona. Make him sweat. Make him cry!"

Oh, but it was easy to mislead the young. "I will, my friend." He slapped Haral on the pauldron so hard the thing almost fell off the boy's damned shoulder. "I will."

Haral lifted the tent flap and Jona ducked into the brig. There was a burst of black in front of his eyes, and the plate of food toppled out of his hands.

"Careful," said Zular.

Jona blinked. "What? Oh, good catch!"

Zular held the plate a few inches off the ground, despite being chained to a post in the ground. "Thank you, my friend. For me?"

"Sorry, it might have gone a little cold. And there's not much fat on it, but it's the best meat we can muster now the butcher has finally died."

Zular gave a nod of interest, and Jona's heart leapt. "The butcher you say? Well, Jona. It looks delicious." Zular took up a piece of horse meat and chewed quietly on it. He looked like a king, which was confusing seeing as he was chained to the floor. "How have you been?"

Jona tried to lean against the post, but it shifted so he stood. "Since yesterday? Alright. What was that cloud I saw when I came in?" He closed his eyes, analysing the pattern on his retina.

Zular chewed slowly then swallowed. "My friend, those wonderful eyes of yours must have just been adjusting to the darkness."

"Maybe I've just been working too hard," said Jona. "I have been stoking the fire all morning."

"You do your fellow soldiers a service. You truly are a leader of men. I can only hope that they appreciate your sacrifices." Zular took the bread, taking a slow bite—savouring the butter, no doubt.

"I am a leader, or at least I deserve to be. More than that kumpani witch who leads at the moment. I hope Haral has not been bothering you?"

"He is just eager to please his superior." Zular shrugged. "Do you think you might get me a thicker blanket? Or perhaps a shirt?"

Jona smiled, and tugged on the cloth tucked in behind his leather waistcoat. "Here you are, my friend."

"Jona. You are too good to me. Thank you. It has been cold. Especially in the evenings."

Jona slipped out of his waistcoat. "I tell you what. Take this too."

"You are too kind. I shall put it on, next time I am unshackled."

"You really think I would make a good leader?" Jona played with the thought of it. Imagining himself wearing a commander's coat, the stripes of command upon his shoulder.

"I have no doubt at all, my friend."

Doubt filled Jona's heart. "They wouldn't listen to me."

"I think they would, my friend. All you need is an audience. They need a strong leader. Someone who will take their futures and fill them with promise!" The shackles and chain clattered as Zular held out a fist in front of him. "Look within yourself. Do you not see great things lurking there, waiting to be tapped? I do. I see it. You would care for this camp as though they were your own. You've certainly looked after me when no others would. When anyone else might do me harm."

"JONA! ARE YOU IN THERE?" The scream was so loud it made Jona's ears ring. It came from just outside the brig, and scuffling too. Haral was chattering about something or other.

"What the..." Jona stepped out of the brig. Before his eyes had even adjusted, he was seeing stars.

Yewla, Alis's mother, stood there readying another slap, but this time Jona was ready and he jabbed his fist into her face. Haral protested, but he stepped forward into the next one, planting a haymaker that swept the woman off of her feet and into the dirt. Alis jumped back, holding that stupid bear.

Jona roared. "How dare you hit me—"

Yewla booted Jona in the shin, it shouldn't have hurt, but suddenly he was falling back into the canvas of the brig and the whole lot was falling down around him. "You bitch!" Drowning in the tent canvas, he shouted. "HARAL! HARAL GET ME OUT OF HERE!"

The young guard rushed over and lifted Jona out. His leg hurt, but his pride was more bruised. What's more, a thickening crowd stood about them, watching. "What's your bloody problem Yewla?"

Yewla was standing again, her dark eyebrows pulled together and her olive skin bright red. "You tormented my little girl! That's the problem!" She lunged but Haral muscled in, pushing her back.

"Stop it!" growled Haral.

"Get off me!" She pulled herself free and spat in Jona's face. "Who torments a child when their father has just died? Who? You are scum, Jona!"

A hush fell upon them, and Jona turned to see Zular stepping out of the collapsed brig. The shackles at his hands were glowing brightly, dripping metal hissing to canvas and mud until they fell away as molten lumps. Zular rubbed his still smoking wrists. "It seems you have the audience you were waiting for, Jona."

Jona looked around. Zular was right. Half the camp had appeared to see what was going on.

"You see?" roared Jona. "You see what happens in the wake of our good Captain's absence? Confusion. Disruption. Fear." He gestured at Yewla, who snarled silently back at him. "We are only as good as the best of us! Only as good as the one who calls himself leader!" Jona stopped to take a breath. He was apprehensive. He was scared, but never before had he felt so much resolve. It was as though he were being held up from behind by some massive force that urged him on. He would be the best he could be, he would lead and take this union of men and women to the Bohr and smite them down.

"Derval," he shouted. "Our beloved butcher. Father to Alis, husband to Yewla, is dead. Our Captain would have you believe that he died of some magical disease. That some stranger in the night came and stole the man's soul while he slept?" He laughed. "That's the kind of heresy that gets people put away for being mad!" He shook his head. "Derval died because he has been living here in the bloody cold for a decade! He died because he was mistreated and ignored by his commander. And his wife."

"You utter filth!" screamed Yewla, wrestling against Haral's grip.

Jona forged on. "Derval's passing marks the end of this life and the beginning of a new one." He stepped by Yewla towards the main body of the crowd. Faces he knew stood and watched and listened.

"Now is the time for us to begin anew, with a new leader. We shall return to Raeven's Torr and recruit. We will draft if we have to. And when we are ready, we will march upon the Kemen front lines and by the blood of the Forbringr we will tear the bastards down!"

A roar erupted from the crowd. Soldier upon soldier banging their shields, plates and weapons in unison. Jona's heart leapt with joy. This was the absolute defining moment of his life. Nothing could stop him now. "Nothing will stop—"

"JONA!"

He snapped around to see Eris stalking towards him. He'd seen this woman as naked as the day she was born. He'd held her and those wonderful breasts of hers and slept upon her naked chest.

She stopped a few feet in front of him. "What are you doing, Jona?"

Jona shook his head. "Seizing."

Eris looked him up and down then turned towards the crowd. "We have found a way through the wall!" Murmurs spread through the soldiers. "A way in!"

Jona panicked. "What good will that do us if we all die from the cold!"

Eris shook her head. "We will survive. It will be hard but we will—What is he doing free?" Eris pulled her sword and marched towards Zular.

Jona stepped in her way, the blade stopping a hair's breadth from his chest. "Don't Eris. He's one of us."

Eris's eyes widened with each word. "Jona, he is a Bohr spy."

"I am no more a spy than your dear Atalfia." Zular spoke calmly, his words delivered with the authority and grace of an emperor.

Eris snarled at him. "Careful, spy."

Jona placed a hand upon Eris's sword pommel. "Eris, it doesn't have to be like this! The more we fight amongst ourselves, the deeper the shit we live in. Derval died this morning."

Eris stared long and hard between Yewla and Alis, the two clutching each other, sobbing. "Yewla I—"

Jona seized once more. "Look at what we are reduced to! We are worth much, much more than this." He gestured to the camp. "We are strong. We need leadership. They need me. And I...I need you."

Eris glanced at the crowd, at all the pieces of Jona's creation before settling on Zular. "I just...I just don't know anymore." Her hand drifted to her stomach. "Jona..."

Jona stepped towards her, then he was there, his arms around her. Feeling her warmth once more. He shut his eyes. "Please, Eris."

Eris's breaths were shallow. "I...I cannot let our child grow up here."

Jona pulled back in shock. A thousand emotions bursting forth all at once, disgust chief amongst them. "You are with child?"

Eris took Jona's hand and placed it on her stomach. "You are to be a father, Jona."

The sides of Jona's world fell away from him like wet cake; the core of him left bare in what should have been the most triumphant moment of his life! He stared at Eris, uncomprehending. The news of it, the sound of the words. They were important, he knew it, but they didn't make sense in the order they had been spoken. Jona looked around. The whole camp was there. Faces he knew and respected, all watching his world fall apart.

"Jona," Zular's smooth tones washed over Jona like warm sunlight. "Listen to me. Do not look at this as a burden. Look at this as an opportunity." He turned with him and presented Eris like a prize. "She is so strong and beautiful. Look at those features, that nose and those high cheekbones. If ever there was a Queen to your king..." Before Jona could speak Zular slapped Jona hard on the back and declared. "Your leaders are to be parents!"

The Fifth Union erupted in cheers, and Jona reeled. Even Eris looked proud, as a Queen should. Proud of Jona. Her king. Clouds of warmth permeated the air and Jona felt his loins stir at the prospect of it all.

He held up his fist and proclaimed to the very Forbringrs themselves. “I AM TO BE A FATHER!”

53

FLASH

The Red Isles held onto the sky's fire for longer than any other sunset Abika had ever seen, until the violet night finally dragged a blanket of stars over the Myathar.

The currents dragged them one way and then another, but Vasta knew when to let the sea win and when to fight it. Their short trip around the bottom of the island had thrown them well off course, and as the air grew cold she thought of her room back at the commune, the warmth or her blankets, and the shape of her mattress that fit her so well.

She shifted on the unforgiving wooden benches of the Myathar. "Why didn't Rothmarr fight?"

Vasta stood across from her. He had spent most of the journey so far jumping back and forth from the left to the right of Rothmarr's boat whenever the boom swapped sides. It was getting irritating. "I don't know."

"And those daemons...They were—"

"The people of Minerva. The people of the Red Isles."

"Why were they acting like that, though? Killing their own. Eating each other." She shook her head and laughed. "The city was hardly a paradise before that, but what happened to have caused—"

"What do you think, girl?" snapped Vasta. "What has changed since we arrived on the island? What was there, and is now...not there?"

Abika swallowed. She might've have gotten used to the fool Bohr, but he was still a Bohr, and he could end her life anytime he liked. "You think the crystal tower did this?"

"That crystal tower was a beacon of energy." Vasta looked away, and Abika was reminded of Rothmarr when they had first boarded his vessel. The wistful out-to-sea look was apparently something that came with the role of sailing. "The loss of the tower meant the release of the energy holding The Red Isles together. I couldn't have fathomed how deep that reliance went." Vasta was more talking to himself than Abika. "For it to affect the people so indicates that the tower is only part of something bigger. Energy is what focuses the world. If we are made of matter, then energy is what gives us purpose. Take it away..." He shrugged.

"And what? We become murderers?"

"We become shells. Like Rothmarr."

"You're talking of souls. Rothmarr had a soul. I saw it in his eyes."

Vasta shook his head doggedly. "Souls imply a keeper. There are no gods, child. We are alone. We are the arbiters of our lives. There is no deity to rely on. Those who do only waste their lives. Minerva should have proved that there are no gods. If you wait for intervention, then you will die waiting."

"Poetic," said Abika. "Souls or no, those daemons had nothing left. They were something else."

"That we can agree on," said Vasta. "The peoples of Minerva were wrought from the fires of hell, a disease drawn up from a place or thing, that your crystal tower was keeping at bay." The same look of fear she'd seen before was painted upon his face. "Whatever it is, terrifies me deeply. Whatever could affect a whole island is truly powerful. We saw it, when we landed. The decay, the disinterest. The latent rage. But also, physical markers. The midpass. The currents that suddenly became impassable. The loss of flora and fauna on the island. Do you remember hearing a bird? Or seeing any wildlife? I didn't." The great Bohr sighed. "Even Brenax, in the short time I knew her, was sad deep in her heart."

The sea had calmed, the waves dropping low enough that the great canvas above was reflected back. They could have been floating in the sky, surrounded by stars. "I saw raevens in the orange grove, Vasta. Besides, you can't tell me that we're all made of energy?" She tapped her forearm. "That doesn't sound like something a scholar would say. More like a heretic."

Vasta scoffed. "Energy is the lifeblood of reality. It brings life wherever it is, and whenever it is taken away, it takes life with it."

"Rubbish."

"Look at a fire. It burns only for as long as we fuel it. All energy wants to become inert, Abika. We are just here trying to stop it from doing just that. For as long as we can. And to your raevens, the orange grove was closest to the tower. It was the eye of the storm, and within the eye there are different rules. The ironic truth of rules is that they hold only while it suits them."

"You're talking in riddles again, scholar."

"Am I?" The boat rocked and Vasta peered over the side. "The wind is dying. We may have to sleep here tonight." He stretched and looked upwards. "But there are worse places to be."

Abika looked up. "Like the Red Isles, you mean?"

"I will mind us for a while." He threw a blanket at her. "But you should sleep, while your gods allow it."

She narrowed her eyes. A thousand responses came to her, like stars of their own twinkling into existence. Trying them on for size and looking at his possible reactions to each led her to only one conclusion. "Good night, Vasta."

"Good night, Abika."

The waves slapping against the Myathar dragged Abika from a fitful sleep full of panic and pursuit. Beneath the blanket though, she could have been in another world. It was warm and the smell of the sea was fresh. She might have stayed there forever had Vasta's careless stumbling not interrupted her thoughts.

She concentrated on the gentle sounds of water—being lost at sea was certainly not as bad as she'd heard it was. When she was younger, some city children around Abika's age had escaped from their parents and drifted out to sea on a makeshift raft. They were never seen again. It hadn't bothered her all that much—they should've been more careful —Freja and Jekob sobbed the night that they'd heard about it. Their quiet muffled tears had awoken her like the waves had tonight, and she'd crept through to find them in each other's arms. The image of her foster parents crying should have filled her with regret, but it didn't. How could it? They were not the people she ever thought them to be. Still, it didn't explain that deep despair churning up her stomach.Was it Lorith? Did she miss that idiot boy? Was he even alive? The answers were like objects in the mist, hiding from her.

A tin cup fell to the deck near her head and she rolled her eyes. Fool Bohr! Then something wet slapped down in view. Abika was already picking what curses would be fit for Vasta's clumsiness, but they stuck in her throat. A heap of gore, fresh and oozing black blood, colourless in the moonlight slid towards her with the boat's movements. Abika's heart thumped as the urge to slip gently into the water overtook her.

Abika pulled her feet in so the blanket covered her completely. "Where are you, Vasta?" she breathed.

Another chunk of flesh splatted to the deck, and Abika shivered as an urge to cough took over her body. She sucked in her stomach, willing the itch in her lungs to abate. Her breathing became shallow as she tried to fight it, but her reflexes were not something she knew how to abate. Holding the cough back had tripled its intensity, and it popped out of her like a cork from a bottle.

Grasping fingers pulled at the blanket, then a chilling scream filled Abika's ears and she spun on her back, kicking out as hard as she could. The daemon reeled and clattered to the deck alongside pots and huge fishhooks. The safety of the sea behind beckoned at Abika.

Fumbling, Abika pulled the soulblade from her pocket, grasping the melted, blackened half of it like a handle. The daemon lunged forward, bending her wrist with the force, and the soulblade fell uselessly to the deck as they both fell back against the galley wall. Holding it back, the daemon snapped at her with broken teeth, mouth opening and shutting mechanically. Its eyes were empty of life. Vasta had been right, whatever it was, it was not human, not anymore. Abika slipped under its grasp, and it fell face-first to the deck.

The sky flashed, making silhouettes of the boat, the sail and the daemon as it turned, snapping, grasping.

"Vasta! Help me!"

If you wait for intervention. You will die waiting.

Vasta's words in Abika's head were like forks of lightning themselves. She was alone.

She took a breath.

"I am the storm," said Abika to the daemon.

The soulblade was in her hands, blue and glowing.

"I am the storm."

The daemon stepped towards her.

A rumble filled the sky as the thunder of the first lightning flash caught up with Rothmarr's boat. The daemon cowered, dropping his knife and pressing its hands to its head and wailed.

"I am the storm." The words came harder with the belief. The flash, the thunder, the power of the sky hung about her, and Abika felt it keenly in every part of her body. Not just in the smell of new rain, or the buzz of an ocean storm, hers was the power of the Gods themselves!

Abika raised the soulblade and the lightning crackled down to meet her. The daemon cowered, drawing itself beneath the bench she had been sleeping on, and Abika felt pity, then her head was at once filled with memories of a life she had not lived.

A middle-aged woman walks into a terraced house, covered in oil. She'd been fixing the boat until she'd heard that noise. What was it? It had to be that bloody girl again! She'd bloody show them. Sneaking into her son's room like that. This would be the last time! The mother barges the door open to find them there, naked and embarrassed, then pulls off her shoe and chases them both out of the house, onto the street. The two run away. It was the last time she ever saw her son again.

The woman is old now, sitting by herself in a broken kitchen drawing deeply from a pipe and inhaling the blue smoke down into her lungs. It used to help, but not anymore. All she has left is her own sadness to keep her company.

Another flash, the old woman dropped her pipe, the room vibrated, the sky outsider her windows shone bright for a moment, then her soul was leaving her as mist, drifting away and leaving her body standing alone as a daemon...

The daemon stared dumbly at the deck, drool and blood dripping from its lacerated mouth. Its hands had the same wrinkled skin Abika had seen in the memory. It was the same woman sitting bleeding upon the deck of Rothmarr's boat. The same woman who had chased her own son from her home, and now, she was here.

Abika reached inside herself, and she took hold of the power. Her legs and arms grew heavy and warm. Tears pricked at her eyes. "I release you."

The daemon lunged, and Abika lifted her soulblade towards it. Light flashed from the knife. She blinked away the dots of colours to find the daemon standing in a daze. It lunged again.

"No!" Abika held out a nervous blade, but the daemon was too strong. Another flash signalled more lightning from the storm on the horizon. She just had to survive another few seconds for another flash! She pulled her feet to her chest and kicked out, but the daemon was ready and grabbed her, and sunk its teeth into Abika's leg just below the hip.

"Argh!"

The daemon fell back screeching and wailing as the light intensified. Abika lifted herself up, holding the soulblade firmly in front of the daemon's face. Lightning burst from the blade, but instead of letting the Thunder just come, Abika pushed it away, to the back of the boat, to the Red Isles, To Rothmarr's father's house, to the orange grove, to Ipiti, to Nord and to the very limits of her imagination. The forks of light burned ever brighter, setting fire to the sail, the deck, and the daemon, with a light so intense it brought daylight back to the Myathar.

54

THUNDER

Abika had become the storm, using the flash of lightning and the thunder to control Soulfire. She had fooled them all by using the Great mother's own gifts against her! Raw power filled her up, but it was different this time. It was though everything that was happening was could not have happened any other way.

Even as the feeling spread through her bones, the daemon struggled against the fire, so bright that it seared flesh to bone. Abika no longer cared that the daemon used to be a person—the woman who banished her son and broke her family. Abika would punish her for her sins. If the woman's daemon face suddenly grew remorseful and then she pleaded with Abika to spare her life, Abika still would have turned her down. All that mattered was the feeling, as Soulfire tore through Abika, making right what was wrong. She drew deeper, and the flames intensified, turning the daemon to ash.

The Thunder followed soon after, ripping the sky. If the Flash was the conjuring of her Soulfire, the Thunder was payback from a debt borrowed. Abika had delayed the Thunder's return, sending it as far as she could imagine to give her time to kill the daemon, and like the cough that had burst out of her, delaying the balancing force had multiplied its strength.

Splinters of wood crackled, as the wood of Rothmarr's vessel expanded. The force of the Thunder tore through the matter that made up everything around Abika, and the Myathar burst apart.

Sea spray and wind whipped about Abika, the world spinning, colours and shapes moving too fast, until the painful slap of water. She should've scrambled for air, fighting to stay alive. The desire to live was, after all, knitted through every fibre of her, but she didn't. The water enveloped her, stealing the heat from her body as she sank below. Abika didn't struggle because this was her own debt, bought and now paid for. A life for a life. If the Thunder was the balancing force, then her death would come, and she would welcome it, because somewhere deep within her, she knew it to be fair and just.

Even as the resignation pressed in upon her, there was a piece of her that said no. Splinters of memory, killing the pig, escaping the citadel, stabbing the guard, letting the vendor who sold her the singing sculpture die, the man who drowned in the canal, they were all shards that pierced her mind and her lungs.

A voice sounded deep inside. Was it hers?

Balance may exist for them. But not for us. We are imbalance. We choose our own path. We are one-sided. We are.

Abika pushed up through the water towards the flaming smudge high above, fighting the urge to draw in lungfuls of saltwater. All she saw was that fire, flames that led back to air and life. She pulled herself up through the water, gnashing teeth, clouds of red swirling from her mouth.

The darkness below called to her but she wanted to live! The world needed someone to tip the scales, but the cold was sliding up her body, grasping at her skin...

Vasta surveyed the still-flaming boat from the side, looking for a way on, but the wood was damaged all around. He dropped the fish from his mouth, and paddled towards the outboard, but it too was missing. The Myathar was done for.

"Abika!"

It was the eleventh time he'd shouted her name with no response. He was a Bohr of sound reasoning, even in the face of the blood-deep instincts that drew him to kill and maim and torture. If his blood could have it, he would have lived in the woods chasing deer like some animal for the rest of his days, but he refused to be him. He was a scholar, and that man told him that Abika was dead.

"ABIKA!"

Vasta grabbed the smouldering wood and hauled himself out of the water. The deck creaked underfoot as the fire worked its way around the vessel. There was a smoking pile of ash, slowly burning its way through the close wooden planks, and the sickening smell of charred meat. A great force had hit the boat. The gunwale was all bent, the boom and mast had been pushed almost completely over, but in the same direction. On the other side, there were signs that an explosion had pushed everything away. Rothmarr's boat was well made and might even survive this fire, but whether or not it would still be seaworthy was another question entirely.

Then he saw the daemon's face lying pressed up against the corner of the deck. A piece of human flesh, cooking on the charring wood.

"Vasta!"

Vasta jerked around. "Abika!" He threw himself into the water and swam over to her as best he could. "Come here, girl!"

"Leave me!" shouted Abika, pushing him off. "Leave me, I'm alright."

Vasta ignored her, and dragged her like a drowning cat back to the boat, all but throwing her onto the smouldering deck. "You are not alright. You look like death. Watch the flames."

"I thought that was a good thing," she croaked.

Vasta leant back and kicked his legs furiously, splashing water over the deck. It took some time, but eventually the fire began to wane and die out. When he pulled himself up, Abika was sitting, steam drifting up from her wet farmer's clothes. "Abika, what did you do?"

"I killed her."

Vasta knelt at her side. She was so small. "No, Abika. It was no *her—*"

"You're wrong," said Abika, resting her chin on her knees, she had her shard blade out in her hand. "It was a woman. She had a son." Spots of colour rose up on her cheeks. "And I killed her. I used my power to kill her. The Flash. The Thunder." She laughed and her lips pressed together. "Who would have thought that her life would end here?!" Tears fell freely down her face. "Upon a burning ship in the Middle Sea, burnt to cinders by someone like...me."

Vasta felt the conflict deep in his bones. "This was not your fault. It was mine. I should have foreseen that one of those things could have grabbed the hawser. A scholar thinks, knows. Predicts. I should have seen it."

Abika stabbed the shard blade into the deck. "Do not try and take ownership, Vasta! I had as much a part in it as you." A glow surrounded her.

Vasta moved back. "Abika you're sick. You cannot reach for Soulfire when you've already used so much. What you were exposed to at the shard, the crystal tower, was enough energy to destroy the island. That tower was all that was keeping the island safe, and when you accessed it..." He didn't know how to finish. The line of thought should have led to an answer. It always did, and yet he could not fathom it. "It should have killed you." The haze around her shifted and the points of light dwindled like morning stars. Vasta's whole body relaxed. "You are truly God's gift, Abika."

The girl swallowed, the youthful energy of her own body giving her strength he wished he had. In truth the fishing had sapped much of his strength, and now the adrenaline was wearing off, he was beginning to flag. But he dared not show this girl. She had to still think of him as stronger than she.

"What do I do now?" she said, a child oblivious to her own potential.

"You must learn to control this gift, Abika." Vasta took a long breath, the hesitation as surely plain as every emotion he was feeling. "And while I cannot wield the energy of other worlds, there are few who can, I will do my best to teach you how to control yourself."

He wanted her to throw her arms around him, and to cry out all of her fears. He would hold her, and comfort her and guide her. But Abika just blinked at him.

"Alright, Vasta," she said, quietly. "Teach me everything you know about Soulfire."

PART III

KAVIK and JUNIPER

55

DIGGING DEEPER

The wind was relentless. Zunqai's streets had become tunnels of pressure and force that even the Bohr seemed to be avoiding. Kavik strode on past the huge doorways, the fountains, the effigies and statues of Bohrblood battles, until the dark day grew even gloomier.

Zunqai was largely circular, arranged in a grid centred around the palace, but navigating was tiresome. The Bohr seemed to know what they were about, at least on days where the heavens were closed, but even after eight cycles of life here, Kavik still had trouble finding his way. Worse was that he couldn't show it. Weakness shown would get you killed faster than getting lost, and so he strode on.

For all of the tearing bloody weather though, Kavik's heart was light. Empty streets in Zunqai were such a rare thing that he might have walked all night had he not a job to do. But, like most good feeling in this bloody town, it didn't last long.

He reached into his coat pocket and pulled out a fist-sized cage. "Alright, boy," said Kavik, talking to the bird inside. Juniper hopped back and forward excitedly on the perch. "I've no idea what awaits me here, so it's best you wait for me outside. Find somewhere high and cosy." Unclicking the clasp, and holding the spring to stop it from collapsing, he pried open the door. Juniper hopped onto his palm. After a quick feather shake, Kavik let the conure nuzzle his fingers before bringing him to his mouth and letting him drink from his tongue.

"Remember, if all goes south you find someone else. Alright? Someone who you might help like you helped me." The conure danced a little. "Don't wait on me, you hear? I ain't worth waiting for. Now, boy, be off with you. And listen for me." Kavik waggled his fingers just so, and Juniper took flight in a blur of green and orange, disappearing over the rooftops towards the aviaries. He shook his head at the energy of youth. A game of pursuit that had long passed by Kavik. "Fool bird." With the slightest pressure, Kavik pressed the cage into a flat disk and folded it, then slid it neatly down beside his wallet. He allowed himself a short moment before pounding on the door.

Almost immediately it creaked open and a yellow eye regarded him. "You the Horsemaster?"

"Aye, but I mind horses no more."

"And?"

Kavik rolled his eyes. "The weather's always bad."

"And."

"And the Bohr are a shower of shits."

The door flung open. "Welcome, Bohrwan!" The misshapen doorman stood, arm's welcoming. That yellow eye was all he had and it bulged nearly all the way out of his head.

Kavik took off his hat. "Stand aside. Unless you mean to leave me out in the rain?"

The doorman thought on it, like there was a riddle hidden between the lines and, satisfied there wasn't, nodded emphatically. "More than that, you're welcome. Not all who knock this door get an answer and even less get to see the inside. But news travels before ye, Bohrwan." The doorman grabbed Kavik's shirt and yanked him with surprising strength, slamming the door behind him. Then his hands were all over him, checking for weapons. "You're not armed."

"I don't need weapons, doorman. If we're going to fight, I'll throttle you dead with my bare hands."

The doorman's grin was like an old wound reopening. "Is that right?" He punched Kavik in the arm, then nodded approvingly. "I'd wager you might last a round or two with me! You sure you're not a Bohr yourself, Bohrwan?"

"Take it back, doorman."

A high voice cut him down. "Frog, leave him be."

Kavik turned to see an angel walking towards him. A fair woman, but rough enough that she might have lain with him, should he have cared enough. "You're Danna?"

The woman stopped in the dank hallway tilting her head. Auburn hair fell over a scarred but beautiful face. "Not what you were expecting?"

If Kavik had learned anything in Zunqai, it was when to keep his mouth shut. "You've seen some action." He shook his head at his own idiocy.

Danna smiled, creasing the scars over lip and nose. "I have. I will." She looked Kavik up and down. "I see why Fia kept you around, Bohrwan. Someone your size would be hard to kill."

Kavik gritted his teeth. "I'm no Bohrwan."

"I know," said Danna, dryly. "If you did have Bohrblood in that big chest, you would have probably tried to kill me by now. And you certainly would have had a go at Frog here. That's why he's such a good doorman. He's a good filter."

"Only a human would put up with my shit," said Frog, pointing at his crusty eye socket. The doorman turned and stumbled over to a table and began dunking his bread into a bowl of tablebroth. He took a wet bite and grinned again. "Oh, and he says he's no Horsemaster either. You sure he's our man, boss?"

Danna moved the wisp of hair from her green eyes. "Oh, I'd say so. According to Eris there'd be no mistaking him."

"Eris?" said Kavik. "So, the fifth are in touch with you?"

Danna nodded. "The fifth. The fourth. All of them. Always."

"Fucking unions," said Frog.

Danna touched Kavik's arm. "So, you're a Horsemaster who has given up on his animals?"

Kavik shook his head. "I hate animals."

Danna stared at him, working him out. "We all lose faith in our gods at some point or another, but they usually always come back when we need them." She gestured to the dark passage. "Come."

The hallway ran on for the length of the old house, which was much deeper than it looked from outside. "We are within the hillside."

Danna kept walking ignoring him. Kavik tried his hardest not to let his eyes wander over her curves. She probably expected him to look, but if an enemy wants you to do something, you're always better not to do it. Laeb had taught him that.

"Definitely not a Bohrblood then," she said, stopping abruptly.

Kavik lifted his gaze. "Just a man."

"And some man at that."

"Your doorman," said Kavik. "He's stronger than he looks."

"Frog keeps us safe. You only underestimate the union once."

"This isn't a union." Kavik scoffed.

Danna blinked at him then turned and carried on through the dank tunnel. The makeshift hallway had changed from walls and ceilings of stone to wooden boards and mud, with a thick rope that ran the length at waist height.

"You're not afraid of small spaces, are you Kavik?"

Kavik ignored the quip. "If this truly *is* a union, how many of you are there?"

Danna stopped to light a lamp hanging on the wall, which caused all the connecting lamps to blink into life. "Many of us consider this to be the only *real* union, Horsemaster. We have the oldest claim to Zunqai."

"Outside of the Bohr."

Danna turned on him. "Did our mutual friend really send you here to mock us, Horsemaster?"

"No, I came here for resource."

Danna shook her head. "Resource? Is that what you call it these days? I call it aid, support. I call it standing our ground. Staying alive. Creeping through a hornets' nest is what I call it!"

"Are you a member of the rebellion or not, because I know for a fact that not all the unions care for the resistance."

"A plain talker then." Danna shook her head. There was a flash of something metal near her hands. "Everyone dances to *her* tune. I fight for humans."

Fatigue gripped Kavik, but he kept on. "Then you *are* part of the rebellion. You are Tsiorc."

"The Tsiorc are long dead, Horsemaster!" Danna held a thin copper blade up under Kavik's chin. "Your Tsiorc have no place amongst the unions. They were destroyed in Tyr, and never returned. A last beacon of human hope destroyed by the gods themselves. No, we are the rebellion now, and the rebellion *are* the unions."

"Are you going to kill me with a letter opener?"

Danna's teeth flashed. "It doesn't matter how big the blade is, Horsemaster. I thought someone with your *experience* would have figured that out by now."

"Then do it." He spoke calmly, because he was calm. Juniper would be fine, and that was truly all that mattered. "Plunge your little blade up through my skull and into my brain."

Danna looked thoughtful. "Do you really want that, Horsemaster? I can deliver it if you so desire."

"And I'm sure I would join a long line of men you have released from this life." Kavik sighed. "But, no. This is what the Bohr want, Danna. They want us to waste time fighting each other, because then they don't have to. They can simply stand aside as we eradicate ourselves." Kavik stuck his chin out, feeling the point of her blade cutting his skin.

Danna pulled away, but that copper blade stayed out in her hand. "It's not much further. Just watch though, it gets slippery up ahead. Use the stones."

"And now you're concerned for me?" Fia had been right to remove this woman from the ranks so long ago. Kavik checked the nick for blood and sucked his finger, then followed, ducking low, stepping upon the half-buried flag stones to avoid the mud. He cursed himself for choosing his best leather riding coat, now scuffed and mud-splattered, he would have to take it through the back streets to that tailor—

The next flag stone fell away with his weight. Danna leapt forward but there was no time to protest. Kavik fell into a trap hole, riding the flag stone down into cold, stinking water that reached up for his mouth and nose.

"Argh!" He coughed and spluttered, looking up at an open trapdoor. "What are you about!?"

Danna stood at the edge of the hole, a good ten feet above his head. "Sorry, Horsemaster. But I've got to be sure. There's too much at risk to let you into our world without proof of who you say you are." She reached out of sight and pulled a bucket to the edge of the hole.

Kavik spat. "What are you doing, Danna? This was not—What have you in there?"

Danna tapped the bucket. "My helpers. How did you hear of us?"

Kavik swallowed bitterness. "You know how—"

Danna shook her head and pulled a cowl over her mouth. "Sources. Horsemaster, do you know how many people have died in that very hole? It's more *essence of liar*, than it is mud and water. Now, I know you have sources. I want names!"

Kavik shook his head. "You know fine well, girl!"

Danna pulled on a thick glove and reached into the bucket. "Don't call me girl." She sounded bored, and that scared Kavik more than anything else. Even when she pulled an eel from the bucket, wriggling and shiny.

"What's that?"

"An eel. But a fascinating one. As one animal lover to another. It has these little teeth that extrude from its mouth. They latch on to flesh and expel their stomach, leaving their whole outer bodies completely, so they can enter yours through the wound. Then they just...eat until they can eat no longer."

"I bet they taste good grilled. Most things do."

Danna tilted her head. "Who told you about us, Horsemaster?"

"If this is truly is a union, then you would know that you just can't be sabotaging the Bohr in their own stronghold without notice." She watched him, quietly. It was unnerving. "Alright." Kavik smashed his hand into the water, splashing his face with muck. "Atalfia. Atalfia sent me. The lord's army is being remade by Queen Kaliste and Captain Atalfia, the leader of the tearing Tsiorc, sent me here to talk to you, Danna."

Danna shook her head. "Fia minds the Fifth Union, not the Tsiorc, and the lord's army was destroyed in Tyr along with your Tsiorc almost thirteen cycles gone. You're a fucking liar!"

"I don't lie, and it's called the *Queen's army* now. Don't you dare tell me you haven't lost contact with some of your members? Because I know THAT would be a lie you tearing bloody fool."

Danna studied him, that twisted mouth pouting. She was probably very beautiful once. "And what does *Atalfia* think I can give you, Horse-master?" The eel had stopped wriggling, and it stared down at him with as much expectation.

"Communication between each of the major quadrants of the city has run dry. At the centre of each of those quadrants is a human union with a leader who should be spying and leading and training humans for the long fight!" Kavik sighed. "And you, Danna, were sold to me as someone who could get me a seat at the table. Clearly Atalfia was wrong. This is no union, and you are no union leader."

"I don't believe a resourceful fellow like you isn't already in the pockets of every union leader in Zunqai! The Northerns, Southerns, Easterns and Westerns? They would fall over themselves to have a spy like you."

"The unions stopped talking to me five cycles ago. And don't you dare ask me why or so help me, I will climb out of this hole and tear that pretty head from those shoulders!"

Danna raised an eyebrow then threw the eel. It plopped into the murky water in front of him.

"Argh!" Kavik pushed away, until the muddy side was cold against his back. There was another splash as Danna emptied the bucket into the traphole.

"What're you doing, you tearing idiot?!" Kavik grabbed one of the wriggling shapes near his chest, but it was too slimy to hold. It flashed a row of tiny little razor teeth before sliding out of his grip. "Get me out of here!"

But Danna just watched, leaning on the upturned bucket like a proud parent watching her children playing.

Kavik stopped and closed his eyes. Nothing had bitten him yet. He was yet to have his body invaded by these awful things. He had to control his panic and lower his heart rate.

When he opened his eyes, the water was calm. In fact, he might have even tricked himself into believing that all was right with the world. He was just out for a swim...in a rancid muddy hole.

"A man who meditates," said Danna. "I never thought I'd see the day."

"They're not biting me."

"No, and they won't." Danna pulled a copper timepiece from her waistcoat pocket and tilted her head. "Not for another hour or two."

"Nocturnal."

"They'll sleep on the bottom until hunger wakes them. I just have to decide if I leave you in there until that happens." Danna stood and pocketed her watch. "What do you want from the unions? Because you can damn-well believe that is the question they will ask me if I try to get you an audience with them."

"I want in." Kavik sighed.

"Into the union?"

"Into the Queen's army."

Danna sat on the bucket. "And so the truth will set you free."

Kavik spat into the water, ignoring the wriggling near his feet. "I need to get into the ranks of the Queen's army to see what the Bohr are working on. Something is different this time. They are working on something. Something insidious."

Danna frowned at him. "What do you know?"

"Oh no. You let me out, and then we'll have a discussion."

Her eyes narrowed, but she reached behind her and threw down the rope that lined the tunnel. Apparently, it had been built just so, to help people out of this hole. The irony was not lost on him.

With great difficulty Kavik hauled his bulk out of the hole one slow, slippery step at a time. When finally his feet stood upon the flagstones, he looked up to find Danna's copper blade under his chin once more.

"It seems that biggest isn't always best after all, Horsemaster."

Kavik wiped the rancid water from his mouth and spat into the hole. "Yes, well, when you spend your life as the biggest eel in the hole and then suddenly you're not, you learn a few things."

"You're not that big, Horsemaster." Danna tapped Kavik's soaking wet coat. "In fact, I'd say you were skinnier than you should be."

"In my day, I could lift an adult nara above my head."

"I can quite believe it." Danna lifted Kavik's hat from the floor and brushed it off. She ran a finger along the rim. "Being a spy is difficult when the Bohr know we're here, it must be very hard for you."

"It is." Kavik graciously took the hat back and placed it on his head —now that it was the only dry clothing he had. "And the long fight is coming regardless."

Danna gestured back along the tunnel. "Then it's probably time you met the union leader."

56

A SHIELD OF LIGHT

Rothmarr's boat drifted along the coast of Sulitar, dragged by the currents until eventually Abika and Vasta were pulled past the shelter of the Red Isles completely. Frantic paddling had made no difference to their course, and even as strong as Vasta was, he would never replace a strong wind.

"We're being pulled out!" shouted Abika. "Go faster!"

"I...am not...a fish." The waves had picked up again, slapping over Vasta's face as he kicked from the back of the boat. There was nothing close to gauge their progress either.

"We're not even moving!" She squinted at the hazy hills of the Red Isles, no longer purple but a soft blue that merged into the sky. "I could use Soulfire." She reached inward again, closing her eyes.

"No—" Vasta stopped kicking.

Abika shook her head as the waves cut Vasta off. "All I can see are flames anyway."

"No, girl," spluttered Vasta. "Just because you have access to something...powerful, doesn't mean...you bring it out at every opportunity! Soulfire will not help us here."

"Then what bloody good is it?" shouted Abika. "What good is it to be able to wield such power? You told me that there were those who could level mountains with it! Destroy armies!"

"The Banèmen. Yes. They were born to do those things, but they still pull their trousers on and eat with eating sticks!" Vasta leaned forward and grabbed a plank, hauling himself back on deck. "The world is made of matter." He rapped the plank with his knuckles. "Soulfire is part of the energy that sits beneath all that we see. All that we touch. It imbues everything. The plants, the animals, humans, Bohr. A wise man once told me that we are all just pockets of energy and our job here on Rengas, in existence, is to experience as much as possible. Doing so changes the nature of that energy, so when it returns to your Great Mother, the Forbringr or whoever it is exactly that deigned us to be here, it is renewed. Of a different...frequency, as it were. We have added to the great ether. Some say Soulfire is a flavour of that great ether. You take, and so you must give back."

"Then why can't everyone touch it? Why me?"

Vasta wiped his face, then shrugged. "I cannot answer that."

Abika picked up the shard of crystal she had taken from the tower and rolled the lump over in her hands. "You mean you will not answer that. You don't trust me."

"You're right," said Vasta, smoothing back the hair on his face and head. He looked like a drowned dog. "I do not trust you, but that is not why I cannot answer."

"Then why?"

"The question is so fundamental, as to be completely unanswerable. Scholars more clever than I have mulled over the question for cycles and not come up with anything resembling an answer. Even my take upon the roots of Soulfire is completely subjective."

"So you made it up?" Abika sighed.

"It is a theory based on my observations of life. Of everything. Learn, progress. Observe and extrapolate."

Abika padded over the burnt deck to the broken planks, and stopped as the remnants of Rothmarr's boat creaked sideways. "You must have a theory about why some can touch Soulfire and others can't, Vasta? I don't believe that you would have lived as long as you have—How old are you anyway?"

Vasta's bushy eyebrows raised. "I do have a theory."

"And..."

He seemed to think on it, then his eye was drawn back to the waves. "We are drifting again!"

Abika's heart leapt into her mouth. "Well, get back in there!"

Vasta shook his head. "It won't make a difference, girl! I cannot fight the currents of the sea any more than I can fight the clouds in the sky! There is no land in the Middle Sea! We will perish upon the open—"

"Toss me."

"Toss you?"

"I delayed the Thunder when I killed the woman."

"How?"

"It was like lightning that strikes first, the Flash, with the Thunder coming after. Except I delayed it and it let me go deeper. I thought of all the places I've been since I left the commune, the road, the city of Ipor Dan, the Red Isles..." To Abika, it was a straightforward question with a straightforward answer. "The further I could imagine, the further I could push the Thunder away. It just responded whenever I thought of a new place I had been. I think the Thunder must always return."

"Balance," said Vasta. "You take, and so you must give. Then what did you do?"

"Then, while I was imagining those places, I simply asked for the fire to protect myself, and it came. I willed it forward against the daemon woman and she died. It connected me to her, Vasta. It let me see inside her as she burned. Whatever those daemons are, they are alive. They are not walking dead. They are something else."

"The soulless. Still, your fire will do us no good here, girl. We sit upon an ocean on a pile of sticks."

"It's not just fire, Vasta. It's force," she said, nodding towards the vast ocean behind her. "I'll make a wave."

Surprisingly, vast nodded then turned and began scrambling around in one of the few remaining cupboards. He pulled out a handful of lead fishweights and began tying them to Abika's feet. "You'll be high up, girl. Hitting the water on the way back down from that height will be like hitting stone. These will ensure it is the surface tension that breaks and not your legs."

Abika nodded, but fear gripped her as she became suddenly aware that she had to do this. "Vasta, how do I—"

"Don't try, girl. Just do. Just like you said. Hold it back. Consider everywhere you have been so far, and use it. Use your experience and hold back the Thunder. Just be sure to direct the force into the sea to create the wave." He straightened up, considering the sea as Rothmarr and every sailor that ever existed had done. "Keep it small. Don't try and create a huge wave, or it'll travel inland, getting bigger and bigger until it wipes out the shorelands."

"We don't want that," said Abika, thinking of the commune. She tried to move her feet, but the weights were heavy. "What if—"

"You won't drown, child. Just try not to set the boat on fire again." Vasta tied the strapping around her ankles, bringing them together so that even if she wanted to, she could not have pulled her legs apart. "Ready?"

"Go, Vasta."

Vasta picked her up, and threw her straight upwards. The wind roared past Abika's ears. Her stomach lurched with the speed and force of Vasta's toss. She looked down and couldn't help the scream that followed. She could have been flying for the incredible height she was reaching. Clutching at Soulfire was like trying to grab a greased pole! She scanned the horizon, and her eye fell upon a distant shape, hazy and mostly hidden by the curve of the world. The wind's rush lessened as she reached the peak of Vasta's toss, and as it did, Soulfire filled Abika's veins with power. Fire was there, accessible without any kindle, even in the cold air above the Middle Sea, warmth spread throughout her. Stoking a fire was something she had done a thousand times, and the warmest fires had to build, but there was no time for that. The Flash came first and light poured out of her. Abika drew as much Soulfire as she could and directed it into the sea. The glow that surrounded her shot away from her like a beam of sunlight, smashing into a spot in the ocean a few hundred paces away. The water sizzled and steamed, but there was no wave.

Abika drew more Soulfire, so much that her skin felt afire, so much that the air around her seemed to crackle. The force of it kept her floating there, as the gods of the earth tried to pull her back down. The air thickened, then turned solid. Adjusting her footing, it felt as though she were standing on the ground. Soulfire was giving her strength to fight the elements, and she could feel the force of it as she channelled more and more of herself into the beam of light. Blue lightning crackled along its length, smashing into the tunnel of whirling water, spinning so fast the seabed beneath began to show.

You take, and so you must give.

The wave was not coming. She had failed, but perhaps there was another way. The Thunder was on its way now, leaving her very little time. If her fight with the old woman had taught her anything, it was that the Thunder was inevitable. If this was the Flash, then the Thunder would...

"That's it!"

She let the Thunder come. Her skin tingling in anticipation. If the Flash was the effects of the power within her, then, as Vasta said, the Thunder was the balance. But if she could direct that too—

The air began to hum, vibrating as the world sought out balance to her debt, and Abika willed it on. Willed it faster, and so it came. Shockwaves hurtled towards her from every direction, dragging the clouds and ready to crush her into dust. Abika changed her stance, then drew the Flash back into herself, the only thing she knew how to do, sucking in the beam of power as the shockwaves of Thunder tore through the air. She imagined a shield of light around her, and she began to glow. Things looked suddenly clearer—the shape on the horizon was a land mass, an island. She could see it now staring back at her, watching with great interest as this strange being stood upon the air, battling the forces of this world. The shield of light dimmed as the Thunder smashed into it. Ringing filled her ears, but Abika directed it all, Flash and Thunder, towards that island in the centre of the Middle Sea.

The rushing wind returned with aplomb. Gravity had finally won her back and she was falling. The wind roared again, and as the world greeted her once more she tucked her arms in. Cold water smashed into her, claiming her for its own. The weights dragged her down some of the way, then miraculously the knot around her ankles tore away. They spun away from her, dragging the rope like a ribbon, twirling into the darkness below.

Abika swam upward, towards the light, but her arms were so tired.

Her very bones felt tired. She was the old woman, bone-weary and finished with it all. A blurry shape appeared above, all arms and legs flapping around like a fish, then she was being dragged upwards to the surface.

Before long she was staring up at a bright blue sky, breathing heavily. "Did it work?"

"No. It didn't work," scoffed Vasta. "I tossed you up, and you fell back down."

"That...that can't be." Abika stared at Vasta, at his big, stupid animal-looking head. "I was up there...I stood, made a whirlpool using Soulfire."

Vasta didn't dismiss her, didn't shout at her or say she was wrong. He just stared back at her. His inquisitive eyes scanning her face, searching for weakness. She supposed it was a trait of all Bohr, to find that thing, that point of failure in whoever they spoke to. Whatever it was, it made her feel like prey.

After a long while, he finally spoke, albeit quietly. "Soulfire can be tricksy."

Abika blinked. "Tricksy? That's all you have?"

"That's all I have."

Abika flung her arms up. "You, the great Vasta. The Bohr the Order of the White Dragon wanted as a figurehead?! The fountain of all knowledge! And your explanation is *tricksy*?" The Bohr didn't react, making her even angrier. "You're a fool, Vasta! A bloody fool." She turned back towards the Red Isles, the tops of the mountains only barely visible now. "So, what do we do?"

"Nothing," said Vasta. "We do nothing."

Abika fell back against the galley cupboards, the only part of Rothmarr's boat that had any sort of backing to it.

Vasta looked down at her. "You could try and make a wave from here? Or I could toss you again?"

"We have no more weights. I'd flail around like a broken bird." That wasn't the reason at all. The truth was Abika could no longer feel the awesome torrent of power that was Soulfire. Usually, it felt like she had somehow caged up the wind and could release it at will. That power of potential, the knowledge of what she *could* do, gave her strength and will. But it just wasn't there anymore. There was not a scrap. Some part of her panicked at the thought of never touching Soulfire again, but in truth, she was so tired she could barely acknowledge it. She stared at the palm of her hand and Abika knew, as sure as the ocean was deep, that this was the end of them.

57

UNIFICATION

The union tunnel continued for some way into the hill, before finally leading to a cosy square garden with an open skylight above showing the bruised Zunqai sky. Creepers ran along the sides, delicate things with purple flowers that filled the air with pollen scent. Kavik was no gardener, but when you were covered in shit-stinking mud from head to toe, everything else smelled like roses.

He squinted at a man standing with his back to them as Danna closed the mossy door closing with a soft thud.

"Sir?"

The man turned and Kavik took the measure of him. A book in his hand, pressed clothes, and eyeglasses resting upon his nose. A scholar. The union cross hung around his neck, marking him as a union leader, but he looked more a boy than any other Kavik had met so far, despite the salt and pepper grey at his temples.

"I'm Kavik."

"You are northern?" said the man, ignoring Kavik's outstretched hand.

"As much as you." Kavik hated one-sided introductions—everything and everyone deserved to be equal in this ridiculous world, there was no time for anything else. "Was it the name or the face that led you to that conclusion..."

"The face." The union leader closed the book, taking care to mark the page first. He favoured his left arm, but it didn't look natural on him. He stepped forward, studying Kavik. "You are—"

"Don't you dare say it," rumbled Kavik. It was impossible not to appear grouchy in the face of pretension. "A man needs a name before judgement passes."

An emotion passed through the union leader's deep eyes. Women would have no doubt found those chiselled features and the long body attractive, but to Kavik he was just another face. "It's in our nature to be hesitant of new people. There's too much at stake to let just anyone in here." He gestured to the walled garden. "You know where you stand, don't you?"

"You'll tell me that now, because I stand in the body of a union, that I must bow to you? That I must beg for your employ? Perhaps you may even give it to me, but then we start as master and slave. If we stand upon the same side then let us get on with it."

The union leader picked up a small pair of scissors. "These flowers only exist here because I cultivated them. They are native to Sulitar, and yet they grow here in Kemen where it is too dry and too hot."

"Speak plainly."

"I do," said the union leader, dragging his gaze back to Kavik. "I might take longer to get there then a pragmatist like yourself, but I will...get there."

"Then, in the name of pragmatism, give me a tearing bloody name!"

"I don't think it has one." The union leader considered the flower once more. "At least not one that I know."

Kavik growled deep in his throat. "Do not play games. You say there is much at stake? Then realise that you are not the only one with life invested in this city."

The union leader snipped the flower from the plant and let it fall to the cobbles. "Then let us talk plainly. I know who you are, Kavik, and I know you've been talking with the other unions. What say you to that?"

Kavik glanced back at Danna, and she winked at him. "You ask when you know the answer?"

"I'd like to hear it in your words, Horsemaster." Another flower fell to the floor.

Kavik grappled with the words in his head. He had never been a great thinker, but sometimes a little finesse was useful when dealing with people like this. "The Queen is building an army, with Bohr fighters."

The union leader seemed unimpressed. "We were right then, Danna. The Bohr are assembling another army."

"That's not all," said Kavik. "Humans are being drafted in too. And not just mercenaries. People with families. Fathers, mothers." The relevance landed because the union leader's eyebrow raised. "The long fight is on its way. And the Bohr will win, whether we're ready or not. This army of mercenaries and Ruffin will—"

The union leader stopped Kavik with a finger. "Ruffin?"

"Hundreds of them. Each with a Rider trained in the use of Soulfire."

"This is a lie!" Danna scoffed. "You really trust him?"

The union leader picked at Kavik's wet jacket. "I see you've sent him to the hole already. There must have been some quality to him that you agreed to." He tapped Kavik's shoulder. "You were lucky, she's been known to leave folks in there with the eels until dark."

"Only men," said Danna, dangerously.

"So, what is it that you want, Bohrwan of the north?"

Kavik took a deep breath. "The best place to learn of your enemy is within their own ranks, standing shoulder to shoulder with the men on the ground. I aim to penetrate the ranks of Queen Kaliste's army. To learn and fight from the inside as a spy. To stand beside them until the last, and then kill every single last one of them." His own words had become sharp. He stepped back, giving the union leader space.

The union leader smiled. "I can see why they want you too. A Bohrwan would slay many of our kind on the battlefield." He turned slowly. "You know, I used to fight."

"Is that right?"

"You don't believe me, of course."

"What weapon?"

"Bow. And very good I was too. Although, I haven't touched it since."

Kavik nodded, understanding. "War leaves its mark and not just on our bodies."

The union leader rubbed his right shoulder. "Well, we can't help you. The Northerns don't know anyone in the Queen's Guard. Our contacts have all been killed or lost..."

"So the Northerns can't help me. What about the other unions?"

The union leader's face creased into a strained smile. "You wish to make friends? We could all learn much from you, Horsemaster."

Kavik shook his head. "You know, I've been in every square garden of every union in Zunqai. I've spoken to every up-themselves union leader, the Westerns, Easterns and Southerns, and now the Northerns, with your kaldi presses, your garden scissors, your books on tactics— Yes, I saw the cover." Kavik poked the book under the union leader's arm. "Is there anything in there about unification? Because if the unions spent as much time cooperating as you do fighting and spying on each other, the Bohr would be a relic of history long forgotten." Then something struck Kavik, like the first droplets of rain in a desert. "You are Sami."

The scissors paused, hovering either side of a tender stem. "I am. You can see it in my—"

"You were in Tyr, weren't you?" Danna's feet shuffled behind him, but more worrying were the folds of cloth being moved around a sheath. It was a noise Kavik knew very well. "You do not look old enough to have been part of the lord's army. Which leads me to ask which side you fought on?"

The scissors clamped shut, but awkwardly, and the tender stem caught between them, uncut, holding on for its life.

"The Kin." The union leader looked up, but where Kavik expected to see anger or suspicion, he saw only sadness. "I was young and I lost more than I care to say."

"So, you stood on the Way Bridge, weapon in hand. Locked out from the city gates? Kavik took a step to the side, keeping Danna in his peripherals.

The union leader frowned, seeing Kavik anew. "There was a man who was glimpsed the night of Tyr's demise, the Kin who escaped with their lives say the man was seen sabotaging the gates."

Kavik cleared his throat. "Hearthsalt. Aye, that was me. After crawling through the sewers of Tyr so that I smelled much the same as I do now, but Kin or no, surely you must have realised that by fighting with the Bohr you would be fighting your own people? Is that what this is? Recompense?"

The man opened the scissors and the flower drooped. "I was young."

"Youth does not forgive a lifetime of sin."

"Forgive?" The man had crossed the short distance between them in a heartbeat. He held the scissors up at Kavik's chest. "I don't need forgiveness!"

Kavik had always found it easy to stay calm in the face of anger. Just the presence of it was like a float he could hold onto in an ocean of unfamiliarity. Even so, He wished desperately to call for Juniper. "You anger quickly for one so at peace."

The union leader's expression relaxed. "I am Sami and I fought for the Kin, arguably the wrong side, but does that change things? Do you still wish for a seat at the union table or not?"

"When I put my life on the line for someone, I like to know who I'm dealing with. Some call it a failing."

"Some?"

"I'm not in the business of keeping people happy."

The man smirked. "Then we have at least one thing in common, Kavik. Tell me more of this opportunity to join the Queen's new army."

Kavik spoke at length of the Bohr and the union leader and Danna both listened closely. Of his conversations with palace guards, with kitchen workers, with servants, and valets. He had used a variety of different techniques to draw information from the humans who worked beneath the Bohr in their own capital city, but the answers to his questions were all the same, that the lord's army was being reformed, but with one very big difference.

"And what is that *difference*?" asked the union leader.

Kavik approached him, reaching beyond and plucking the flower from the ruined tenderstem. Inside the folded purple petals was a round, solid seed, which he rolled beneath his fingers until it was released. "That the long fight is coming." He let the seed roll into his palm then whistled loudly. Within a few seconds Juniper was fluttering around them. The colourful little bird stopped upon a branch high up, cocking his head at the three humans and their tense poses, but his boy knew when his master was safe and when he was in peril, so Juniper fluttered down to Kavik's thumb, and snatched up the seed. Even so, Kavik was still ready to waggle a signal for Juniper to escape.

"A Horsemaster who has given up on his animals?" said Danna, smiling wryly.

"You trained a conure?" said the union leader, bemused. "A bird I'm told is nigh on untrainable."

Juniper returned to the branch amongst the purple flowers still holding the seed with his claws, and began tearing it into strips before eating. "It's always best to present a new front to those you are yet to trust," said Kavik. "You talk of uniting, and yet our brothers and sisters, who are all ready and willing to fight the Bohr, join your unions only to be drawn into an cave of self-defeatism. Spying on each other. Attacking each other. The Bohr *want* us to stay fragmented. They need us to. The unions are making it easier for it to be so."

"And who is going to draw us together?" snapped the union leader. "You? The Westerns wouldn't listen to any leader that wasn't born in Kemen, The Easterns are so left-minded that any conversation regarding money or resource sends them running! I won't even get into the Southerns, but I can tell you that they are the least likely of all four of the great unions to listen to anyone."

"Five unions. You forget the rebels holding the Hatàrian border."

"Holding the border?" Danna laughed aloud. "They are as useless as old fruit in the sun, and their captain is—"

Kavik squared his shoulder and turned towards Danna. "Ready and willing to fight, and if you know what's good for you, you'll not say another word about it."

"Then tell me, Horsemaster," said Danna, indignantly stepping forward to meet Kavik—a whole foot below him. "Is she still stymied by the wall? Unable to climb some flat stone? Forgive me if I don't spare the Fifth Union another thought!"

Kavik reached over and plucked another seed from a flowerhead and held it up for Juniper. The little bird fluttered down and retrieved it, but stayed there this time, his needle claws holding tight to Kavik's calloused thumb. "The Bohr have decided that they don't need humans to survive, or at least that there is a level of survival they are willing to accept that doesn't include us. Unification is our only way through. If you don't, then no human will be tolerated in Zunqai, or perhaps even Kemen. The Bohr will spread like cancer through Nord, but they will do so not as the fragmented forces that failed in Tyr, but as an unstoppable whirlwind that will leave the world devoid of human life. Their ships will leave the Horn Dol Zunqai ports and spread around Rengas infecting all. The Outer Isles will fall last, and from what I hear, there are already sympathisers that side of the Middle Sea. Humans who actually *want* to be governed by the Bohr. *We* are fast becoming the minority. Draw the five unions together under one banner and unite the humans of Zunqai." Juniper fluttered away to the floor, nipping at the flowers lying there.

"I can see why the other unions kicked you out," said the union leader.

"Then be the change, and do what they refuse to do." Kavik placed a light hand on the union leader's shoulder. "And who better than a veteran who fought the Bohr in Tyr, *and* a former Kin." The union leader's expression grew grim. "And now that we dance and sing the same tearing tune, a man needs a name!"

The union leader sighed long and hard. "Call me Hasaan."

58

SHADOWS OVER ZUNQAI

"You are radiance, my Queen," shouted V'olpar over the hammering rain. The upper windows of the Palace could surely take no more of this blood-awful weather.

"I feel radiant, V'olpar." Kaliste stroked her rapidly expanding stomach.

V'olpar's words might have been considered blasphemous at any other time and from any other person, but his master V'Laerk's connection to Kaliste protected him to an extent. Whether he knew that was another story.

The tiled hallway sang like a choir of children ringing them on their way. "Life is an unusual construct, isn't it?" mused Kaliste. "One minute we're here, working together, fighting for the same cause. The next we are ash, drifting into the sewers."

V'olpar was still basking in Kaliste's presence, looking around to see who could see them. "You mean it is...unusual. Life? What makes you ask? What has happened?"

"Oh, nothing," she tapped her stomach. "I've just found that even after as many cycles as I have lived, I can still be surprised."

"You talk of the child in your belly, my Queen."

Kaliste grimaced. "No. I do not. V'olpar, What do you know about Ge'Bat?"

"The island off the coast of Kemen?"

"Unless you know of another place named so?"

"No." This time V'olpar grimaced. "Of course, apologies, my Queen. Ge'Bat is run by two emperors. A brother and sister who famously do not get along."

Kaliste shook her head. "Fortensa and Forthing. They used to fight like tomcats, but I can tell you that those times are long gone. The urge to battle and fret over every detail has left along with their youth. What do you know about their economy?"

"Only that it is well known amongst the Council that they do not get along with Sulitar. Their little island is not worth troubling ourselves over."

"Ge'Bat sits atop a subterranean reservoir of black oil, which seeps up from the ground and, treated properly, is very combustible. They use it to power everything from lights to machines that can throw and lift many times that of a Bohr. It has made Ge'Bat a very wealthy place indeed. A *little island* with lots of wealth would be an easy target, or are they more like..." She paused in the hallway. "Dragons minding their gold."

V'olpar frowned so deeply his horns looked they might come together. "There hasn't been a dragon in Rengas for a thousand generations—"

Kaliste shook her head silently then carried on. "You need to read more books, V'olpar. Tell me, what of the army?"

"We've had trouble, my Queen. The weather is an onslaught—"

The armoury opened out in front of them as they walked, spears, maces and all sorts of heavy weapons hanging from the walls behind the three Bohr smiths working amidst the steam and smoke of the ground forges.

"V'olpar, you can't tell me that you're letting a little water hold you up?"

V'olpar stopped. "An unnatural shadow hangs over us, my Queen. The rain falls from heavy clouds that refuse to move despite the wind. Kemen earth was never meant to hold so much water. It has held us back in recruiting, but we have forged ahead regardless, despite the anger of the Forbringrs."

"You think the gods are causing this weather?"

V'olpar nodded, then held a fist to his hairy forehead.

Kaliste blinked. "You have many layers, V'olpar. I can see why V'Laerk keeps you close." V'olpar bristled, standing taller and puffing out his chest. She nodded forward. "Then let us see where we are at."

They walked the final corridor to the square and V'olpar pushed open the wide doors to the courtyard. Kaliste should have been shielding her eyes from the brightness of the sun—aside from the servant tunnels beneath the Palace, the armoury was a stone box with no windows—but it was dark outside. The courtyard of the Central Palace was jammed full of dull steel, black leather and red flags that stood like stalks of wheat amongst the grass, gently flapping in the wind. The Queen's army was a tide awaiting the storm.

The squad captains stood high above the humans, but there was no need for them to be sneering so. These men and women were mercenaries, bred for war, led by some of the hardest Bohr that ever lived.

V'olpar raised his hand and a wondrous, splintering crack filled the air as thousands of feet stamped to attention. If the Bohr underling had been bristling before, now he exalted, stiff-backed like a peacock displaying its feathers.

"Where are the rest?"

V'olpar turned towards her. "The rest?"

"The rest," growled Kaliste. "There are a million humans in Zunqai, and here I barely see one hundredth of that. Where are the rest, V'olpar?"

The sky flashed as lightning struck somewhere deep in the heavy clouds. "Bands of resistance have formed. Cells who spread warnings about the drafts. They're organised."

"THE UNIONS SHOULD NEVER UNDER YOUR CONTROL UNDERLING V'OLPAR!" Kaliste closed her eyes and gathered herself together—the morning's good feelings were slipping away. "V'olpar." She took a long breath to steady herself, but it didn't do much good. "Your position carries an expectation. V'Laerk knew it. You need to do more. This army must be complete before the long fight. Do you understand me?" She let go of V'olpar's arm, unsure of when she had grabbed it. Black scorch marks showed where her fingers had dug into his thick skin, and a fetid meat stink touched her nostrils. Anger was coursing through her veins like wildfire through dry brush. "Where are the Ruffin? Where are the Banèmen?"

V'olpar looked suddenly unsure. "This is an army of human fighters, humans fighting humans. The beautiful arrangement." His coarse voice did no justice to the word *beautiful*.

In the absence of the Bohr King, killed in Tyr, Kaliste had taken the throne almost without resistance. Perhaps the lack of a fight had softened her. Perhaps taking something so easily after a hundred lifetimes of struggle and poverty had led Kaliste to think of herself as more than she was. She stood in front of thousands of men all waiting to do her bidding. Jagar might have had plans, but *she* was the one standing here. Wherever Jagar was, he had power but he could not leave, otherwise it would be him standing here with a pen hovering over the ledger of history! Kaliste was Queen of the Banèmen. Queen of Zunqai.

She grasped Soulfire. Holding back the forces and energy of other realms amplified the effects greatly, and so she held them back. Her fingertips and toes began to tingle, as the nerve-endings in her body interacted with the power coursing through her. It should have obliterated her, that force, but she was built differently to the rest of these beings, and that was why she was here, and they were there.

V'olpar stepped back, his hand hovering over the longsword at his hip, his expression flickering between conflict and fear. The first few lines of the army standing only feet away began to shuffle, their own resolve breaking in the face of the Queen's power. She clapped, her hands drawn together like lodestones, and a shockwave exploded forth as waves tearing through the falling rain. The power spoke through her as she made herself a conduit for the energy. Heat and light poured in through her as forces she could direct.

Kaliste directed the stream of Soulfire upwards at the bruised sky. It pulsed, the edges of the clouds evaporating. But then Kaliste hesitated. A gloom was returning, the clouds in the sky, the depth of vapour hanging above Zunqai. The wind began to spin whipping the Queen's army this way and that, sending the Bohr toppling. Dirty tunnels of roaring air reached downwards, first as tendrils of cloud burgeoning out and inflating into tornados that began tearing through the city. Something deeply powerful was holding the clouds to Zunqai. The amount of Soulfire Kaliste directed at them should have vapourised them completely.

"Jagar is doing this." Kaliste could feel it, deep inside.

She reached out towards V'olpar to tell him so, her mind was still coursing with Soulfire. Pain stabbed at her stomach and heat blossomed at her hands. Spots of light appeared in the space between her palms, circling one another, fusing together until a ball of fire hovered there, rotating as a tiny sun, it should have been beautiful but Kaliste was no longer in control. Panic clutched at her heart as her own power was wrenched and directed by another force.

Unwillingly, her palms were being drawn apart, the pressure pulling more Soulfire through her, syphoning it into a fireball that was now as big as her head. The power began feeding off of itself, sustaining the flames until the great sun was as tall as she was. She stood behind it, a slave, her arms outstretched like a praying clergyman.

The flag stones melted beneath her, the archway of the Palace door cracked and split. The Bohr wrought iron and wood splintering to pieces. Kaliste felt as cool as a fish in water—whatever it was that directed her power, was also protecting her. V'olpar lay on his back behind her, smoke rising from his still form. Soon his ashes would be drifting towards the sewers!

Some of the front lines of the Queen's army tried to run, but their captains cut them down. The rest stood, entranced by the unearthly fireball rising up over their heads.

Kaliste's jaw clenched as she fought for control of her own self. The child inside her was fighting too, but fighting for more Soulfire. Enough to burn down the Palace and then Zunqai itself! If Soulfire was a stream directed at will then Kaliste had to use her experience of the flow if she wanted to control it again, but she was fighting the new life within her. Deep feelings of pride filled her to think of so powerful a being coming from her own womb. What terror this new child would being to Rengas! Kaliste rose up off of the charred ground as she concentrated on the intricate patterns in her mind, the shape and colour of moving energy as it coalesced and combined, broke apart and drifted, distorted and twisted, each form unique, each...She knew this ride. It took barely a thought to see the gap between the streams as they moved. The pattern repeating over and over. She reached in with her will and took hold, swimming with it, directing her own life force inside it and drawing the power back within herself, expanding and exerting her control a little at a time until once more the stream belonged to her. There was only one thing to do now, as her army were slowly being baked alive by Zunqai's new sun, but still she could not do it. The sound of ten thousand humans screaming was too delightful to let go of—

Let go.

The stream of Soulfire stopped abruptly, and the force that was holding her upright faltered. Kaliste crumpled and fell into a shallow crater of blackened stone. Her body was grazed and sore, but nothing could have prepared her for the loss of so much power. Tears fell freely from her eyes as, transfixed she watched the new sun floating up towards clouds above Zunqai vaporising them all. The tornado's spun away into nothingness.

Before Kaliste could howl in abject horror at her loss, V'olpar appeared. He dropped down and dragged Kaliste up and out of the crater. The right side of his face and body was a mess of red and char, and still he lifted Kaliste away from the ruined Palace entrance and back towards the armoury.

"Are you alright, my Queen?"

"I am the Queen!" screamed Kaliste, grabbing V'olpar's tattered jacket. "I decide. Not you, not them! Not fucking Jagar. I own this city, and you will conjure the biggest army Rengas has ever...ever seen! Do you understand?"

"I understand, my Queen." As V'olpar nodded, pieces of his charred skin floated down to the smithy floor. "And it will be my life's honour to serve you."

59

BLOOD AND ORIGIN

"This is hopeless," sighed Hasaan. "Utterly hopeless."

Kavik spared Hasaan a glance. "Quiet."

Hasaan shrugged doggedly. "How are we to ask these people to help sneak you into the enemy's army if they won't even agree on who is fighting?"

Kavik had never considered himself particularly clever, but even as the speakers disappeared down rabbit holes, only to reemerge, neither wiser nor closer to a solution, he still followed all without issue. Perhaps he had been living in the thick of political intrigue too long, or perhaps, as he had aged near sixty cycles on Baeivi's green earth, he had grown accustomed to everything taking much, much longer than it should do. Still, it didn't do well to show it. Decorum had to be maintained for the duration if he was to be taken seriously at this particular table. He lifted his head and took a sip of tea, checking each union leader.

The Westerns leader was Kemen-born, and a pompous and self-righteous stick figure of a man with a sallow face and dark eyes and skin. The Easterns leader was younger and female, with olive skin and a mild manner, but those sharp blue eyes were keen, and she watched the proceedings like a hawk, saying nothing. Kavik liked her even less than the Southerns leader, a woman who had thrown an objective point of view to every single point raised so far.

She adjusted her neck scarf, a commodity far removed from the overbearing heat of the room. "And what of the fives? What does Atalfia think?"

"The fives?" scoffed the Westerns leader. "The remnants of the Tsiorc? What help exactly do you suppose the Fifth Union would bring to fight?"

"The Tsiorc is not dead!" The union leaders stared at Kavik, surprised by his outburst.

The Southern's leader spoke next. "Whatever they choose to call themselves is irrelevant. They have no bearing here. This is the table where decisions are made. The four quadrants of Zunqai, four pillars. If they didn't think it prudent to attend—"

Hasaan spoke before Kavik could even ready his reply. "The fives are on the Hatàrian border, Attis."

"No names!" snapped the Westerns leader.

"Where along the border?" said the Southerns leader.

Hasaan put his head in his hands. "The fives would be here if they could be. Some might even argue that their work on the border is—"

"What?" asked the Southerns leader. "Far more important than ours here in Zunqai?"

The conversation spun like a top for much of the morning, and no matter who interjected, or who raised their voice, the same spirals of position and authority continued to bandied around. Kavik cleared his throat loudly, and when that didn't work, he brought his fist down on the table. Plaster drifted down like snow from the low ceiling revealing beams of light.

"We are not here to argue." Warmth spread through his palm and he rubbed it away, suppressing the grimace. "We are here to work together. I drew upon many methods to speak to you. Southerns, I had to lie to get you here. Or at least, I had to be economical with the truth, a skill I am yet to master. And I fought by one of the greatest tacticians alive, Commander Laeb hisself." He turned to Attis. "Westerns. I lured you under the pretence that the Northerns were in dire straits! That death hung about their doors and their throats like a wolf waiting. You practically begged me to come after learning the peril your brothers were in. And don't make that face, Attis. Yes, I used your tearing name!" Kavik turned the Easterns leader. "And you! You have yet to say barely a word! Not participating does not—"

"Not all words need to be spoken, Horsemaster. Like not all fights need fought."

"What does that even mean? You talk in riddles, all of you!" He kicked the chair back and marched over to the small blind, tearing the rag from the window. Golden light poured in, highlighting faces, walls and bare wood. "We are standing upon the edge of our extinction and all you can do is fight over chits and chattels. The Queen has demonstrated that she has power that no one being in the world has ever wielded. Look at it!" He gestured to the raging ball of fire hovering below the high clouds of Zunqai. "It is a declaration of war. It is a sign to unite the Bohr under one banner. Forces which were once fragmented are drawing together to fight in an army the like of which has never been seen before." Kavik took a wearisome breath and placed the rag on the windowsill. The new sun was quite beautiful, as most terrible things were. "Inaction will be our undoing and indifference will be our legacy."

The room stayed quiet until finally Attis broke the silence. "You call them so, but your chits and chattels are the details upon which life continues or does not. I'm not just talking about currency either. I talk of the roles within the city. Who teaches, who learns, who deserves to stand upon the council—"

"Distinctions which are important to our way of life," added the Southerns leader. "Besides, we have all of us been successfully disrupting the draft into this new army. If it wasn't for us, a great many more humans would be standing in line forced to fight their own kind."

Hasaan's expression became grim. "It's Tyr all over again."

Kavik let out a long sigh. "Well, at least you're agreeing about something. Let us move back a step. First things first. Names, and backgrounds. All of you. I am Kavik, and I have said, so far, more words than all of you have said to each other in your lives, so no more needs said. Attis. Your name is out, now your background."

Attis looked uncomfortable. "I fail to see the point of this. But…I will comply. I am Attis."

The Southerns leader shook her head and adjusted her scarf. "Tell us something new you fool!"

"I am thinking upon the relevance," said Attis. "Extraneous information can be used against me."

"Your first mistake," said Kavik. "This room is safe. This house is safe. Our fight is the same."

"So it is," said Attis. "Fine." The Westerns leader's mouth twitched. "I have a partner, who works in the palace. He is a kitchen worker, and he helps…feeds me information from the Bohr regime. We met at the marketplace. I adored his attitude to life. There was this old woman who had her foot stuck in a grate and he—"

Kavik shook his head then changed it to a nod. "Too much, but good." Kavik turned to the next one. "Now you."

The Easterns leader clasped her hands together, colourful bangles and beads scratching the rough wooden table. "First of all, this room is not safe. It is what, a hovel of some kind? A disused building, or living quarters?"

"It is hidden," said Hasaan. "The Bohr don't come here, they prefer more lavish settings."

"Well, I don't want to be the one who causes the fuss. Privacy is of paramount importance."

"Name," demanded Kavik.

"Ye'toya. Leader of the Easterns, lover of kaldi and chai."

"Great," said Kavik, lifting his hands. "Thank you Ye'toya. I already feel like I've known you all of my life. Now you."

The Southerns leader looked uncomfortable. Perhaps it was that all eyes were on her, or perhaps she was a Bohr sympathiser.

She adjusted her scarf once more. "I am Pling. Born in Ge'Bat, raised in Bakla and now union leader in Zunqai. My father worked hard to keep me from the hassles of common life. People need leaders who are wise and rich. He was a powerful leader and warrior and I learned much about warfare and the practices of royal investment in the people."

"The monarchy?" said Hasaan. The table turned towards him. "Not sure I agree, but in the vein of moving forward. I am Hasaan. Sami by blood and origin."

"A Pathwatcher?" asked Attis. "It is said your kind are map makers?"

The table was suddenly quiet. All eyes on Hasaan. "Maps are illegal. If the Bohr discovered maps in any of our unions, all of the hard work we have done to unionise, to create a dialogue with them would be lost! Besides, I left that life behind me when I joined the Kin. I spent many months on the road with them and lost many during the events of Tyr."

"You were at the Battle of the Bridge?" said Pling. "You saw the Forbringrs reclaim the cursed city?"

"With my own eyes." He lifted his shirt, revealing a heavily scarred torso. "As I say, it cost me my family, my friends and almost my life. My perspective here is unique, flawed perhaps, but unique. Kavik came to each of us in turn because we each control a great many of the humans in Zunqai."

"Good," said Kavik. "How many do we serve?"

Ye'toya spoke first. "Eleven thousand."

"Fourteen," added Attis, perhaps a little smugly.

Pling raised her chin. "Two hundred and fifty thousand."

Kavik had to hide his surprise, and by the looks of it so did Hasaan. "That is significant. What is that, a fourth of Zunqai's human population?"

"Roughly," said Hasaan. "Add in the Northern unions which stand at around fifty thousand and we're talking a third."

"These are not members though?" asked Kavik, confused. "Surely they would speak of the unions to the Bohr otherwise?"

"Oh, the Bohr know of us," said Attis. "It is expected that, as humans, we would have some discourse over how we live our lives. So they grant us the freedom to choose, to an extent, what those freedoms are."

"Who grants us that power?"

Pling's voice was almost a whisper. "The master V'Laerk."

Ye'toya was next, whispering like they were being overheard. "We meet with him, annually. Although he tends to send his underlings."

"V'Laerk met with me," said Pling. No one responded.

"And does the power he bestows include enlistment?" Kavik tried hard to keep the excitement from his tone, probably failing.

Hasaan shook his head. "It does not, Horsemaster. If it were that easy, I would enlist you into the army myself."

Ye'toya chuckled. The sound was so unusual that the entire table stared at her in surprise. "*That* is your endgame? That is why brought us here, together, so you may join as a foot soldier in the ranks of the Queen's army?"

Kavik rolled his eyes. "By all the Forbringrs of tearing Rengas, yes! Bloody yes!"

"Well, that makes this meeting very simple!" Ye'toya stood up and reached out for a valet to pass her jacket. There was of course no valet, so she walked over to the coat hooks and pulled it off herself, the sequins sewn into the hems glittered in the sunset light.

Pling stood too. Then Hasaan, and Kavik watched as all of the work he had put in over the past half cycle disappeared in a moment. "Wait! Where are you going?"

"It can't be done," said Pling, standing at Ye'toya's side.

"Why not?"

"Only the Bohr may enlist. That is the mantra of their kind. They say when, where and how. Zunqai is *their* city. We just rent the space. We work for them. If you want in, then you have to be at the wrong place at the right time."

Attis stayed seated as the two female union leaders walked out. Nothing about their tone gave Kavik any indication he could get them to come back. This was it. The end. He fell into his chair. "All that tearing work, for nothing."

Hasaan stood in the hallway, watching as the pair marched down the stairs. There was the sound of the building's front door opening and then slamming shut, and snowflakes of plaster were once again drifting down.

"There might be a way," said Attis.

"How?"

"Yes, how?" said Hasaan, closing the door.

Attis's eyes darted around, as though the pieces of his plan were hovering in front of him, invisible to everyone else. “There’s a ledger, but it will be dangerous. Very dangerous.”

“Try me,” said Kavik.

60

THE OBSIDIAN SHARD

There was fire, of that, Abika as certain. Was it the soft crackle of flames, or the sound of wood splintering? Perhaps it was the smoke in the air, eager to blind her regardless of the position she sat in. The smell of the sea lurked behind, and the sound of waves breaking against the beach outside the commune.

A hazy figure sat with her. Meorith. Abika's commune sister drew a pipeful of blue smoke into her lungs before disappearing into a cloud herself. Laughter filled the space, echoing around and distorting. The cloud dispersed, then rushed back into a new form, a daemon, with grey skin, reaching hands, and mouth agape in a silent scream.

Abika didn't run, but panic set in. Her heart pounded, but the fire was there. She took in the flames, feeling comfort in their presence and the fire wound around her like a snake protecting its eggs. A blink was all it took to send the punishing tongues away to surround the daemon, burning it alive until there was almost nothing left.

Her fingertips disappeared into the fine ash, already cool, and lifted the solid object inside. A figurine. She recognised the bearded man chopping wood, and it brought comfort.

A voice, soothing and musical, drifted towards Abika over the rising smoke, lifting and falling with the air currents. "A camp fire?" Stepping into the light, neither of the two figures above Abika looked like the voice's owner.

The woman had fierce eyes that stood slanted upon a sharp face. The man standing at her side was as handsome as she was unapologetic. Brown hair and hazel eyes against fair skin. It was his smile though that disarmed Abika.

"Who are you?" asked Abika.

"I think you know that already," said the woman.

"You are my parents."

"We are," said the woman.

"And this place?" Abika looked around. She had been mistaken. There was no commune, and the bay was not the sea, but a lake. Somehow, it still felt like home.

"Is important to us," said the man.

Abika held up the figurine. "What is this?" It didn't feel like a question she should ask, or that her parents would even understand, but for some reason she asked it anyway.

"Only she can answer that."

The outline of another appeared, dark and hazy.

"Who—" even as the first word formed, Abika knew who it was. "WHY IS SHE HERE?" Abika was up, swiping her hands through the air. The apparition sat on the log next to her, unaware of anyone's existence, she was holding something.

The woman's teeth showed, but it was not a smile. "You will do as you're told." The man moved to speak, but the woman held up her hand. "Sit down, daughter."

Abika stayed where she was, folding her arms. She would not be cowed, regardless of who these people said they were. This place was not hers, she had no part in its creation, but she could still decide. Choice was her weapon, and she would wield it and cut and maim with it. "I thought a mother was supposed to be kind. Caring. You remind me of Freja."

The woman scowled at her. "I never met Freja. But if she raised you like any Sulitarian parent, then you have her to thank."

"Thank!" Abika spat. "She made my life hell! She ruined me, and moaned and—"

The woman slapped Abika hard across the face. "Careful, child. I am Lyla, the product of a Kemen mother and a Sulitarian father. I grew up in Sulitar where our litters are grown as the rocks. Your father, Isak, is Nordun, and together we stand against the gale, to push back against the current. And you,

Abika, are of us. You have the wildness of earth and the fortitude of the sea within your veins. You are God's gift."

Abika glared at the apparition of Kyira beside her. "Then how were you so easily cut down?"

Lyla looked hurt, but it was Isak, who spoke. "It was a misunderstanding. Our journeys were cut short."

Abika tried to follow the movements of Kyira's hazy form. She was whittling, sharpening something from wood. "What is she doing?"

"Creating an effigy of her father," said Lyla. "The blade was partly her father's, reforged with the god-killer," said Lyla. "And now it keeps her as it kept him.

"She stood stick to something she's good at. Like destroying homes."

"You might not agree, daughter, but you owe much to her."

"I owe her nothing."

The apparition looked up. Was she here? Could she hear them? If it really was Kyira, then maybe Abika could find out where she was. She just had to ask the right questions.

"Why is this place so important to you?"

Lyla reached for Isak's hand and grasped it firmly. "I sat here, at this fire, with you in my lap and in that moment I decided to help Kyira. Her path was forged upon this spot. That is why it is important. She made the choice, right here, to carry on. To push forwards. As you must."

"Kyira is not important. And some random place in the middle of nowhere—"

"This isn't just some random place!" growled Lyla. "Here we stopped after the fire tornado in Makril, a whole town of people, looking after one another. A town, Abika, where you were born! You brought fever to me and illness. I almost died."

Abika swallowed, and turned to Isak. "Kyira killed you...And you forgave her?"

Isak nodded.

"It was an accident, Abika," said Lyla. "Don't let your fury lead you astray. Please."

Abika reached into her pocket and pulled out the chunk of crystal she had taken from the shattered shard. The apparition that was Kyira looked up at her, and all at once, Abika was aware that the world had stopped. The fire had frozen, tongues of flames hanging in the air, the smoke wisps completely solid above. Her parents were both standing, both fearful, their frozen eyes locked upon the rock in Abika's hands. Abika thought back to the cell, to the tune that she had heard Vasta playing in his shop. How had she heard him that night? Freja's necklace had given her answer, Soulfire. The tang of it tickled her senses and Abika held the crystal to her chest, using it to draw upon. Soulfire trickled into her.

Focusing, she thought of Vasta's shop, thought of the smell, and the neatness of the place. A line of light appeared, thin at first, but thickening. That was the thing about Soulfire that she was beginning to understand. More Soulfire didn't mean more power, it was the conjuring of it that was important. She could stretch Soulfire across the world if she chose.

The line split, becoming a ring of light, distorting the world behind it, but as black as night inside. The frozen faces of her parents looked on, unable to help, unable to stop her. She reached for it and stepped inside.

Wind. Rain. Salt.

Abika licked her lips. It was dark when she opened her eyes, but there were shapes around her. Seawater broke over them, the waves threatening scatter the few planks that remained of Rothmarr's boat. Abika squinted against the downpour, looking for Vasta's shape somewhere, but everything was the same colour. There was no sign of the Bohr anywhere. Echoes of images whirled and gnawed away at her mind, but all she could remember was her mother's and father's faces, faded and unreal, while the constant scrape of metal on wood buzzed in her ears.

She stood, wobbling as the broken deck of the Myathar slid under her, and dragged herself off the boat and onto the rocks. Unkind they were, mottled and sharp, and soon her hands were grazed and sore. There was no trace of land beyond, just thick cloud and mist obscuring all against a black and white world.

A break in the mist revealed a towering shadow above. She was on the island of black rock standing on the fringes, and in the centre stood a tower of pure black glass, obsidian black tall against the violet sky in its centre.

The mist rolled on, stealing the scene away and whispered a name along with it.

"Abika?"

"Vasta! Over here!"

The Bohr appeared above her, peering down from a plateau above the rocks, banks of heavy sea mist rolling around behind him. Abika skipped over the outcrop between them, avoiding the huge holes where sea spray erupted like geysers.

"You see that tower, Vasta? I saw it from the sky when you threw me! How did we get here?"

Vasta shook his head. "Abika, I looked everywhere for you. I've walked the full circle of this island, twice. Where were you?"

"On the boat, you fool!" She pointed at the broken deck for good measure. "Are you blind?"

Vasta lay on his stomach and reached down to help her up. "I checked the boat. You were not there. You should have waited for me."

Abika refused Vasta's hand and climbed the short rockface herself. "I didn't go anywhere you fool Bohr." When she reached the top, she pushed the Bohr away. "You always do this, Vasta! You always preach at me. Tell me what to do. Well, enough! Stop it. I'm not a child."

"You are a child, girl."

Abika felt the urge to reach for Soulfire, but she quelled it. "Where are we?"

"It's another shard," breathed Vasta, looking up at the obsidian tower. He sounded strange. Dangerous.

"Like the one on the Red Isles?"

"Not exactly." Vasta picked up a loose piece of the black rock, shaking his head slowly. The boulder looked tiny in his giant hand. "No. This rock, this place. It doesn't belong..."

The Bohr loved rocks, and he'd picked up many on their journey away from Ipiti, studying them and even sometimes tasting them, but this was different. He fingered the rock, moving it this way and that, apparently fascinated by how the murky light moved over it. He held the rock closer, hiding it from her, as if he was afraid she would snatch it away. "I told you, girl." His head twitched. "There are no islands in the

Middle Sea. All of this grew...around...that shard." His voice was changing, growing deeper, and coarser like an animal.

Abika gently touched his arm, his pulse was racing, visible on the veins of his straining muscles. His whole body curled around the rock, his head and face hidden in the depth of his chest. The wind stole away most of the sounds, but she could hear him muttering, whispering. Growling.

Abika glanced behind her. It was only a few metres back down to the geysers, but she couldn't jump it. She would have to climb down, and carefully. She tried inching around Vasta to go the other way. She had to get away from him.

Vasta spun towards her, snarling. "Where are you going?"

Abika stepped away from him, unable to look away from the Bohr's face. She knew him so well, and yet this creature was not him. "The shard. I...I need to see it from another...angle."

"Are you afraid?" Vasta snapped at the words with sharp teeth.

"No."

"Liarrrr!"

"I don't lie," said Abika, taking another sidestep back towards the edge.

"Death is a gift! A blessing of the shadow. And if you truly are God's gift, then your Great Mother will be glad to see you again!" On the last word, Vasta surged forwards. Abika fell back awkwardly, and the rocks grazed and bit at her as she tumbled back down to the geysers. There was barely time to wait before Vasta followed, dropping to all fours like a huge bear scrambling down towards her, his eyes murderous.

Abika dragged herself up and over the puddles of seawater. "Vasta! What are you doing?"

The Bohr growled deep and low. "What I've always wanted to do, Abika! I am fear. I am fire. I am hungry!"

The ground tore at Abika's bare arms and legs as she ran, and with every step a plume of seawater burst out of the rocks nearby, drenching her. Her breeches and shirt clung to her skin, leeching away what little warmth she had left, but warmth didn't matter. The Bohr chased her, moving as she did, changing directions as she did. A fountain of seawater burst out of the ground between them, and Abika leapt up, turning and running as fast as she could, but still Vasta's guttural pants pressed in on her from behind like a predator chasing prey.

The rocks parted, revealing a narrow hole where the ground had split, it was a channel of water that looked deep, Abika swung left towards it, choosing her footing carefully then leapt as high and far as she could. The opposite side of the hole rushed to meet her, and she slammed into it. Scrabbling, she managed to hold on to the hole's side, but she could hear Vasta behind her, his sharp claws on rocks, then silence. He leapt, landing softly on all fours in front of her. He turned and snapped, tattered clothes whipping about him, clawing at the air where Abika had just been.

The roiling water slapped painfully at her back. She dove down and dragged herself through the water, fumbling for the channel. The world was blurry beneath the surface, but instead of walls of rock caging her in, the rocks sat atop the water like black ice. Vasta had been right, it was a floating island grown from the shard. Abika swam beneath as far as she could, following the currents as they dragged her backwards and forwards. The breath inside her wanted out, but she couldn't let it, she had to hold it. There! Another hole where the water was white and foaming.

She burst through like a geyser herself and let her breath back out into the world, the she was diving once more, until she found the next hole, and the next, until finally she dared to look back. Vasta was gone.

61

PLAYING THE GAME

Kavik shuffled uncomfortably beneath the smithy's long stone table. He had once worked in the mines of Nortun back when he was still a youngling himself—it was back-breaking work for one his size, but worse was the acidic air. Breathing in powdered stone for weeks and months at a time took its toll on the body. Some of his old friends had died in their thirties and forties from lung rot, a festering disease where growths and lesions filled the chests of mine workers, and all for a few shiny stones! The Forbringrs had, for some reason, spared Kavik all so he could, once again, squeeze into space he had no tearing business being in!

The cloud of thick sulphur stink that hung about him stripped the skin from inside his nostrils. While the rhythmical pounding of hammer and stone rang in his head. An hour must have passed before the blacksmiths finally stopped and the three Bohr left. The echoing boom of the oaken door still filled the hall when Kavik crawled up and out of the manhole into the armoury.

"Horseshit, the lot of it." He reached into his pocket and pulled Juniper's cage out. "There you are my boy," said Kavik, opening the entrance. "Have a look around." The little conure hopped around excitedly then fluttered up to the ceiling, before dropping deadweight and catching the fall with a single flap of his wings and landing back on

Kavik's thumb. "The air is thick, boy, I know. Let us get this done before we both succumb."

Kavik peered back at the loose slab that covered the tunnel beneath the Palace smithy. It looked normal enough, hidden in the shadows below the armoury table. Most eyes would have been drawn to the metals and glass glittering upon the table's surface rather than the uneven cracks upon the floor. Still, he banged his heel on the slab. It only budged a hair's breadth, but the act served to bring him some peace.

"What did Attis say was next?" Kavik picked off each thing on his hand. "One, climb the tearing palace wall; two, find and crawl through the tearing tunnels beneath the tearing fountain; three, lift the tearing bloody slab in the armoury... " Kavik lifted an evil looking glass mace with tempered spikes protruding through from a metal core. Say what you wanted about the Bohr, but they had been forging for thousands of cycles longer than humans. "Three and a half, grab a tearing weapon or two."

The glass was incredibly smooth, but he was no mace man, so he gently placed the mace back down, and took up a newly forged karambit instead. Still black from the forge, the curved handle and circular blade fit snugly in his palm. The beauty of the Karambit was that it didn't look like a knife. In truth, you weren't supposed to try and stab with one, you fought with sharp fists and cut and sliced your way out of trouble, but it could still deliver a very nasty wound if thrown properly.

"Much better. Now, where was I..." Kavik waggled his fingers and Juniper dived down from a beam at the ceiling, then fluttered around his head. "Ah yes. Four, slip into the tearing south corridor." His gaze fell upon the oaken door.

Daemon eyes from gargoyles and Bohr long dead followed each and every soft step he took, and the armoury's high ceiling amplified every breath. He was just deciding upon which wall was closest when voices sounded from behind the south wall.

He ran towards the dark corner just as the oaken door opened. The Bohr who entered glanced over the dark space, but those slitted, goat-like eyes passed over him like he wasn't there. It could have been a ruse, perhaps the Bohr had seen him and was preparing an attack, but this looked like some kind of servant Bohr. Kavik had never seen a Bohr so small before. It had the frame of a young man in his twenties, slender but strong, and was garbed in folds of white cloth expertly tied around its pale grey fur. It even wore cup-sized shoes, hiding hooves beneath overlapping straps of well-tended white leather. A loop of keys jangled at its belt.

Kavik easily picked out Juniper's green form against the ceiling and directed a raised thumb at him. The little conure took the meaning and fluttered down to the goat Bohr, all flapping wings and screeches.

Confused, the goat Bohr acted as any human might've and started flapping his arms around to shoo Juniper away—he didn't see Kavik creeping up behind him.

Kavik pushed the oaken door shut then grabbed the Bohr's horns.

"Atttaaaa—" The goat Bohr's cry was cut off as Kavik pulled his wrist hard into the creature's windpipe. Its movements became frantic, it punched and kicked, launching a tiny cup shoe into the air. It bent forward, but Kavik stood to the side and the next back kick went wild, sending them both to the floor. Kavik pressed his bulk down on it, pulling the sharp of his wrist hard against the goat Bohr's throat, until finally the twitching and wheezing ceased. Kavik might've held on, pulled tighter, waiting for the ruse to end, but he'd seen enough death to know the difference. Every creature acted the same when their maker came to visit. He let go and the Bohr's head fell loudly to the stone floor.

Juniper gave a sweet chirrup from above and fluttered down at Kavik's request. "We need out of here, boy. The sulphur is finding you."

Kavik took the keys, then dragged the Bohr back to the long table. The flag stone was lifted and dropped back into place before the echo of the goat's body found the bottom of the tunnel floor beyond. The oaken door on the south wall had locked itself, but there was only one key it could have been, and soon Kavik was standing in the south corridor. The conure sneezed releasing a cloud of yellow dust from his feathers.

"Forbringr's blood, I'm sorry, boy. I shouldn't have taken you." Juniper chirruped and shivered as Kavik preened him as best he could. "There you are, boy. No more armouries. I promise."

Beyond the corner was a set of stairs that led up five levels. By the time Kavik reached the top he was out of breath. He stopped short of the final corner. "Now, boy, according to Attis, beyond the corner just there, this corridor stretches for a good eighth of a league. Backbone of the palace he said, so it will be busy with more of *them*." Juniper flapped and hopped up onto Kavik's shoulder. Kavik waggled his fingers again and pointed. Juniper obeyed, gliding to the corner and then fluttering back. "Right shoulder? You saw someone?" The conure danced. "Yes, then."

Kavik padded over and peered around. Sure enough, there was movement, but it was too dark to see who. The corridor was narrow at his end but seemed to grow much wider as it left the south side of the Palace.

"Attis wasn't wrong, dear boy, this place is a warren. We'll need to be careful if we're to find the Royal Quarter without being seen." Kavik tried the first door, grabbing the huge ring in the door's centre and twisted it. It was well lubricated, but still stopped about a third of the way round. "Right again, Attis." He tried is best to imitate the union leader's accent. "The first door is always locked. We're in the right place, Juniper."

Kavik carried on, walking with purpose, but kept his hands behind his back for Juniper. "Sixteen doors in." He whispered, mocking Attis's Kemen accent. "Keep your eyes down and you'll be fine. Bloody fool." As union leaders went, Attis wasn't the least trustworthy of them all, but he still didn't feature high up on the scale. Kavik hadn't always been so mistrustful—before joining the Tsiorc under Laeb he had worked in many professions, but ultimately in a rebellion you went where you were needed. The nara and horses in his care kept him, as he kept them; they were all the Great Mother's creatures. It was his own kind that Kavik had always mistrusted. They betrayed, lied and sought nothing but coin and power. What was his role in all of this madness? To stop the Bohr so humans could carry on their ways? It was a question he had no answer to, and yet here he was playing their games.

"Sixteen." Kavik stopped at another large oaken door and grasped the ring. It clicked as he twisted it, and the door creaked open, revealing a room lit by a single candle.

"In!" urged a sharp voice. The candle rushed forward, flickering over the face of an impish looking man. "In!"

There was a flash of green and orange as Juniper found the crack of the closing door, and then they were all alone. "Five. Meet the contact in the sixteenth room. Attis—"

"No names," said Imp.

Kavik shook his head, then shrugged. "Fine. I'll just call you Imp."

"And I shall call you Bohrwan." The man must have been thirty cycles younger than Attis—the Northerns union leader clearly liked his fruit before it was ripe. "Well, Bohrwan?"

"How old are you?"

"Old enough." Imp pulled a kitchen knife from the knotted folds of his hak and held it out.

Kavik snatched it off him before he could say anything. "Don't point what you can't use." He handed it back, handle first. "Now, Attis told me you'd be here, and here you are. How do I get to the Royal—"

"I can't get you there."

Kavik blinked. "But I need into the Royal Quarter if I am to—" He stopped himself. He didn't know this man.

Imp crossed the room to a window and drew a chain down. Golden light flooded in. The study looked down over the bay. A ship was drifting across the Horn Dol Zunqai, Zunqai's own private inner sea, past the fleets and fishing vessels and towards them, near the mouth, and entrance to the Middle Sea. "The Queen is leaving."

"That is not the Queen's ship."

Imp shook his head enthusiastically. "I knew it wasn't! We were all talking of it earlier in the kitchens. It's a charter. She's travelling incognito. I wonder where she's going."

"What does this have to—" Suddenly it all made sense. "Wait. The Royal Quarter is locked down?"

Imp tracked Juniper as the conure fluttered between every perch in the small study. "There's no way in. Anytime the Queen leaves the palace, the Royal Quarter is locked down. No entry, not even for servants. Pan Guards stand at every entrance."

Kavik grimaced. "That's a problem."

"No, *that's* a problem." Imp nodded to Kaliste's sun, shining down upon the Queen's ship. "When she leaves, do you think it will it go too? It fills us all with fear."

Juniper must have sensed the unease as he landed upon Kavik's shoulder. "All I know is that it is a symbol of everything we fight against. It is an abomination. To create a sun defies the Great Mother. She is the creator and none other. It fills you with fear? It terrifies me to my very bones."

They both held a fist to their chests, muttering prayers to the Great Mother, the blinds were being drawn, and they stood once again in the dark. "Imp, I need to get to that ledger."

Imp's face crumpled in confusion. "The ledger? That is why you were trying to get to the Royal Quarter? You're trying to enlist some poor enemy of yours into the Queen's army?"

Kavik ground his teeth. "The *locked* Royal Quarter. Yes. Didn't Attis—"

"Tell me? No." A smile formed on Imp's face. "The drafting ledger isn't in the Royal Quarter."

"Where is it then?"

"It's in my old gaffer's office. I know that, because I was there this morning."

Kavik drew a wearisome breath. "Well, can you show me the way?"

Imp's hands were abruptly stretching out towards Kavik, stroking his chest, and shoulders. "I can show you more than that, dear Bohrwan..."

It took only the slightest movement to draw the karambit up between them, its hook-blade reversed so the point could rest upon imp's windpipe. "You need not show me anything I didn't ask for."

Imp stepped back and rolled his eyes. "You've got to give me something, Bohrwan." Imp pointed at Juniper. "I want the bird."

Kavik laughed. "Juniper wouldn't go with you even if you were composed of mainly seed and perches."

Imp shrugged. "Then I can't help you."

Kavik let him shove by, then pressed his fist against the door. The karambit still sat snugly in his closed palm. He considered what words to say, what threats to swear, but fear would only serve to stand this asset against him. He needed Attis's little friend on his side.

Kavik brushed the blade lightly against imp's cheek. "Cold steel. Warm bodies. Lad, if you get me to that ledger, then we'll see what can be arranged."

Imp's devilish eyes shone in the candlelight. "Then you'd better get undressed, Bohrwan."

"I said after."

Imp smiled. "And I said *before*. If you intend to walk through the palace. Then you'll need to look like one of us." Imp walked over to the large cupboard, revealing rows upon rows of uniforms hanging within. He pulled out a set of white robes, hanging all the way to the floor. "Now, let's get you out of those old clothes."

62

DARK VOICES

Ae'thria was a dark space. It literally meant *dark voices*, and was a hidden place for those who knew how to get there. But other than the thin layer of water upon the ground, it was devoid of life and death. It stood between places as neither real nor unreal. Some said Ae'thria had been carved out of reality, and that none but the Banèmen knew of its existence.

Wars had been decided in Ae'thria, the history of humans was an echo of the words uttered in here, but it had quickly fallen out of favour as ships became faster, and as raevens became domesticated. Ae'thria remained a realm of silence.

Drizzle floated down from somewhere high above, the droplets too small to disturb the shallow water splashing around at Kaliste's bare feet. The very air in Ae'thria washed away any Soulfire, so no one in could wield power against another. Kaliste sat upon the stool of black stone that had appeared as she had entered. She was naked—nothing travelled to Ae'thria that wasn't your own, including your clothes. It was a place of equality.

She sat, crossing her legs on the lone stool, and once again reconsidered her decisions, disposing of the arguments one by one to expose the core of her goals. It was a fine tapestry, with layers upon layers of reasoning and purpose, around a shining central light. Ae'thria allowed Kaliste to bring her web of thought into existence, each thought and memory a gravitating thread of possibility that she could move and manipulate like a seamstress. The web revolved slowly the interconnected lines of her mind a complex pattern of pulses and globules that held her deepest desires. She examined each thread: the war, Jagar, V'Laerk, The Order of the White Dragon, Akosh (damn him) and of course, the humans.

"This is the only way."

She *had* to break the laws of the Banèmen, there was no other way. She beckoned the hovering structure around to focus on the link between her and V'Laerk. Inside it was a rainbow of emotion: lust, companionship, and was that love? Kaliste didn't know or care. He was hers, and she was his.

The first sign that he had heard her began to trickle down the connection. Not words, but rather a flavour of the Bohr she had chosen at the Evesgiving. The threads vibrated with his frequency, and Kaliste focused more.

"V'Laerk."

The essence of him solidified into a response and his words echoed around Ae'thria. *"My Queen. How are you doing this?"*

Kaliste dragged at the line between them like a rope, urging it into Ae'thria. Another stool rose out of the shallow water and V'Laerk's Bohr form coalesced until he sat there as plain as day. He moved to get up.

"No," said Kaliste, holding out her hand. "Don't get off. If you touch the water, your body will be brought to Ae'thria too, and here you will stay forever. This silent realm is hidden, but unforgiving."

V'Laerk nodded, shuffling just enough so that he could bring his legs crossed beneath. He looked around. "All I see is darkness."

"It's about as private a place as you could wish to have." said Kaliste.

"Private, and yet I cannot touch you?"

"I didn't say that," purred Kaliste, crossing the short space between. "I said you should not touch the water." V'Laerk's lips parted in a snarl, then her lips found his, passing through as if he wasn't even there.

V'Laerk drew back. "I cannot feel you. I wish to feel you."

"Then do it."

It took a moment for the Bohr to begin feeling her touch, but it was quite clear when he did. She ran her hands over his skin, and down to his crotch, wishing that she could throw him to the ground and fuck him senseless. The projection might not have been him, but it was the *essence* of him and the smell of him. Kaliste's eyes burned, her Soulfire might not work in here, but there were parts of her that worked absolutely fine. And she was not projecting like V'Laerk.

"I want to feel you," he breathed, "from the inside." His hands moved slowly over the curves of Kaliste's body.

"Where are you?"

"Your neck," said V'Laerk, lustfully. "I can smell you."

"No," breathed Kaliste, tilting her back and exhaling. "Where are you now? Where is your body?"

"A road just south of Costra Dae."

Kaliste pulled away. "Sulitar?"

"The same," breathed V'Laerk.

"You are still only in the north of Sulitar?"

"The Order of the Dragon are not quick. I have executed three of them already, but—"

Kaliste screamed. All of the frustration and anger of the last day poured out of her. The echo came back distorted as the sound smashed against the unseen distant walls of Ae'thria but she kept going until there was no breath left inside. "It's alright," she said, placing a warm hand upon her stomach. "Sleep child. Sleep."

"My Queen—"

Kaliste shook her head. "No, V'Laerk. No. I will talk, and you will listen." The Bohr sat back, but sat straight, looking ridiculous with his legs crossed beneath him like a naughty child. "You need to move faster. The Order of the White Dragon must—" She stopped. A thought had occurred to her. "How many of you are there?"

"A ton."

Kaliste's intention had been to send the Order of the White Dragon straight into the fight alongside the lord's army but Sulitar was too large to traverse so quickly. As much as she wanted to peel V'Laerk's skin from his body she had to give him credit. A ton-weight of good strong fighters with a will to fight could outclass even five-ton of Queen's army soldiers. Perhaps not the Ruffin though.

"Can you make it to two-ton?"

V'Laerk frowned. "Possibly. Through drafting. Sulitar has many fighters." He stopped." Why would the Order join the humans? They fight for the Bohr!"

Kaliste felt V'Laerk's frustration as keenly as if it were her own. "Jagar wants me to drag every human out of every corner of Zunqai and draft them into the Queen's army."

V'Laerk nodded. "That is a good idea."

"It would be, if they were fighting for us!" She couldn't help kicking the water. "Jagar wishes the Queen's army to join with the humans as a force. He wants me to just hand them over to the resistance!"

"Why?"

"I DON"T KNOW!" screamed Kaliste. She closed her eyes, regaining her composure. "Wherever Jagar is, he is trapped. But he has access to some sort of power."

"Soulfire?"

"No," said Kaliste, through a uncertain breath. "Something more powerful. Never did I think there could be a force more powerful than Soulfire, but Jagar has it, and he can wield it. What is more, I think he that power is affecting the Common Realm whenever he conjures—the clouds of Zunqai were unnatural—but then Jagar was a master player, capable of anything. He could convince even the most resolute of the Banèmen to do his bidding, and he never did *anything* without reason, and so often was that reason cloaked in a thousand million different layers of subterfuge." She considered her own shining goals for a moment, a master plan itself still to be worked out. "I guarantee that his plan is not what we think it is. Handing over an entire force to the enemy will not stand. I will not do it. I will betray him."

"You are my fire, my Queen." He held out a hand and Kaliste stepped towards him, allowing his astral form to caress her stomach. "Our boy will rule as you do." He pulled away, looking more like a king than any other. "I will draft into the Order of the White Dragon. Three tons."

Kaliste felt V'Laerk's face, imagining she could touch his skin and leaving a trail of failing light wherever her skin broke the projection. "And I believe you can do it my love. But please, no drafting. We need more. Those who fight for the Order must be converted! Proselytise these people, V'Laerk. Set them free. Sulitarians are known as the best fighters in Rengas. We need to be able to direct them at our enemies. They will not fight their own without will. They must join you, they must see in you a God of men. You must rule them!" Ae'thria shuddered and a shockwave parted the falling drizzle. V'Laerk's form faltered as the connection was tested by the imminent entrance of another. Another stool rose up."V'Laerk, show me you understand."

"It shall be done, my Queen."

The drizzle stopped, and an echoless voice cut through Kaliste's body. "Kaliste. How good it is to see you."

"Akosh. You made it."

"I did," Akosh's naked form appeared out of the shadows like a ghost in the night. His black eyes drifted over towards V'Laerk's projection. "A Bohr? In Ae'thria? You know the rules, Kaliste."

"The rules." Kaliste folded her arms. "You seem to dwell on some past notion of me caring upon rules. Especially when *you* speak of them, Akosh."

Jealousy returned through the line, not as potent as before but strong enough for Akosh to notice. That was the problem with Ae'thria, the Banèmen that came here shared everything.

"This place is sacred. It should be a haven, not contaminated with the blood of lesser beings."

V'Laerk snarled.

Kaliste lowered her hand. "Dearest, V'Laerk. Don't let Akosh test you."

Akosh grinned. "It's what I do."

"I brought you here to discuss something important. If history has indeed been decided in this Ae'thria, then let us write new lines in that ledger. Doorways are opening between places. It started in Tyr, destroying the city and many of our kind in the process, both Bohr and Banèmen. But now we must work together. As beings we must make use of these doorways while they remain. While they are inert."

"Inert?" Akosh was still standing, and listening intently, but his words were like ice, if not so transparent. "You call the tearing of our world *inert*? These *doorways* may function as tunnels for us to make use of, but they are not here to aid any being that walks upon Rengas's soils. The doorways are a side-effect of this world's dying breaths."

Kaliste shook her head. "You think the world to be dying, Akosh? I know you are fast, but your speed must be waning in the later cycles of your life."

"These doorways are here for a reason, Kaliste. Do not think that they may be abused without comeback."

"Akosh, I have never heard you so serious." Then the answer stood between them like a moonflower blooming. Kaliste smiled. "You are afraid of them."

"No—"

"And now I see why. Is it because now, suddenly, there are those who can beat you to the destination? Akosh, is no longer the fastest of our kind? The fastest moving being in Rengas."

Akosh's eyes were fury. "Speed is—"

"All you have," said Kaliste, going for the throat. "It's all you ever had, and now it is at risk." And just like that, as one thought led to another, Kaliste saw the truth. "*You* approached Jagar. You asked him to save you...to include you in his plans."

Akosh looked suddenly uncomfortable. "You laud upon yourself, *my Queen* but you are no slayer anymore. Just another worn-out royal, scared to lose the last piece of land she has left."

Any other time, it might have made Kaliste angry, but the truth laid us all bare, and when it was known, it could not be unknown. "No. You didn't go to him. He came to you. Tell me, what is your task, Akosh?"

"My *task*?"

She held out her hands, showing her pregnant body in all its glory. "We are all equal here, Akosh. Tell me your task, the task the Great Father deigned upon you."

Akosh took a long breath through his nose, dark eyes flicking towards V'Laerk's still-hazy form. "The Great Father asked me to take a force of Bohr and reduce the numbers of the human army in Bakla."

"Which force?" asked V'Laerk.

Akosh sneered. "The Kresh'ae."

"I know them," said V'Laerk. "How many remain?"

"Almost fifty."

"Against how many Republicans in Bakla?"

"Five thousand."

V'Laerk nodded to Kaliste. "The Kresh'ae are some of the most brutal Bohrkind. They will lose, but they will badly damage the Republican army in Bakla."

"By how much?" asked Kaliste.

"A fifth at best, or a tenth at worst."

Kaliste turned back to Akosh. "Jagar asked you to help them win?"

"The Great Father is worried the Republicans might find their way to Zunqai."

"That's not it," said Kaliste, thinking aloud. "Why would Jagar want me to send the Queen's army to join the ranks of the Republicans, and then send you to reduce their numbers? It doesn't make sense."

"Jagar is playing you against each other. Telling you each one thing, so he may achieve another goal. It is classic deception. You must understand why Jagar wants to betray his own kind and what his endgame is if you intend to best him."

Kaliste blinked, then turned to V'Laerk. *"You can hear me?"*

"I can," said V'Laerk, through the link. *"Don't trust Akosh."*

Akosh frowned at them both then smiled, replacing his smug expression, the very same she had wiped from his face. He might play games, but he was not winning this one.

"You have something to say Akosh?"

"Your link is so strong with your sire, Kaliste, that even in Ae'thria where Soulfire cannot be touched, the two of you can still communicate telepathically with one another. This is truly magic of old! It reminds me of Jagar and Aashvi. Now there was partnership of ages! The two strongest Banèmen in existence." He waved away Kaliste's response before she had a chance to rebuke him. "Anyway, this is getting boring. What do you intend to do about the doorways, Kaliste?"

"The doorways?" Now it was Kaliste's turn to look smug. "The doorways that so frighten you?"

But Akosh had worked it out too. He stared at her. "You intend to change them. Don't you?" He shook his head. "I wondered why the place was standing so thickly upon your lips. You caressed the word."

V'laerk spoke aloud. "What is he talking about, my Queen?"

Kaliste glanced at V'Laerk, but now it was her turn to stand in the light. "Dearest, I must go somewhere soon."

Akosh shook his head. "She's going to Tyr, Bohr." He was walking circles around her now. "It can't be done, Kaliste!"

"It can be done, Akosh. And I will do it."

"It should not be done!"

"What, my Queen?" V'Laerk sounded desperate.

Akosh beat her to it once more. "This mistress of yours believes she can change the endpoints of the doorways that are ripping Rengas apart."

"I knew this." V'Laerk moved his feet, almost touching the water.

Akosh shook his head. "But you cannot change just one. You must change them all. Not just whichever doorway you found, Bohr. All of them. Every single doorway that the Bohr wish to use to mobilise and conquer Rengas." He turned towards her, water sloshing about his bare feet. "The problem is, Kaliste, that our world is already showing signs of the suffering brought by the doorways from The Great Father's realm. The lines between reality are thinning, strange things are happening. Ancient boulders, the hardest surfaces in Rengas, splitting in half. Great towers of soulglass growing out of the earth like trees, each a beacon of power that might eclipse even the Great Father himself! These are truly magical objects, greater and more powerful than the sum of their parts. They call upon energy in such a way—"

Kaliste snatched at Akosh's throat, and she held it tight. "Quiet."

"You will bring ruin upon the world!" croaked Akosh. "You will hasten the break up. You will—"

Kaliste held tighter, pinching the windpipe beneath her fingers. "As always Akosh, your words are poison."

Akosh didn't retaliate, instead he only smirked at her, shaking his head in disapproval until finally his form vanished beneath her fingers in a cloud of spiralling black smoke.

Kaliste turned back to V'Laerk, and her chin started wobbling. She hadn't cried in a hundred cycles. "Dearest. I must go. I will contact you again, once more before the end. But just promise that you will do as I have said. There is more at stake than just you or I here."

V'Laerk swallowed, his expression unreadable and the connection keeping his form here fluttering like an injured raeven. "Our boy."

"He will live."

"And you..."

"Goodbye, V'Laerk." She severed the connection, and the projection that was V'Laerk blinked out of existence, and the shape of him lingered against Kaliste's eyes as more tears fell.

63

DISTRACTIONS

Concealing a tiny bird cage in a folded bedsheet knotted in a few hundred places about his body, had been the easiest part of Kavik's day so far. Even crawling through damp tunnels and hiding in a room filled with Bohr that could have sniffed him out, was simpler than this.

"So, I'm your..."

"You're my cousin! How many times must I say it?" Imp's words were as sharp as the karambit poking Kavik's lower back with every step.

"And I'm..."

"In Zunqai as part of a servant exchange." Imp paused and turned. "No. Actually, you're a traveller, keen on joining the new ranks of the Royal Servants." Imp was already shaking his head at his own words. "That will never work..."

Kavik scratched his behind. "Why not."

"You can't just join the ranks of the Royal Servant, Bohrwan." said Imp, words dripping with smugness. "It is a sought-after, cultivated role, that only a few—"

Kavik grabbed Imp's arm. "These are distractions, lad. Work it out."

Imp frowned deeply, but set off at pace. So fast that Kavik had trouble keeping up with the slender man, dipping between wings of the palace, spiral staircases and secret passages. The white cloth of the servant did however, protect Kavik from any unwanted glances as they moved along the south corridor.

He smelled the kitchens before he saw them, and by the Great Mother he was hungry. The passage from the servant quarters ended with a tiny door barely big enough for Kavik to get a leg through, never mind his belly.

"You're right," said Imp. "Maybe cousin *is* too specific. I mean, you're hardly going to be related to me. Unless..."

Kavik ignored the rest, and concentrated on not catching his dangling nethers on the stone as he opened his legs to exit the passageway. "Don't forget why we're here. This isn't some play, or act. People's lives—"

"No. We *could* do cousin," said Imp. "Second cousin. Ghani! Ghani, wait!" Imp rushed off, leaving Kavik to rearrange the rapidly loosening folds of his servant uniform, before returning with a young girl with beautiful ebony skin. A friend. A close friend Kavik hoped.

"A Bohrwan?" said the girl, her arms laden with steaming bowls of delicious smelling food. Kavik's eyes took it all in. Steamed rolls filled with meat and cabbage, venison sausages. "Are those roasted potatoes?"

The girl shook her head slowly. "Oh, don't be so stuck up, Ghani. They won't notice a single potato—"

"Don't you dare," said Ghani, slapping away Imp's wandering hands. "Who's this?"

"He's my cousin," said Imp.

Ghani nodded slowly, the whites of her eyes growing. She pressed her lips together, suppressing a smile. "You don't need to lie to me, you know. I won't tell." Her raised eyebrows told Kavik that this wasn't the first of Imp's *cousins* that Ghani had met.

The decor had changed from the dirty white of the servants' kitchens to auburn and wood. There was no mistaking the tastes of old, powerful men, when money reached a certain age, all it wanted was mahogany and red drapes. Kavik stepped away from his entourage and began down the hallway.

"Wait!" said Imp, catching up. "Wait. We had a deal!"

Kavik glanced back just in time to see Ghani roll her eyes and disappear into the kitchens, and then the karambit was out. He held it up against Imp's neck. "Remember what I said? You need not show me anything I didn't ask for."

Imp didn't speak. Kavik just held the karambit hook over Imp's windpipe, much longer than was necessary. Anyone could have walked out from the busy kitchens and seen them, but Kavik was betting that no one would. Imp had the same look on his face.

"Do you ever get the feeling," said Kavik, "that you are thinking the same thing as someone else."

Imp swallowed a lump past the unmoving blade. "I will scream."

Kavik shrugged a little. "You would be dead before your blood hit the floor. And even if I were somehow caught, I would live on. At least for a time. And then, should they decide to execute me and we were to meet as ghosts in the afterlife, I would still not give you what you want."

Mania was as potent a tool as any knife, and Kavik had many, many cycles of awful experiences to draw his madness from.

He glanced right at the new section of hallway. "Your gaffer's office?"

Imp nodded silently.

"Good," said Kavik. "And the ledger?"

"It's...It's just in there."

"It better be," growled Kavik. "I found my way in here once, and I wager it wouldn't be too difficult to locate where you sleep."

Imp's eyes grew somehow even wider, then as Kavik loosened his grip, the man skulked away, disappearing after his friend and back to the safety of the kitchens.

Spotless weapons hung from the walls in the gaffer's office like with not a single mark or notch.

"Hot from the forge," said Kavik, closing the door. The broken lock rattled on the other side; Kavik kept the karambit handy. Juniper fluttered up the top of a tall clock, nodding his head in time with the pendulum.

There, on the gaffer's desk, stood the ledger. A book, almost as big as the desk itself, and open in the middle. Kavik rounded the desk and ran a finger down the neatly etched lines and names. "Children, stolen from mothers. Husbands, stolen from wives. Juniper, my boy, this is a book of death." He reached for the pen and found the last name. "Aged twelve. By the Great Mother—"

Juniper squeaked in alarm.

A door opened.

A voice.

The Ledger Keeper, a thick-set man with two chins, bellowed so loud Kavik's ear's rang anew. "Intruder!"

There was barely time for a heartbeat before the door burst open and a Pan Guard ducked in. The face of a hawk, the body of a goril, and twice as big as Kavik. Imp stood in the hallway behind it, smiling.

Kavik threw the karambit as hard as he could, not waiting to see if it landed, then hurled himself against the office wall, tearing off an ortaxe. He jumped up, swiping back and forth, holding back the Pan Guard as best he could.

Juniper fluttered down, flapping, squawking, squealing in the Pan Guard's face, and Kavik rushed forward. The spike on the head of the ortaxe found its mark and punctured the Bohr's rough hide. Kavik yanked it free, and chopped again, swinging wildly, and somehow the shining axe found its mark once more. The copper smell of blood filled the air as Kavik dipped and ducked beneath the Pan Guard's wild grasps. Imagine it! Kavik, keeper of horses, as nimble as a—

His eye fell upon the tiny orange and green body of a conure lying upon the oak floor, unmistakable, awful, heartbreaking. Kavik's joints became weak and he fell to his knees, the orate clanking to the office floor.

"Juniper, NO!"

Then Kavik was being lifted up from the oak panels. Juniper's body falling away. Twitching, fluttering. He was alive! Even before the thought had materialised, the conure was up on his feet. Kavik brought his knees to his chest and kicked away from the Pan, knocking the Bohr back and himself loose. Kavik fell to the desk, rolling backwards across the drafting ledger, tearing pages and pulling the huge book backwards onto its side and straight through the office window.

Kavik pointed to the window. "Go, boy! GO!" And Juniper disappeared through the hole and outside into the open air. He turned, grabbing a handful of broken glass, holding it out in front of him at the Pan Guard. “Come on!” he roared. “Come on!”

The Pan Guard didn’t fight. It stepped back, its beak making an awful clipping sound, drawing a clawed-hand over the wounds on its thigh and calf, and stared back at him with an expression Kavik couldn’t place. The Pan Guard tasted its own blood, and when finally it spoke, it was like wood splintering. “So that is what my blood looks like. You fight well, Bohrwan.”

The Pan Guard ducked back out of the gaffer’s office, and stopped to admire Imp’s body pinned against the wall at the neck by Kavik’s karambit. “Impressive,” growled the Pan Guard. “Draft the Bohrwan, Ledger Keeper, I want him in my squad.”

KRASK
SACOA
ZUNQAI
BAKLA
KOPEMA
Horn Dol Zunqai
iron road
KALAKA
EMPIRE
CRACKED WASTES
KOA'ART DOL ART

Diary entry

Lost

I have no appetite, but worse are my dreams, which are plagued with pillars of light that hold my heart and mind prisoner.

I think my time in Bakla is coming to an end. It is time to run once more. Will I ever find a place that is mine?

64

TRUST

Kyira's knife hovered near the rough edges of the chunk of wood, promising a shape. "I am no artist, Milli." Milli tilted her head. She thought of Tor, and the wonderful figurine he had given her so long ago. "I'd be as well leaving the sculpting to those who know how to do it."

The beds to her side—cushioned mattresses filled with goose down—were empty but well-kept, meaning that people had been in and out of the tent while she had been sleeping. Even now, at barely an hour past dawn, she couldn't have slept if she wanted to, and by the blood of the bloody Forbringrs themselves, she wanted sleep. Fatigue soaked through from her skin leaving her exhausted, and worse, nothing felt real anymore. Her choices, her path, it all fabricated as though this reality was somehow created only for her.

A young farmer boy burst into the medical tent and she dropped the wood and blade clattered to the floor at Milli's feet. "Lands! At least announce yourself!"

"Sorry, Kyira." The boy held out a pair if shears from the door, too far for Kyira to actually reach.

"Are those for me?"

The boy coughed. "For the dog, I'm told." He dropped the shears down on the chest at the end of Kyira's bed and turned to leave. "Sorry, camp's busy. Just give the shears back to the commander when you're done."

Kyira scoffed and the boy made a hasty exit. "You hear that Milli? Even the children are war-weathered." Milli looked up at her. "Well, at least I'm not covered in fur. It's far too hot for all of this now." Milli looked up Kyira gave her a firm stroke, her lolling tongue dry from panting. "Come on, girl. Let's get you sorted."

The shears were blessedly sharp—blunt blades were no fun for shearer or sheared. The wide scissors squeaked with each cut, not from the spots of rust flecking the steel, but from the tightness of the nut holding the two blades together. After an hour of cutting, Milli was only half done.

Kyira had moved to the floor for better purchase. "Oh, Milli, we can't leave you like this now! Your bottom will be cold, and your head will be hot!" Milli's tail wagged anyway, but that tongue was still lolling. Kyira stood and walked over to the water bucket and brought the whole thing back over. Without hesitation Milli shoved her whole head inside. "You silly dog. Come on, we're nearly there."

"Nearly there, indeed!"

Kyira jerked up. "Fiskal." The commander looked drawn, his chiselled face grey and hallow. "You look...well."

He eyeballed her. "A sarcastic Nordun...Nay, a sarcastic Sami? I never thought I'd see the day! You have been here so long, Kyira, you are one of us now! But you are forgiven. I am used to much worse." He pulled a cloth bag from behind him, and the wondrous scent of fresh bread wafted with it.

Kyira took the bag graciously. "Thank you, Commander. Your talents really do have no bounds." She peeked in to see four crusty cobs of various colours. "You used different flours for each? It must have taken you all morning?"

Fiskal just shrugged. "When I can't sleep, I bake."

"But you do look tired, and like you slept in your uniform. You need to change."

"I did," croaked Fiskal. "But there is also much to do in the camp." He leaned awkwardly against the main tent pole. "Although I am thinking now I prefer your attempts at sarcasm compared to your brutal truths."

"Then you should sleep more."

"You're right, of course. We are mobilising at the moment, and it involves every part of the camp all at once. One minute I am answering questions about the longevity of grain in humid conditions, then I am an apparent expert in horse-shoeing, smithing, and cooking." He shook his head. "A young gentleman asked me to officiate his union with another soldier. I have no problems with such things, of course. But a half day to say words for people I barely know? It is time I do not have, and thusly there are those who think less of me because of it." He gestured to his face. "Hence."

Kyira ran the shears through Milli's fur around her nape, getting as close to the skin as she could. "Mobilising? Are you going somewhere."

"Of sorts. Drills mostly."

"I guess you can never be too careful."

"That's exactly it." His demeanour changed suddenly. "Have you thought any more on my offer?"

"What offer?"

"Don't be coy." His familiar, charming grin returned. "You know what I mean. I want you to join the Republican army. I want you to be our eyes. To lead us—"

Milli yelped as the steel nicked a patch of skin under her snout. "Oh! Milli, I'm sorry." She slammed the shears down and took Milli's head in her arms, holding her tight. Milli licked Kyira's ears.

Abruptly Fiskal was there. "Here, let me."

Kyira sat up on the edge of her mattress as the commander of the Republican army got on his knees in front of her. Initially, Milli looked doubtful, but before long she was lying in his arms as the shears worked their way skilfully around her fur.

"My father was a farmer," said Fiskal. The shears seemed to be an extension of his hand, slicing easily through Milli's fur and so close to her pale brown and white skin. He moved them up to her face, and Milli growled. Teeth bared, Fiskal lowered the blade and instead just sat stroking her. After a moment, he switched hands and used the shears themselves to pet Milli. The handles had rounded edges that must have felt like heaven beneath Milli's ears. "The trick is to use the stiffness as a means of control." It took Kyira too long to realise he was talking about the shears. "It is tough on the fingers, but where there is pressure, there must be force. This is a natural law of our world, no?"

"If your father was a farmer, why aren't you a framer too?"

Fiskal chuckled. "That's the Sami in you talking. My father managed a chain of farms around Bakla. We may have settled here in Kemen, but in my blood, I was always Nordun. Whenever I see the hills of Nord I know that I am home. Even with such fondness for Bakla. The two are lovers; two sides of one coin. The coin of my heart. My father grew deep roots in these flatlands. Come to think on it, I couldn't have been older than Leenar when he passed."

"Leenar?"

Fiskal held up the shears. "The boy who brought you these."

"I did not realise you were so deep, Fiskal. It is a trait of the Sami to become so linked to the earth."

Fiskal watched her as she spoke, listening intently. "Not just the land. I know enough of the Sami and know how important family is to them." His eyes probed her for a moment, but Kyira stared back. She hadn't told him of the hardships she had endured with her brother and father, and when she gave nothing away, he carried on. "My father was a working man. A proud man. I still talk to him sometimes. Is that strange?"

Kyira chuckled. She couldn't help it, it bubbled out of her like froth from a steaming cup of kaldi. "Oh, Fiskal! We are all of us strange. I also talk to my dead father." Milli looked up at her, tongue lolling, clearly confused as to why the commander had paused his shearing. "Every day."

"You do? It is wholesome, talking to the dead. It helps us in life, I think. It helps me anyway."

Kyira took a long breath, she felt good. "And what of your mother?"

"I never knew her. She left when I was babe, and I'm told she had another family" Fiskal shook his head, but kept smiling. "My father blamed her for everything! I'm not sure it's healthy to curse the good name of those who cannot defend themselves, but then she did leave him to raise a child all by himself, losing any right she had to be remembered."

Kyira shuffled on the mattress, aware of every fibre of herself. "I left someone behind once. A daughter."

Fiskal paused, the shears held in suspension. "Where?"

"The details don't matter."

"Details are everything. They decide the winners, the losers, the dead. The living."

Kyira glanced at him sidelong, unsure what to say. She had told Darc far more for reasons she couldn't fathom.

"If you don't want to tell me, then don't. I know it is in my nature for people to trust me." He stopped. "What? Don't look so surprised. I know myself well. It is how I built an army. Getting people to trust me is what I do."

Kyira shook in sudden outrage. "Is that what this is? Is that what you're doing here? Lulling me into your army? Because I already—"

"No! Please, Kyira. Forgive me. It is who I am. And I could not change it as much as I could change the course of the moon through the night sky. People follow me because I tell the truth. I put myself out there. I trust in life, and life trusts in me. And it rewards me with opportunities that others might not see." Milli dropped her head back on Fiskal's hand and let out a long sigh. "It is never my intention to deceive."

"But it happens anyway." Kyira shook her head at herself. "I'm sorry, Fiskal. My walls are up." She suppressed a smile as Milli's leg started to shake. "Perhaps leading an army was not your Forbringr's call after all." She was trying to be sweet, but it came out stiff and strange. She had never been good at sweetness.

"Milli trusts me. As you should, Kyira."

"I'm afraid I will need more than just a haircut and a rub behind the ears before I hand over my life to you."

"Kyira—"

"No." She swallowed, wishing somehow that her tone could be stronger, but when her best friend was drifting off to sleep in her assailant's arms, it was difficult to feel anything but admiration. Iqaluk would have been stronger. He would have known how to handle a situation like this. She had to be stubborn, like him. "I have fought in someone else's fight, Commander. I have killed for others, and it brought me no peace."

"There *is* no peace to be had in war, Kyira, but our fight is not about peace. It is about survival. We fight the Bohr because we have to. Without a human force to stand against them, they will destroy us all. The ones who are left will find themselves enslaved."

"You sing the same song as Laeb, Fiskal. And it is a tune I have heard before. I cannot fight with you."

Fiskal's eyes dropped. He picked up her diary, reading the line of her last entry. "Lost. Are you lost?"

"No more than you." She held out her hand, waiting for him to give it back, but he held on to it.

"These things that you must do. They are described in here, yes?"

"Wise men do not pursue a woman's secrets."

"Ah, but secrets keep only their keepers."

Kyira snatched the diary out of Fiskal's hand, realising that it was exactly what he had wanted. "Then mind your own, Commander. And it might be a good time to tell you that my time here has come to an end. I'll be leaving tomorrow at dawn. I may have to drag Milli away from you, but she will come with me eventually." She had no idea if she was trying to amuse the man or scathe him.

Fiskal gave Milli's head a final rub then set her now skinny body gently down on the ground so she didn't wake. "Then blessed be your shadow, Kyira." He stood and turned to leave, then stopped near the end of the bed. "I've always wondered what that meant. Blessing someone's shadow. Is it blessing the darkness within? Or perhaps it is acknowledging our presence." He studied the pole, picking pieces of peeling paint from the wood and examining it, as if searching for clues. "Really though, I like to think that blessing someone's shadow is acknowledging that the light is shining down upon them. That the good graces of the gods above watch over us, and the shadow is our presence in their light."

"Commander. I will not change my mind. Bakla has left an impression on me. On the both of us." She petted Milli's head. "More than you know. But it is time for me to move on.

"And so you will run." Fiskal crushed the paint between his fingers. "It is, after all, what the Pathwatchers were meant for, wasn't it?"

"How dare you—"

"Don't you wish for more?"

Fiskal's comment caught her like a sudden slap, but her head was too full, and the truth was, he was right—running was all that she had left, and by the Lands Kyira wanted to run. "More of what, of this? Of death, where there should be *life*? You are right, Fiskal I do wish for more, but I won't ever get it from you." She had completed her thought, and the words had felt just, but now they were out for both of them to hear Kyira regretted them deeply. Iqaluk would have chided her for her pride, but what did her fool father ever know about what was fair? She stood, a statue of resolution. "Commander, would you please tell Darc that I'm leaving tomorrow. I'd prefer not to bump into him again."

Fiskal blinked. "And that is final is it?"

"It is."

"Kyira of Nord, we could have achieved so much together..." He motioned to leave then stopped himself. "I put my trust in you, and you have thrown it back in my face."

Kyira wanted to much to sling more hate at him. He deserved it, but her anger had evaporated like water on a plate of scorching mud, leaving only sadness. Her eyes filled with tears. "Tell Darc that—"

Fiskal thumped the pole in anger. "Darc? Who is this Darc? I have not met anyone of this name! You know, Kyira, we're done here." Fiskal held his hands out. "I shall let you *move on*. If there are truly other friends here that you have made, I implore you to tell them yourself you are leaving. You owe them that."

Kyira's heart pounded anew, and the cloth entrance of the tent seemed to flap forever after Fiskal had left.

65

BARGAINING

Fiskal closed his eyes in annoyance. What did he have to do? What concoction of events did he have to initiate to get the damned girl to listen? Kyira didn't trust him, and he understood why, with everything she had been through. She was as impressive a specimen as he had ever laid eyes on. He wanted her more than he wanted to breathe. Not just for her skills, or her instinct, but for her. Imagine the children they would have! He slammed his ale down on the inn table.

"Sir?"

"What?"

Leenar looked affronted. Any other time Fiskal might have offered him an apology—not today it would seem.

"There's a...guest."

"Tell me boy, why must you always interrupt me? Everywhere I look I see you shadowing me. I'm the commander of the Republican army! I have people baying for my attention in each and every corner of Bakla. Give me some space." The rant ended with a bitter taste, and finally his brain caught up with Leenar's words. "Guest? What guest? Where?"

"Here."

Fiskal stood immediately. The chair falling to the old oak floor. "Akosh. Please, come in."

The whites of the Banèman's eyes grew stark in the room, as though nothing else existed. "Are you inviting me?" said Akosh, softly.

Fiskal's heart hammered. "Of course not, sir. My city is your city. It belongs to you." The Banèman seemed sated at this, but danger hung in the air. "Your usual?"

"Need you ask."

Fiskal ushered by as the Banèman lifted the fallen chair, deliberately placing it just so before sitting down in front of Fiskal's ale. He lifted the glass and sniffed it, then placed it back down and raised his eyebrows expectantly. "Shall I get it myself?"

"No, of course not. Leenar?" The boy hadn't moved. "Get the red. The thirty-one." Leenar hurried away. "It's in the basement." Behind the bar, Fiskal helped himself to the glasses beneath, choosing only the nicest and scrambling around for a cloth to buff it a little before Leenar came back with the wine. If this had been Fiskal's inn, he would have kept it far cleaner; the owner let him use the space during the day for meetings and to escape the beach and the army stationed there. "You look well, Akosh."

Akosh blinked. He sat there, a devil in the shape of a man. The shape of him was where the similarity ended though. The long dark hair, the pointed fingernails on long fingers clasped neatly in front of him upon the scratched wooden table, the flawless complexion, and eyes that seemed to change colour depending on what angle they were seen from. Not that one looked at those eyes for very long—he'd made that mistake the first time Akosh visited and it had almost cost him his life.

Leenar burst through the back door, pale-faced and eyes wide. "We're out of the thirty-one."

Fiskal's heart hammered anew. "Out?" he hissed. "How can we be out! There's only..." he bit his lip to contain his anger. "There's only one who drinks it. How can we be out?"

"I...I'm not sure, commander."

Fiskal lowered his eyes to the dusty floor, spots of red marked the boy's toes.

"Turn around."

"Commander..." stammered the boy.

"I said turn around!" Fiskal took the cloth he had buffed the glass with and tied a knot in the end. "Lift. LIFT."

The boy lifted his shirt and braced himself against the bar's back wall. There could be no hesitation here, but still, he should wait. He held the cloth above his head and waited for Akosh's signal.

Akosh nodded, and the cloth came down. Again and again, Fiskal whipped Leenar's back, watching the boy's pale skin change colour like tempering steel—white, red, deep red, then blue and finally purple. The boy took it silently.

Akosh nodded again and Fiskal stopped. Sweat dripped from his brow and his arm ached with the effort, but he waited where he was.

Akosh stood up and approached the bar. "Go outside, boy. But don't leave."

Leenar went even paler as he pulled his shirt down, but he nodded and sheepishly left the Banèman and the commander to themselves.

"The wine can wait."

"What will you do with him?"

No words, no emotion. Just a flat stare.

Fiskal had never thought of himself as courageous, he was a practical man. Pragmatism was one thing, but in the face of duty he had to look after his people. It was his number one concern. Without them, he was nothing, so when Akosh tried to speak, Fiskal spoke over him.

"Comman—"

"The boy has a family," said Fiskal. "A mother and two grandparents."

Akosh tilted his head. "You mean to say..."

Fiskal went for broke. "I mean to say, that the boy is important to many people. Myself included."

The inn grew dark, the fringes of Fiskal's peripherals blurring. Shapes and light surrounding the most beautiful eyes Fiskal had ever seen on either man or woman. "And would you give your life for his?" The words slithered out of the Banèman's mouth.

"Y...Yes." The inn returned, bright and full of wonder and life. A seed of hope began to grow in Fiskal's chest.

"Then," said Akosh, "I shall spare him. But I shan't see him here again." Akosh took Fiskal's hand. "Some call me impatient. Not many.

But some. But with you, Fiskal, I find myself at peace. I couldn't say why either. There are not many upon this good land who inspire such feelings within me. I can move faster than any being ever in existence. Faster than the frames of your vision." A full glass of wine appeared in Akosh's hand, the liquid inside completely still. "You did have another bottle of the thirty-one by the way, it was tucked away in the back of the cellar. Next to a little box which contained two bottles of a very plummy looking twenty-nine." Akosh swirled the glass and sniffed it. "You've been holding out on me!"

The floral bouquet of it filled the air and Fiskal's eyes pricked with tears. "That...is a good cycle."

Akosh moved to sip it, then stopped. He upended the wineglass and the wine splashed upon the floor, disappearing through the cracks. "Time is a construct. Do you understand? Only I control it." Akosh stepped forwards, his teeth bared. "None other." A wry smile crept onto the Banèman's face. "I left you the other bottle, but do not keep things from me again."

"Yes, sir."

"Good! Then, to business. Are you prepared?"

"Yes. Yes, we're mobilised and ready for your attack. But..."

"Yes?" Akosh's teeth flashed. "Come on! Get on with it."

Fiskal was trapped but he had more than himself to think of. "Can you give me something, Akosh? Anything that will help my troops stand up to your forces?"

"That is not part of the game and you know it." Akosh frowned, those shining irises burning gold through red and green, before finally resting on the exact shade of purple of poor Leenar's bruises. "And if anything, it is you who owes *me* a debt." A wine bottle appeared in Akosh's empty hand. "On second thoughts, maybe I will take the twenty-nine. For the road. Oh, but I left the box down there, I imagine it has some sentimental value for you."

"Please, Akosh. I beg you." Fiskal's legs were shaking. The Banèman could end it all here and now, but the Republican army needed Fiskal more than they knew.

The corners of Akosh's thin mouth twitched, as though the whole debacle was a hilarious game. "You know why I came to you. You,

Fiskal. You were an obvious choice in the grand scheme. Your family's simple past. Their fair-weather child, who grows into the man with the silver tongue. Give yourself credit, Commander! You drew together an army to be truly feared in the face of overwhelming odds. Men and women who pledged their lives to your cause. A simple one but a *just* one." Akosh disappeared from the spot he had been standing and reappeared at Fiskal's side. He threw an arm over Fiskal's shoulder and pulled him close. "I hear that you also have in your possession the very soul who killed the great Jagar. Is this true?"

Fiskal kept his eyes down. "Yes. But...But she wavers."

"Commander, I don't believe a man of your *skill* is unable to recruit a lowly Sami into the ranks? Because I can tell you first hand, that the Great Father would appreciate her presence within your...army." Akosh slapped Fiskal's back heartily. "I'll leave it with you, friend!" He turned to leave then apparently thought better of it. "Ah, but I am being cruel. What is debt between friends? Here is a gift, Commander." Abruptly, the Banèman's face became expressionless. "The Kresh'ae will attack Bakla tomorrow, before dawn. Be ready." The Banéman vanished, and the only indication anyone had been there at all was the inn door slowly closing.

Fiskal swallowed, and closed his eyes. "Leenar, are you still there?"

The boy's face appeared at the door. "Yes, Commander?"

Fiskal pulled Leenar into a long embrace, and when he finally let him go, both of their eyes were wet. "Leenar, go and inform the officers that tomorrow the Republican army will be attacked by the Kresh'ae Bohr."

"The Kresh'ae?" Leenar's young face went pale. "Yes, Commander."

"And Leenar, if you believe in the Forbringrs as much as I, you will do me a favour and pray for our souls."

"Why, sir?"

"Because soon, they may be all we have left."

66

THE MASTER OF FEAR

Abika stumbled around the island sticking to the rocky crops and water wherever she could, but the cold was eating its way into her. With Soulfire she could have lit a fire with it by drawing points of light from her palm and *hardening* them so they became sparks—there was no other way to describe the feeling. It was the same process she used to kill the daemon, just on a smaller scale. It felt wonderful too, delaying the Thunder so that the lightening could fill her up with power like a well. With every league she travelled and every new place she saw, it gave her more places in her mind to push the Thunder back to, amplifying her strength.

Even if she could touch Soulfire, any fire she made would just go out, there was no wood to be had anywhere. Maybe the rock would burn, but what good would that do without a way to bring fire in the first place? She stared at her throbbing hand, the cuts and grazes still raw, willing something, anything, to happen. The ease of which she could touch Soulfire when she sat upon the bay smoking tom'ra seemed a world away. If she had some of Lorith's finest quadruple-grafted green right now she could fall into a pool of Soulfire, command it and will it and run across the sky until she was back in Ipiti! To hell with Kyira, and Vasta. To hell with everyone!

Once, she fancied she caught sight of Vasta in the distance, prowling like a wolf at the base of the shard, a tiny figure stark against the thrumming tower of obsidian which was so tall it looked like a spear driven through the belly of the sea, reaching for the sky, but it might have been her eyes playing tricks, but what if he *was* waiting for her? He'd been at sea the same time as she had, and she was so hungry she was considering licking the rocks.

The floating island was made of a sort of porous material that was hard and brittle, but somehow very buoyant. It wasn't that long ago Abika had admired Vasta's rock collection in his shop. It was hard not to be impressed—the Bohr was obsessive, and had collected a colourful and varied stack of the things—but all that time spent studying, watching and observing had been so he could keep the animal inside at bay. Looking back, Abika could see it in every interaction they'd had. Everything he had said was manipulated and conjured, carefully picked from a collection to suit the situation, and she had let him. That, above all, was what made Abika more angry than anything else.

She laughed. Then she cried.

It was all of it, too much. She wanted to scream, but it was her own choices that had brought her here! That anger was a puddle compared to the wave of sadness drowning her. Through it all, there was only one of beacon of light, and that was Kyira. The woman who had started it all, killing her parents, and leaving her for dead with a foster family that didn't want her or love her. That was the only way to stop the sadness. She had to find Kyira, and she had to kill her.

Stepping around a rise, she found Rothmarr's boat where they had come ashore, gently banging against the rocks. Maybe the sea *was* better. At least she would die in sunlight, warm and free, and not trapped upon this island—

A sound.

Was it the blood rushing through her veins? Her heart pounded in response, unhelpfully. Shaking uncontrollably, she peered around the rocks.

Footsteps. Vasta must have seen her! Abika skirted around the rocks, skipping as fast and hard as she could, in her mind she pictured Vasta close behind her, jumping upon her, tearing her open, feasting on her—

"Wait."

Abika stopped. The voice spoke, and she simply did as she was told.

"Turn."

Once more, she obeyed. A man stood there. He was well-dressed in a suit of pressed wool. His face was sharp and chiselled, but it was his skin that stood out the most: painted like a map with black and white. Not inked, like Sulitarian warriors, but rather as though he was affected by some strange disease.

Abika swallowed, the urge to run making her legs and hands twitch, but too many questions burned in her mind. "How are you so clean?"

The man smiled warmly. "Now, of all the things I could have guessed you'd ask, that is not what I thought it would be." He strolled towards her, fine polished shoes delicately placing upon the flat areas of rock, his hands outstretched. His grey eyes took her in. "You've been through it, haven't you? Here." He pulled a white apple from his jacket pocket and tossed it towards her.

The apple hit the black rock and rolled away, the noise alone bringing grumbles from Abika's stomach. "You didn't answer my question."

"No I didn't. And a good question it was too. In fact it's rather a beautiful way of asking me a great number of things, the answer of which would instruct you immediately upon my desires, goals and threat level." He nodded approvingly. "You are as smart as you look."

A roar sounded far off, in the direction of the shard, and Abika ducked. "No!" she breathed.

The man held his hands out again, stepping closer. "It's alright. Your friend won't bother us." It was hard to read his expression with his skin as it was, but Abika felt at ease with him. "The Bohr is leaping around on all fours like an angry bear," continued the man. "He's a war to wage with himself before he poses any threat to you or I. We'll be fine as long as we stay out of his way."

"Who are you?" snapped Abika.

The man seemed to wrestle with something for a moment, then apparently gave in to it. "I'm...not really here, in truth. I'm able to visit, but for the foreseeable future that's as much as I can do."

"How can you not be here?"

"Like this." He vanished, then abruptly was standing beside her. Abika jumped back, standing on the apple and tumbling to the rocks, opening a fresh graze on her knee.

"Ah!"

In an eyeblink the man was back where he had been. "Sorry, my fault. I forget sometimes how bound by the physical you mortals are. Forgive me..."

He stood waiting politely for Abika to give her name. "Itraeka," she said. I am Itraeka."

"Itraeka." He sounded amused. "Obviously, I'm not here, but I also have to conjure this body and face to speak for me. Sometimes I can make use of a host, but I didn't think it would be helpful this time seeing as the only other person within a hundred leagues wants to eat you. This time I chose to project myself."

"Lucky me," said Abika. "Wait, *mortals*? What are you then, if not mortal?"

"Immortal." The man sat down and crossed his legs. "Free of death. Why? Does that bother you?"

"No. And you don't need to speak to me like that. Like a child."

"You're not a child?"

Abika shook her head and nauseous hunger made her head swim. She took a long breath to steady herself and her eye fell upon the boat.

"You can leave," said the man, gesturing. "I'm not here to stop you."

"Then why are you here?"

"I've asked myself and others that same question more than you know. In truth, I came to meet you. The abandoned girl."

Abika barely knew herself what was going on, and now this stranger was confessing he knows all about her life? She rounded on him. "What can you possibly know about me?"

"Itraeka, if you listen, I will tell you." The man grinned, revealing a bright, wide smile of perfect white teeth. "It's true that you're playing my game—Isn't that how the world turns?"

"That's how you lose, by playing games in the first place. Like, if you say you're not really here, and yet you're here to meet me. So you knew I would be here. You must have been watching me, which means you've seen everything I've been through and done nothing to help. You are an enemy."

"Faultless logic," said the man, smiling. "Faultless. Wonderful! You're right, of course. I am an enemy, at least I could be. Or I could be the greatest companion you have ever known. Either way, I will tell you plainly how I came to know of you." He shuffled forwards, like they were telling stories around a campfire. "From one unbalanced force to another, it was destiny that we should meet."

Abika reached down and lifted the apple, examining it. "Unbalanced?"

"Your effects are already altering the realms. The things you've done and the choices you've made." He tapped his lip. "I'd wager that part of the reason that I stand before you now is partly because of your actions. And I have to say, to see where you've come from and to see you now, and with your spirit so intact. It's clear to me why she fears you."

Abika sighed. "Who?" This was getting boring. The apple felt real enough and was unscathed from its fall and when she had stood on it. She bit into it. It was wonderfully sweet—the best food she had ever eaten! The juice dribbled out of the fruit as she devoured it, seeds and all. With the last swallow she noticed the man watching her intently, hungrily.

"How is the apple real, but you are not?"

"The apple wasn't real. But it is now." More riddles. He smiled again. "Just a nifty bit of Soulfire."

Abika almost choked on her own spit. "Soulfire? You can wield it too?"

The man nodded. "Amongst others, yes."

"Others..."

"There's a few flavours to what you call Soulfire, Itraeka, but they're all the same thing, essentially. The way we, you, access them is different in each case. Depending on what you want to achieve."

"You make it sound like work."

"Oh, you have to work for it. It's a tool, to help us silly beings to our own ends. It can make lives easier, or it can destroy just as easily. You know this, I can see it in your heart. And that's what strikes me about you, Itraeka, even with the short time you've been aware of Soulfire's existence, I can see you already understand it in ways that others spend a lifetime trying to master. Your potential is higher than this shard." He gestured upwards like a grandiose street magician. "Higher than the sky! This shard stands upon sacred ground. We are pilgrims to this great stone. It has called us here." The man turned towards her, his slender form silhouetted against the shard's strange light. "Abika, I'm trying to do something, and there are a lot of people out there who are trying to stop me."

Abika's heart almost stopped at the sound of her real name.

"They see me as a threat, because they don't understand what it is I am trying to create. They fear what they do not understand!" The man held his fist out. "I have enemies on both sides, Abika, Bohr and human." He started pacing as he spoke. "I've tried my best to negotiate with them. To lead, to punish, to stand aside, yet every time, I'm met with resistance. And yet the problem remains, I am not really here!" His laugh was cruel and unusual. "And I cannot lead from a place I do not exist in! You see, I was given a gift. Or rather I took it for myself. Seized it. But it would seem there are many levels to corporeality, and there is still so much I cannot do. I need to stand on the same land, to feel the grass of your world between my toes, to feel real blood in my veins. I am ready though, Abika. My bags are packed. I just need someone on this side to help me open the door."

"Someone." Abika folded her arms.

"You, Abika. You. And don't look so surprised! I know who you are. There are those who make the waves and those who drown in them, and when one such as you appears, well, it's not difficult to to follow those ripples back to the source. Indeed, I know a great many things about you, little bird. Of course, you are not *my* Little Bird, but the name is still fitting, because I still remember the sound of your fluttering, foetal heartbeats. Even wrapped in the safety of your mother's womb, I knew, one day, we would meet again." He held out his hands and smiled. "And here we are."

Abika held in her frustration and surprise as best she could, but it still felt like it could burst out of her. "You knew my mother?"

The man smiled, and his map-like features seemed to swim across his face. "I did. I do, but that's another story entirely. Look, nobody should have to work for free. So, if you help me, I'll show you methods and means that only those you call the Forbringrs know. Soulfire's many flavours will come as easy for you as they do the God's themselves." The man picked up a loose rock. "As easy for you to wield as a blade." The rock melted in his hand, changing form into a blade of fire. He held it high, and it floated up and out of his palm until abruptly evaporating into a puff of smoke.

"If I were to run...?" said Abika. "Leave and never want to see you and your *ways* again? You'd let me?"

"I would not stop you. In fact, at this moment you could likely overpower me. You are flesh and bone. I am but a trick of the light." He finished with a flourish and a smile.

Abika turned to the Myathar. It was broken, and she didn't need to be a shipman to see it. She might try it anyway, but she would never avenge her mother and father's deaths by leaving this world as fish food on the bottom of the Middle Sea.

"If you're afraid of me—"

"Ah, I never said I was afraid."

Abika walked towards him. "And you know that I am more powerful than you."

"Again, I—"

"And you've been watching me." She stopped in front of him. "Then you know who and what I am. What I've done. Do you know what I think? I doubt it."

"Well, No—"

Abika took the man's hand and it was as real as any other. "Because if you have, then you *should* fear me."

"I faced down the Great Mother herself, girl. I am the master of fear."

Abika smiled. "Then show me everything. I want to know it all."

67

MOTHER'S MILK

Kaliste fingered the tassels of her Princess's cloak. It was old, but then so was she. You had to respect the ancient things of this world, especially a Banèman of nearly a thousand cycles. Humans thought of her as immortal, but then it was easy to rule when you outlived even the most persistent kings.

The Reliathar was as solid a boat as a Queen could ask for, but it's fleet of shoreboats couldn't have been more poorly made. And Banèman or no, the cold still found her, especially when in her human form. Kaliste tried to focus on the waves, and the water rushing by the broken Way Bridge in the distance, but the shining doorway kept coming to her mind, as magical as it was. Except it wasn't magic. It was science. Theology. Philosophy, all rolled into one. Each were one and the same—different names for the same functions. The choice of word was simply a matter of stance.

"And education," she said quietly to herself.

The doorway waited for her Queen's army, floating above the cold cellar floor, a mysterious force balanced against two places awaiting her order. But still, it required her intervention or else ten thousand men and women would emerge on the far island of Dor and find that the only enemy awaiting them was a few stubborn vines. The doorway's vibration fizzed through Kaliste, even at the great distance she now found herself from Zunqai, it still called to her.

It knew what she was about to do.

Jagar's words tickled at her mind, niggling and biting like an insect.

If this is to be the last battle. The last stand of the humans, then it should be a good one. Wouldn't you say?

She had spent much effort in forging an army to finally rid Rengas of the human scourge, and Jagar wanted to just hand them over to the rebellion? To this Commander Fiskal? A human waste, unable to create an army of his own? That was the problem with humans, they were lazy. Always looking for the path of least resistance, not least when it came to their own survival.

She had dissected Jagar's motives, pulling apart the pieces and reconfiguring them like a game of Chinaes, and still the reasons for handing over the Queen's army to the humans was completely unclear. The army would of course fight in whichever direction they were aimed, and Jagar knew that. He knew that a quarter of Zunqai's strength lay within those ranks, and still he wished to remove it from the Bohr's arsenal. There had been nothing in history that Kaliste could draw upon to understand it, the act itself was as unnatural as...creating a new sun.

The biting wind and the rolling deck of the shoreboat brought Kaliste back to her senses. She shook her head and slipped her hand between the fans of her dress, resting it on her stomach.

"The *Great Father* plans something." The swollen life inside her moved. Even her unborn child knew of the threat Jagar posed to the realms.

Tyr grew larger and larger with every gust of wind until soon the black cliffs of Terävä loomed above, the mountain's razor peaks sharp and uninviting. Only the monkeys that lived between them could find solace and shelter in such a place.

Kaliste stepped off of the shoreboat and onto the coarse black sand of Vasen, which sank deliciously into the gaps between her human toes.

"We can't stay long, my Queen." The Bohr captain of the Reliathar was slight, and not weatherworn enough. His hands were soft, and he tried to make up for it with more growl from his hyena-face. "The Kanava currents will drag us all the way to Anqamor should they get the chance."

"You believe the Way is still dangerous?"

"When the Kanava flipped upon Tyr's demise, they sped up at the same time. Most boats wouldn't stand a chance upon the Way. My Queen." The captain looked back to the rocking ship anchored a half league off the shore. "The Reliathar might manage it mind you."

Kaliste gritted her teeth. She needed her energy. "Will that cave entrance take me into the catacombs?"

The Captain turned. "Aye. It ought to take you right in."

Kaliste padded over to it, avoiding the razor rocks. "Stay here."

The air was thick and the ceiling low. Kaliste ducked as far she could until she was forced to crawl. In her human form she could have revisioned herself to not look pregnant, but what a disservice that would do to the child within. Each ache and pain was a silent prayer to her and V'Laerk's creation.

The cave twisted and turned until finally the sound of sluggish waves indicated a flooded cavern. The entrance involved squeezing through a gap between two ton-weight boulders, each holding a small fortune's worth of charn vein inside. The famous Tyrian charn here should have been plundered long ago, and yet no human dared approach the Way, nor the remnants of Tyr. Fear of what happened to this once prosperous city kept away even the most insistent of pirates.

The ceiling above shone, but as large as the cavern was, it was clear it once stretched for leagues beneath the hillsides. The remains of Vasen, the Domst, the homes of the political elite, Bohr and human alike, sat now beneath crystal blue waters. It was an illusion of light and magic though. Who knew how far down the seabed lay after the doorway of Tyr was forced shut?

Kaliste pulled her straps loose on her dress and let it fall to the rocky cavern floor. Little red crabs scuttled away from the loose garments. She stepped into the blue pool, admiring how the images of ruined buildings far below broke apart as the soft waves disturbed the still surface.

"Let us hope there is enough of me left by the time we reach the doorway." She touched her bare stomach. "Let us hope, son, that the doorway is still there or this will be all for nothing."

Kaliste took a few long breaths then dived. Coldness enveloped her, and her human self flickered away. Sleek and powerful, she was herself again, and she swam deeper and deeper until the light above was but a smear. The walls of the catacombs reached out with arms of steel and broken stone until they too were left behind. The water thrummed with power, a vibration of ages that even a lowly human would have noticed, but it was not what it should have been. The power of the doorway that closed above Tyr and destroyed the city should have wrought a tower that reached the clouds, but something happened that day that brought it down.

An unnatural glow began to fill the space around her, growing in intensity. Kaliste's chest spasmed against the lack of air, but she didn't fight it—that would only hasten the end—instead she swam deeper until everything told her to stop and turn back.

Kaliste powered forwards, until the edges of the broken shard appeared. Sharp like the broken stem of a wine glass. Keeping her heart rate as low as she could, she dropped down feet-first upon the black seabed.

The shard was raw energy held in suspension and each piece of it would provide the wearer with unspeakable powers, and here she stood at the foot of a broken tower at the bottom of the sea. Her chest spasmed again. The clock was ticking.

Kaliste drew and Soulfire flooded into her lungs, infusing her blood with new oxygen.

Her fingertips found the glass, and the shard glowed eagerly in anticipation, copying the shape, first of her hand then of her entire body, the hazy outline of her Banèman form becoming clearer with every heartbeat. It pulled her closer like an impatient lover, and her feet slid on the seabed until she was embracing the walls of the sunken ruin. It started as a tingle, the interface, growing in intensity and lighting a fire upon every single nerve ending. Blue forks of light crackled like tiny electrical storms, each nightfork growing thicker as the shard's impatience grew. Kaliste held back a moment, teasing the force of nature. She was in control here. Not it. And just like a lover on the brink of madness, the shard too began to shake with frustration, vibrations pulsed out from it, each shudder a hundred thousand times more powerful than any Soulfire she could conjure. Without her, the shard was as inert as the void. Only she could be the spark to the tinder.

"Obey me."

The shard shivered again.

"Obey me."

Yes.

Kaliste drew deeply from her well of Soulfire, and like a hungry animal, the shard's forces grew exponentially. The surface of the sunken tower was no longer shiny and smooth, but murky and matt. The solid physical barrier of the atoms between them was the only thing keeping them apart, and now that was changing. The shard was trying to draw her in and consume her. Kaliste's feet slid through the sand, pressing her in. Her left hand broke through the surface, and immediately began to break down, becoming one with the shard. Her blood, veins, tissue and bone all crystalising.

"Obey me!"

The connection between Kaliste and the shard grew suddenly fuzzy as the shard drew upon Kaliste's well of Soulfire too. Unfathomable amounts of energy burned through her. She was a conduit for energy from realms unseen, seeking to enter her domain through her. The shard pulled more and more Soulfire through her until her skin began to burn. The seawater bubbled ferociously.

"OBEY ME!"

The shard didn't respond. It was no longer cogent and the interface between them was unbreakable. If it could not consume her directly, it would burn her to a cinder by drawing enough Soulfire to level a continent. Kaliste's heart thumped from exhaustion. There was nothing for her to do!

Then she thought of the Bohr from the alleyway in Zunqai. Her unborn child had broken that Bohr to pieces, and even as the memory flickered to life, so did the life inside her.

The shard could control the flow of Soulfire, but Kaliste and her unborn child would direct it. It would burn her, but maybe the child might live...

Kaliste's son kicked frantically in her womb as Soulfire filled his veins. The water was turning to steam so quickly that Kaliste could breathe, and a dome of air grew out from her. The black sand beneath Kaliste's feet smoked, filling the dome with dangerous gas. And still the child kicked harder and harder, drawing more. Kaliste was being pulled by two of the most powerful forces in existence. Whatever was going to happen, was now inevitable.

The seabed cracked open, but Kaliste was no longer bound to the ground. She floated above the fissure, in a dome of air suspended beneath Tyr's violent waters, as the broken shard fought to consume her. Her glowing skin became hard, as her body burned. This was it. Like an out-of-control ship crashing through waves, Kaliste directed the energy of a thousand other raging realms, dragging it back and holding it. She pictured the doorway in the basement of the house in Zunqai and aligned her vibrations with it. The interface opened up, giving her access to them all, every doorway in Rengas was hers to command. There were so many!

Colours, sounds and smells almost too numerous to quantify assaulted her senses. Kaliste ignored them, and her senses dulled as they were burned away. In the dark of her mind the connections between each doorway shuffled like cards. The doorway in Zunqai now opened somewhere in the Middle Sea, but that wasn't useful! She tried again, flicking through the options, trying to force the doorway in Zunqai to exit in Bakla. There was a new doorway there, very new. But the interface was slippery and the stacks of doorways shuffled away. They were sentient, and they were denying her!

A splash of water landed on her forehead. Kaliste drew in an outstretched arm and wiped her eyes, and through blurred vision saw the dome had thinned. Her trapped arm was a shard of living crystal, all the way to her bicep, and growing. The fissure below steamed and roiled, a crack into nowhere. To the centre of Rengas? She didn't want to find out. Closing her eyes again, she saw the doorways had settled once more.

Kaliste reached out one last time, her concentration a dagger penetrating a maelstrom of sensations. The doorways were there once more, and this time she let them choose their own connections, changing naturally to fall as they wished without intervention. It was so easy; they wanted to move.

The end points began to switch again, the doorway in Dor, the doorway in Zunqai, the Middle Sea, Tyr, Nord, Makril, Lumael, Kyotho —they were everywhere. Akosh was right! If this truly was the end of our world, then these were the holes that it would evaporate through.

Kaliste watched as the shuffling connections carried on endlessly within the interface, the doorways flashing every time they connected and disconnected, creating a strobing pattern on the inside of Kaliste's eyes.

Dread filled her head at where this might lead. Was Jagar's goal really worth destroying? Was this all worth it just to send the army through to Bakla? Either way it was too late.

The flashing slowed as the endpoints settled once more, the doorway in Zunqai grew bright, a flash of blue, then through all the hues of the spectrum before finally stopping on a yellowish orange. The colour of fire. She followed the connection in her mind's eye and smiled at the realisation that it led to the beach in Bakla.

The dome collapsed. A billion tons of water smashed in upon her. Soulfire took over, but her body's needs were ignored. The shard burned brightly as it drew the power through her, and it would not stop. Kaliste tried to swim upwards, a mechanical reflex to try and escape and stay alive, but the shard would not let go of such worthwhile prey, so Kaliste closed her eyes and let it take her, and in that moment of surprise Kaliste prompted the interface one last time.

The blinding echoes of those doorways were still there, thrumming with power and renewed vigour. In their whole existence, they had never been changed, and new life pulsed excitedly away from them. Kaliste might have absorbed some of it for herself, but she was too far away, and the child would die. She focused. She pushed. Prodding for weakness. This was a negotiation and she was here to claim the debt—

she had brought to them new life and they would take from her new life.

Each doorway flashed by, ignoring her and refusing the exchange, but she just needed one out of thousands of doorways for it to work. Her lungs burned, and the child within her kicked in frantic panic.

"Quiet, my love."

The doorways flashed again through the interface, as connection after connection was refused.

Just one.

All she needed was one. Another denial. And another. Her lungs screamed, even a Banèman needed air to breathe. Desperation clutched at her heart as the fear of what would happen started to become reality. The kicks inside her were growing weaker as her body began to die, as her son began to die, but she pushed and pushed with Soulfire, probing every corner of the interface for a way through. Her own soul was at risk, but without this one final act, her and V'Laerk's line would end here.

Queen Kaliste pushed as hard as she could, wielding power beyond that of any being before her, and just as the kicking stopped, one of the doorways accepted her exchange.

Her and V'Laerk's creation was taken from her womb, a gift, not only to the realms, but to her son. As Kaliste let go, and as the lines between realms faded, she knew she had finally beat Jagar. She had betrayed him, and won, and as much as it had cost, it was worth the price.

68

BLOODLIGHT

The sulphur of the smithy wafted into V'olpar's nostrils well before his feet found the soot-covered flagstones of the armoury. He had been checking weapon allocations on the wrong side of the palace when the darkness came.

The smithies stood solemnly as V'olpar threw open the doors to the palace square. The statues of his ancestors grimaced in a deep red light, and V'olpar too shielded his eyes against the remnants of Queen Kaliste's sun. The light was waning, moving through gold and red like a sunset. He pulled his axe from his belt, unsure what to do with it. Aside from the litter left behind after the lord's army, the square was empty as V'olpar crossed it, and keeping one eye on the waning sun and one eye on the street, he made his way through Zunqai, humans and Bohr alike parting for him like Pulier parted the Horn Don Zunqai at the great battle of Pulier's Pass!

His gleaming, golden armour told them all who he was, but most knew by now. The famous V'olpar, student to the Queen and King of Zunqai themselves!

He hurried as the Queen's sun grew smaller, trying to get a better vantage point yet with each step he took, the great ball of blistering fire contracted. He imagined that somehow it was tied to him, and not Queen Kaliste, and as he padded over the dry cobbles, he searched for a way within himself to bolster it, and perhaps halt its last breaths. But of course, there was nothing. V'olpar was a simple creature, a practical Bohr who used his hands and wit to achieve his goals. He didn't have the magic of Banèmen, and so he could do nothing but watch as the Kaliste's sun withered and died.

He turned the last corner towards the Fountains of Kalcoon and stopped in awe. The circle was full, edge to edge with soldiers. There were so many of them, clad in their dark leathers and carrying shining steel swords and spears, that the fountains were completely obscured. Two Ruffin stood near the centre, their lizard-like forms almost as long as the circle was wide, their Bohr riders, painted in white and red.

V'olpar made his way through to them, leaving a wake like a shark through a school of herring. He stroked the closest Ruffin's neck, marvelling as the creature's scales shone even in the dimness.

"Report," said V'olpar.

"It is bloodlight," hissed the Rider through his slitted helmet.

V'olpar stood straighter. "Bloodlight. What of the doorway?"

"Awaits," said the Rider.

"I want to see it."

The Rider heeled his Ruffin forward and the creature hissed. The lords parted hastily for them, as they led V'olpar down a narrow street by the remnants of buildings that once stood. Past piles of rubble and stone and a single red door and frame that stood against a ruined home with no roof and barely any walls.

"There," hissed the Rider, pointing. In the hole that had once been the basement of the old house, sat a shining sphere, flashing intermittently.

"You!" snapped V'olpar. "Come here and open this door."

A proud soldier standing nearby jogged forwards and nodded at his king, keeping well back from Rider and Ruffin. The soldier touched the door then was thrown back agains the wall on the opposite side of the street. He began shaking and screaming, then the black armour was blistering, then his skin, hair and before long there was nothing but a smoking corpse lying on the road. The Ruffin turned, presumably to help itself to the remains.

V'olpar shook his head at the Rider. "I wouldn't go near him if I were you. Those flames are not visible to any but those who wield Soulfire, but they are there, make no mistake, and they will burn for some time yet. The entrance to this building was trapped with Soulfire, one of Kaliste's traps. Which confirms that it was she that found this place, and that she knows of this doorway."

"Commander?"

V'olpar turned, ready to educate the Rider on what he had worked out from Kaliste's plans, but his eye was drawn back to the Queen's sun. A noise like metal being twisted and torn emanated from it, echoing down the streets. The Queen's army roared in agony as the soldiers clasped at their heads in pain. V'olpar and the Rider watched silently as the fiery sun swallowed itself, collapsing inwards. V'olpar closed his second eyelids against the blurring light, and a fiery shockwave exploded forth, blowing the clouds away.

"One. Two. Three. Four. Five. Six—"

The buildings rattled as a gust of hot air blew through the circle and down the streets, bathing Zunqai in the sun's final breath.

"We have lost the sun," hissed the Rider. The Ruffin tossed its head, testing the air with its forked blue tongue.

V'olpar adjusted his gleaming armour, wiping dust from the shoulders. "I think we have lost more than that, Rider." He turned and marched back down the alleyway, not stopping until he stood in the centre of the circle. The Fountains of Kalcoon had lost a few heads, apparently the stone used in the water feature was not as good quality as the buildings. Shame. It would still bear him regardless. And so V'olpar climbed. He set his feet upon the remains of his ancestors and roared aloud.

"Soldiers! Hear me. I am V'olpar. I talk to you now not only as commander, but as King of Zunqai!" Applause filled the circle and the roads beyond as the populace of the great capital filled the streets. V'olpar waited, savouring the attention. This was the single greatest moment of his life. "Today we lost a Queen, and as such I rename you. From this day, and in the honour of Queen Kaliste, blessed be her shadow, I rename you the King's army!"

The applause came again, louder this time. The whole city was caressing him, feeling his words. The gods would know him, the leader of the greatest city in Rengas and ruler of the world! The thought brought warmth to his chest, and when he spoke next, the words boomed forth with their own power.

"TODAY, WE FIGHT THE REBELS. WE WILL FACE THEM DOWN AND DESTROY THEM!" He clenched his fists and he relished it as the crowd before him reached and screamed and yearned for him. They would bleed for him, die for him, and V'olpar owned it all.

He jumped down from the fountains, arms raised, exalting. Walking backwards through the crowd. He stopped at one who looked scared. A human man, bigger than most and with a painted face. He stared up at V'olpar's greatness, unsure of what to do or say. The man hadn't clapped.

"What is your name, human? I give you leave to reply."

The man blinked. "Kavik."

V'olpar's eye twitched. "Then kneel, Kavik."

The man seemed to hesitate for a moment, hand hovering over his pocket. V'olpar urged him to release a weapon, but the soldier bent the knee. Luckily for him. The two soldiers either side of him did the same, and a wave rippled outwards as every member of the King's army kneeled to their new king.

69

HALFWAY TO THE HILT

"How are the nights so cold?"

Jekob shook his head at Vard, then shuffled closer to the flames. He wanted to strangle the man. The fabric of his gloves was soaked through, dripping water and somehow drawing fresh marks on his already ruined boots. His thin scarf hung limp about him like a dead snake, but he had nowhere else to store it. During the day the heat and humidity of Sulitar pressed in, following them league after league until night came, when it became unbearably cold. The time where life could just comfortably exist, lasted no longer than ten minutes.

"How are you unable to talk of anything else?" snapped Jekob. He was retreating into himself, and he knew it. He could see it happening and yet there was nothing he could do but watch.

Losa threw a burning log and it landed beautifully in Vard's lap. "Yes, be quiet, Vard."

Vard jumped up, and the log fell to the frozen earth. "At least you two are agreeing for once," he quipped, brushing off burning embers.

Losa breathed into her cupped hands. "Will you give me an answer please, Jekob?"

Jekob pulled the gloves and scarf off and steam curled up from them, broken only by his own smoking breath. "No. That's your answer. No. I will not ask him."

Losa shook her head in disgust. "You're afraid of him. Don't deny it! I've seen you searching around as though he might skewer you through the back and give you that honourable death you've always wanted!"

"Of course, I'm afraid of him," hissed Jekob. "V'Laerk is the biggest Bohr I've ever seen. You'd be fucking stupid not to be!" He glanced around. "Where even is he?"

"He wandered into the forest."

"We're all in the forest, Vard."

"The dark side," quipped Vard, "where all the branches are close and you can't move for being scratched to pieces. I guess it's better than the inland forests were the trees are so big they make bloody ships out of them!"

"You afraid of some trees?" scoffed Losa, holding her hands over the campfire.

"No!" squeaked Vard. "But maybe the giant bloody spiders!"

Jekob studied Vard's face. His ginger beard was already flecked with grey hairs, probably as he spent most days skittish and afraid. It was to be expected, after the ground that they had covered in so short a time. You couldn't move one thousand soldiers over a sea and through a place like Sulitar without a few hundred panic attacks.

"Although if you were to ask me to turn around right now and head back to Costra Dae. I wouldn't say no." Vard sat up. "In fact, I'd bloody-well run there. To the great Palace of Sulmar, and once I was there, I'd knock at the door..." He elbowed a soldier at his side who offered him a reassuring laugh. "And I'd find myself a nice princess to call my own and spend the rest of my days making that woman as happy as could be!"

"Jekob." Losa clicked her fingers in front of his face. "I asked you a question."

"Damn it, Losa! I'm not doing it! If you want to make a suggestion to V'Laerk, then you bloody do it. I'm not an errand boy."

"A suggestion?" She leaned in. "He's going to kill one of us, Jekob."

She was worried. Those big, dark eyes were wide and desperate. He wanted to say she was out of her bloody mind. But he couldn't. He glanced over at the other fires. Mucky white coats sat huddled around each one.

"If you do it, Leader Jekob, V'Laerk might spare you." Losa wasn't just saying words anymore, this was a cultivated response. "He owns me and will kill me should I ask anything of him. Vard is too dense to ask the right question, and that leaves you, Jekob. The great Leader Jekob. It has to be you, Leader. It can only be you. With you, we may all live."

"Forbringr's blood!" said Jekob. "I will ask V'Laerk if we can split forces. If it just means you'll stop bloody talking."

Both Vard and Losa sat back and breathed deeply, until they noticed each other, then Losa was up and walking off. She turned back after a few steps. "Thank you, Jekob. Sincerely."

Jekob feigned a smile. "Yeh. Fuck you, Losa. Sincerely."

The woods around Low'rind were of a tree Jekob had never seen. The trunks reached upwards, and some to an incredible height, but they had grown in sections, each one smaller than the one before it. Making them very easy to climb. At the top, huge nuts grew in clutches, surrounded by deliciously sweet orange flesh. They were constantly falling all over the place, thwacking to the ground, so that sleeping around them became a game of will-the-next-one-hit-me-or-someone-else. Jekob had escaped them for the most part, but a few others had taken some nasty bruises from the falling nuts. Huge spiders lived up there too, so if it wasn't nuts falling on your head, it was spiders as big as your hand. They roasted well though, and had no fangs, so there were at least some things to be grateful for.

By all that was holy, he missed the commune. He even missed Meorith, Thio, the bloody cook! Abika...She was more complicated. That girl scared him like no other. Since their arrival in Sulitar, Jekob had been watching the trees constantly, waiting for Abika to appear. She had wiles, that one, and worse, it wouldn't be a straight up assault in broad daylight, but a sneak attack while he slept. The scarf he wore was threaded with sea silver, invisible to the naked eye but as strong as steel, and it had cost him most of the coin he had taken with him from

Ipor Dan, but it was a price he was willing to pay if it kept his neck safe from a knife in the night.

Jekob shuffled through the archways made by the reaching tree limbs, ducking low and dipping beneath, then sliding between until all at once the smell of blood stopped him in his tracks. He had developed a good nose for the stuff recently, having been the one to discover two of the three dead fellows that V'Laerk had lost his temper with. They had all been so broken there was no coming back, and fear had spread through the ranks like gut rot. The officers in each squad put pressure on Losa, and Losa, in turn, came to him to rectify, and that was what had led him here, to this quiet, hidden place, all alone with the biggest bloody Bohr in Rengas.

There were bodies of animals strewn across the ground, their innards adorning the branches. Fruit spiders crawled amongst them, sucking the meats dry. Jekob froze. In the middle sat V'Laerk, his massive bulk hunched over.

"V'Laerk." The Bohr didn't react. Jekob took a tentative step forwards. "V'Laerk. We...I need your wisdom."

"Wisdom," rumbled V'Laerk, his voice as dry as the brown palm leaves crushed beneath him. "Wisdom comes from experience. Experience comes from longing, and I long for nothing."

Jekob swallowed. "The Order longs for leadership."

"The Order matters not."

That one stung. "The Order is the reason for all. The reason we dragged ourselves across the sea, and through the fields of Costra Dae. Only the mountains of Sulitar stand between us and the south. And you, V'Laerk, stand at the centre of it all. You are at the centre of the Order. Without your leadership, we do not exist." The words were real, Jekob felt them deep in his soul.

The Bohr inclined his head. "You truly believe that?"

The Order of the White Dragon was self-perpetuating now that it was affiliated with the Queen and King of Zunqai, which alone, would be enough to multiply its followers a hundredfold.

"As truly as I trust in you, V'Laerk." Speaker Ohalo might have wished them to follow Bohr doctrine, but deep in his heart, Jekob wanted more. The humans of this world could forge a path by themselves, as sure as the sun was in the sky.

V'Laerk stood. His bunched mail corset dropped like handfuls of pennies to swing from his hips. "Give me your sword."

Jekob resisted the urge to back away, and did as he was ordered, pulling his blade from its sheath and holding it out hilt first. It looked like a toothpick in V'Laerk's hands.

"There is to be a war to the south, and our great Queen Kaliste..." V'Laerk seemed to falter, as though the words caused him pain. "The Queen ordered me to halt our movements south and draft. Sulitarians are good fighters, and once we have enough, we are to travel the Middle Sea across to Bakla and join the Bohr ranks, so we can finally end the human rebellion. By then, we will be cleansing the towns all the way back to Kyotho."

"Sulitarians are hard," agreed Jekob, "and their hearts harder."

V'Laerk ignored him. "I accepted this order without question because she is our Queen. My Queen. My Kaliste." The Bohr's lips pressed together, and tears began to fall. "My Queen and my son have passed. Their lights have gone out, and so must mine, for there is no life without her. A king without his Queen...I cannot go on."

Jekob set his jaw. "V'Laerk, I'm so sorry—"

"DON'T PITY ME!" The sudden change in V'Laerk's tone chilled Jekob's blood. V'Laerk stepped back, but the snarl remained. "Don't you dare pity me, human." He took a long breath. "Humans are as flawed as we are. I see that now. We reign above you, and our strength and stature projects visions of gods." V'Laerk rested the sword on Jekob's shoulder. "But we are as you, just beings, lost in the majesty of life, searching for purpose." The sword moved up to Jekob's forehead, hovering above his eyes. "And I can only assume that whatever powers handed us these forms did so for good reason."

Jekob stepped back despite himself. "You wish to mark me?"

V'Laerk snarled. "I wish nothing. I *will* mark you. Before I leave, I will transfer power back to an individual whom I respect. They will lead the Order of the White Dragon as I have done. You are that individual Leader Jekob. There is no other human whom I respect as much as you, as so it was a simple choice. I pass your associate's life unto you."

"What about Ohalo?" Jekob blurted out the question before he could think.

"I sent a party to *unseat* Ohalo from the Speaker's Chair soon after we left. The high seat of Order of the White Dragon is no place for a weak old man."

V'Laerk raised Jekob's sword again, and this time Jekob stayed where he was, wincing as the tip of the blade pierced the skin of his forehead, cutting across into his flesh.

"You may wonder why we do this," said V'Laerk. "Why the Bohr mark those who mean something to our kind." V'Laerk moved back, shifting away the furry carcasses and crawling spiders at his feet. "The Bohr have no gods, and a people who have no gods have no reason. We make and forge our own paths. Those who we deem worthy must be as seen, feared and respected as we are. This mark then will give you power, Guardian Jekob. All who see it will know, and they will act to your will. Bohr will treat you as an equal. Humans will quail to your order. You are as us." V'Laerk dropped to his knees, and swung the Jekob's sword so it was pointed at his own chest. He placed the point under his armpit, took a long breath and slid the blade in. Halfway to the hilt, V'Laerk let go and raised his chin. "Finish it."

Jekob's heart hammered as he clutched the sword. There was nothing else to do, but as he was told. And so he did. He pushed with all of his might feeling the Bohr's mighty heart within yield to his sword. V'Laerk's eyes rolled back and the Bohr fell away to the forest floor leaving Jekob standing above, sword in hand.

"Jekob?" If Losa's tone was fearful before, now it was terror embodied. Her brown eyes found his and Jekob smiled as gingerly she lifted a hand towards the bleeding cross on his forehead. Realisation swept over her like the waves of an ocean, breaking upon her bow. "Jekob, what have you done?"

Bloodlust coursed through Jekob's veins, he wanted more. He wanted to end them all, to attack Losa, and cut her to ribbons. He wiped his own blood dripping down his face. "Get the Order prepared to leave."

"Where are we going?" she uttered, her lips shaking.

Jekob's heart leapt, but the value of V'Laerk's words had yet to find a home in his mind. They were strange things, intangible and unreal, but they were his nonetheless, and that was all that mattered.

"We have work to do, Losa. V'Laerk's dying wish was to augment our ranks with Sulitarian blood. Forced conscription." He shook his head. "That was what even V'Laerk, in his infinite wisdom, never understood, for as similar as Bohr and human are if we are to ever coexist, they must first see us as *equals.*"

"Jekob, what are you saying?"

"The Order of the White Dragon will not *conscript* Sulitarians, we will liberate them! I will bring the Order to the lives of all humans, exactly how we did on the Island of Ipiti. Tonight, we will travel to Costra Dae, to the great Palace of Sulmar. We will rest. We will eat. And we will entrench ourselves in their lives until Sulitar belongs to us!" Jekob stepped up to Losa. "Do you walk with me, or do you fight me?"

Losa looked down at his bloodstained blade. The colour was returning to her face. Could he trust her? He didn't need to vial of poison to do the work out here. He could finish her with the same blade that had slain the might V'Laerk, King of Zunqai, then leave her here to the spiders.

Losa smiled. A wry smile that spoke of dedication, loyalty and something deep and primal. She pushed the blade aside and rushed into him, and then they were embracing. Her warmth pressed against him, her lips and her curves, moulded perfectly against his body. Jekob reached around and grabbed her behind, lifting her up, and she wrapped her legs around him.

"Sincerely, Jekob," she purred in his ear. "I walk with you."

Diary entry

Nordun Terns

Fiskal and Darc are lying to me. They are working together. They have to be. But why? I've packed my things, but I can't leave yet. Not yet.

70

THE LAST REPUBLIC

Bakla beach was the most expansive piece of land Kyira had laid eyes on. She had walked for near two hours before the dawn, and still the Republican army had remained in view. Her feet were cold but the sand was fine, if not a little muddy. Milli was probably still fast asleep, and while leaving her was sadness itself, Kyira felt an urge to be by herself.

The wind danced and whipped about her enjoying the fun of fanning her along, and leading her further from people and their problems—she had enough of her own.

The Republican army was a smear of black against red, a machine filled with people, milling, smithing, cooking, sparring, and she'd had her fill of them. She had always daydreamed, running the hills of Nord in her mind. The *sisters* she used to call those hills and ridges, but apparently she'd lost that as well. Their ancient snow would crunch underfoot, new snowcricks would chirrup and dragonlights would scar the night sky. Nord was far away. She could leave right now...

"And never return."

Her feet took her on along the beach of Bakla until she stopped by a dry plate of mud. Lifting it carefully, she found more of the mudworms the boy had shown her when she had arrived. She might have eaten some, but all she could think of was Darc.

Calling out for him would be easy; she would interrogate him and throttle him to within an inch of his life! But then...what if he did appear at her call? What being could appear to someone at will like that? Her grandmother, blessed be her shadow, had hallucinated towards the end of her life, talking and interacting with people only she could see. She went mad before the end.

"Only the Great Mother," she mumbled. "The Forbringrs!" She spat at the sky, and the spittle rained back down on her. She was her own worst enemy, but the gods still deserved her wrath! Her eye was twitching, a muscle caught in spasm that threatened to drive her insane with incessant throbbing. She rubbed it, scratched at it, then slapped herself hard across the check. The warmth lingered, and her eye lid fluttered gently.

She wanted to curse Darc's name! Had she really imagined him? He was so real? She thought back to every interaction she'd had with him, racking her brain, but she couldn't recall Darc ever speaking to anyone directly, and that left only one truth...

There had to be more to her path than this!

She composed herself, thinking of her past and how she had come to be here in Kemen. The smuggler's vessel brought her from Lothri, but before Ge'Bat she had joined the refugees travelling from Lumael in the south of Sulitar. The journey through Sulitar had almost killed her a number of times. Before that, she'd been working the fields of the Red Isles, Dor and Ipiti. Those times seemed simpler now, but she knew they were not. She'd almost died from poverty on Dor—it was pure luck that she had managed to find a vessel willing to take her to the more prosperous island of Ipiti and more luck that had led her to the commune.

"Jekob." She hadn't thought of him for a long time, but the commune wasn't ever far from her thoughts, because the baby was never too far from her thoughts. Abika had been so young when Kyira had left, but Kyira was no mother, however hard she had tried to be. The call of a Pathwatcher's life away from the paths of Nord had dragged her away from Jekob and Abika so she record the world of Rengas. What a fool she was!

She dropped the mud plate and scanned the horizon. Was this just who she was now? Belonging neither to Nord, nor Sulitar, nor Kemen? If Darc wasn't real, then was any of it real anyway? How could she trust anything that had happened in her life, or any choice she had made if she was just a slave to everyone else's choices?

Perhaps she *should* just listen to the fates and the Forbringrs, and do as they willed because there was no peace to be had within. The horizon stared back, unhelpful and immense, a cursed illusion that extended the beach flats to eternity and back again.

"Iqaluk," she uttered, under her breath. "What do I do? Who is Darc?"

There was no response, because that was stupid irony of need. When you needed someone, they were nowhere to be found.

She started back towards the army, her feet moving of their own accord, her mind unready and unwilling to decide upon a future she held no control over.

A familiar flap of wings caught Kyira's ear, and a tern dropped to the sand in front of her. It padded around, unperturbed and unaffected by the danger of the quicksand.

"What are you doing here?" The black and white tern was from Nord; she had seen thousands of them in the past, but never any outside of her birthplace. The bird cocked its head at her, seemingly unafraid, and the realisation hit her. "You migrate here?"

Kyira always thought the terns lived short lives, dying in the coldest winters of Nord, but here it was. Its coat was dusted red with Bakla's sand, but there was no denying what it was. It cracked its grey beak into the mudplate, cracking the mud and pulled out a long, wriggling mudworm from the hole.

Nordun terns flew to Bakla to bask in the southern sun and gorge themselves while Nord was assaulted by hard winds and cruel snow!

Kyira laughed aloud and the tern squawked and took flight, lifting up on the wind to join a flock hanging silently above. "It is time for me to go home."

AKOSH

71

GOD-KILLER

The sun was still red and low as Kyira marched through the dusty streets of Bakla. Reluctance clung to her from the fatigue still lurking in her bones, or maybe because she would miss the place—She couldn't tell how she felt about anything more. Every decision she had ever made buzzed around the inside of her head, sapping what little energy that remained. Was this the curse of a Culdè, adrift and without purpose?

"How long has it been Milli? A month since we arrived? Two?" Milli cocked her head. "Somewhere in between I should say. Six weeks of the Republican army. It's time we went home..."

Kyira peered around as the words trailed off, as though the commander might pop out of appear at a street corner with promises of a better life and victory against the Bohr. She might have stayed for him —Fiskal was an impressive man, but one unlikely to change, even for her. Kyira of Nord was a pragmatist, and she needed someone who would fight back when she needed to be fought.

Worse though was that Fiskal was lying about knowing Darc, which meant they were working together for some reason. But why? To trick Kyira into joining another army? The alternative was that Fiskal didn't know Darc, because he couldn't see him—Kyira just conjured the man out of her own mind.

Neither option presented her with much hope, and so here she was, once more running away from her life. A tern returning home with a bellyful of mudworms.

As the beach flats disappeared around the corner of the first street, she gave her pack and map tube a tap, then touched the knife at her belt. "A blade can decide your fortunes. That's what Iqaluk always said Milli. Well, this blade has done nothing for me so far."

Her sandals made short work of the already busy streets, and soon they were standing at the main junction where she had first met that other treacherous liar, Darc. Kyira crossed the street to the alcove where the family had been sitting the day Darc had entered her world. It looked like any other, empty and unlived in. There was no rug, no washing line, no children, and it was cleaner than it had been. She struggled with the meaning of it all, knowing that truth lay mere paces away, yet she couldn't see it no matter how hard she looked. Darc was an enigma, but there was something so familiar about him.

She dragged herself away from the despair of it all and looked on down the main road to the city gates. This was the right thing to do—she'd made up her mind.

"Are you ready, girl?"

Milli ignored her; she was watching the swallows dip and dive through the first rays of the rising sun.

A wisp of wind touched Kyira's neck and she jerked around, her blade was in her hand. Milli blinked at her confused but alert, which cooled Kyira's blood, but the unease remained. Stepping back into an alcove, Kyira studied the passersby from the shadows. Workers, mothers, fathers, all living their lives, earning, working, dying. Through the throng, her eyes locked with another. The colours of him were all wrong, dark hair, pale skin—

"Akosh!"

"Kyira." The words rang in her head as though he were standing at her side.

She tried to maintain some sense of self, but it was impossible when her heart was hammering so hard. "Why are you here?"

Akosh stood amongst the crowd across the road. He shouldn't have heard her, but his rasping voice echoed in Kyira's mind. *"To fight. Of course."*

There was a blur, and a shadow burst into the alcove. Akosh abruptly stood in front of her, holding her knife. "Nice blade," he said. "A god-killer if ever I saw one, stained red with ichor."

Kyira tried to step back but found herself frozen. She tried to speak, but her lips wouldn't move. Akosh smiled. "You're wondering what's happening." Gently he placed a thumb on Kyira's chin and moved her head. The street outside the alcove was frozen in time. A swallow hung in the air just beyond, its wingbeats so slow. "When you can move as fast as I can, you control *everything*." He blinked at her in normal speed, unaffected. "And everyone."

Kyira's mind seemed to be working, but the words wouldn't form fast enough.

"Save your energy," said Akosh. "You'll be needing as much as you can spare soon enough." He stroked her chin. "So, *you* are Kyira. And here I was thinking, I have to meet this *one* who brought such chaos to the world! This *one* who killed the Great Father and to whom Fiskal so dotes upon. Imagine then, my surprise to find the same Sami girl who I let off in that ruined little town."

"Kamsin." Kyira tried to snarl.

"Kamsin. Broken teeth is all I remember." Akosh bent and whispered in her ear. "What a wonderful crossing of paths though. Who would have thought we'd meet again. I mean, really. The Great Father was practically invincible here in the Common Realm. Jagar, leader of all Banèmen. I don't mind telling you dear Sami, that it was rumoured that not even the gods themselves could harm Jagar in his prime, until you, Kyira, and you managed far more than a simple cut. You killed the greatest Banèman who ever lived, and that, my dear, makes you very special!" Akosh jumped back gleefully. "Now, Kyira, let me enlighten you. You've been wondering why the wonderful human city of Bakla has been creeping under your skin like insects burrowing. Well, girl, there is a doorway here. A hole in reality. Right here somewhere in Bakla. There will be more too as the Common Realm's death draws ever closer." Akosh turned towards the entrance and extended his hand to the frozen swallow. “The ability to move anywhere in Rengas, from one side to another, in the blink of a swallow’s eye.” He drew the tiny bird into his fist, slowly crushing its wings and body. When he released it, the bloodied mess hung suspended in the air. “Speed is power, but if you control the doorways, you control Rengas. It remains an unfortunate allegiance. Fiskal knows about it too. I’m almost sure of it. He didn’t tell you, did he? He keeps things from people, does the commander. He always has an angle you are yet to see. Had the Great Father not been so specific, I would have tortured the location of the doorway out of him.” His expression grew dark. “You know, in the state you find yourself in, Kyira, I can do anything. Torture is much more fun when the body can’t just die. I could separate it limb from limb, one piece at a time, and you would feel everything in real time. It’s why your mind can witness me, Kyira, but the rest of you cannot.” Akosh leaned in, his hands slithering over Kyira’s body. “Of course, it’s not just about pain. There’s pleasure too. Pleasure you cannot even imagine, spread over cycles. I’ve lived a hundred lifetimes walking amongst the spaces of time, and you could join me as my Queen between time.”

Kyira released a string of curses, each a blob of sound that made no sense.

Akosh shook his head. “Fiskal is afraid of you, you know? I can see why. What the commander doesn’t know, is that you, Kyira, are much, much more than you seem. I can smell it on you.” He leaned in again, turning his head to the side so they were cheek to cheek, staring out into the street. “We are two swallows, you and I, chasing each other in the day’s first light. We would make a formidable team.”

Kyira tried to speak again, grinding her teeth, pushing against his power, but still her body would not obey her commands.

“No?” Akosh stepped back. “Fine.” He moved Kyira’s head so she was looking down. Milli was frozen mid-snarl, the whites of her teeth bared.

Akosh squatted down at Milli’s side. Kyira’s heart should have hammered, but she existed between heartbeats. There was nothing she could do as Akosh ran Kyira’s blade over Milli’s snout.

Kyira tried to move, to fight and to kill this inhuman, vile being. But she was bound by Akosh, even if her mind was free to think. Akosh dragged the knife tip scraping over Milli's fur, leaving peculiar patterns that quivered against time. He turned to look up at Kyira as he did. The sinews and ligaments in Akosh's pale hand tightened, as the muscles readied their response, he blinked, his eyes closing as he began the action, his monstruous mind instructing his hand to stab, the blade would enter Milli's body and there was nothing the poor animal could do about it.

She was helpless.

Another blink came, but it was slow, and like a candle bursting into existence, the structure, reason, and power all aligned. Kyira understood! She could see it all, laid out before her.

"Wait."

Akosh scoffed, and stood upright. "Kyira? My dear? Was that you?"

"Wait."

Akosh smiled widely. "Soulfire? You see, Sami. You *are* more like me than them." He held up Kyira's knife and let go, and it held there, bound once more by the frozen timeline of the world. If Akosh's touch was enough to control time then just maybe Kyira could use that to her advantage. She looked inward, deeper, beyond the darkness of her mind. The portal that had told her to let go, the shining flame that Kyira denied in the city of Tyr. It was still there. Waiting.

She reached out.

The broken swallow began to fall, and the air moved over Kyira's skin once more.

Breathe.

Her heart caught up. Akosh looked confused, but Kyira was ready. She snatched the blade from the air as it started to fall and lunged, not directly at the Banèman but to the side, between him and the stone archway.

Akosh's form blurred, but the echo of the Banèman's power still lingered in Kyira's mind, and she used it as he did, the fire inside amplifying her movements, pushing her muscles to move faster than they had ever moved before. She locked her arm and strengthened her stance, for the briefest of moments moving as fast as even the great Akosh could.

Akosh's eyes rolled towards the exit onto the street, then the

Banèman reeled, not expecting to see Kyira's blade in the way. The blur around him increased as Kyira's power waned, then he struck her, and there was no mistaking that familiar sensation of meat on steel.

72

THE BELLS OF BAKLA

Kyira was sent spinning to the floor. Dust and sand and stone scraping against her skin. Then she collided painfully with the archway, but when she looked up, but both Banèman and Milli were gone.

"Akosh!" she roared into the street. "You coward! Come back!"

"Kyira."

"Where are you?" She scanned the faces on the street, grabbing at anyone with dark hair. A woman turned and shouted something but the words were—

"There are not many who could wound me." Akosh's word echoed once more in Kyira's mind. *"So, I leave you with a gift. And a choice. Leave now, and I shall return your friend."*

Kyira looked inward—the fire was easier to see this time—and she replied also through her mind. *"You are afraid, Akosh."*

Laughter filled Kyira's head. *"So, that is your choice? Well, the Kresh'ae Bohr are about to engage Fiskal's Republican army upon the beach. Come join us. You never know, Kyira, perhaps you will bag yourself another Banèman."*

Even as the words were reclaimed by Kyira's panicked imagination, the bells of Bakla started to ring. The roads emptied as the throngs of people disappeared into the heart of Bakla, running home, protecting their loved ones...

"Milli!"

Her eyes filled with tears. Milli was a kind soul who didn't deserve to be cheated by a stain like Akosh! Rage took hold of her and she screamed as loudly as she could, but there was no one to comfort her.

A stinging in her hand drew gaze down. Her blade, her father's blade was broken. She found the pieces, ignoring the dark red staining the metal and dropped them in her pack. She stashed the pack and her map tube in the rear of the alcove, and she put her hair up in a bun.

"Milli, my love. I'm coming."

The streets tore by as Kyira sped back through Bakla towards the beach flats. Panic had wrapped its cold hands upon the people of Bakla, and the bells rang bold and shrill, urging its people, fight and protect all you have!

Kyira was filled with a raw purpose that she had never known. She would fight, and she would kill every single Banèmen that had ever walked upon the Ringland!

A gang of children were screaming as she passed by a Domst. A Bohr stood in the middle of the lane, surrounded by people, each of them had sharp things, spears, forks, axes, none of which were meant for fighting, and yet every one of those tools found a mark, poking holes in the giant creature. It side-swiped, knocking over half of the crowd, but the effort had thrown it sideways and the Baklinians jumped on, climbing it like a tree. Kyira almost felt pity as those tools cut it down.

She sped on through the streets until the tufts of long grass that marked the dunes appeared. Behind them, dark columns of smoke billowed, rising high as tar burned. Stone gave way to sand and the beach flats of Bakla opened out before Kyira as a field of death.

Knots of Republican soldiers scuttled between fights, unfocused and unsure, each knot of fighting centred around a single Bohr, but there were dozens upon the beach flats, standing amongst the sea of soldiers as great towers, dragging their huge clubs, forks and blades through the clamouring Republicans. There was no order, no direction and no force. The Republican army was a hammer without a handle.

Sickness rolled over Kyira. She staggered forwards and her knees wobbled sending her to the sand. Struggling, she held the contents of her stomach down. What was it? Something was draining her strength! She looked inward once more, but the fire was out.

Breathe.

Left foot.

Breathe.

Right foot.

Her steps became faster, the long dunes disappearing from her peripherals.

Breathe.

The Bohr of Kresh'ae were merciless. Broad, bulging and heaving, they bludgeoned their way through the human fighters, cracking skulls and bones and leaving piles of wounded about the reddening sand.

Kyira grabbed the closest soldier from the knot of soldiers in front —a man in his thirtieth with a fresh laceration that led from his ear and down the back of his steel armour. He spun, murder in his eyes.

"Join them!" Kyira pointed to another bigger knot further down the beach. "Cluster together, otherwise they—"

The soldier spun away, pushing forwards. Kyira grabbed his topknot and yanked him back by the head, almost sending him to the dirt. This time his spear followed, but Kyira was ready and knocked it away.

"What?! You're stupid, girl!"

Kyira slapped the soldier's face, drawing a fearsome noise that drew attention from the back of the knot. "You cannot win here," she roared. "Join the other knot! Cluster the forces!"

The soldier's eyes flicked back and forward between the knots then he nodded, understanding the advantage. "Come on! She's right."

Two more soldiers stepped out of the knot, making the same leaps as the first. They grabbed two more each, and word trickled into the knot. Soon, the group of soldiers were pulling away from the huge Bohr at the centre of the fight and joining the other knot. The Bohr left standing blinked at Kyira. It was a pale thing, covered in blue spots and patches of fur, but it was tall, like something between a horse and a goat standing. She stared back at it, and reached for her belt blade—the only sharp thing she had. Her blood ran cold.

"A blade can decide your fortunes." She held her fists out in front of her, unsure of what else to do, but the Bohr's lazy gaze rolled away from her like a drunkard deciding on which way to stagger home. Something caught his attention and he roared and charged forward. Kyira leapt sideways, rolling it off and jumping back to her feet, fists ready, but the Bohr was running towards another knot further down the beach.

A cheer rose up from behind as near fifty men and women hacked the downed Kresh'ae Bohr to pieces. Scattered soldiers who had been sprinting around the beach made for the knot, arms and weapons raised as if the battle was already won.

"Move on!" shouted Kyira. "Move on and get to the next one! Send them to hell!" The Republicans roared in answer, notched, bloody blades dripping over steel helmets. Kyira had only to point after the Bohr and every single man and woman charged after it.

Kyira ran after them, heart beating, legs burning, mustering the smaller groups and coordinating them to the bigger knots. Word moved quickly, as the smaller knots became bigger—the Bohr didn't think to fight together. Maybe they were too tribalistic, or maybe Forbringrs were with them.

"The Kresh'ae are being controlled!" She snarled again. "It's Akosh. It has to be him."

Kyira scooped up an abandoned sword and shield near a broken corpse and slammed into a small knot of fighters. A woman turned to meet her, front teeth missing and dried blood on her chin. Kyira growled at her, throwing her towards the bigger knot. The woman nodded, understanding much faster than her male counterpart had. She took half the knot with her, and soon this Bohr was left standing alone as the Republicans abandoned it to join their fellows.

Kyira stared back at a white-eyed Bohr. It was more feminine, but with the same sling of fabric and netted steel armour as the rest. In its hand was a sword as wide as Kyira's own hips, but this one stood dumbly, the blade and its odd-shaped square tip sinking into the sand. Kyira waited for the charge but the thing just stood there. A quick look around told her the knots were all distant now. She had run the length of the beach, standing near the dunes where Fiskal had taken her.

Drawing a ragged breath, she stepped forward, banging the shield with the shortsword, but the Bohr didn't react. Another step, and another, until she stood at the creature's feet. Drool dripped from its mouth, running down its scaly neck. Its yellow face had a slight snout, so it was more animal than human, but everything else was human-like, just exaggerated, as though a child had been asked to draw its nightmares.

Her sword hand twitched as she listened to its body, a stomach gurgling, a great barrel chest breathing, then she was reaching out, touching the Bohr's solid thigh. A pulse thumped through, deep and steady.

Once, back in Nord, she'd had to put down a broken mare after the birth of its foal had gone wrong, and Kyira, barely eight, had been tasked by her father with ending her pain. The mare's breathing was deep and long to begin with but became shallower as the hours wore on. It held on until dawn the next morning. She had sworn on that day she would never leave an animal in such pain again.

Kyira raised her sword and placed it beneath the Bohr's chin. "I'm sorry."

"You can't help her." Akosh's paper tearing voice was hot in her ear.

She spun, but her sword met nothing but air.

"Fight me, you coward!"

A breeze blew past her, then bright pain as a cut opened up on the back of her neck. "Ah!"

His voice sounded from behind the dumb Bohr, his dark jacket and pale skin flashing for a moment between the Bohr's legs. "A graze, but my blade can go deeper." Another breeze, and he was at her ear again. "You look resolute, Kyira," he whispered. "A fine quality in a soldier."

Kyira lowered her sword. "Where is she, you coward? Where's Milli?"

Akosh appeared in front of her, edges blurring. "She's safe, for now."

"If you've hurt her..."

"I never understood this human *need* for animal companions. Dumb creatures who just...follow you around." Akosh winked knowingly at her, then winced as the red wound on his face opened. The

Bohr standing over Kyira staggered then caught itself, staring dumbly at its own feet, white eyes drooping.

"What have you done to them?"

Akosh flashed his teeth, his gums as colourless as the rest of him. "I tell them things. They listen. You forget that the Bohr are as simple as humans."

"We are not all so simple." She drew a line across her cheek with her finger.

Akosh's forced a smile. "You are an enigma, dear Sami." He began to pace. "You say one thing, but your mind seems to think another. It's true I cannot tell what it is you think, but I know when there is a difference. A hundred lifetimes upon the soil of Rengas have taught me many things about your *kind*."

Kyira lunged, but her sword hit nothing, and she fell to the sand.

"Missed," came a whisper in her ear. Akosh kicked the back of her and Kyira was back in the sand.

She pulled herself up and more bright pain at the ankle. "Argh!"

"You cannot win against me, Kyira." Akosh sauntered out from behind the Bohr, holding his knife under his nose. "But I admire your tenacity. Although I'll admit I never really understood it." He tongued the blood on the metal, savouring it.

Kyira lifted herself up, the knees of her breeches damp. There was a slice through her leather moccasins. Death by a thousand cuts. "Perseverance is for—" She threw the sword forward—a lunge that should have skewered Akosh through the upper chest, but this time she kept back some effort and pivoted, throwing the weight of the weapon over her head. The sword sailed past her left arm and caught something behind her. She spun to meet it.

Akosh stood a few paces back, his fingers running along the edges of a fresh cut in his white shirt. "Twice!" he snapped. There was no smile any more, just anger. "Kudos to you." His eyes went white, swirling with a whirlpool of purples and blacks and the Bohr turned mechanically towards Kyira, raising its blade high.

Kyira did the only thing she could and raised her own sword. The Bohr's wide blade smashed the little shortsword to pieces sending Kyira spinning sideways. Sand filled her mouth. She tried to roll but a deep ache in her arm pulled a scream from her guts. "Argh!" Backing away, she held the shield in front of her, glancing down at her ruined arm.

"Bones," said Akosh, smugly. "They're only really useful until they're not. Am I right?" The Banèman's eyes went white again and the Bohr advanced. Kyira shuffled away, but nausea quickly overtook her senses. The world spun as the pain in her limp arm spread up her shoulder. The shield weighed a ton weight, the sand held gave no purchase, the Bohr lifted that blade again...

A new sensation filled Kyira's head, separating her from her body. Every fibre of her remembered it, and while Fiskal wasn't here this time, the same familiar sickness washed over her as it did before.

Fire.

Panic.

Breathe.

Eyes open.

Awake.

Blue light stole the world from her.

It was happening again.

The doorways were an abomination. Even so, Akosh couldn't look away as the Common Realm tore in front of him. Even to his experienced eye, the shape of it seemed a paradox of geometry; spherical, existing on all three dimensions, but also flat, and he couldn't focus on its boundaries.

His hesitance and deliberation was why the Kresh'ae Bohr was so punished. As luck would have it, the air had split right where the Bohr had been standing, mangling its body and slicing it in two through the middle. Hilariously, there was no time for even the Bohr's remains to fall before they were sucked away into the dark hole.

The Sami girl was lying dumbstruck in the sand twenty paces from the doorway. Akosh squinted, then gasped in horror. "No! It can't be!" Her eyes were white. She was in control. She was doing this! "NO!"

Kyira struggled with the forces, trying to understand what was happening inside her. The stark memory of Tyr was as bright and fresh as if it happened yesterday, but this portal upon the beach of Bakla was very different. This was a hole that led to nowhere. She knew it because she could *feel* it. The darkness inside pulsed eagerly, waiting to consume her. Her fingers caressed the air before it, like a firesnake tasting the air with its tongue. Somewhere an echo of pain registered, but transfixed, she walked towards the portal, feeling every pulse, bringing it line with her own heartbeat.

Breathe.

Breathe. The portal breathed with her, as she knew it would.

Breathe.

Breathe.

Akosh stood nearby, backing away. Kicking up sand. Falling backwards. From the side the portal was disk-shaped, if it could be said to have any shape at all, so Kyira willed it to rotate, using her hands to suggest the direction, and the portal turned towards the Banèman. Akosh backed away, and Kyira drank in that fearful expression; the thin lips, those dead, dark eyes, the long hair whipping around. His power began to pull away from him as a black wind, sucked inside. Kyira pushed forward, palms out, and the portal moved with her, melting the sand beneath into glass.

Akosh did not run because he couldn't. Kyira knew the portal was holding him, drawing away his power like iron filings to a lodestone. The black wind deepened in colour as the portal moved closer, and Akosh let out an inhumane wail as the two met. His fate was magnified as through glass as slowly, from the feet up, the portal consumed Akosh. Deep red burst from his mouth and left his pale contorted face as droplets, drawn inside, and as it reached his chest, the motion slowed, whether by itself or from some sick pleasure derived from the depths of Kyira's mind, requesting it so. She savoured Akosh's last moments as it sucked his vile presence away into nothingness.

Breathe.

Kyira brought her hands together, but the portal shook. Denying her.

"Close," she commanded. "Close now."

The portal denied her again, and rotated, swinging towards her. Kyira gazed into the blackness. Having witnessed Akosh's death she should have been petrified as her path finally came to an end, but instead there was calm. The surface was smooth and cool, yet warming —a contradiction of existence. A hole that stood out as an object, a thing she could interact with and move. The darkness within was absolute, it had taken Akosh, but it had not Kyira's doing. As Akosh had directed the Bohr, Kyira had directed the portal. But she was no Banèman!

Dots of light appeared in the dark beyond the iridescent surface. Something was moving inside. Was it Akosh? Was he really dead?

The dots of light moved as one, a single line snaking this way and that, the closest growing bigger with every heartbeat. The first few lights blinked out, then, as she watched, some of the snake's body began to dither and wane.

Breathe.

Breathe.

Kyira reached out, drawing the lights towards her. She didn't know what she was doing, but the connection was so deep, it had to happen, because that was why it was here. It was why she stood upon the beach of Bakla at this moment instead of a road in the middle of Kemen, or a sister of Nord. The paths of her journey were a line that all led here.

Breathe.

Breathe.

The lights flickered. They were reflections from somewhere else, and they turned from white to red as they came closer, flocking towards her through the nothing, their bloodlight filling and replacing the darkness. Sound followed, screams, heartbeats, fast and panicking, like her own. The pulsing quickened, contracted, and Kyira backed away. She'd seen such contractions before, before the birth of the foal from the mare, from the mother Lyla as her daughter, Abika, entered this world, and now here one world gave birth to another. The reflection resolved into shapes. Bloodlight upon steel. Swords, helmets and shields. Silver buckles, matte leather, and the shapes of soldiers. Their forms filling the space inside.

Kyira backed away, as Akosh had done. Pushing the sand away with her feet, scrabbling backwards as the first soldier emerged, passing through the portal. He fell to the sand, as awkward and fumbling as a new fawn, looking around with misty eyes. Kyira stumbled up and ran as fast as she could.

73

LET US TAKE BACK ONCE MORE WHAT WAS OURS

The sand felt good. Like home. There was something about the grains in the province of Bakla that were finer. V'olpar couldn't say why it was, nor did he really care, but it was at least clear that his faculties were slowly returning after the violent trip through the doorway. The feeling of home and familiarity was so welcome that he had to stop himself from lying down and rubbing his neck glands on the beach.

It smelled different though. Like humans. Like rotting seaweed and decay. And meat.

The doorway had pulverised the body of some Bohr, so the sand of his homeland was already red with blood! "It is a sign!"V'olpar knelt down at her side and pulled up handful of hair. "May you learn in the afterlife what you could not here. Blessed be your shadow."

He cast his eyes about, breathing the salt air deeply. The horizon was far, and the beach flat. It would make a good killing ground. In the distance a human woman sprinted away from them, no doubt terrified at the army that had emerged seemingly from thin air.

The Rider and the Ruffin appeared in the doorway next, behind the stream of King's soldiers milling through from Zunqai. The edges of the doorway growing to accommodate Rider and beast.

V'olpar stepped aside to give them room. "The Queen really has outdone herself."

The Rider growled in acquiescence, and the Ruffin snarled. "You were right, my King. The doorways have been opened."

V'olpar shook his head. "They were always open. But now we can control them."

More soldiers were stepping through the transparent skin of the doorway. The big human, Kavik, stumbled out and promptly emptied his stomach. "How many did we lose during passage?"

"Half," hissed the Rider. "They were weak."

V'olpar closed his eyes in annoyance. "Where did they go?"

The Rider's pointed teeth flashed beneath his battered helmet. "Lost."

"Three ton of men?"

"We are left with only the strongest of them, my King," said the Rider, "and we will still take Bakla! Will you fight, my King?"

V'olpar growled. "No. I will not leave this doorway. It is ours." He had hoped this would have been easier. The lines of humans in the distance were already arranging themselves into ranks along the beach. Their numbers comparable to the King's. "Hopefully our brothers and sisters from Kresh'ae have not softened our prey too much..." He turned away at the last, trailing off. It wouldn't do well for the new King's first engagement to be a failure. "Sort them, Rider. We are here and these humans will feel our wrath. Let us take back once more what was ours!"

74

ASCENDANCE

"Soulfire has nothing to do with soul." The girl looked confused. "Look, it's really very simple."

"It doesn't sound simple."

Frustration filled Jagar like water to a jug. He leaned against a rock, head in hands and ignoring the rolling waves smashing against the floating pumice. "You don't need to know why it's named so. I have been using Soulfire for a thousand of your lifetimes and I've never asked that question."

"Then you are a fool."

For the hundredth time, Jagar wished he had the strength in the Common Realm to teach her a lesson. A real lesson...He took a step forward and his foot flashed, the leather shoes on his feet changing colour. Taking a moment to remaster his form, he began to talk. "Let me tell you a story." The girl rolled her eyes. She really was a viper, this one. "Have you heard of a stallo?"

The girl nodded. "A Forbringr?"

Jagar shook his head. "No. A stallo is not a god, a stallo is a celestial being. Legend says that they lived on separate land masses and were so powerful and strong they were able to pull the lands of Rengas into the Circle of the World we know today."

The girl was concocting a plan, Jagar knew it because that's what he would have done too. Besides, most of her questions had been set up to distract him.

"So," mused the girl, "this *stallo* used Soulfire?"

"I didn't say that. I said they were strong, girl. Strong. They used their great muscles to move the landmasses." Before the question could even come, he shot it down. "It's a legend, a story. The Bohr also believe they were formed from the first stallo. Ancestors of Forbringrs. Pulier's Pass? No?"

"You said they weren't any gods."

Jagar screwed his eyes shut. "The devil is in the detail, you're right. They were not gods, but the Bohr believe they were, because it helps inflate their egos. Imagine telling a story to your children, and your children's children of how you descended from the heavens."

"The Bohr tell night stories?"

"So I'm told." She was doing it again. "Do you want to know about the secrets of Soulfire or not?"

This time the girl stood, she turned towards the shard. "I know the secrets of Soulfire. I walked on air. Stood on it like it was rock, high above the sea."

"And that's how you intend to get home is it? Running across the sky?"

The girl gazed off into the middle distance, beyond the glowing shard. "Well, I did it once."

Jagar felt sympathy for her. Real sympathy, and while that was surprising, it also meant that something else was happening. He padded over to her, noting how the ground beneath his feet felt just that little more solid than when he entered this realm. "Abika, I admire you in many ways." He placed an arm around her, but she pushed him away.

"I don't need—"

"Yes, you do, girl. You need me. Soulfire is tricky to understand. It's not like learning how to stab someone or kill or maim. It's like learning how to breathe. Your body already knows what to do." He hated talking like this, like father to child, but he'd tried everything else. He'd tried candour, anger, even ignorance. A trinity of ways to manipulate this horrid creature, but it was only when he started preaching like a father that her attention flickered to life like an oil lamp igniting. He was the Great Father after all. "This is why I talk of stallos and of gods. They are the *creators*. Soulfire started there and is a necessary component of life, like how fire comes to being when the smoke is thick and fast, combustion, spark and flame. Heat, power and glory."

Abika had let the man talk—he did so like to talk—but now he was waiting for some answer. The shard necklace in her pocket had been steadily growing warmer as she trickled Soulfire drop by drop into it. At first, when she had been bored by the stranger's unceasing monologues, she had just rubbed the shard necklace. It had given her a strange feeling in her fingertips, and she had felt the urge to do something with it. Channelling Soulfire meant closing her eyes, but that was easy when you were being bored to death. Perhaps he was a god, descended from the heavens, or banished by Baeivi. Either way she knew that he was dangerous.

She pulled something deep and meaningful sounding from her head, open-ended and vague enough to keep him going. "I guess that I just want to go home. I miss the familiarity of life."

Home. Jagar had been thinking of home more and more. He'd been here in so many ways and forms now that he could have called it home. Baeivi, the Great Mother herself was, of course, nowhere to be seen, and chaos had reigned in her absence. The souls of lives, left unchecked, flew freely between realities, energy transferring between realms as cosmic dust, and while it was the most beautiful scene to behold, it was not what interested Jagar as his soul lingered on the fringes of the ether. Holes, as black as night, stood amongst the chaos of energy and multi-coloured clouds. Negative space was easy to spot because life did nothing but move. Everything alive, all the way down to the elemental particles of life, was always moving, jumping from here to there, but these holes were as still as pins on a pinboard, while the papers flapped about in the wind. If Soulfire was elemental, these holes were the pillars of all existence. The underpinned structure of it all. The souls of men and women emerged from the edges of those holes only to disappear inside.

Perhaps it was because his identity was being stolen from him, that Baeivi had tried to pulverise him into soul dust. He was just about to talk more on the matter, when he felt the first souls enter the doorway.

The stranger floated there quietly, eyelids quivering. Abika had seen his flashing clothes, like he were a dreamlike apparition she'd conjured, but as she watched the man became more and more real. He was being infused with something new and dangerous.

Abika took the glowing shard from her pocket, ready to let the Soulfire out. First, she would set it upon him, then she would bring down the shard mountain standing tall above.

There was nothing that could have prepared Jagar for the elation as the barriers between realities opened up before him, not lines or borders, but ethereal planes of existence, more like clouds of nebulae forming and unforming, coalescing and breaking apart in infinite regress. His great plan was finally coming to fruition, as the souls of the damned piled on through the doorway. He couldn't tell which doorway and nor, at this particular moment, did he care, so wonderful the feeling was. It started as a trickle, as so many things did, but soon the new souls of those lost between realms imbued and fed him. It was an important event, because it had never happened before, not in a million lifetimes, but also because it signified one very important fact. Kaliste had betrayed him. At best, she thought she had done it of her own accord.

At worst, she wanted to hurt Jagar. Either way he had to thank her for playing her part so well.

His eyes closed in eternal ecstasy, and Jagar's mind retreated into the realm of the Great Father searching the ethereal plains for Kaliste's form, sniffing her out. Souls of Banèmen looked different to the souls of humans and Bohr. It wasn't so much how they looked, sounded, tasted or any other dull human sense, but rather a combination of all five The first time he'd contacted Kaliste through the ether she'd shunned him, refusing his connection, but that was when she was corporeal. Now that she had passed into the realm of the Great Father, she would be floating about through the clouds and mists with no impunity. All he had to do was summon her. He took a moment to admire the holes, visible now in every realm, be it here in the realm of the Great Father, the Common Realm or Ae'thria—they were everywhere, and they were beautiful.

He drew his great hands across the spiralling arms and their sparkling points and drew her in like a fish to a net. The ether reacted to his presence, souls rushing towards him like flies, buzzing around in the hope he might grant them permission to go back. They wouldn't thank him for it, if he did, but then they were the new souls, still expectant and in denial.

One such soul stood out from the rest, iridescent yet almost solid. He drew it forwards.

Kaliste. You betrayed me.

Kaliste's soul drifted closer, the clouds coming together in form so that they mimicked the features of her now long-gone face. Her eyes screwed together as she tried to focus.

"I...I betrayed you."

You changed the doorways.

"Forgive me."

You sent my army though the doorway, didn't you? You disobeyed me.

"Forgive me."

I forgive you.

The cloud of dust took on an expression of surprise. *"You forgive me?"*

I forgive you, Kaliste. You played a part in a much larger game, and you played it perfectly. I don't care about the humans. I don't care about the forces of men and whereupon their lives lie on the maps of Rengas. I don't care even that you changed the doorways so that you could betray me. Because Kaliste, it was my hope you would do these things. It was my hope that you would ignore my word and stand against me. I fought the Great Mother and beat her. Trapped her for the rest of time. I became the Great Father in her stead. But I wished to escape the shackles of her making and live corporeally in any realm or reality I chose. But to do that I needed you. Watch.

The cloud of dust that was the remnants of Kaliste's withered soul rotated around at Jagar's will. The holes were consuming everything now. Their blackness bloating as they filled with the matter.

"What is happening?"

You see, Kaliste. I needed new souls to enter the doorways, but their placement across our world was not one where they would encounter many people. Some doorways were underwater, some were hidden in the jungles of Sulitaria, high above the ground. One stood inside a great mountain of Nord. But, lo! You came along and changed the doorways, against my wishes in the hope you could protect the legacy of our forebears. And as noble a proposition as that was, it was by design. You did it because you think you are better than me, Kaliste. You always have. Jagar relished this. The monologue. The final act. It filled him with immense joy as he circled around to watch Kaliste becoming aware that everything she had done was part of his plan. What was the point in planning so much, to such a degree, only for it to go unnoticed? The final act had to be liberated, it had to be observed. He gestured back towards two black holes as they expanded and merged together, sucking in souls from all around, humans, Bohr and all else.

You see, like Baeivi, I'm also trapped. I can leave only to inhabit the form of another for a short time, animals are easier, but less useful. But humans? Surprisingly they strike the balance of autonomy and energy, and I could spend almost a half day wandering around pretending to be human. Imagine it!

"I'm proud of you."

Jagar bathed in Kaliste's approval, soaking it in like warm rays of sunlight. *Every time someone passes through a doorway, they leave a piece of themselves behind. Some don't make it through at all, they get lost in the nothing between places. It is they who give the greatest gift of all.*

Kaliste smiled. "*You truly are the Great Father. Let me help you.*"

And there it was. Self-preservation. Jagar swallowed the distaste down. *No, Kaliste. Your part in this is done. Your role is complete.*

Jagar extended his hands and willed Kaliste forward into the influence of the now massive black hole gaping before them. The dust began to spin as the impression of Kaliste's form twisted and contorted. He watched and relished as she screamed at him, first in anger, then fear at what awaited her immortal soul. She would feed him well.

I will cleanse this realm, Kaliste, as I will cleanse all of Rengas! When I am finished the doorways will have exterminated not only human life, but Bohr too. Banèmen and all. And when every being, dead and undead, have passed through a doorway and are lost to the nothing inside, I will recreate the world. I will be as the Stallo and as the Great Mother, a creator. A God!

The black hole's influence tore at the substance of what remained of Queen Kaliste...

As Kaliste tumbled towards oblivion she was content. The Great Father had done what she expected, but in doing so, he had unknowingly given the seed of a Queen and King a fighting chance. Her line would not only continue, it would reshape the realms. The ways of those who shape the worlds, shape... us...all...

The effect was immediate. The great, glowing blue shard upon the island in the centre of the Middle Sea filled Jagar's vision, but the confusion that came when moving between realms was gone. That was the first sign. This was as clean a transition as he'd ever had. The girl still stood in front of him, a dagger of blue glass in her hands.

He extended a hand, as he had done on the fringes of Baeivi's realm, and lifted the girl from the dirt, as he did, his own feet touched down. The ground was solid, but there was more. He could feel the grains of pumice, so clear and present beneath each foot. He knew the journey each grain had taken to be here, to witness his ascendance. He focused in on one of those grains, lifting it from the earth, rotating it above his palm. A planetoid of infinite possibility. Of infinite power and energy.

"What have you there?" he said, as content as he had ever been.

The girl writhed, trying to fight his influence. "Nothing."

"Oh, don't put yourself down, girl. Come now."

"You know what it is," she hissed.

"I do," said Jagar. "A blade. Wrought of Soulfire. A blade you no doubt forged from Freja's necklace."

"You know Freja?"

"I know everything."

The girl relaxed, and in doing so began to drift to the ground. "And Kyira?"

Jagar ground his teeth. His hands shook. He wanted to reach up and drag the lightning from the sky at the sound of her name! "You wish to exact vengeance don't you?"

The girl blinked, unsure. "My mother came to me in a dream and told me it was an accident." The girl fingered the tip of her new weapon.

Jagar's laughed. "The madness of dreams. Ask me, dear Abika. Ask me again what I know of Kyira, the Pathwatcher. The Sami girl from Nord. Daughter to Iqaluk. Ask me."

"What do you know of Kyira?"

"The Pathwatcher killed your family. I know, not because I am all-knowing, but because she told me so herself. She confessed to me that she is a murderer, and she had no remorse that I saw." The girl nodded meekly. "She killed me once." Jagar tapped his temple. "The wound here, it never healed." He fingered the scar. "Healing is no longer a problem for me now, but I shall keep *this* as a memento, a purpose of my own. And when once again mine and Kyira's paths cross, I shall remind her of the pain and suffering she caused me."

"What if she is innocent?"

"I have been with her, girl. I called myself Darc, and followed her for some time. Playing with her mind and her body. She is evil, girl and she chose to kill your family! She murdered them in cold blood." Jagar moved towards her, and embraced her. "Trust me and don't despair! Hold onto your anger as a life raft in turbulent seas. It will fill you with reason and purpose, and what greater purpose is there than bringing justice and balance to the world?" He stepped back so as not to frighten her. "My dear you are my God Soldier."

A roar filled the air. Jagar raised his arms as the Bohr leapt upwards from the shadow of some nearby rocks. To any other it might have looked like Vasta the Bohr was about to catch him off-guard, but Jagar had known where he was the whole time. He had brought him here, pulling at the Bohr's heart, drawing it closer to the sound of Abika with the promise of a meal.

Vasta hung in the air between them, jaws bloody and rabid and foaming like an angry wolf, but it was Abika's reaction to it all that fascinated Jagar. He couldn't read or control her as he could the Bohr. So when she stepped back away from Vasta, frozen in time and hovering above them, the Great Father, in all of his infinite power, could do nothing but watch.

"You are not my father," said Abika. She moved forwards to the Bohr, hovering in front of him. Slowly, but resolutely Abika pushed the blue blade into Vasta's side, without resistance. "You are a Bohr." Again she stabbed, this time in Vasta's back, severing the spinal column. "You brought me here and looked after me." Abika plunged the Soulfire blade up into the Bohr's stomach, walking around him as she spoke. "You made the mistake of trusting me." She paused now. "But I cannot be trusted." The blade entered the Bohr's neck, and the spell broke. The Bohr dropped like a lump of lead to the ground and remained there.

Jagar cricked his neck. "There are not many who surprise me, Abika. Not many when I was a Banèman, and even fewer now that I am a God." He lifted her once more from the ground, but this time he used her own Soulfire to do it. He gave her control of her own destiny. "I can tell you where Kyira is, if you like. But you have to make me a promise. For I do not give, without being given. You must promise me, that when you are finished with her, and you must make her death last a long, long time, that you will come back to me. You will stand by my side, and I will give you more than you ever could dream. I will give you more than anything this realm can offer. The Common Realm, Ae'thria, The realm of the Great Father, they could all be yours to use as you wish. Worlds within worlds, dimensions living in the folds of space so intricate your human mind could never comprehend."

Abika's smile widened with each word, her physical expression the only indicator that Jagar had. Even her heartbeat was masked to him. If he had closed his eyes, he wouldn't have known she was there. She was an enigma of time, matter and energy. The remainder of an unbalanced equation, readily ignored and as equally inconsequential.

"I promise," she said, flatly. She had not a hint of remorse as the Bohr's blood dripped from her murderous hands.

Jagar breathed deeply, then he drew upon the great shard, the mountain of glass standing in the island's centre. This by-product of an old portal still, ironically, contained enough frozen Soulfire that it could melt an island, or boil a sea. To Jagar, though, it was as easy as lifting a hand. He pulled the Soulfire away from the shard, and it came to him, leaving the mountain of glass as a wind of blue and green, drifting like the waves of the aurora towards him. As the first rays of it touched his fingertips, he let it run through him, passing through his arm, along his radius and ulna, down his humerus to his heart, and through his chest and lungs to the other side. The grain of sand lying on his palm vibrated and thrummed as the power filled the atoms therein. The great shard flashed and winked out as the last of its frozen Soulfire was taken, then shattered. Jagar closed his fist and the great shard held together, millions of pieces ready to fall upon his will.

Abika held her hands over her head. "No!"

"Don't panic, girl. You still have a few moments yet."

The grain in Jagar's hand glowed blue, giving off a pleasant and cool light. It had begun its life in the heart of a volcano, eons ago. Before life had walked. It had clumped together with some others, unaware of its existence, until it was shot out to land upon the seabed of a flooding plain. Weathered by the sun and rain and sea, it shrunk from boulder to rock, and rock to stone, until finally when the portal under this island closed and the seabed was raised up, it held on to be here, now. Now, other than the Great Father himself, it was likely the most powerful single object in existence. A jewel of power, shining. Jagar allowed the grain to take on any form it liked, and the matter and great energy within reformed itself into a red crystal. A ruby, the size of his thumb.

He padded over to Abika. "Here. This is for you. My guess is that one day you will not need the power held within it, but for now..."

Abika brought the hilt of her wrought knife to the ruby and they snapped together like lodestones. The light of that blade became purple and strong. Jagar could *feel* the blade through space and time. It existed as a token of power, a thing he could track on a girl he could not.

"For now though, I think you know what to do."

Abika nodded. She cut downwards through the air, frowning when nothing happened. "It doesn't work."

"You must cut with your mind, girl."

Vasta's body lay still in front of Abika, a monument to her destruction. She studied the purple knife. It was most beautiful thing she had ever seen. She could feel the life surging through it, and by the looks of expectation upon the stranger's face he expected her to use it.

Closing her eyes, she let her body relax. There were no threats anymore. She was free to do as she willed, and so she did. The face of the daemon woman from Rothmarr's boat appeared in her mind. Vasta had said she was an empty shell, but Abika knew different. She would make her own choices now. All of her life she had been pushed and pulled one way or another, and now it was happening again! She forced herself to relax, seeking a dark spot within, a place for her and her alone.

The first part was called the Flash, the second part was called the Thunder.

The Thunder would bring with it a force that would correct the Flash, returning equilibrium to the world, and Abika could feel it building. The air seemed electric, and tiny forks of light lifted off her skin, each one a pinprick of pain and pleasure. Then it was coming, hurtling towards her faster than the fastest horses. Abika imagined that force, the Thunder, held back, and sent it away. Sent it beyond everything she knew, beyond the island, beyond the Middle Sea and The Red Isles, beyond her home in Ipiti and the commune upon the lake, beyond the jail in the city of Ipor Dan and Vasta's shop, each place she had seen allowing her to push further. The Thunder blew away from her at a speed she couldn't fathom, land disappearing beneath it, oceans a blur, then blackness and stars, spheres of earth floating amongst a black canvas that seemed impossibly long and never ending, and then further still. Rengas was a just speck of dust upon a blanket of stars.

"Worlds within worlds," she said to herself.

Opening her eyes, she drew the blade down through the air and cut it as simply as slicing cloth. The slice curved in on itself, it was a hole floating on every dimension. The stranger stepped back, staring aghast from the dagger at her feet to the cut in the air. Beyond was a beach, long and flat, where thousands of men and women were fighting. Soldiers clad in black, wielding swords and shields and spears, cutting their way through the ranks of another army, while huge lizards with riders tore and hunted anything that moved.

"Kyira is down there, isn't she?" Abika already knew the answer.

"Move the doorway, girl. Find a place nearby."

Abika imagined herself as a bird, swooping over the battle, the scene below moving as the window above the two armies changed position. It gathered some speed as it rolled over the sea of fighting men until finally she found a spot near some dunes. If she was a bird, she would have set down, but the window sank into the ground, blackness filling half of the view.

"Matter does not matter," said the stranger.

"What?!"

"The portal does not see the ground as the final stopping point as you do. You may live upon it, but the window can travel freely through any matter. And so you have to guide it."

Abika imagined the window lifting, and painfully slow, the viewport began to rise too, inching back up from the smoking sand. The back lines of the army stood off in the distance.

"What now?"

"Now?" The stranger walked over to her once more. "Now, you walk through." Abika moved to step in through the window she had cut, but the stranger stopped her. "Wait. Use the blade on Kyira as you used it on Vasta. The edge will never dull, and anyone who it kills will find themselves drawn to me in the afterlife." Abika pulled away, but the stranger didn't let go. "Do it slowly. She deserves nothing less."

"What do I call you?"

The stranger grinned more widely than ever before. The maps on his skin moved, swimming over his skin, combining and splitting into new shapes while others sank below. "I go by many names, some more permanent than others. But you can call me *father*."

"Then thank you, father." Abika turned and stepped in through the window and onto the sandy beach of Bakla.

75

BLOOD, SAND AND RUIN

Blood, sand and ruin reigned. There was nowhere to stand, let alone direct upon the beach, shuffling shoulders and the weight of hundreds of bodies pressed in from all sides as frenzied fighting ensued.

Kyira had no idea even if she was going in the right direction, or simply awaiting her turn to die. The knots of fighters had mostly combined, into long lines of attackers, but Fiskal was still nowhere to be seen—chaos was Kyira's only partner in this.

She thrust her sword out towards the left side and screamed. "STOP THE SIDES FROM ADVANCING!" Some of the nearby soldiers shuffled managed to shuffle left, but the orders were lost in the cacophony as the maelstrom of bustling bodies awaited their turn to fight. The King's army's painted faces gave them a haunting appearance, and they moved with the same practised motions, like they were controlled by a single mind. Akosh might be dead, but was there another Banèman on the killing field? Kyira needed to get higher if she was going to make any headway.

There was an ancient boulder behind her, the only one for leagues, but before she could force her way through the lines a whistle blew hard and long. She turned, terrified and she felt the soldiers around her hold their breath.

The King's army had split down the middle. A Ruffin had leapt out from the midst of the fighters, and was barrelling down a newly formed channel between the rows of its own army, its lizard-like legs alternating and kicking up sand.

Ruffin and Rider smashed into the front lines of the Republicans, tearing through armour, steel and bone. The creature was six rows deep before the friction of bodies finally slowed it, and there it stayed whipping around, and using its thick neck and long tail to main, kill and break up the Republican ranks. The Republicans retreated from the Ruffin's wide foaming jaws, watching in horror as it scooped up anyone who was too slow to back off. Leenar, the young boy who had brought Kyira the shears, was one of those unfortunate souls, and the Ruffin extended its massive jaws over him, crushing him to a pulp from standing.

"Hold!" cried Kyira.

As the space grew wider, the Ruffin's Rider leapt off and began swinging a huge scythe, cutting great circles.

A gap appeared and Kyira thrust forwards into it, stumbling to at the feet of the great Rider. Its battered helmet was of wrought iron, and it stood two heads taller and a chest wider than she, worse though was its wicked smile, which took up most of its narrow face.

"I'll take this one for myself," hissed the Rider, its voice lingering. The Ruffin backed off, snapping at the circle of soldiers, and banging its tail into the sand.

"Here!" A high-collared officer standing at the edge of the circle threw Kyira some steel. A shortsword, but blessedly sharp. "Behind you!"

Kyira ducked, feeling the wind of the scythe, and rolled sideways, leaping backwards, stretching out in the air into a back flip. The sand came up to meet her too soon, and she crumpled to a heap near the Ruffin, which hissed and snarled. It could have taken right then, but the Rider's orders kept it at bay.

As Kyira struggled up, the Ruffin Rider yanked the scythe free from the sand where she had been. The world was still spinning from her jump, and while the Rider didn't know it, had he lunged just then, Kyira would have been too disorientated to dodge him. But the Rider hesitated, for on the end of his scythe was a mud crab, skewered through its shell. He plucked the poor crab from the end of the blade and crushed it

Breathe.

There was another flash of cloak.

Breathe.

The attack should have come from another direction this time, but this Rider was shrewd.

Breathe.

Kyira rolled forwards, away from the scythe's blade. The Rider swung again cutting swathes of other soldiers across the middle, forcing them back, forcing the circle bigger, but Kyira was inside, and by the time the Ruffin Rider realised, it was too late. Kyira shoved her short-sword up through the Rider's groin, twisting the blade. She had no idea if these creatures had the same bodies as humans, or if that area was as delicate as any other, until the Rider fell to his knees. The scythe clattered as it landed, and boots and swords descended. Kyira yanked her sword free and left the Rider to his fate.

The riderless Ruffin leapt out of the Republican lines like a frog as the walls closed in around it, stumbling across the sand and limping away towards the distant water. An enterprising band of soldiers chased after it, and then abruptly it was rolling over, thrashing around in the sand. Plumes of dust erupted around it as the escaping gas below burst, dragging the lizard down.

"YES!" roared Kyira. "Quick sand!" She watched as the great beast struggled against the sinking mud, and then as quickly as it had started it was over. It was gone.

The Republican soldiers all turned back towards the rest of the advancing Bohr army, and Kyira moved to join them, roaring in unison, relishing the chance to cut more of the enemy down.

"I saw you!" shouted a man over the din of death and steel. The voice caught Kyira off-guard. She spun to meet him; it was the high-collar from the circle. "I saw you beat that Banèman," said the officer.

She didn't know this man. "Another mystery man who appears at just the right time." She grabbed the nearest soldier, a woman with bright red hair. "Do you see this man?"

The female soldier looked flummoxed. "This man? Of course, that's Dier. Captain Dier, sorry, sir." There was a roar from deep in the lines and the female soldier ran off, melting in the lines.

Kyira held the sword up to the man's high-collared neck and chisel-jaw. "Then *Captain Dier*, Help or go." He had the most feminine eyes she had ever seen on a man. If it wasn't for the long scar that marked him from cheek to cheek, Kyira might have called him handsome.

Dier stepped back, placing a careful hand on Kyira's blade only to find it unmoving. "Held up by my own sword by my own soldier?"

He had to be real, Darc had never once tried to manhandle Kyira, probably because he never really existed. "I'm no soldier."

"No," said Dier. "You're more far than that—You're a Sami. You fought alongside the great Commander Laeb in the Cursed City—and Fiskal told me all about you, Kyira. You need to pull back the flanks." The man had a smooth way with words, there was no denying that. "This force appeared from nowhere whilst we were finishing off the last Kresh'ae Bohr. Kyira, they caught us unprepared on our own turf!" Dier held out his hand. "Where the hell did they come from?"

"There is a doorway on the beach," said Kyira. "A hole in the air that leads from somewhere else. The King's army came through it, but I think they lost half their force in doing so."

Dier went pale. "If this is only half, then humankind is in serious trouble. We do not have the numbers—"

"Numbers are not everything!" snapped Kyira. "Where is Fiskal?"

"Fiskal's gone." Dier spat on the sand. "The great commander Fiskal left us to rot." His eyes fell side long and he roared an order of retreat to the flanks. A flagbearer appeared behind her, and Dier took the flag off him.

"Then we are here alone."

"You are not alone." The man brought his fist to his chest, and handed the the flag to Kyira. "Captain."

Kyira took the flag of the Republicans army, the soul of the human resistance against the Bohr, and held it high. Regardless of whether she had chosen this path, it was here, now, and the only way path Kyira could walk.

"Send in more riders," snapped V'olpar to his second. The Rider nodded, and the Ruffin licked its lips in anticipation. "Fill the gaps it leaves with humans, and get the Bohr lines ready to come in after." The Rider nodded and rode off, the Ruffin loping away, eager to kill and to eat. Starving the creatures was not his idea, but Kaliste's. She was as viscous as a firesnake and half as trustworthy, but as the saying went, there's no snake like a dead snake. "And tell them to watch out for the quicksand!"

He clapped his hands together, and a spear was dropped into his palm by a soldier to his left. A king did not engage in battle, but sometimes it was nice to stretch the muscles. He leant back and launched the spear through the air, clapping his hands again for the next one. Before throwing, he watched, gauging the landing.

"Good throw, my King."

V'olpar back-handed the human across the head, feeling the man's skull break. He careened into the group around him, landing in a heap of twisted limbs and blood. "It was short!" said V'olpar.

He readied another throw then leant back and let fly.

The world spun. Purple light filled Kyira's head. Fear. Panic. Resolve. She couldn't hold it any longer!

She turned and emptied her stomach. She was fighting herself, but she had to push forward. It was Hasaan's bloody cliff face all over again, frozen halfway up and halfway down, unable to move and unable to speak.

"Kyira! Spear!"

Kyira recognised Dier's voice over the din of death and steel. A spear was flying towards her, silhouetted against pale clouds, and growing larger until it thumped into the sand at the foot of the boulder. The thrower, a huge Bohr on the back lines of lord's army, smiled as he threw spears the size of trees into the mass of fighting bodies.

"Kyira," shouted Dier. "We need you! Stand and direct! The enemy have us in a bind. Their beasts are knocking holes in us, your soldiers need your collective reassurance that we can still win this. These are mercenaries we are fighting, they are skilled. But they will not do any more than is necessary, and that is why they will fail. Kyira, are you listening?"

"There's someone out there."

Dier looked up and frowned. "Who—"

Over the thousands of fighting men and women and the beach beyond, a lone girl was striding towards them. The light around her changed, growing darker, the sun vanishing behind clouds that only minutes ago were not there.

Kyira realised too late. "She has a weapon—"

A crack of thunder split the air. The boom rolling through Kyira's entire body, from head to feet, vibrating the core of her. It banished the sickness away like waves stealing the beach, and she and two armies watched silently as the girl walked towards them all.

Abika could still feel the window's presence behind her like a throbbing, beating heart.

The wrought Soulfire knife glowed purple, pulsing with the red core inside. What incredible power thrummed off of it! Her own Soulfire lurked beneath the surface of her skin, but the soulblade could flatten both of these armies, had that been her goal.

She cared only for Kyira though. The woman at the centre of it all—her mother and father's killer. Abika could see her now, and yet Meorith's words was the voice she heard.

"Why are you so bad, Bee?"

A different life. Abika's own decisions had led her here and no one else's. Not Jagar's, not Jekob's, not Freja's. Not even her mother and father's. She was a product of her own choices, and she would have her vengeance. Now.

Blue sparks emerged from her hands, crackling in the air. There was pain somewhere, but not enough to diffuse the power. The clouds above her answered in unison, drawing together and bringing darkness to the beach. Lightning forks crackled down, smashing against the sand and leaving smouldering craters.

"I'm coming for you Kyira of Nord!"

"What was that?" shouted Dier. "How did she—"

"She's a Banèman," said Kyira, unable to tear her eyes from the flashing thunderheads.

"She can't be a Banèman, Kyira!" said Dier. "She's too young! Legend says that slayers are born into adulthood!"

"Then it seems the Queen of the Banèman has changed her tack." Kyira swallowed. "I'm not sure what we do here, Dier."

Dier's eyes were wide. "Send in the flanks around the Bohr. Send them running." Dier whistled to the flag bearer boy. "FLANKS!"

Four hundred soldiers on each side ran around the attacking Bohr army, past the fighting lines to this new threat marching along the beach. Weapons clattered, and shouts rang along the front lines like waves but Kyira's hesitation ran deep. Was this truly the right move?

The question was answered for her.

Two groups of fighters came roaring from each side. She couldn't help but step back in the face of so much force, as she had when Vasta had attacked her. Vasta who had seemed so real, but like everyone else, had betrayed her. Abika pointed her soulblade at the right flank and released the Soulfire within.

V'olpar's laugh faded into a scream as a beam of pure light tore through the back of the King's army, burning human, Bohr and Ruffin into dust, leaving holes in the very air, that closed up and brought fire that licked and danced among those nearby, moving like snakes amongst the Bohr and King's soldiers.

V'olpar threw himself backwards, as the bar of light leapt out and up to the sky, an uncontrollable and deadly force of nature wielded by a tiny girl.

He squinted back in her direction, blinking away the colourful lines in his eyes, and grabbed the last spear.

Kyira clutched Dier, as fear clutched her. The beam of light missed her by a few metres. The heat of it crackled and the air was filled with the smell of sulphur. The boulder on which she stood had a perfect hole burned through it, and while barely a foot-wide, it had taken at least a hundred lives of those in front and behind. Chests, heads, and limbs alike had been bore through in a straight line of pure energy that had burst forth of the girl.

"What weapon could do such a thing!" Dier looked more and more fearful every time Kyira turned to him. As well he should. Kyira should have felt fear too as the girl turned that terrifying weapon towards the stunned Republican flanks once more, but instead there was something else. Familiarity. Guilt. Shame.

They had all turned towards her now, running shoulder to shoulder, the feud between them forgotten, murder painted on their faces in blood and coal. The back lines of the black army joined them, until soon there were lines and lines of humans and Bohr tearing towards her, ready to cut her down.

She would make Kyira pay. They would all pay!

Abika imagined the Flash coming back to her, rolling over sea, hill and mountain until it was filling her up. The Thunder was on its way, ready to counteract the Flash, but the Soulfire was already collecting and recharging inside her, ready to wield as a fiery tool of death. The Thunder left her on the beach, passing by the outer islands of Sulitar, back the way it had come, pushed beyond everything Abika knew: the lake, commune, and up into the stars of forever, lost to the eons.

The urge to cut through the air was so powerful, that the soulblade glowed brighter than ever. A torrent of fire filled her veins with so much rage that she gasped in the face of it, choking as if the air around were so thick she couldn't breathe it anymore. Her arms were going red, her veins pumping, her heart hammering as though it were trying to escape her body. She fell to her knees, barely able to breathe and looked up at the clouds above her.

The blue canvas beyond.

The bird in the cell.

Vasta.

Jagar.

It all came out at once starting as a scream, but it wasn't sound that burst the clouds apart, it was light.

A shockwave rolled over the beach, crashing into the lines of soldiers dumbstruck upon the beach of Bakla. The Republican front lines and King's back lines were hit hardest.

Iron helmets crumpled over heads, steel swords burst open like they were made of glass, bodies were flung into the air—both armies fell like broken saplings in the wind.

Kyira and Dier were tossed off the boulder into the regiments behind, leather, sand and metal assaulting them from all sides until eventually they rolled to a stop in a pile of groaning bodies. Salt blood filled Kyira's mouth, her back ached, her legs were pinned.

"Kyira!" shouted Dier. "Are you there?"

Kyira tried to sit up, pushing off a poor fellow who had taken the beam straight through his chest. "I'm here!"

"What do we do?" Dier struggled through the arms and legs of the soldiers lifting themselves back up from the sand, and found Kyira. "She's too powerful. She must be the greatest Banèman who ever lived!"

Kyira took Dier's hand and found her feet. She swallowed back the bitterness filling her mouth. Immense guilt filled her heart."She's not a Banèman."

Dier's chiselled features contorted. "How do you know?"

Through the hole in then boulder was a direct line of sight to the girl upon the beach, and she stared right back at Kyira.

"I know. Because she is my daughter."

76

GIFTS

Abika was readying another Flash when a spear the size of a small tree thudded into the sand next to her. She spun, enraged, and that was when she saw the Ruffin.

Jekob had told her stories of these huge lizards, that could change colour at will and grow big enough to swallow her whole! It loped towards her over the sand its bloody jaws agape. Exhaustion gripped her. She tried to hold out the soulblade, but it was dull and she could barely lift her arm. There was nothing left inside, and there was no time.

The sand dragged at her as she stumbled back towards the window but the lizard and the man sitting atop it altered their course to head her off.

They would get between her and her escape! She skidded to a stop, and held out her hand. The window was too far away! She reached for it, further! She could feel it. It had to obey her. Abika was special. She was meant for something more than this. Afraid for her life, Abika willed the window forwards, pulling at its influence with everything she had.

It had heard her!

"Please!" Tears streamed down her face as the Ruffin's growls filled her head. "Please, help..."

The window chose to disobey, and as it closed Abika realised she was going to die.

Kyira could not only see it all happening, she could *feel* it. That familiar impression inside her had grown from the second Abika had stepped onto the beach. The sickness swirling in her guts might have boiled her up from the inside, and she could barely keep it down, but she knew that soon the revelation would be inconsequential. The Ruffin pounded towards Abika and Kyira could do nothing but watch.

Breathe.

She let the dark in.

Breathe.

The light was there, waiting. A gift from the Great Mother, left with her since Tyr. Kyira reached for it. There wasn't time for anything else.

Breathe.

Dier stood at her side, shouting and pointing, but Kyira ignored him. She closed her eyes, and looked inward, thinking of Akosh, of how fast he moved. Dier's words slurred, getting slower and slower. The very air between them seemed to stop moving, then the battle below was slowing too. A flock of terns above seemed to be held in suspension, hanging in the air as the world held its breath.

Kyira reached out with her thoughts. *"Hold on, Abika. I'm coming."*

Abika jerked around. A voice sounding in her head. "What?! Who are you?"

"Don't move."

"I can't...Help me!"

The Ruffin was nearly on her. Bloody jaws agape. The Rider rode upon its back as though he had been born there, and from behind he pulled a long weapon with a curved blade upon the end. He swung it about his head and roared and the Ruffin roared with him.

It was a single second drawn into the space of a lifetime as Kyira walked on through the lines of unmoving soldiers. After Abika's lightning, none had yet resumed fighting, so they all stood shoulder to shoulder, humans alike, frozen together and staring as their new enemy, a young girl with the power of a Banèman army, faced down a Ruffin and its Rider. Humans and Bohr alike were locked in a moment, as everyone was. Everyone except Kyira.

Kyira lived in that moment, walking and breathing as normal. This had been Akosh's world, living whole lives between heartbeats, but she knew it wouldn't last forever. Akosh had lived a million lives, and while his speed might have served his practised hand for any length of time, Kyira could already feel his great gift waning.

With every second in this world within worlds, the battle of Bakla was speeding back up as the Forbringrs sought to correct the imbalance Kyira has brought forth using Akosh's stolen strength, so she ran as fast as her Sami legs would take her towards Abika.

The distance was still too great, it wouldn't be enough, not for this Pathwatcher or any other.

Kyira had to do something else. Her father would have known, and even if she would never have listened to him she would have trusted him, because he had always trusted her. The words in her mind led her deeper. The sand at her feet. The darkness beyond. The clouds above. Reality was only as real as her own mind. Her thoughts. They crystallised. Listening to the movement of everything, and all at once she began to understand.

77

AE'THRIA

It was the same dark place Kyira had found herself in Tyr, the place that still haunted her soul. A light floated above the water splashing about her feet.

It still felt as though it was of her and for her, but it couldn't have been. This time she had brought herself here, and she could see that it was ancient. She didn't know how she knew that, but it was as obvious to Kyira as the Lines on her chin.

Looking down she saw her hands, her feet, and everything else in between. It was more than just her body though, she was a vastly different person than that young Sami girl who was pulled into the portal above Vasen, so when she approached the light she bathed in the warmth of it.

"It is a gift." The voice that echoed around was sweet. The sweetest, and the still water reverberated with each syllable. "A gift from the Great Mother."

"From Akosh?"

"No, Kyira. You took Akosh's speed. His power is yours now. He doesn't need it anymore." The voice sounded amused.

A shape, blurry at first, stepped out of the dark mists and walked towards Kyira. She wore a dress of flowers and grass that seemed to grow and move as though a garden grew there. She was life, embodied, fair and beautiful, and she held out her hands towards Kyira.

Kyira wanted to embrace her—she'd never had a mother, only Iqaluk—but something held her back. "Are you my enemy?"

"No," said the Great Mother, her lips delicate and rose-coloured.

"Then why do you haunt my dreams?"

"We are linked you and I. Something imparted when last we met. Abika has it too."

"The power of the Great Mother?"

Baeivi laughed, her face terrible yet beautiful all at once. "No, my child. Only Baeivi carries the power of the gods. But one other haunts your dreams. He is a plague!" Her face became terrible once more. Eyes of fire. The dress black as the life died upon it. She stepped backwards, starting to fade.

"Are you are trapped here?"

The voice hesitated. "Yes, but don't pity me. Go, now. Save her."

Kyira held out her hands, pleading, and fell to her knees in the water. "Please, I'm too far from her! I can't reach her."

The mirth disappeared from the Great Mother's voice as the darkness stole her from view. "Then you know that what must be used if you want to save her. And she does need saved."

The still water began to rise, cold moving up Kyira's legs. "Wait! I need to know. How do I use your gift?"

"Save her." The Great Mother's sweet voice was fading.

Kyira shouted as loudly as she could as the water found her stomach, her chest, her shoulders. "But how?! Please."

As the water found Kyira's lips, she heard one last thing. "Only you can save Abika. Only a Pathwatcher who knows the ways."

78

LINES

V'olpar stood at the window's side, watching and waiting for the Ruffin to reach the strange and powerful human girl. He couldn't wait to see the red bursting from her body as the Ruffin scooped her up in its jaws and mashed her to pulp! The window pulsed, and V'olpar took a moment to admire it.

What a marvel of power! A tunnel between Zunqai and Bakla.

Finally, there was a chance for a unified Kemen, and it would be he who brought it all! The war between the rebels and the Bohr would be over in an eyeblink. The halls would rise in exaltation, and he would be the king who finally solved the human problem.

"And we owe it all to you, Queen Kaliste."

"Blessed be her Shadow." The line of Pan Guards stood to salute as the words were recited.

"Indeed," said V'olpar. "And without her, our Queen, we would not have this opportunity to finally—"

The window pulsed again, and V'olpar jumped back. He had seen what it did the Bohr on their arrival, its hunger had also halved the forces of the most powerful army in the world. Perhaps it was reacting to his touch, or his words. The words of a King.

It started moving away, and V'olpar found himself jogging at first then running at full speed.

"Come back!" He panted. "No!"

Kyira stood a shot distance from the broken army lines, reaching out towards the girl she left, the girl called Abika.

She guided the portal towards her as easily as she might have guided moths to a flame. That was Baeivi's gift, and as soon as her mind had returned to Bakla, the answer was as clear as the Laich in springtime. The sickness she had felt was a connection, an interface that she could use to speak to those with power. She spoken to Akosh with it—she used it to steal his speed—and now she was speaking with the Great Mother herself.

The portal was sentient, but still, it knew Kyira's intentions and would carry out her wish because she could ask it too.

"Faster."

The portal quickened slicing through sand dunes as though they simply did not exist. In a way, she considered if they existed at all, if anything existed at all. What difference did the shape of the land make when you could move through it? The question stuck in her mind as she willed the portal forwards.

She had to get this right, or Abika would be cut into pieces by the portal's infinite edge. Only a Pathwatcher could do this. The lines of the earth, the lines of the beach and the shadows, the Lines on her very skin all came together.

"Abika. You need to be ready."

Kyira could sense Abika's hesitance through the interface, but it was fleeting. The girl was already prepared. She knew what was coming and she knew Kyira was behind it. Dark hatred filled Kyira's head from the stream, insidious and threatening as Abika's words echoed inside.

"You killed my parents! And now I shall—"

Abika cowered as the Ruffin finally reached her and pounced.

Its skin shone like sunlight through sea spray, each thick, round scale moving and rolling independently, so it was hard to tell what exactly the Ruffin was doing. The shadow that blotted out the sky left no question though. As did the fetid stink of the Ruffin's breath, and the sounds of its hiss. It was going to crush her and eat her!

Abika screamed and closed her eyes, and a rush of wind blew through her.

She jolted like a fall during half-sleep.

The air was different.

She opened her eyes, expecting to see the afterlife.

It was dark. The image of the Ruffin's bloody mouth still filled her head, but the scene had been stolen from her. Ruffin, Rider and beach were gone, replaced with a wall of mud and brick and wood all stacked that stood tall above her.

Shaking, Abika peered around. The dunes had become a ruined basement in a broken house. Buildings stood tall all around, and even from here Abika could see a tall carved fountain not far away. It was eerily quiet. She tried to stand but fatigue took hold, and her legs gave way. She crumpled back down, and started to cry.

"Kyira," she croaked. "You did this." The thoughts of the woman she had once called Mother were still as clear to Abika as if they had been spoken to her face-to-face.

"You need to be ready."

There was movement, to the left and she jerked away, afraid. The air changed shape in front of her eyes. It was a window, and inside was the fading image of a beach painted upon the cellar wall. Kyira had sent her away. Which meant that the woman who had killed Abika's parents was not as powerless as Abika had thought. Nor apparently as heartless. The window she had sent to save her, and scooped Abika up and whisked her away before the Ruffin had gotten to her. Kyira had saved her life.

"You mistake me," said Abika, as last vestiges of beach drifted away, "if you think that I would ever forgive. I hope you hear this, Kyira, because I am coming for you!" The image winked out, leaving a soft circle upon the painted white brick.

A little bird, colourful and bright, fluttered down to Abika's side and cocked its head at her. Abika reached for her purple shard knife, but it was missing.

She held out a hand and the conure hopped upon her finger. "I'm Abika," she said. "It means God's Gift."

JAGAR

79

EPILOGUE - FALLEN SHARDS

Jagar chuckled as the window winked out. The portals existed as a layer between life and death, but Abika had that same power, and he had been drawn to her like a beacon on a dark night.

She had stolen the Great Mother gifts when she had denied a Baeivi's command over the fateful city of Tyr, although it was clear that she just didn't realise it yet. Aside from himself, the girl had to have been the most powerful being that ever existed, even if, of course, there was still so much for her yet to discover.

She might live outside of his influence, but he would eventually get to the bottom of her. Even if just to know why a tiny little human girl had been bestowed the gifts of a god.

Jagar gazed upward, admiring the mountain of glass. As with so many things, it was by Jagar's influence here and now alone that this, the most powerful soulshard still stood.

"More than the power of a god," he whispered. "Much more."

He drew his arm back and let that influence go, and the shard mountain began to fall apart. Most of those pieces were bigger than buildings and as sharp as razors. Jagar fixed his gaze upon the jagged top of the shard as it plummeted through the cloud, dragging vapour swirling along with it. The dark glass no longer shone blue, the Soulfire was all gone, but the weight of what remained was more than enough to kill him now in this, his *human* form. The first pieces thumped into the earth as the tower collapsed. As it tipped forward, the body of it strayed slightly off course, but Jagar raised a hand and guided it back so the full weight of the mountain would land upon his head.

He knew the weight of it, the smell of it, that tip, the way each crack and crevice had pitted and broken away as the tower had shattered. The weak points in the mixture of frozen Soulfire had created a swirling soup of strong and brittle, which would never have fallen on its own. Like many things, it needed a guiding hand, and that was all he had done. After sucking it dry, he had found that weak keystone in the heart of the shard and with the smallest drop of will, cracked it. The weight of the shard had done the rest.

Worse though, was that there were no others who knew the poignancy of this moment. Not the dead Bohr, not even Kaliste, blessed be the dust of her lost soul. The world would never know of the significance of this day's events, and more specifically what he, the Great Father, had done. It was a strange feeling, to be so clever and so powerful and have no one around to see it. It almost seemed pointless. Almost.

Perhaps he should've beckoned the girl to stay longer so she too could witness this moment, but she was too important to risk. Her path lay elsewhere, away from his for the time being. She had to grow, to live, to kill. He knew it, as he knew the glass, the ground and the sky. It was ironic considering there was so much about *her* that he didn't know or understand. Her heart and her mind were cut off to him, and that troubled him, but her control of Soulfire was unique—it behaved differently for all—but still, it was like nothing Jagar had ever seen before. The Flash and Thunder she had called it.

More shards of glass fell about him, some bursting into smaller pieces, while others smashed through the pumice to sink to the bottom of the Middle Sea far below. The tip of the crystal mountain was almost on him now. Casually, Jagar closed his eyes and drew a thin blanket of air over him, similar to compulsion, but more rigid in form. Jagar opened his eyes, just as the great shard tip smashed into it, the bottom spread outwards, but its own momentum drew it down, and for any other being in this world it would have flattened them to nothing, annihilating them. A light dust drifted down over him, swirling around like soft rain, but not so heavy that Jagar had to cover his eyes. He had to see it all. This was, after all, his doing, his order, even amongst all of this chaos. All that had occurred was thanks to his goals, and his plans. If it wasn't for him, none of this would have come to pass, and oh, there was so much more to come. And yet, he still wanted to know more about the girl, about her fate and her path, and how he could use her.

Jagar smiled as the fateful thought blossomed into life. Some lowlier than he might have considered the thought some kind of gift, handed to him by some higher power, but of course there was none higher than him.

The thought was of his own brilliant making, and with it came clarity, clear as soulglass. He picked his way through the chunks of fallen shard so sharp that an innocuous bump might have severed his arm. The Bohr was just lying where the girl had left him, dead as you like. His body had somehow evaded being completely flattened by the still-shifting remains of the greatest soulshard Rengas had ever seen. A coincidence, or was this moment fated? "There are no fates. Only the Great Father's rule."

Jagar opened his palm over Vasta's still form, sand and blood mixing. The clouds above drew inwards, glowing with the same bloodlight that painted every surface, shining through broken glass, reflecting and refracting an entire spectrum of possibility. Jagar called upon the core of his power, the power of the realm of a trapped god and fire filled his veins like new blood.

Jagar guided it downwards through his palm and into Vasta's body. The Bohr twitched.

"Arise," commanded the Great Father.

The End

GLOSSARY

Ae'thria - Means Dark voices. A realm that exists as a layer between life and death.
Arcez - An island in Sulitaria (The Outer Isles)
Avere - Children without parents cared for by a community
Bakla - The capital of New Bakla, a human republic in Yemen
Baklin - The language of New Bakla
Baklinians - From Bakla
Banémen - The slayers. Bohr who are born with special abilities who are inbred until powers emerge and the exceptional qualities of the Bohr become sed into tools that can be wielded like blades.
Bohrwan - A human who is like the Bohr in some way
Briš - A dice game
Common Realm - The humans' reality, usually referred to as such by the Forbringrs
Dor - An island in Sulitaria (The Outer Isles)
Earla - The old wars name for The Red Isles
Evesgiving - An event where the Bohr fight each other to mate with a Royal
Evesroom - The fighting room during Evesgiving
Forbringr - A god
Fountains of Kalcoon - Fountains in Zunqai

Fyrevin - Whisky
Ge'Bat - A prosperous island
Hak - A kimono-like dress tied at the waist
Háongs - Long thin houses in Ipor Dan
Határ - The Borderlands south of the Way
Határian - From Határ
Hauwi - An island in the Outer Isles, famed for its hard fighters
Hearthsalt - An element that burns bright and strong. Very explosive.
Ipiti - An island in Sulitaria (The Outer Isles)
Ipitians - People from Ipiti
Ipor Dan - The capital of Ipiti
Iporiti - A northern city in Ipiti
Kaldi - Coffee
Kamsin - The ruined town from Broken Teeth near Kyotho
Kartta - An ancient Sami tribe that recorded the lands and carved hidden maps into map boxes
Kemen Empire - The large southern continent which is home to the Bohr
Kyotho - A larger city in Kemen
Lothri - The capital of Ge'Bat, famous for its Gilded Docks and markets
Lumael - An island near Ge'Bat used for smuggling
Maelta - A map box. An intricate box with complex patterns that shift and can be block printed to reveal a map of a location. Created by the Kartta
Maerd - The capital of Hauwi
Mear'pid - Fossilised petrified cow dung
Minerva - The capital of the Red Isles
Myathar - Andra's ship that takes Abika and Vasta from Ipiti to the Red Isles
Nara - A deer-like horse with antlers that can grow very large. Used for riding and farming.
Neubakla - "The World's Gates" in Baklin
Nitba - Nitba is the nocturnal Dayba. A little bat.
Nordun - From Nord
Ongaxe - A double axe.
Ortaxe - One-handed, two-handled axe

Pathwatcher - A Sami tradition of maintaining the paths throughout the continent of Nord
Red Isles - An island in Sulitaria (The Outer Isles)
Redula - The language of the Red Isles, spoken by Freja when she gets upset.
Rengas - The Ringland world, with all continents combined
Revision - Change the appearance of
Ringlander - Someone who comes from the mainlands (predominantly Nord and Határ.)
Ruffin - Long dragon-like lizards that can grow very large. Often used in battle, and can confuse prey with their iridescent scales.
Soulfire - The power
Soulshard - Hardened Soulfire
Stallo - A mythical god-like plant giant from the old wars
Stoytree - a tree with a weird check pattern rings when cut. Used for Chinaes boards
Sulitaria - The family of Islands that includes Sulitar, Hauwi, The Red Isles, Ipiti, Dor, Taraunteen and Arcez.
Sulitar - the largest of the Outer Isles
Sulitarian - from Sulitar
Taraunteen - An island in Sulitaria (The Outer Isles)
Terävä - The poor side of the cursed city of Tyr
Teräväen - from Terävä
The Guard of the White Dragon - A faction of Bohr sympathisers from Ipiti
Tom-ra - A powdered drug made from crushed leaves
Torqa - A cart pulled by a human
Tsiorc - The original rebel resistance brought together under the triangle/cross sigil to fight the Bohr
Tyr - The cursed city which fell into the Way after a portal opens above
Underling - An understudy, mentored by a master Bohr
Vasen - The rich side of the cursed city of Tyr
Zunquai - The Bohr-run capital of the Kemen Empire

www.ingramcontent.com/pod-product-compliance
Lightning Source LLC
Chambersburg PA
CBHW020505310726
48979CB00016B/2785/J

9781739914943